HUBRIS RISING

Echoes of Tomorrow
Book 2

ALEXANDER TITUS

SEAN PLATT

STERLING & STONE

HUBRIS RISING

Chapter One

THE LAKE'S surface looked like polished obsidian, reflecting the periwinkle sky streaked with violet clouds.

Phoebe stopped for a moment and glanced at Lucas beside her. "It's so beautiful."

"The iron oxide and manganese particles suspended in the water create an unusual light refraction pattern."

"Or you could just say it's beautiful."

He smiled. "It's beautiful."

They were approaching the lake from the southern hill, traversing the loose scree angling down toward the water. A large group of Hyperionites had already gathered on the shore, their scaled skin shimmering in shades of blue, green, silver, and violet. The adults sat in a loose cluster, braiding fibers into rope as younger kids waded in up to their waists and stood shivering, their arms wrapped tight around their chests. A few bolder teenagers threw caution to the wind, diving in and disappearing into the lake before surfacing farther out. Flutter and her friends prepared to launch a raft from a small dock extending from the jetty several dozen meters past the adults.

Flutter waved for Phoebe to join them.

"As we agreed, I'll return for you in three hours," Lucas announced.

"You don't have to come back. I know my way home."

"I told your mother I would accompany you."

Phoebe refrained from rolling her eyes. "She worries too much."

"Possibly, but my presence alleviates her concerns, which means you can visit with your friends."

"Fine." Phoebe sighed. "Where are you going?"

"To scan the higher elevations for new mineral deposits."

"That sounds super boring."

Lucas smiled. "You won't have to share a tablet with your siblings if I'm able to discover extractable neodymium deposits. We'd be able to manufacture new ones."

"You've been saying that forever."

Lucas didn't reply, only continued along the path and up the side of the opposite hill.

When was Samara going to realize Phoebe was old enough not to need an escort? She knew the area better than the back of her hand. Besides, Flutter and the other Hypers were her friends. She couldn't be safer here.

But her mother worried about everything all the time, as far as Phoebe could tell. If she was ten minutes late for dinner without checking in on her comm, she got a lecture. If she put one foot outside the colony's perimeter sensors by herself, lecture. If she forgot to take her morning dose the second she woke up, lecture.

She wished her mother would trust her for once. She'd had the same safety training everyone else had, gone through the same survival classes and passed the same certification test. But Samara acted like she was a toddler who didn't know the difference between an edible berry and a poisonous one.

Phoebe ran towards the jetty, kicking up loose stones and sending them rattling down the slope ahead of her. Her foot twisted, her arms flared and she half-slid, half-sprinted the rest of the way. The last few strides turned into a controlled slide until she hit stable ground with a thud that rattled her teeth.

Once down the hillside, she slowed and then paused at a formation of rocks near the shoreline to examine a cluster of fleshy, tubular structures emerging from a central bulb growing out of a crack in the stone. The tubes pulsed slightly, contracting and expanding in a slow rhythm.

She knelt and brushed her fingers over the tubes, which curled slightly in response. Had she seen this plant before? Maybe in passing? She couldn't recall. But she might as well take a sample for Renata. Maybe her mother would find it interesting too, although Samara rarely had time for anything these days beyond her lab work.

Phoebe shrugged off her backpack and retrieved the collection kit she always carried, unzipping the compact case to reveal the array of tools that Renata had taught her to use before she could read, including sterile forceps with molecule-thin tips, a laser scalpel barely thicker than a pencil, and collection vials filled with clear preservation medium that could stabilize organic samples for up to three weeks at ambient temperature.

"Sorry," she muttered as she used the scalpel to cut loose a small section of the tubule and placed it in the vial with the forceps, along with some of the amber fluid that welled up from the wound she'd inflicted. Then she sealed the tube, labeled it with the date and location, and packed everything back into her kit for later.

She heard clapping and glanced up.

Flutter waved at her again. Less patiently, this time. They were waiting for her.

Phoebe got to her feet, hoisted her bag over one shoulder, and sprinted the rest of the way to the dock, built from eighteen crooked planks salvaged from old crates, anchored to the shore by metal poles hammered into the lakebed. The whole thing listed a few degrees and creaked with every footstep, but it was stable. When it finally wore out, the Hypers would rebuild it with whatever they could find. They were like that, constantly trading for the colony's scraps and turning them into something useful.

Flutter waited for her on a small wooden raft that had been lashed together with rope and sealed with sticky resin from ironbark trees, using laser cutters to drill through to the softer phloem inside. The resin hardened into a flexible, waterproof coating that helped to keep the raft buoyant despite the high mineral concentrations in the water. Flutter had told Phoebe that before her people had arrived, the Hypers used to pack hot coals around the trunks to soften the tough bark so it could be penetrated with metal drills.

Flutter was tall for her age, her scaled skin shimmering in tones of blue-green and silver, the ridges along her forearms and neck more defined than those of the younger children. Her dark, fathomless eyes brightened when Phoebe arrived.

Poke stood ankle-deep in water beside the raft, reflecting light off the lake glinting on the bronze flecks that dotted his dark green scales, while Tally crouched near the center of the raft, fiddling with a device that Phoebe had never seen before. The iridescent sheen of magenta and violet waxed and waned across her indigo scales as she moved.

Phoebe signed their names, and they both grinned in

welcome. Like Flutter, they had the same delicate, angular features and deep-set, dark eyes that seemed to drink in the light.

Flutter reached out, gripping Phoebe's wrist, helping her onto the raft. The planks dipped under her weight, but that didn't stop her from throwing her arms around her friend and hugging her.

Flutter pulled away and began signing in their language, "Did you bring it?"

Phoebe grinned and sat next to Flutter, shrugging out of her backpack. Then she opened it up and pulled out a small bundle wrapped in waxed paper. Inside were pieces of dark, amber-colored candy. It was chewy and sweet, made from sugarcane syrup and native tubers dried and ground into a powder, then flavored with petals from a flower that only bloomed for a week in the spring, which gave it a faintly spiced, almost floral aftertaste. Renata had perfected the recipe over the years, and when Phoebe was younger, she'd begged to help harvest the flowers; she'd spent hours in the kitchen with both her mothers, making batch after batch.

But for the last few years, Samara had been too busy in the lab to help, and lately, Phoebe found herself bored by the time they poured the first batch into the trays to harden.

Now, she'd rather be outside. When she wasn't hanging with Flutter and her other Hyper friends, she volunteered to go hiking with the biological collection teams, just to get out of the colony proper. Samara was usually too busy to notice so she'd risk sneaking out by herself to explore the ruins of the Hyperion colony, where the Hypers had been created. It was mostly rusted-out prefab buildings and a defunct lander that the Hypers had stripped of every usable component long ago, but it was better than being home where Samara monitored her every breath.

Flutter bounced up and down with impatience, signing, "Please, please."

Phoebe broke off a chunk of the candy and held it out.

Flutter snatched it, popping it into her mouth with a pleased trill. Phoebe laughed as Flutter's expression shifted to delight.

"Sweet. More?"

"Not yet," Phoebe signed. "Let's make it last."

"Ready?" Poke signed.

Phoebe nodded and Flutter signed for him to take them out.

Poke untied the raft and reached over to where he'd stored a long wooden pole wrapped in strips of treated fiber for better grip. He jammed the unwrapped end into the water, digging it into the bottom of the lake, and gave a powerful shove. The force sent a ripple through the raft as it lurched free of the dock.

Shiny, eggplant-colored water swirled around them. Each of Poke's pushes sent them farther from shore.

Tally hunched over a clunky device that looked like it had been cobbled together from at least a dozen different machines, connected by a wire to its cone-shaped receiver.

Flutter pulled more salvaged tech from a hay-woven satchel at her side. The scratched screen had buttons running along the lower edge. The lettering on the sides of the case had completely worn off, giving Phoebe no clue as to what it had once held.

The raft drifted, passing by a cluster of teens playing nearby. Poke flicked his pole, sending droplets of water spraying at them and breaking the rippling reflection of the sky in the mirror-like surface of the lake. They laughed and splashed back in return.

Phoebe glanced at Flutter's tech. "What's that for?"

Flutter signed a sinuous, waving motion.

Phoebe frowned. She hadn't seen that gesture before.

"Fishing?" she guessed, though the sign didn't quite match the one she knew.

Flutter shook her head. "Sweet?"

Phoebe smiled, digging into her bag and passing her another piece, then two more to the others and another for herself.

It wasn't long before Poke brought them to a stop and secured the pole to the side of the raft. Tally lowered the cone end of her gizmo into the purplish water and started fiddling with the controls. Meanwhile, Flutter produced a wire, plugged one end into her screen and passed the other to Tally, who connected it to the larger device.

Flutter's screen flickered to life. Abstract images appeared; small blobs moving across the display in various directions. She twisted a dial, adjusting it. After a minute the smaller blobs disappeared. And a half-dozen larger, slower-moving shapes came into focus.

Flutter trilled.

Poke turned to look at her.

She turned her screen so he could see it.

Poke stiffened, then stood, balancing himself on the raft. He grabbed the pole, smacking it against the water's surface. The teens turned to look at him.

Phoebe's stomach tightened. Something was wrong. She leaned over Flutter's shoulder, watching the blobs move across the screen.

Poke tucked the pole against his torso then signed something, too fast for Phoebe to follow.

The teens in the water exploded into motion, heading to shore. Most of them made it. Except for three who'd been having the splash-fight earlier.

One of the boys disappeared so fast it looked like he'd been hooked from below, his outstretched arms vanishing in an eruption of foam. The second twisted mid-stroke, his expression changing into one of pure shock before he too was yanked below.

The third teen, a girl, stopped swimming and looked back. Then she took a deep breath and dove beneath the water.

The only evidence that they'd existed were the ripples left behind by their disappearance.

Hyper parents ran to the water's edge, yanking out children that had been splashing in the shallows.

Phoebe got to her knees, scanning the water, waiting for the three teens to surface, but nothing. Then the ripples smoothed out, leaving behind only the gentle rocking of the raft.

The seconds stretched. Too long.

She tightened her grip on the edge of the raft, pulse quickening, watching the water.

Where were they?

A flicker of movement caught her eye. A shadow shifting beneath the surface, quick and sinuous. Then another. But the teens still weren't coming up.

A cold spike of panic shot through her. "Where—"

One of the boys broke the surface of the water, wrestling with something that looked like a large eel. It thrashed, ten feet of sinuous body, sharp spines running behind its head and down both sides. Its wet skin gleamed like leather. Its mouth was lined with needle-like teeth that snapped at the air.

Now Phoebe understood the sign that Flutter had made earlier.

The boy clung to it, trying to keep the creature under control. But it buckled and thrashed, spines raking across the teen's arms and chest, carving thin, crimson lines into his skin. He bellowed but refused to let go even as his blood mixed with the swirling water around him. Phoebe shot a panicked look at Flutter, but then another teen burst from below, gripping the eel-thing's tail.

Then the girl surfaced, a sharp stone in her hand. She closed the distance between her and the eel-thing in seconds. The first boy shifted his grip, forcing the creature's head up, exposing the pale flesh beneath its ridged throat.

And the girl struck.

She drove the stone into the creature's exposed throat. It ripped through layers of sinew and cartilage with a wet, crunching sound.

The creature convulsed, its ridged body flailing in a final, desperate attempt to escape. Spines flared along its sides. But the teens held on.

The girl didn't stop.

She drove the stone into the creature's flesh again and again. The eel-thing shuddered, its mouth gaping in a silent, drowning scream. Dark, inky blood burst from the wound, spraying across the girl's face.

Then the creature jerked. Once. Twice. And went still.

For a moment, there was silence. Just the ragged breaths of the teens, their bodies slick with water and blood.

Then, a rising trill filled the air.

The three swam toward shore, taking the dead eel-thing with them. A woman ran over to greet them, inspecting their wounds.

Phoebe mimicked the sinuous sign Flutter had made earlier, then signed, "Can you eat it?"

Flutter grinned wide, eyes bright with amusement, and patted her stomach. "Smoke, eat later."

Poke glanced at Phoebe with a look she wasn't sure

how to interpret, then began pushing them back toward the shore with his pole while Tally disconnected Flutter's screen from the larger device.

She wasn't sure what it was with Poke these days. Sometimes it seemed like he didn't want her there. Other times he was as friendly and playful as the others. Maybe he resented her, an outsider, watching the hunt. Samara was constantly reminding Phoebe that no matter how friendly the Hypers seemed, they had different rules and they thought differently. Phoebe had to be extra-careful to avoid causing a cultural misunderstanding.

Another totally unnecessary lecture. They'd studied the Hypers in school, starting with how they'd descended from the original colonists and how their culture had evolved into something unique over time. Most of her classmates thought the Hypers were disgusting, but Phoebe had been fascinated. So she'd begged Lucas to take her with him when he visited the village to study them, and he'd somehow persuaded Samara to give permission.

She felt at home with them in a way that she never had with her own people.

Phoebe turned to Flutter and signed, "Want another lesson?"

Flutter nodded, handing her screen off to Tally.

Phoebe reached into her own backpack and pulled out her tablet, tapping the screen the app she'd been using to teach Flutter to read. It was meant for toddlers with its bright colors, oversized letters, and a-little-too-cheerful effects, but it worked.

First, she wrote a word on the screen with her finger: *Crap.*

Then she signed it.

Flutter let out a high-pitched, oscillating sound, a trilling noise that was unmistakably laughter. When she stopped, she copied Phoebe. Her handwriting was shakier, but her control was improving. The app let out a cheerful trumpet sound, the screen flashing a shower of digital confetti before the word disappeared, making space for the next attempt.

Tally turned toward shore, signing. A minute later, everyone was back in the water. Poke glanced over his shoulder at them—he had that look, again—then he got up and stripped his shirt off before diving into the water.

Flutter signed, "Asshole."

Phoebe wrote it on the screen: *Asshole.*

Both girls laughed.

"Alright." Phoebe hit another button and handed the screen to Flutter. "Let's try something more difficult."

She wrote: *Phoebe wants to swim.* Then she pointed to each word and signed it to Flutter, who copied them on the touchscreen.

"Excellent," Phoebe signed as another confetti shower appeared. Then she wrote several more sentences, making the signs for each one once they were written: *Are you hungry? Do you like candy?* And finally: *Poke likes Flutter.*

Flutter looked embarrassed, but happy. "Who do you like?"

Now it was Phoebe's turn to feel embarrassed. "No one."

Flutter signed, "Sad."

Phoebe flipped Flutter off. Then they both laughed.

She glanced over at Poke as Flutter loaded the next level and began playing on her own.

All the boys Phoebe's age in the Vitruvian colony were just… boring. And she wasn't attracted to any of the girls, either. Renata kept telling her she'd "blossom in her own season," whatever that meant, but Phoebe had been feeling more and more isolated, drifting away from the people she once felt connected to: her schoolmates, her siblings, her parents. The more her former friends focused on relationships and starting families, the more she wondered what was wrong with her.

Why didn't she want the same things they did?

Maybe it was just Lucas' influence. He always made her feel there was more to life than simply accepting what was given. Together, they'd gaze at the stars, contemplating the vastness beyond. And Phoebe knew there was something more for her.

She looked down, her reflection wavering. Samara had been on her case for weeks to pick a vocational track.

"Genetics makes the most sense," she'd said yesterday. " You've already logged 324 hours in my lab, you understand the equipment, and we need more researchers for the next phase of adaptation studies."

But Phoebe's first apprentice session fixing ventilation systems with Maeve had been more fun than all those lab hours combined and the astronomy lessons with Lucas where they'd used the telescope they'd cobbled together from salvaged Hyperion lenses and colony-manufactured mirror arrays was what she really looked forward to.

But Phoebe would feel guilty if she didn't follow in Samara's footsteps.

Samara Makinde was the woman who'd engineered human survival on DaVinci, and everyone expected Phoebe to follow those impossibly large footsteps.

And the worst part was, she was good at it. Which meant that they were all probably right.

The raft rocked beneath her and she leaned forward, dipping her fingers into the water. More than anything she wanted to see the Borlaug, the colony ship that Samara and Renata and all the other adults had traveled on to settle DaVinci, which was still orbiting above them. But they had to conserve shuttle fuel for emergencies, and the ship in orbit was powered down to preserve its energy stores. She'd been brokenhearted when Lucas explained that the colony wouldn't have the capacity to refuel and refit the Borlaug for a trip to another world in her lifetime.

That infrastructure would take a few hundred years, at least. Not to mention everything they'd have to mine, starting with the radioactive material, plus scaling food production far beyond the colony's needs in order to preserve enough for a full crew to have years' worth for traveling.

It wasn't fair.

Poke surfaced right by her fingers.

She jerked back, startled. He grinned up at her, treading water. Then held up what looked like a handful of deep green seaweed with ribbon-like tendrils. Phoebe took a piece from him. It was slimy to the touch. She held it up to her nose and sniffed. It smelled like a combination of fish and something metallic, with an undertone of sweetness that seemed entirely wrong.

She glanced at Flutter, who shrugged.

Phoebe nibbled a tiny piece. Bitter. She gagged and spat it into the water. Flutter, Poke, and Tally all laughed.

Phoebe signed, "Asshole."

Poke grinned and dove down again.

Flutter nudged her, then signed, "Poke likes Phoebe."

She flushed, watching the ripples where Poke had disappeared in the water.

Maybe. But Phoebe didn't like Poke.

Not like that.

Chapter Two

THE GREENHOUSE always hit Atlas with a wall of competing smells: the sharp tang of tomato stems (limonene and alpha-pinene compounds), the earthy stink of compost (breaking down at 40°C in the decomposition beds), and the metallic undertone of the hydroponic nutrient solution (pH 6.2, optimized for leafy greens). Each climate zone maintained its own precise environment; Section 3, where he stood now, kept a steady 26°C with 65% humidity for the nightshades.

He pinched off another yellow aphid — *Myzus persicae*, one of six Earth pest species that had made the journey to DaVinci as stowaways in the settlement's seed stock. The tiny insect's exoskeleton gave way with a microscopic pop between his fingers. It was the twenty-seventh he'd found today, a troubling 18% increase from yesterday's count.

Atlas wiped the remains of the aphid on his pants and turned to the next plant. The ventilation system hummed overhead, cycling air through filters designed to keep native contaminants out of their food supply. A rhythmic heartbeat that sustained the greenhouse. He barely heard it these days.

Beyond the plexiglass walls, he saw hints of DaVinci's true landscape: jagged mountains set against a violet sky, scattered patches of the dark blue-green vegetation that had evolved on this world. So close, yet untouchable to most of the Naturalists.

"Shift's over, Atlas." Jared stood at the end of the row, already pulling off his work gloves.

Atlas straightened, rolling his shoulders. "Finished your section already?"

"Not everyone's as thorough as you. You coming?"

Atlas shook his head. "I want to finish this row first."

"Suit yourself. Don't miss evening prayer."

"I won't," he said, even though he would rather spend a whole night working in the greenhouse than an hour at worship.

Atlas watched the other workers file out, voices fading as the airlock cycled and sealed closed behind them. Silence settled over the greenhouse in their absence, broken only by the soft hiss of the irrigation system activating in a distant section. He counted to three hundred in his head, giving his coworkers time to make their way through the connecting corridors back to the residential domes.

When the number was up, he counted again.

Five minutes of complete silence confirmed what his gut already knew: the greenhouse was empty.

Only then did Atlas walk to the secluded alcove in the back corner, where a bunch of shelving units were loaded with soil bags, fertilizer, and work tools. His secret lay hidden behind an old tarp on the largest shelf.

The panel looked like any other section of the greenhouse wall, but Atlas had modified it, turning it into a door. He laid his palm against a section that was slightly discolored and pushed.

The panel swung inward with a barely audible click as the pressure seal broke.

Fresh air rushed in.

Atlas stepped outside and inhaled deeply. Compared to the settlement's sterile air, the outside smelled raw and alive: iron-rich soil, the sharp tang of alien vegetation, and that unmistakable electric scent that preceded sporestorms. Nothing about it was safe, controlled, or doctrinally approved. That's what made it perfect.

The greenhouse stood at the base of a steep hill, leading up to a field where the settlement's small flock of sheep grazed during the day. A series of weathered sheds housing feed and supplies stood at the summit. Beyond the ridge lay the Vitruvian colony. Not that he'd ever been there.

He would have to have special approval, and Dr. Basu would never give him that.

Atlas took another deep breath of air that most of his fellow Naturalists hadn't tasted in years. Yet here he stood, immune to the spores for reasons nobody fully understood.

The Divine Blueprint.

It was supposed to make him feel special. He felt like a lab rat instead.

The sun was beginning to set.

Atlas had maybe ten minutes before he'd need to return, or risk being missed.

But the idea of going back inside was almost unbearable. The same faces, the same conversations, the same prayers. Even the air seemed to recycle the same molecules, growing flatter and deader by the breath. Outside, the world was vast and alive and utterly indifferent to human notions of purity. More and more, he hated being indoors, confined by walls and dogma and expectation.

Sometimes, in moments of very dangerous imagination, he dreamt about running away. Heading straight to the valley and abandoning everything he knew. The thought both thrilled and terrified him. There were Vitruvians and Hyperionites out there: dual sources of contamination that could destroy the Divine Blueprint he carried.

But despite the danger, the thought of leaving occupied more and more of his waking hours, making him feel more alive than anything had in years. There were no voices out there telling him where to go. What to do. Who to be.

It would just be him, the wind, and the shifting sky. Valley would give way to hills and mountains and forests and places no one had ever been. Maybe he'd find something out there waiting for him. Maybe he'd become something new. He might disappear, swallowed by the silence, his bones left for the wind to scatter.

Even death on his own terms would be preferable to a life spent trapped in this place with nothing but prayers and sermons about his responsibilities to provide salvation for the entire settlement.

He could hear Dr. Basu in his head, preaching that this was why it was so important to control one's thoughts. Ideas were like the Bloom, the native fungus that contaminated everything on DaVinci. Once they took root, they spread through every corner of your mind until thinking anything else became impossible.

Atlas watched a cloud darken, its edges tinted magenta from the setting sun. He'd give anything to live outside permanently. He'd seen old photographs of Earth, of green trees and blue skies that looked as alien to him as DaVinci must have looked to the first colonists. Had they felt this same sense of simultaneous wonder and alienation?

The light was almost gone.

Atlas filled his lungs one last time with honest air, then slipped back through his makeshift door.

He moved silently through rows of Earth vegetables, aliens themselves on this foreign soil, heading toward the airlock that would return him to his gilded cage.

Everyone knew that he could go outside without an environmental suit, but he'd been forbidden to, for fear that he would carry the fungal infection back in with him.

Besides, the carrier of the Divine Blueprint couldn't be seen to break the rules. He had a responsibility to the future of humanity on DaVinci. Or at least the future of the Naturalists. As Dr. Basu reminded him daily.

The airlock cycled, flooding his lungs with the familiar, heavy air of the colony and Atlas tried not to cough. He exited the greenhouse, walking home through the transparent corridors. He passed the entrance to the Sanctum, the only place in the settlement that even he wasn't allowed to go. Only Dr. Basu and her highest acolyte, Elda, had the entry code to the place where the Divine bestowed its blessings and its punishments. As a child, Atlas had been terrified of the whispered stories about what happened to the impure or imperfect who tried to sneak into the Sanctum.

By now, he was pretty sure it was where Dr. Basu herself prayed for hours at a time, and that was far more of a discouragement than tales of divine bogeymen.

A few children ran through an intersecting corridor as he turned the corner, their laughter bouncing off the curved walls. They fell silent when they saw him, slipping past, as though not wanting to disturb him.

Atlas flushed.

Everyone in the settlement knew who he was.

His ability to survive on DaVinci without the immuno-suppressants that all the other Naturalists depended on was supposedly proof of divine favor. Dr. Basu said his very existence proved that rejecting genetic engineering and trusting in *purity* was the right choice. He wasn't allowed to just be Atlas. He was the Divine Blueprint, a walking prophecy, the colony's salvation wrapped in human skin.

Atlas wasn't a person to them.

He was *something else*.

Something sacred.

Even the youngest ones understood that much.

Scientists in the Vitruvian colony probably had a technical explanation for his immunity: gene mutations or adaptive responses. But here, uncertainty bred faith. His unexplained resistance made him special, chosen, *responsible*.

A walking miracle that validated every restriction, every rule, every sacrifice the Naturalists demanded.

And Atlas *hated* it.

The only good thing about having the Divine Blueprint was the ability to go outside.

The residential dome came into view, a bubble of reinforced polymer stretched over a metal framework. It was located in the second ring, closer to the center than most. Another privilege of being the Divine Blueprint.

He felt a flicker of guilt about bypassing the full decontamination process after his brief time outside.

But he'd been going outside for two years now without subjecting himself to the chemical spray down that would erase the scent of the outdoors from his nostrils. He'd been careful to avoid contact with anyone until he'd showered, and he washed his clothes immediately himself, so no one could accidentally touch them and pick up a random spore. And no one had gotten sick. Not because of him, anyway.

Atlas arrived at home.

He heard voices from within.

There was only one person who'd dare call on them this late.

He pressed his palm against the sensor and the door hissed open to reveal an ambush. His mother sat ramrod-straight on her meditation cushion, hands clasped in her lap. Dr. Basu occupied the spot beside her, radiating authority despite her small frame. And there was Dr. Basu's daughter, Hyacinth, completing the triangle of judgment, her eyes fixed on him with unsettling intensity.

Atlas stiffened.

Why was she here?

Lately, Hyacinth had developed the unnerving habit of materializing wherever Atlas went, like she'd installed a tracker under his skin.

She'd appeared across from him in the dining hall three days running. Rearranged the prayer circle to claim the spot facing him. Started asking detailed questions about greenhouse shifts she'd never shown interest in before. The pattern was too deliberate for coincidence, and too persistent for Atlas to ignore.

They had little in common beyond their mothers' positions in the settlement's hierarchy. Hyacinth was devout in a way that made even his mother seem lax, reciting doctrine with a fervor that bordered on fanaticism. Their conversations, if they could even be called that, consisted mainly of her agreeing with whatever he said, then steering the topic toward settlement traditions and worship circles.

Now Hyacinth sat beside her mother, hands folded in

her lap. Their eyes met and she looked… happy. Happier than he'd ever seen her.

He found it unnerving.

"Atlas." His mother rose, gesturing for him to sit. "We've been waiting."

"I was finishing my shift in the greenhouse," he said, remaining near the door. "What's going on?"

Dr. Basu stood, smiling. "We have wonderful news."

The cold knot in his stomach tightened. Whatever they considered wonderful news was unlikely to align with his definition of the word. "About what?"

"After extensive analysis and prayer," Dr. Basu said, "we've determined that you and Hyacinth are the best genetic match for procreation. Congratulations, Atlas, you're engaged."

Atlas glanced at Hyacinth, who didn't look even a little bit surprised.

"But… I'm not ready to get married. Right, Mom?"

Dr. Basu glanced at Briar, and Atlas saw the surrender in his mother's eyes. "No one is ever ready, Atlas. But at some point you have to take a leap of faith."

What was he supposed to say to that? He doubted this "genetic match" had anything to do with actual compatibility; it was about power. Dr. Basu wanted her bloodline directly linked to the Divine Blueprint, ensuring her grandchildren would be first to inherit immunity.

"There's much to be done before the ceremony," Dr. Basu continued. "The official announcement, of course. And once Hyacinth enters the Sanctum, she will not speak to outsiders, not even you. Her days will be spent in prayer and reflection, cleansing body and soul in preparation. When she's ready, the ceremony will be held. You will become husband and wife."

Husband and wife.

Atlas heard the words as if from a great distance.

This couldn't be happening.

He wasn't ready for marriage.

Especially to Hyacinth.

"I'm honored to be the first to receive the Divine Blueprint," she said.

"As you should be," Dr. Basu said. "After your union is blessed, all women of childbearing age will be spiritually wed to Atlas."

Hyacinth blinked. "What?"

Atlas felt like he'd been punched in the gut. He spun toward his mother, the betrayal burning in his throat. "Mom?"

Briar dropped her eyes. "Dr. Basu knows what's best for our people."

Atlas caught the slight tightening of her fingers, the flicker of something — *discomfort?* — as she shifted on the bench.

"Justin would be so proud," she added.

Ever since his father had died, Atlas' mother had developed the habit of invoking his theoretical approval whenever she sensed that Atlas would balk at doing what she wanted.

It had worked when he was younger, but the older he got, the more he resented having to please someone who'd died when he was three.

"The Divine Blueprint must be shared with as many worthy vessels as possible." Dr. Basu said. "But do not fear, Hyacinth. You alone will be his wife in body. The others will only be joined to him in spiritual ceremony, to allow the Divine Blueprint to be transmitted to them."

Hyacinth swallowed. "Yes, mother."

The room shrank around him. His chest tightened as if

the air itself was turning solid in his lungs. Panic clawed up his throat, hot and desperate.

"No. I won't do it."

Dr. Basu's face hardened. "This isn't about what you want, Atlas. It's about the survival of true humanity on this world. You've been blessed with the Divine Blueprint. With that blessing comes a certain responsibility to all Naturalists."

"One I never asked for," Atlas said.

"None of us chooses our purpose." She shifted into her sermon voice, a hypnotically silky cadence she used to make doctrine sound like gentle suggestion rather than absolute command. "The Divine chooses and we accept. Your immunity is not random chance, Atlas. It is a gift that you will share with all of the children of the next generation."

Atlas stared at her.

Children?

He wasn't even married, and she was already ordering multiple kids? Atlas turned back to the door, grateful he hadn't taken off his shoes. He hit the sensor and the door hissed open.

"Atlas!" His mother's voice cracked like a whip. "Where are you going? This discussion isn't finished."

"It is for me."

Atlas bolted without looking back. His feet carried him toward the greenhouse automatically, instinct seeking the one place where he could breathe.

He needed space. He needed clarity. He needed a way out.

He eyed the security cameras that watched every corridor. Dr. Basu insisted the cameras were for protection, in case the Hyperionites attacked or the Vitruvians tried to sneak in and sabotage them. But no one had seen a Hyperionite this far south in years, and when members of the other colony visited, Dr. Basu insisted they have an armed escort. Atlas suspected the cameras were really there to make sure no one wandered off-message.

The relentless red eye blinked down at him. He resisted the urge to stick out his tongue.

"Atlas, wait!"

He heard Hyacinth's footsteps behind him in the corridor, but he didn't slow down. She caught up to him at the junction, nonetheless.

"Wait, please." She raised her hands, palms open. "Just talk to me."

He stepped back, afraid she'd touch his clothes and possibly pick up spores. There hadn't been a sporestorm for weeks, but just because he didn't want to marry her didn't mean he wanted her to die.

"There's nothing to talk about," he said. "They've decided everything for us already. Don't you resent that?"

Hyacinth ignored his question. "I know it's sudden, but… it doesn't have to be terrible."

"Doesn't it?" Atlas studied her face. "How long have you known about this?"

"I found out an hour ago."

She seemed sincere, but Atlas wasn't sure if he believed her.

"I'll be a good wife to you," Hyacinth said. "I'll do whatever you want. I'll make you happy."

The edge in her voice made Atlas uncomfortable. He looked at her. Really looked at her. She was pretty enough, with dark hair and eyes that matched her mother's. But there was no spark.

No connection.

Atlas saw only a trap.

"I don't want a wife."

Her face fell. "What do you want, then?"

Her question caught him off guard.

What did he want?

Freedom. Air that didn't taste recycled. A life where he wasn't defined by some genetic anomaly. But how was he supposed to explain that to Hyacinth? Or his mother? Their entire worldview was shaped by scripture.

"I don't know." He shook his head. "But not this."

"We're getting married, Atlas. My mother has decided."

"Then she can find someone else to play the groom."

"There is no one else." Her expression hardened. "You're the only one with the Divine Blueprint."

"I don't care," Atlas said before walking away.

He broke into a sprint once he rounded the corner, his footsteps echoing down the empty corridor. He listened for pursuit, heart pounding in his ears, but she didn't follow. He might not know what freedom looked like yet, but he knew with absolute certainty it wasn't wearing Hyacinth's face.

His entire body ached for escape. Not just from this conversation, but from the smothering confines of settlement life. From the expectations crushing him from all sides. From a future that had just been handed to him like a death sentence dressed up as divine purpose.

It was dark out.

And still hot.

Summers were always like that on DaVinci.

Atlas slipped out through his greenhouse escape and made his way up the hill to one of the sheds, walking around to the side where an old wooden bucket stood. He stepped up on it, then hoisted himself onto the sloped roof.

He lay down on his back, staring up at the sky.

The first stars had started to appear: pinpricks of light

in the gathering darkness. All his life, he'd been told that his immunity was a gift. A blessing. Divine intervention that proved the rightness of the Naturalist's path. But lying here, watching the sky, Atlas could only think of it as a curse. A genetic prison that had shaped every aspect of his existence.

He would give anything to be free of the blueprint, but there was no escape from what and who he was.

Atlas watched the stars emerge in their full glory as darkness descended.

He might not have long, but for tonight, he was free.

Chapter Three

Dr. Ayesha Basu closed her office door, walked to her desk, and settled into her chair with a frown. What was she going to do about Atlas' defiance? Youth always clung to the illusion of choice, as if wanting something badly enough could make it real. But choice was indeed an illusion, especially in matters as important as this. There was only what needed to be done. The sooner he accepted that, the less pain he would cause himself and everyone else.

She had spent years preparing him for his role in the colony, shaping his understanding of duty, laying the foundation for the Divine Blueprint so that he would step into that responsibility when the time came.

She hadn't expected Atlas to hesitate.

But he had.

Hesitation was a cancer that needed to be cut out quickly. Atlas still clung to the childish notion that he was an individual with choices, rather than accepting his role as a vessel for something greater. He couldn't see that personal desire was meaningless compared to collective survival. But he would learn. Hyacinth would guide him, soften him, reshape his rebellion into acceptance. And if gentle persuasion failed, Ayesha had other methods waiting in reserve.

Ayesha reached for the comm on her desk and keyed in Katherine's code, pressing the transmission switch until it clicked into place. The tuning dial cycled through frequencies, searching for a signal. Static hummed through the tiny speaker, punctuated by the occasional blip of interference.

No response.

Ayesha adjusted the dial, fine-tuning the connection, then tried again. Tapping her fingers against the desk, she waited.

The comm finally crackled to life.

"It's nearly midnight." Katherine sounded tired.

Ayesha almost laughed. "Come, now. We both know you're still up working."

A heavy sigh broken by static. "What do you want?"

"The status of that tractor component I sent with last week's shipment. The oats are ready to harvest but we're falling behind doing it by hand. I need the tractor to work now."

"Maeve's team is still trying to find the right kind of processor to swap in. None of the ones we have will work."

Ayesha's fingers tightened around the comm. "This sounds like sabotage."

"Why on earth would I sabotage your settlement?" Katherine sounded irritated.

"If we can't bring in enough food for the winter, we'll starve. Then we'll have to come to you for help. We'll be even more dependent on you."

"It wasn't my idea to split the colony. And everyone who went with you chose that path. If you don't have the people to fix your tech, then you have no choice but to rely on our abilities and timelines."

"'I told you so?' After all your talk about cooperation?" Ayesha pulled the smooth yellow prayer beads from her pocket and ran them through her fingers. They slid between her fingers like worry stones, their rhythmic movement the only thing that kept her from saying what she really thought about Katherine's excuses.

Katherine sighed again. "We've got plenty of food in storage if you need it. All you have to do is let me know how much you need to cover the shortfall."

Ayesha grimaced. She'd be grateful when her settlement had grown large enough that they no longer had to rely on the Vitruvians at all. "How does our next delivery stand?"

"Food, medicine, and fertilizer. All as ordered. I'll send an update on the tractor component when I have it. But if you'd like to renegotiate the trade deal—"

"I didn't say that." Her jaw tightened. Of course Katherine would bring that up. "And you know very well that you depend on what we give you as well. And you can't afford for your people to find out either."

Katherine was silent.

Ayesha smiled. *Gotcha*.

"Everything will be delivered on schedule." Then Katherine signed off.

Ayesha set down the comm and paced her office, prayer beads clicking softly between her fingers. Self-sufficiency remained frustratingly out of reach. Katherine had been right about the soil quality, a fact that burned worse than admission of failure. They needed twice the acreage to produce the same yield as the Vitruvian fields. Her people were already working sixteen-hour days, harvesting grain by hand while swaddled in environmental suits that turned the simplest task into an ordeal. Without that tractor component, they'd face a critical food shortage by winter. And if dependence on Katherine's "generosity" became the norm, it would be the beginning of the end.

Ayesha would not allow it.

She paused at the window, looking out at the residential domes glowing in the dark. Her people deserved the dignity of self-sufficiency. Because as much as she hated to admit it, fear had a way of eroding conviction. If things got bad enough, some of her people might start whispering about going back to the main colony where "things were easier." Ayesha had seen it happen before, how quickly faith crumbled when stomachs growled. How easily devotion gave way to pragmatism when children went hungry. She had not led her people into the wilderness only to watch them crawl back to Katherine's embrace. The Divine had tested her plenty. This was simply another trial to overcome, another chance to prove her worthiness. She would find a way to feed her people, with or without Katherine's help.

Failure was not an option when the alternative was extinction.

Chapter Four

SAMARA FELT the high-pitched whine of the insect before she spotted it. Her hand lashed out reflexively, slapping her skin with a force that stung her own flesh.

It darted away.

Then landed on her arm.

Culicidae stellaris.

Star mosquitoes.

Renata had named them that for the swirling blue and white patterns on their chitin-covered abdomens that had reminded the xenobiologist of Van Gogh's *Starry Night.*

She slapped at the insect again. Then lifted her hand. Had she gotten it? Yep. There was a smear of dark purple blood across her forearm, the red of her own mixing with the indigo of whatever native creature it had fed on first.

Samara flicked its crushed body away, watching it spiral to the floor. Its translucent wings, torn and useless, fluttered one last time while six needle-thin legs kicked frantically at nothing before curling inward like a dying spider's.

Summer on DaVinci brought a plague of the damned

creatures. Thankfully, their bites didn't itch much and in a month or so, they'd be gone.

The common hall's cooling system wheezed like an asthmatic patient, running at maybe thirty percent capacity after three weeks of malfunction. The fans spun frantically beneath the curved metal ceiling, accomplishing nothing but circulating hot air from one miserable corner to another. Someone had propped the long windows open with metal rods, a pointless gesture in the dead, stagnant air.

The hall had been the first permanent structure they'd built after landing on this planet, and the now-modified walls displayed a peculiar marriage of Earth's technology and DaVinci's materials: polished metal struts framing sections of gray-hued wood native to the planet that had replaced the original metal walls, which had been cut up into smaller pieces and repurposed.

Vitruvia's leadership council slumped around the scarred wooden table, sweat plastering their shirts to their backs and darkening their collars. Samara fought against heavy eyelids as Mahmoud droned through geological details, his tablet projecting wavering 3D maps that seemed to shimmer in the heat haze. Twenty minutes into his presentation, and the only thing keeping her awake was the persistent buzzing of another star mosquito somewhere nearby.

"—and that's when we discovered the vein running directly beneath the eastern section of the lake." His voice finally penetrated Samara's haze of exhaustion. "Initial scans indicate approximately sixty metric tons of copper ore. Assuming eighty percent extraction efficiency, we're looking at potentially forty-eight tons of refined material."

Samara jolted to attention. Copper meant circuitry.

Circuitry meant repairs. Repairs meant functioning equipment, maybe even new medical devices.

"However," Mahmoud said, rotating the projection with a flick of his fingers, "extracting it presents significant challenges. The vein runs deep, following this fault line here." He pointed to a red line cutting beneath the blue representation of the mountain lake. "If we blast in the wrong spot, we could completely disrupt the topography of the lake floor."

"How disruptive are we talking?" Katherine asked from her seat at the head of the table, fingers steepled beneath her chin.

"Worst case?" Mahmoud grit his teeth. "The plains would flood. *Catastrophically*."

"What are the odds of that happening?" Katherine asked.

Mahmoud shrugged. "With our current equipment and limited geological data? I wouldn't recommend we put explosive charges anywhere near that lakebed until we know exactly what we're dealing with."

"What do you recommend?" Katherine asked.

"We need to delay further extraction until Maeve's team can construct LIDAR devices that will give us more accurate readings of the substrate layers." Mahmoud gestured toward the projection again. "Meanwhile, we focus on the iron deposits in the western ridge. They're more accessible, and we've already established safe extraction protocols."

"The LIDAR equipment could serve multiple functions, once constructed," Marcus argued. "We could adapt it for broader prospecting, locate other potential extraction sites. Maybe even other minerals."

Katherine turned to Maeve. "Timeline?"

"Couple of months, minimum." Maeve fanned herself

with braided tree fronds. "We're scraping the bottom of the barrel on circuit boards that can be recycled. Unless we can cannibalize some components from the ship's systems."

Katherine's jaw tightened. "We've taken as much as we're going to from the Borlaug unless it's an emergency. Which this is not."

"At what point does it become an emergency?" Maeve leaned back in her chair. "We're holding this colony together with duct tape and wishful thinking. Half our critical systems are running on borrowed time. The comms array drops signal if someone sneezes too hard. Power fluctuations trip the hydroponics pumps three times a week. Water filtration is running at sixty percent capacity. We don't need another mining operation, we need basic infrastructure that doesn't threaten to collapse every time there's a sporestorm."

Katherine eyed her. "The Borlaug is our last lifeline. If we ever need to evacuate, or if the Bloom mutates again and we can't find a cure, we need those systems operational."

"We don't have enough shuttle fuel to evacuate the whole colony to the ship, let alone enough food and water stores to keep everyone alive until we solve the problem," Maeve said. "And we're even farther from finding what we'd need to make more fuel than we are from mining that copper."

"The answer is no. We're tabling the Borlaug for now." Katherine glanced around the table. "Mahmoud, proceed with your assessment of the iron deposits, and if you need a bigger team, you've got it. Maeve, do your best to move up the timeline for the LIDAR equipment. We'll revisit the resource allocation later if necessary."

Mahmoud nodded, ending his projection with a tap.

Samara shifted in her seat, trying to stifle her disappointment. Her gene sequencer glitched as often as it worked these days, and Lucas seemed less and less confident that he could repair it. They couldn't afford to keep recycling components forever.

Lucas was the only machine on the planet that didn't seem to need constant repair. Was that because Hofstadter had built the android to last?

Or was it possible that Lucas was secretly repairing himself?

He was too damned good at keeping secrets.

"Moving on." Katherine wiped the sweat from her brow. "Harvest projections?"

Leo straightened in his chair. "Better than expected. Renata's new vegetable strains are thriving. The sorghum and millet we planted in the southeast fields are showing remarkable drought resistance. Overall yield should exceed our projections by about fifteen percent."

"And the sheep?" Katherine asked.

"Milk production is up from last year. We've started experimenting with cheese cultures again, which should give us a way to preserve some of the surplus."

The meeting dragged on as each department head rose to deliver their reports. Irrigation yield statistics. Power consumption trends. Birth rates versus mortality figures. The lifeblood of their little civilization, reduced to columns of data that grew blurrier by the minute as Samara's attention wandered.

Her genetics lab had become a glorified screening facility. No emergencies or breakthroughs. Just routine embryo checks and minor tweaks to the genomic library they'd spent twenty years building. Most days, Samara found herself assisting Renata with tasks any second-year apprentice could handle.

Was this how she would spend the rest of her life?

Working as a technician rather than a scientist?

She glanced at Renata, who was gesturing enthusiastically about crop resilience, one hand cradling her six-month pregnant belly. Dante, their son, carried both women's genetic heritage, thanks to the somatic cell nuclear transfer Samara had performed in secret. The procedure existed in a gray area of colony law: not explicitly forbidden, but far beyond the conservative parameters Katherine had established for genetic work.

As far as Katherine and the others knew, Marcus was Dante's father. And he would be in every other way that mattered. Only the three of them knew the truth.

A sharp kick to her shin jolted Samara back to reality, the pain radiating up her leg like an electric shock.

She glanced over at Renata.

She raised her eyebrows.

Samara looked around and realized that everyone at the table was looking at her.

"Sorry," she said, straightening in her chair. "Could you please repeat that?"

Katherine sighed. "Your report, Samara?"

Heat surged up Samara's neck and into her face. She'd been caught doing exactly what she'd criticized others for in the past: checking out when decisions were being made.

She wanted to say she was starting to feel like dead weight. That the lab work that had once filled her with purpose now felt mechanical.

There was nothing harder for a scientist than the absence of discovery.

"And Phoebe?" Katherine asked. "How is she doing?"

The question threw her off guard; she wished Katherine hadn't asked it. Because now she had to lie. And she hated lying to Katherine. "Fine. The medication Leila prescribed is managing her migraines."

But it was true enough, in the way that half-truths often were. Phoebe's headaches were manageable. For now. But they were getting worse. More frequent. More intense.

And Samara had no way to stop them.

Two decades of trying, and she still hadn't found a way to reverse the off-target effects of the genetic manipulation that had allowed Phoebe to survive before they'd found the cure for the Bloom.

She could almost hear Ayesha saying, *I could have told you it was a bad idea.*

"Good," Katherine nodded. "Is that everything?"

A murmur of assent circled the table as chairs scraped back and people gathered their things. But Samara stayed seated, staring at her reflection in the polished tabletop.

Twenty years as the colony's savior, and what did she have to show for it?

A daughter suffering from a condition she'd created and couldn't cure.

A career that had stagnated into routine.

And worst of all, the growing suspicion that her greatest achievements were already behind her, fading into colony history like colors in a photograph left in the sun.

Chapter Five

Phoebe squinted into the microscope, studying the cellular structure displayed on the slide. The lab lights were too bright, and a dull ache had settled behind her right eye. But she couldn't dim them because she needed to see the details of her specimen. So she did her best to ignore them.

At least the lab was cooler than the rest of the colony, maintained at a precise 19°C to preserve samples and create optimal growing conditions for some of the plant specimens. Rows of climate-controlled growth chambers housed various experiments along the walls. Phoebe's occupied the smallest one in the corner.

She straightened, rubbing her eyes.

She really needed to stop. The headache was getting worse. She reached for her tablet and tapped through a series of gene sequences, comparing them to her notes.

"Come on," she said, sliding her finger across the screen to highlight a section. "Why won't you take?"

The culture before her contained modified cells from what colonists called the "Crown Willow." In its natural state, the tree grew in a mesmerizing pattern, with branches that arced upward before curving back to touch the ground, where they sprouted new roots and trunks in perfect circles. If Phoebe could enhance that natural architecture, these trees could become living shelters, living domes requiring minimal materials to transform into permanent structures.

But something was wrong.

Again.

She leaned back in her chair, the metal creaking in protest. This was her fourteenth attempt. The previous batches of modified seedlings had all died before they developed beyond the initial sprouting stage. And this latest sample looked to be heading in the same direction.

The cells on the slide already showed the telltale signs of deterioration: fragmenting organelles, compromised membranes.

Death at the cellular level.

Phoebe pushed away from the workstation, rolling her chair over to the climate chamber. Rows of small pots contained what should have been vibrant green sprouts. Instead, most showed only withered, blackened stems poking through the soil. A few hadn't broken the surface at all.

She tapped her tongue against her teeth. "What am I missing?"

Phoebe loathed the thought of failing again. She was the daughter of Samara Makinde, the geneticist who'd saved them all. But she couldn't even do basic modification of a plant.

She opened the climate chamber's control panel, adjusting the humidity by a fraction of a percent. Not that it would make any difference now. The damage was already done at the genetic level. She'd tweaked one gene too far. Or not far enough. That was the risk when you started editing before you understood the whole system.

Which was exactly what her mother had done to her.

She hated that she was killing them.

She had adjusted their genetic sequences to shape their growth, make them stronger, ensure they were more resilient. She had mapped the sequences, made careful edits, accounted for every variable she could think of. And yet every time, death was her result.

Phoebe had been edited to survive on DaVinci. She was supposed to grow into something better, something useful. But the process had left flaws. Off-target effects that no one had predicted or solved. Not even her mother.

Genetically altered with the best intentions.

Doomed by something lurking in the code.

Breaking down despite every effort to fix it.

Phoebe wanted to believe she wasn't like the plants. That she wasn't just another experiment gone wrong. That she wasn't *doomed*.

But there was no such thing as guarantees. Not when it came to life and death.

How long did she have?

Days? Weeks? Years?

Stop.

That line of thinking led to nothing good.

And right now she needed to focus on her school project.

Something in the combination of adjustments she'd made was triggering cascade failures in the plants' cell walls. She needed to adjust how the microtubules created trusses across each cell so that the vertical and horizontal growth trajectory was programmable, as well as the overall organization of the cells within larger structures. She just couldn't figure out how to get the proteins to fold the way she wanted. The genes she'd targeted controlled branch growth patterning and root formation; they had nothing to do with basic metabolic functions, so this shouldn't be happening. There had to be some unforeseen interaction, some off-target effect she couldn't see.

Her head was now pounding.

She needed to take her medication, but she'd left it too late, thinking she wouldn't need it today. The idea was to catch the migraine before it bloomed.

"Stupid."

Was she talking about forgetting her pills or about herself? She wasn't entirely sure. The distinction seemed unimportant. She was just another failed experiment, after all. Why was she trying so hard?

Because she was trying to be like her mother.

The brilliant, logical, analytical Samara. Phoebe had chosen this project because she thought it would make Samara proud, not because she cared in the slightest about genetics.

She reached for the nutrient solution, her fingers fumbling as pain stabbed behind her eyes. The glass vessel tilted, teetered on the edge, then plummeted toward the floor.

Phoebe lunged, catching it inches from shattering, solution sloshing dangerously close to the rim.

A shadow fell across her workstation.

"Still at it?"

Phoebe started, looking up to see Renata.

"Yeah." Phoebe gestured at the dying plants in the climate chamber. "Not that it's doing any good."

Renata walked over to her, examining the withered seedlings. "*Hmm.* Same problem as the last batch?"

Phoebe nodded. "They make it to early germination, then just … die. I've checked everything. The gene splicing took. The growth hormone levels are balanced. The soil composition is perfect. But as soon as they start developing roots, they collapse."

Renata peered at the genetic model still rotating on Phoebe's tablet. "That's the thing about science right? What doesn't work is just as valuable as what does. We'll try something else."

"Why can't I make them grow?" Phoebe stared at the plants. "What's wrong with me?"

"Stop it." Renata hugged her. "There's nothing wrong with you. You're working with an alien genome. We shouldn't take it personally when we discover that we still have more to learn."

"I guess so."

Renata studied her for a moment. "Are you feeling alright?"

"I'm fine. Just tired."

Renata didn't look convinced. "Wrap this up, it's almost dinner time. Marcus made chili."

Phoebe nodded.

Renata leaned down and kissed her head, then left the lab.

Phoebe reached into her pocket and pulled out her anti-migraine pills. It was probably too late to take them, but she'd try it anyway.

She shook one out of the container and swallowed it dry, grimacing at the bitter taste. She stared at the dying seedlings, feeling as though her brain was made of dying seedlings as well.

In a surge of frustration, she swept one of the plants off the shelf. It crashed to the floor, dirt spilling across the tiles.

Regret washed over her.

She knelt on the floor, eyeing the plant. "I'm so sorry."

She stuck the fragile seedling back into its pot, then scooped up the spilled dirt and tucked it around the roots. It wasn't the plants' fault that they were dying. It was hers.

Once she cleaned it up, she shut down her equipment, logged her failed results, and headed for the door, turning off the lights as she left.

She would try again tomorrow.

Maybe Renata was right and there was a solution she hadn't considered yet.

Or maybe some things just weren't meant to be messed with.

Chapter Six

After dinner, Phoebe slipped out of her bedroom window and into the hot summer night. Thankfully, the medication had worked and the pressure in her skull had eased, leaving only a dull pulsing at the back of her head.

She'd waited until Renata and Marcus had settled in front of their movie before announcing she was tired, yawning repeatedly as she backed toward her bedroom door. They trusted her completely, which only intensified the guilt gnawing at her insides. But she had to get out.

Samara wouldn't notice she was gone, either. She'd probably spend the night hunched over her workstation, forgetting to eat or sleep. That made the guilt worse, because Phoebe was probably the puzzle she was trying to solve.

Phoebe crossed the compound, sticking to the shadows between buildings. The colony had no clear rules about being out alone after dark; everyone was trusted to use common sense and follow the safety protocols.

But it was different for Phoebe. Samara had forbidden

her to leave the house at night unaccompanied. She'd go nuclear if she discovered her daughter's midnight escapes.

But Phoebe wasn't doing anything dangerous. She just wanted to hang out with her friend without an adult telling her what to do.

She got on her dirt bike and rode in the direction of the Hyperion ruins, hoping Flutter had managed to get away too. It was just under fifteen minutes from the Vitruvian colony, but it felt a lot longer in the dark.

Within minutes, the terrain flattened out and she left the last of the colony's structures behind. She kept her eyes out for the half-buried irrigation pipe that had been abandoned years ago, her marker to turn. Somewhere to her left, something small skittered through the undergrowth.

She rode on, spotted the pipe, then turned right. The twin moons cast enough light to navigate, turning the land silver blue.

Within minutes, the ruins emerged from the dark.

Phoebe got off the bike and walked it between the first two buildings.

This was the spot of humanity's first failed attempt at colonizing DaVinci. Despite the fact that Phoebe had spent a lot of time here looking at stars with Lucas, the site had an eerie stillness, as if time itself had frozen at the moment of its abandonment.

Phoebe wound between the decaying structures, slowing when she reached the bowl-shaped clearing behind what had once been the Hyperion colony's medical labs. Beneath this soil lay a mass grave of deformed humans, mostly children genetically engineered with DNA from different Earth animals with highly effective immune systems. Humanity's first desperate attempts to survive the Bloom. Phoebe would sometimes find offerings here from the Hyperionites. Small tokens. A scattering of polished stones. Once, a crude wooden carving of something that might have been a child.

Yet the Vitruvians rarely spoke of this place, and when they did, as if it were something shameful to remember; a mistake, rather than the tragedy that it seemed to Phoebe.

But the Hyperionites would not let their dead ancestors be erased.

Phoebe took comfort in that. Maybe when the time came for her own death, Flutter and Poke and Tally would choose to remember her this way. Hypers lived much longer than humans, thanks to the longevity experiments that had been performed on the original colonists before they'd left Earth. There was a good chance that Flutter would someday meet Phoebe's great-grandchildren and tell them stories about the first Vitruvians, long after Phoebe was gone.

Jeez, she was being morbid today.

She spotted Flutter sitting in the shadows on a broken step across the site.

She waved, running toward her friend.

But as she got closer, she realized she'd made a mistake.

That wasn't Flutter.

It was a boy.

Phoebe froze mid-step.

The boy sat perfectly still as she approached, his posture betraying neither fear nor aggression so much as cautious assessment. She could make out lean features in the moonlight: close-cropped dark hair and skin so pale it seemed to glow silver. He seemed to have none of the stan-dard-issue gear that any of her people would carry while leaving the colony at night: comm, head lamp, medical kit, baton or stun gun for protection.

He was a Naturalist.

Contact with him was forbidden. Not just for her, but for all Vitruvians, unless Katherine had given formal authorization. Because the Naturalists were religious fanatics who denied the very existence of truth and who hated science and technology and progress. She'd studied the Schism and the Naturalist Fallacy and Dr. Basu's cult in school, and she'd even heard her mothers' stories about the first days of the colony. Dr. Basu had tried to kidnap her when she was a baby, and had almost succeeded, until one of the Hypers had rescued Phoebe. Then the genocidal cult leader had started a war to eradicate the Hypers. Samara and Lucas had helped stop it.

She should be terrified of this boy, who might hate her enough to want to kill her just for existing.

But she wasn't.

They stared at each other for a full minute before either spoke.

"You're a Naturalist," she said, then immediately hated herself for stating the obvious.

He nodded.

"Where's your environmental suit? I thought you were all terrified of the Bloom."

"I don't need a suit."

She raised her brows. "That's not what I've heard."

"Well, maybe you don't know everything about us."

Phoebe lifted her chin "Well, I know a lot. And you shouldn't be here."

For a moment he didn't say anything. Then he gave a slight nod and his shoulders dropped. "Yeah, you're probably right. I just didn't expect someone from the other colony to be out here."

"Vitruvia," she said. "We don't just call ourselves 'the other one,' you know."

The ghost of a smile touched his lips, then vanished.

"Well, I've heard a lot of different names for your settlement."

She probably didn't want to know. She should probably leave now. But this might be the only chance she ever had to talk to a Naturalist.

To somebody who was different from everyone else she'd ever met.

And he didn't *seem* dangerous. The way the adults talked about the Naturalists made them all sound like braindead lunatics who couldn't be reasoned with.

Maybe he was pretending to be reasonable?

"What are you doing out here anyway?"

He hesitated. "Exploring."

"At night? All alone?" She'd been taught that the Naturalists never left their compound without suits. What if that was a lie to make her people feel safer? What if he'd been sent out to do something to hurt the main colony?

Or was he acting on his own?

"Did Dr. Basu give you permission to be out here?"

He scowled at her. "Did you ask for permission?"

He had a point. They were both breaking the rules, and neither of them had any more right to be here than the other. But she still felt annoyed that he'd intruded on what she thought of as the one place she could get away from the rules and expectations that followed her around the colony when she was there.

It was unreasonable to think of this place as *hers*, but for some reason she did.

"This is where I meet my friend Fl—" Naturalists thought Hypers were subhuman because not only were they heavily modified, but the modifications came from non-human DNA. "—sometimes."

"I should …" He gestured into the dark.

She shrugged, to show she wasn't scared of him at all. "You don't have to leave on my account."

"Are you sure?"

She nodded, leaning against a broken wall. "What are you doing here anyway?"

He shrugged. "I sneak out sometimes."

Phoebe raised an eyebrow. "Yeah?"

"Yeah." He scuffed a boot against the dirt. "I like the fresh air. Especially when I need to think."

"You did look lost in thought. Bad news?"

He stared at her, then nodded.

"What's your name?" she asked.

"Atlas Shan," he said.

She held out a hand. "Phoebe Makinde."

"Samara's daughter?" He recoiled. "The first…"

Phoebe rolled her eyes, dropping her hand. "Yep, the first successful genetic modification that allowed humans to exist on DaVinci. That's me. Patient Zero."

Atlas stared so long, she almost glanced over her shoulder to see if there was something behind her. "Problem?"

"I thought you'd be … different."

"Different?"

"I dunno, deformed." He flushed.

"Deformed how?

"It's just …" He looked embarrassed. "Dr. Basu describes the contamination as something visible. But you're …"

"Normal?"

"*Beautiful.*" He winced, looking like he wanted to take the words back as soon as he said them.

Phoebe felt herself blush. No one had ever called her beautiful before.

"Sorry. I hope I didn't make you feel uncomfortable."

"Of course not, I hear that all the time. Wherever I go. *'Oh, Phoebe, not only are you the smartest girl in Vitruvia, you're also the most beautiful.'*"

"You do?"

"No!" She snorted. "But thanks. And besides, no offense taken. I kind of expected you to be …"

"What?"

She shrugged. "Less civilized?"

His eyebrows shot up.

"Everyone in Vitruvia talks about the Naturalists like you're superstitious savages."

Atlas laughed and the sound was surprisingly warm. "Well, *we're* told the Vitruvians are soulless scientists who'd dissect their own children for research data."

Her mouth dropped open. "That's what your people think?"

He nodded.

She crossed her arms. "I'm beginning to think we've both been told a lot of things that might not be entirely true."

"Like?"

"How the Naturalists are all sickly and inbred because they refuse medical care."

"Or how the Vitruvians replace their real emotions with chemicals so they don't have to feel anything."

"I heard Naturalists don't even name their kids until they're a year old because they might not survive that long."

"At least, we're not like Vitruvians, whose genes are so scrambled, their buttholes are where their belly buttons are supposed to be."

They both burst out laughing at the same time.

"That's the dumbest thing I've ever heard," Phoebe said when she could breathe again.

Atlas wrinkled his nose. "Me too."

Phoebe sat on the crumbling stair and patted the empty space behind her. Atlas glanced over his shoulder into the dark as though he were thinking of leaving. But a second later, he joined her.

"Now that I know what Naturalists aren't," Phoebe said. "Tell me what they are."

He thought for a moment. "Faithful. We believe in something bigger than ourselves. Or we're supposed to. Everyone works hard to be worthy to live here." He hesitated, like he wanted to say more, but instead, he asked, "What about Vitruvians?"

"The same, except the something bigger isn't about faith, it's about scientific progress. We get that we have to evolve if we want to survive. We're responsible for the continuation of our species."

"So are we," Atlas said quickly. "We're preserving true humanity by keep our genomes uncont—"

He stopped, looked away.

Uncontaminated.

That's what he'd been taught, that the Vitruvians were contaminating their humanity with genetic engineering. It wasn't his fault, he was just ignorant.

"There's so much genetic variation within any population that the idea of a 'true human' is meaningless." Phoebe tried to channel the patient voice that Renata often used with her when she was being particularly clueless. "But we have strict rules to limit when genetic engineering can be used and what genes can be altered. We know that every time you change something there can be off-target effects—" Her least favorite words in the world. "—and we only do it when there's no other way to preserve health. Or life."

"Isn't your mother the prime example of how you don't do that?" Atlas asked.

"Don't you mean me?" Phoebe snapped. "I'm the prime example. But it was life or death for the whole colony when Samara modified me."

"If she'd been patient, she wouldn't have needed to," he blurted, then looked away again, turning redder than a fireberry.

"Why not?" Phoebe asked.

He shrugged. "Never mind."

A minute ago, they'd been laughing. Now she was furious with him. His certainty that he was right. His unwillingness to listen to her point of view and engage in a rational debate.

Well, that was fine, because she wasn't feeling rational at all right now.

"No, explain to me why my existence was unnecessary and my mother should never have given birth to me."

"I didn't mean that," he snapped.

"Then what?"

He stared at her like he was furious at her, too. His jaw worked, his nostrils flared, but he didn't move, and the longer he stared, the more she wanted to squirm. Because it wasn't just anger she saw on his face anymore.

"I'm glad that you exist," he finally said. "And I don't want to fight."

"What do you want?"

As he turned his head toward her and leaned closer, moonlight glinted in his eyes, turning the pale irises silver.

Phoebe felt her heart flutter. He'd called her beautiful.

And it wasn't his fault that he'd been brainwashed his whole life. It wasn't her fault that she'd been lied to, either. They were both victims of a fight that had started before either of them were born.

Something shifted in the space between them, an invisible current that made the hair on her arms stand at attention. Her heartbeat quickened, no longer a steady rhythm but an insistent drumming that seemed to echo in her ears.

Atlas leaned toward her with the slow inevitability of gravity, and Phoebe found herself moving to meet him; it wasn't a conscious choice but a physical pull she couldn't defy.

Heat radiated between them, turning the night air thick.

His knee brushed against hers, sending an electric jolt up her thigh.

She cataloged each detail: the slight parting of his lips, the fractional dilation of his pupils, the way his breath caught in his throat as the distance between them narrowed to centimeters.

Her skin tingled, and she was aware of everything, all at once. Including the fact that if she leaned forward just a little more …

Footsteps.

Running.

Closing in.

They both froze. Then turned at the same time to see a figure emerge from the shadows.

Poke.

He stopped running, his dark eyes bouncing from Phoebe to Atlas and back. He signed, too fast for Phoebe to understand precisely what he was saying, but she caught the gist. *HELP!*

Chapter Seven

ATLAS BOLTED TO HIS FEET.

A Hyper had emerged from between the trees and stood ten feet away. Not what he'd expected. It was taller, with limbs just a little too long for comfort. Moonlight glinted off patches of what looked more like fish or reptile scales than human skin. Their eyes were black, unblinking pools that seemed to absorb light rather than reflect it.

Stories from his childhood flashed through his mind. Hyperionites raiding the settlement for food and medicine. Attacking people who strayed too far from safety. Stealing children who misbehaved from under their parents' noses. Dr. Basu described them as monsters created through reckless genetic manipulation, the inevitable result of human arrogance. Abominations who'd turned against their creators.

Atlas lunged forward to put himself between Phoebe and the monster, scooping up a jagged chunk of rubble, ready to swing if that thing came any closer. "Stay back."

The creature's eyes fixed on him. It made a clicking sound that raised the hair on Atlas' neck.

Some kind of threat? Or was it afraid of him?

"It's okay, Atlas." Phoebe laid a hand on his shoulder, and Atlas wasn't sure if she meant to reassure him or restrain him. "Poke is a friend."

Atlas glanced at Phoebe, struggling to reconcile what he knew with what he saw. He still couldn't get over the fact that she was Vitruvian. Let alone Samara's daughter. The beginning of the end for human purity. She was all sharp angles and quiet intensity, with a wildness in her eyes that he would never have expected, given what he'd been told about her people. She looked like she belonged out here, halfway between wilderness and ruin.

She was the kind of beautiful that made him forget what he was supposed to be afraid of.

But the sight of the Hyper reminded him of DaVinci's dangers.

How could she be friends with a monster?

"What do you mean it's your friend?" Atlas couldn't keep the disbelief from his voice. "Those… creatures are incredibly dangerous."

The Hyper gestured something, its long fingers moving in some kind of pattern Atlas couldn't begin to decipher, but he knew it was upset. Did it think the two of them were trespassing in its territory? Phoebe had said she came here quite often.

"*He*," Phoebe said. "Not it. Poke is trying to tell me something. And you're scaring him. Now stop it."

Atlas blinked. "I'm scaring him?"

Phoebe pointed to the rock.

He flushed, lowering his hand.

She hadn't looked for a weapon. She must think him a coward.

The Hyper made more gestures, glancing at Atlas with obvious distrust.

Phoebe gestured back. Then she said, "Poke needs help. Some of his people are sick."

"Are you telling me you can talk to him?"

"They evolved a sophisticated gestural language because the adaptations that allowed them to survive changed the shape of their larynx." Phoebe stepped out from behind him, toward the creature. "Want to come with us?"

His jaw fell open. "You can't be serious about going with it. Him. He's a Hyper."

The creature took a step forward, and Atlas raised the rock again.

It dropped into a slight crouch, shoulders lowering into what looked like a defensive stance to Atlas.

"Stop it!" Phoebe said. "What's wrong with you? He's not going to attack us."

"You don't know that." Everything Atlas had been taught screamed that they were in danger. The creature, whatever intelligence it possessed, wasn't human and couldn't be trusted.

"I've known Poke since I was a child. He's my friend."

Atlas froze.

She'd known him since she was a child?

He looked back at the Hyper. It was watching them but made no more aggressive moves. Was it possible Phoebe was right?

Or was she about to walk into a trap?

"He needs help," she said. "And I'm going."

Atlas didn't know what to do. Dr. Basu had always said the Hyperionites were the ultimate example of what the Vitruvians' approach to scientific progress led to. Abominations. Demons. The end result of playing God.

But the Hyper standing before him contradicted everything he'd been told. Those dark eyes held unmistakable intelligence. The creature communicated with precise hand movements, carrying on a real conversation with Phoebe.

Whatever Poke was, he wasn't some mindless beast.

"It was nice to meet you, Atlas. Have a good night."

Something tightened in his chest. He couldn't bear to let her walk away, not when the world had just cracked open with possibilities he'd never imagined.

"Wait!"

She paused, halfway turned away from him.

"I'm going too, with you and Poke." He dropped the rock. It fell to the ground and rolled towards the Hyper, who stopped it with his foot.

Atlas felt a moment of panic. But the creature didn't pick it up.

Phoebe eyed him. And he was worried that she was going to say no. But then…

"If you're coming, you can't act like an asshole. No scaring Poke, no treating his people like monsters. Got it?"

"Got it."

She folded her arms across her chest. "Good. Now apologize for scaring him."

Atlas swallowed hard. He'd reacted according to his training: see threat, defend against threat. But Poke wasn't a threat. Just unfamiliar.

That his first instinct had been fear bothered him more than he wanted to admit. He'd been programmed to see Hypers as sub-human. And those stories about Hyperionites — that they hunted in the dark like animals, couldn't be reasoned with, and attacked without warning — sounded a lot like the stories he'd been told about Vitruvians. That they were arrogant, godless, obsessed with control.

Barely human.

But Phoebe was nothing like the stories he'd been told. So why did he assume Poke would be?

"I didn't mean to scare you." The words felt stiff and unnatural in his mouth. But maybe that was the point. Maybe unlearning something meant it didn't feel easy at first. "I won't do it again. I'm sorry."

Phoebe signed, translating.

Poke didn't move for a second, then gave a sharp nod.

"If you mess this up," Phoebe said, turning to him. "I'll never speak to you again."

Atlas believed her.

"I won't mess up. I promise." And he meant it. Despite barely knowing her, the thought of Phoebe shutting him out hit him with surprising force. She'd upended everything he thought he knew in the span of minutes, and he needed to know more about her world, and what life was like outside of Naturalist doctrine.

Maybe there was something else pulling him toward her. Something that made his heart beat faster when she looked at him. But he wasn't ready to examine that too closely. Right now, he simply couldn't stand the thought of losing this unexpected connection.

She studied him for a moment before nodding. "Okay."

The thick night air buzzed with insects as a beat of silence passed between them.

Then came footsteps.

They both turned toward the path.

Atlas tensed.

Had someone from the Naturalist compound followed him?

A figure approached through the darkness. Tall, with military posture and a purposeful stride.

"Unbelievable," Phoebe muttered.

The man stopped before them, scanning all three with unnerving efficiency.

Phoebe let out a slow breath. "Lucas. What are you doing here?"

"I could ask you the same question. Your mother thinks you're at home in bed."

Phoebe's father.

She scowled. "How did you know I was gone?"

"You are not as careful as you think."

"So you followed me? Did Samara put you up to this?"

"If Samara knew you were sneaking out, she would undoubtedly put a stop to it altogether," Lucas said, his tone matter-of-fact.

Atlas glanced at Phoebe. So she wasn't supposed to be out either. Wasn't allowed to roam without supervision, just like him. Something they had in common.

"She could try," Phoebe replied.

"Exactly," Lucas nodded. "Another rule wouldn't stop you, so another solution was necessary. Now, what's going on?"

"Poke needs us to come with him," Phoebe said. "The Hypers need help."

"Very well." Lucas nodded again, then turned to Atlas. "Does Dr. Basu know of your nocturnal explorations?"

He considered lying, but what was the point? Unauthorized contact was too big a deal for Phoebe's father not to report it.

"She does not."

Lucas studied him for a long moment and Atlas had the unsettling feeling of being scanned from the inside out, every secret and motive catalogued. "You'd prefer she doesn't find out?"

"Yes." He cleared his throat. "Sir."

"Phoebe," Lucas said, not taking his eyes off Atlas, "I should send you home."

"But—"

"*However*," he continued, "I believe you would be safer if you remained with me." His gaze shifted to Poke. "Where do we need to go?"

"To a cave in the mountains near the Hyperionite settlement," Phoebe answered.

"Then we should leave." Lucas' eyes flicked over Atlas, cool and calculating. "You should return to your settlement before you are missed."

Atlas hesitated. The sensible thing would be to head back to the settlement. But when he looked into Phoebe's eyes, something inside him shifted.

He wanted more time with her. Wanted to see where the Hyperionites lived. It felt like he was standing at the edge of something monumental. He'd been given a chance to understand the world beyond everything he'd been taught.

If he turned around now, he'd spend the rest of his life wondering what might have been.

"I'm coming," he said.

Phoebe smiled, and his heart jumped in a way he wasn't ready to examine.

Lucas gestured toward the path. "Stay close. If you can't keep up, I won't slow down."

With each step taking him away from familiar territory, Atlas felt the distance growing between himself and everything he'd been taught to believe. It was both terrifying and exhilarating, like being in freefall without knowing if there was ground below.

Chapter Eight

PHOEBE FOLLOWED Poke and Lucas up the narrow mountain path. Loose stones shifted under her boots, forcing her to slow down and watch her footing. She glanced back to see Atlas trailing several paces behind.

Poke moved like he'd been born on these slopes, while Lucas kept pace with the graceful precision of an athlete, never missing his footing. But she and Atlas both struggled; every few steps brought another slide or stumble as loose rocks betrayed their weight.

The path tilted upward at a punishing angle, forcing Phoebe to lean forward to keep her balance. Her lungs burned with each breath, the thin mountain air offering less oxygen than she was used to. The headache she'd forgotten in the excitement of meeting Atlas now pulsed at her temples, a dull throb keeping time with her heartbeat.

Lucas paused at a sharp bend, waiting for her to catch up. "Your heart rate is elevated and your oxygen saturation has dropped three points. Is it the headache?"

Phoebe squinted up at him in the dark. It was so easy

to forget that Lucas was an android. "Are you biohacking me again?"

"I'm responsible for you until you're back home."

It was a small invasion of her privacy. But he'd also known she was sneaking out and hadn't told Samara. He'd let Atlas come with them, instead of sending him back to the Naturalist settlement. And he hadn't said he was going to report the unauthorized contact, either.

So she didn't argue with him.

"I'm fine." She brushed sweat-dampened hair from her face. "I just need to catch my breath."

Lucas analyzed her face, his eyes cataloging her symptoms even as she denied them. For a second, she thought he'd call her bluff. Instead, he simply nodded, then retrieved a tiny box from one of his pockets and removed a pill from it, which he held out to her.

"This dose should be sufficient." She recognized the pill. Her migraine medicine. Did he carry it around with him, just in case he happened to be nearby when she had an attack?

As soon as she took the pill and swallowed it dry, he continued on.

Stopping had given Atlas a chance to catch up. He looked nervous.

"Need a break?" she asked.

He shook his head. "I've just never been this far from the colony before."

She raised her brows. "Never?"

He shook his head again.

"Scared?"

"No," he replied after a beat of hesitation. "Not while I'm with you."

Heat flooded her face, the compliment catching Phoebe completely off-guard.

Poke clicked.

"This way," Lucas said, glancing back at them.

Phoebe sighed. "Yes, *dad*."

Lucas didn't respond to her sarcasm. Samara would have. With another lecture.

"After you." Atlas gestured to the path.

The landscape transformed as they climbed. Thick underbrush surrendered to skeletal trees, then bare rock studded with patches of blue-green lichen that glowed with faint bioluminescence, an eerie light that cast everything in an underwater hue. Poke led them around another bend, then off the trail entirely, gesturing toward a narrow passage between two large rocks nearly blocking the way.

Interesting.

Was it natural, or had the Hypers placed the boulders on purpose to discourage outsiders from going farther?

Phoebe had visited their village plenty of times, but she'd never been up here.

All the more reason to do it while she had the chance.

She squeezed through the narrow passage after the others, the rock walls scraping against her shoulders before she emerged on the other side. The temperature drop hit her like a slap as she emerged on the other side. The air here was at least ten degrees cooler, carrying a musty tang that scratched at the back of her throat.

The mountain face had been carved with precision; no natural erosion could create such perfectly straight lines. A rectangular opening, about three meters high and two wide, had been cut directly into the solid rock. Light spilled from within, casting long shadows that seemed to reach toward them like grasping fingers.

The sight sent a shiver down Phoebe's spine. She'd never gone into a cave before. Samara would have a fit.

All the more reason to do it, now that she had the

opportunity. Poke turned toward them and signed, "Others inside. Waiting."

If the Hypers were already in there, that meant it was probably safe, right?

Lucas planted himself between them and the entrance, his posture shifting subtly into something more guarded. Protective. "Wait outside."

"Why?"

"I want to see what we're dealing with," Lucas replied before following Poke inside.

Phoebe looked at Atlas. "Come on. I didn't come all this way to wait. Did you?"

Atlas' eyes darted between the cave entrance and the path they'd climbed, weighing the unknown against the safety of retreat. Conflict played across his features in real time. "Won't your dad get mad?"

"Lucas doesn't really get mad. Not like other people. And he's not exactly my father."

Although he certainly acted like it sometimes. For as long as she could remember, he'd always been there. Patiently answering the myriad questions that bubbled out of her when she was younger. Noticing when she needed help with something and showing her how to do it better. Inviting her to accompany him on his visits to the Hyper village when everyone else was hesitant to indulge her curiosity.

No matter how many rules she broke, he never expressed disappointment in her, unlike everyone else in her life. He'd ask her to explain her decision-making process, then he'd point out the factors she'd failed to consider, the assumptions she'd made without testing them, and the risks she'd underestimated.

Her real father was dead, some anonymous sperm donor that had been left behind on Earth whose only legacy was to have added to the genetic diversity of the colony by providing half of Phoebe's genes.

And while she loved her adoptive father, Marcus, he was more like a kind uncle.

So, Lucas might as well be her dad.

She was okay with giving him another opportunity to refine her decision-making skills. Because whatever was happening inside that cave involved her too, whether Lucas liked it or not. Poke had come to *her* for help.

Plus, she hadn't dragged Atlas all this way just to abandon him outside.

Phoebe held out her hand.

Atlas froze for a beat before taking it. She smiled as he tightened his fingers around hers. Something about the way he held on made her chest tighten, just a little.

They entered the tunnel.

After several meters, it opened into a chamber so massive that the ceiling vanished into shadow, swallowing the light from Poke's candle before it could reach the top. Someone had transformed the natural cavern into a livable space: the floor had been polished smooth, the walls reinforced with salvaged timber struts. A makeshift ventilation system coughed and rattled overhead, pushing stale air through a network of metal ducts that disappeared into the darkness. But the atmosphere still felt oppressive, as if the mountain itself resented their intrusion.

Near the center of the cave, seven Hypers sat in a semicircle on stone chairs. Behind them, something that looked suspiciously like a quarantine chamber, at the back of the cave. Lucas stood next to it talking to another Hyper, and older one, based on the looseness of the scaly skin under his jaw.

"That looks like it's been ripped out of a ship," Phoebe said to Atlas.

"How do you know?"

She gestured to it. "The reinforced seal, the external paneling, the recessed access ports, all standard for sterile containment. And that locking mechanism is designed for pressure variance. It wasn't built for planet side use."

Atlas stared at her.

"What?"

"You're so smart."

She flushed. "Thanks."

Phoebe and Atlas navigated around the seated Hypers, whose eyes tracked their movement with unblinking intensity. Lucas watched the two of them approach, his eyes dropping to their joined hands. He raised one eyebrow. Atlas let go.

Why did Lucas have to look so disapproving? That was Samara's job. Phoebe was about to say so, but then a small glass door in the chamber snagged her attention and she peered through it.

A pair of emaciated forms lay on cots inside: a man and a woman with nearly translucent skin threaded with dark blue veins and mottled with age spots, stretched paper-thin over the bones practically protruding from their flesh. White hair clung to their scalps in chunks. Every labored breath looked painful, their chests rising and falling in irregular patterns. The man's withered fingers twitched against the bedsheet, while the woman's lips formed words no one could hear through the glass.

Whoever they were, they had been here for a long time.

They weren't just old, they were impossibly frail. These people had not aged naturally; they were relics, preserved far beyond their natural span by means Phoebe could not fathom.

"Who are they?" she asked.

Lucas glanced down at her. "Hyperionite elders."

"But they're human."

"Their age suggests they could be original Hyperion colonists," Lucas said. "Though that would make them nearly two hundred years old."

One of the original colonists. The idea that someone who had lived on Earth so long ago might still be alive on DaVinci…

Phoebe turned her attention to the door. It was reinforced metal, thick and sealed shut, with an airlock-like pass-through built into it, sized for small items to be transferred through.

Were these two people prisoners?

Why else would they be locked inside the mountain?

The Hyperionite elder signed, "Eldest Sick. Need Medicine."

Lucas nodded. "Go outside and send a message to your mother, Phoebe. Tell her we need Dr. Callas, a cargo vehicle for two patients, protective gear, and full contagion containment."

"Do you want me to tell her what we found?"

His expression didn't change. "No. The comms aren't secure."

She blinked.

Who would be listening?

The Naturalists? The other Hypers? Someone in their colony?

She opened her mouth to ask, but Lucas locked his gaze onto hers. "Please, Phoebe. *Now*."

She snapped her mouth closed. And nodded.

Then she hurried back toward the entrance of the cave.

Chapter Nine

ATLAS TURNED to follow Phoebe out, but Lucas extended an arm, blocking his path. "A word, if you don't mind."

He stopped. Now that Phoebe was out of earshot, would Lucas warn him away from her?

Maybe blackmail him to stay away by threatening to tell Dr. Basu about catching them together.

To his surprise, Lucas did neither.

"It's unrealistic to think you won't tell your people what you've discovered here," he said. "But I should warn you that these individuals might be ill, and while the quarantine chamber is currently sealed, we do not know if it continues to be effective or if the Hyperionites have been exposed to potential pathogens. Which means that the three of us may also have been exposed."

"I'm not a tattletale." As soon as he spoke the words, they sounded childish to him.

"I have not implied any such thing, Atlas Shan. I am referring to the risk of asymptomatic transmission. Even if your immune system can defeat the potential pathogen, you could be exposed to something here without showing symptoms. If you return to your community carrying an unfamiliar pathogen, they will have no defenses, thanks to the immunosuppressants they take."

His blood turned to ice water. Not only did Phoebe's father know who he was, the man must know *what* Atlas was: the vessel for the Divine Blueprint.

Lucas looked at him without judgment. "You may be a danger to everyone around you. You must weigh the risks."

Phoebe's father was right. And he was leaving it up to Atlas to choose for himself.

Was that why Phoebe was so different from everyone else he knew? Because she'd grown up being given a choice?

Lucas was right, Atlas was endangering his community by being here. He thought of his mother, of the children in the colony, of Dr. Basu, even Hyacinth. He really should have put on a suit before heading outside. But it was too late for that now.

"I recommend that you not return home," Lucas said. "But accompany us to meet with our doctor for a full medical evaluation and possible quarantine."

Go with them? Just like that?

His muscles tensed, flight response kicking into overdrive. Leave the mountain with complete strangers? Walk straight into the heart of enemy territory? His mother would wonder where he was. She'd beg Dr. Basu to send people looking. And if they found out he was with the Vitruvians...

Dr. Basu would see this as validation of her warnings about the Vitruvians. Their corrupting influence. Their godless ways. She believed that they'd steal the Divine Blueprint if given half a chance. If she thought they had taken him, she might see it as an act of war.

"I can't." Atlas shook his head.

Lucas nodded. "Then you must take every precaution upon your return. Decontaminate thoroughly. Dispose of your clothing. Report any symptoms immediately, even if they seem minor."

"I will."

"You bear full responsibility for the consequences of this decision."

His heart pounded even harder. "If you open that chamber and take those people out, you're responsible for whatever happens as well."

"Yes," Lucas agreed. "But I have much greater capacity to deal with those consequences."

Something in the flat certainty of his tone made Atlas' skin crawl. Phoebe's father was right, he should go with the Vitruvians. But he just couldn't do it.

Why the hell had he left the colony tonight?

But without tonight's rebellion, he wouldn't have met Phoebe. So he wouldn't take it back, even if he could.

"I should go," he said, pushing past Lucas.

Breaking free of the cave felt like escaping a nightmare. Atlas gulped in the cold, clean air, letting it flush the stale cavern smell from his lungs. Behind him, metal shrieked against metal, the sound of ancient seals forced open. He ran faster, putting distance between himself and whatever was happening in that chamber.

But then he stopped, unable to bear the thought of leaving without saying goodbye. Where was Phoebe?

He found another path to the left, wider than the one they'd ascended, sloping down toward what looked like a valley. Maybe she'd gone that way?

He followed it. "Phoebe?"

No response.

The path curved through brush and trees. But the deeper he went, the more disoriented he became. The moon was blocked by the mountains and without it, the path faded into patches of shadow. Everything started to blur together.

He stopped. Listened.

"Phoebe?" he tried again. Louder this time.

Still nothing.

Atlas kept going. He caught his foot on a root and went down hard, the shock punching through his hands and knees. He crouched on all fours, heart thundering in his chest.

He hadn't been attacked.

He'd just tripped.

That was all.

He got up.

Which way had he come from? He couldn't tell. Everything looked the same in the dark.

Stupid.

He clenched his jaw.

Turned around. Started walking. Then stopped. Was he doubling back or walking deeper into nowhere?

What an idiot.

He should never have tried to find Phoebe. He peered through the dark trying to see. But it was useless, and the silence made it worse.

"Phoebe?"

Still no response.

Should he stay where he was? Keep going?

He heard a sound to his left.

Was that Phoebe? Or a Hyperionite?

His knees still throbbed from the fall. He wiped scraped palms on his pants and saw the dust sticking to his skin.

He turned around, saw a flash of light.

He went toward it.

It was the cave mouth. Somehow he'd made his way to

the right and gone around in a circle. But at least he knew where he was now.

Thank God.

Then he saw Phoebe.

Atlas was about to shout her name when he heard the rumble of approaching vehicles.

He still wasn't sure if Lucas would report his presence here. But if he didn't, Atlas still had a chance of getting back without Dr. Basu finding out before he could tell her his version of the night's events.

The version that downplayed, if not omitted, his encounter with Phoebe.

He ducked behind an outcropping of rock, crouching down and peering out as a large transport resembling a military ambulance came into view. Reinforced chassis, half-track wheels for navigating rough terrain, and tinted windows that obscured its interior. The cargo section made up most of its body, with access doors at the rear. The smaller vehicle was an all-terrain buggy.

Phoebe approached the glowing headlights, pointing to a wide stretch of dirt. The vehicles rolled to a stop, then their engines died, and a trio of figures emerged.

Atlas recognized Dr. Callas. He sometimes visited the Naturalist colony when serious illness struck. The other two were strangers, both women. By the way one of them strode straight to Phoebe and pulled her aside, he could guess her identity.

Phoebe's mother.

Samara Makinde, the poisoner of humanity's future, according to Dr. Basu.

She looked like an exasperated middle-aged woman who'd been woken up to deal with an emergency, only to find her daughter in the middle of it. She wore the same expression Briar had when Atlas had stormed out of their dwelling earlier this evening.

"What were you thinking?" she asked.

"I was meeting Flutter," Phoebe replied with a shrug.

"You can't keep sneaking out after dark. What if—"

"Nothing happened," Phoebe said. "I'm fine."

"It's not about whether something happens. It's about trust."

Phoebe crossed her arms, looking away. "Well, maybe you should trust me more."

"Maybe I would if you stopped acting like a child."

Phoebe stiffened. "Then stop treating me like one."

"Get in the vehicle and wait for me." Samara sighed. "We'll finish this later."

Phoebe's shoulders slumped.

Her mother joined the others who were donning protective gear. Once they were suited up, they checked each other's seals before walking toward the cave.

Samara paused before entering.

Atlas held his breath.

She turned, scanning the area. Her body went still as her gaze locked onto him.

Neither of them moved, both staring.

Samara's gaze flicked to Phoebe and then back to him.

Her stare hardened. She said nothing, but Atlas still heard her loud and clear: *Stay away from my daughter.*

"Samara!" Dr. Callas called out.

"Coming." She followed the others into the cave.

Atlas finally exhaled.

He should go. The longer he stayed, the more likely he might take something back to his people.

But leaving now might mean never talking to Phoebe again.

He couldn't accept that.

Chapter Ten

WHY DID Samara have to be so unreasonable?

Poke had come to her for help, and she'd only been trying to do the right thing. Now her mother had humiliated her, treating her like a disobedient child in front of Atlas. Heat crawled up her neck as she caught him watching the scene unfold. Perfect. Her first genuinely interesting encounter with a boy, and her mother had to swoop in and demolish it.

Phoebe walked over to him.

"I'm not ready to say goodbye," he said.

Her heart began to beat faster. "Me either."

Phoebe glanced back at the cave. If Samara was annoyed about her sneaking out to see Flutter, she was going to be livid if she found out Phoebe had been in the company of a Naturalist. She held out her hand.

Atlas took it again. His warm skin against hers sent a jolt through her body.

She led him into a nearby copse, where branches created a canopy of silvery leaves in the moonlight.

"Are you okay?" Atlas asked.

Phoebe nodded, though she wasn't sure if that was entirely true. Her heart was pounding out a thousand beats per second. And she was feeling everything: the night air on her skin, the smell of the trees, the warmth of his hand in hers. "You?"

He nodded.

The silence between them felt electric, charged with possibilities neither knew how to voice. Words were inadequate, clumsy things compared to the current running between their braided hands.

He leaned forward. And she did too.

Their lips pressed together.

His lips were impossibly soft against hers, hesitant at first, then more certain. The contact sent a current racing through her body, a live wire connecting every nerve ending at once. Time stretched and compressed, seconds expanding into eternity, the universe narrowing to just the gentle pressure of his mouth on hers, the warmth of his breath mingling with her own.

When they finally separated, she felt fundamentally changed, as if some essential piece of her DNA had been permanently altered.

"I have to go," Atlas said. "My mother can't know that I was here."

"When will I see you again?"

His expression clouded, duty at war with desire. "I don't know. But soon."

"Wait." She fumbled for her comm unit, tugging it from her pocket. "Here. So you can contact me."

He stared at it. "Are you sure?"

"I'll get another one. Then we can talk."

His fingers closed around it as he leaned in and kissed her again, quicker this time. "I'll wait to hear from you."

Then he was gone, slipping between the trees and

disappearing into the darkness toward the fissure in the rocks. Phoebe felt oddly light-headed. It was almost like the dawn of a migraine, but different. A floating sensation, in no way painful. Her skin buzzed with awareness, her lips still warm from his touch.

She pressed her fingers to her mouth, half-believing she'd imagined it all.

Time lost all meaning as she stood rooted to the spot, her body humming with a new awareness that brightened the stars and sweetened the night air.

The call of a bird startled Phoebe from her reverie, and she made her way back to the vehicles and climbed into the smaller one. But instead of thinking about the frail, elderly couple inside, her mind drifted to Atlas.

She had never given much thought to the Naturalists before. Their odd neighbors to the south, avoiding contact and rejecting everything the Vitruvians valued. Samara obviously didn't respect their way of life, that much clear whenever she spoke of them. Phoebe had been raised to feel the same way. Who ignored science in favor of the divine? It was like expecting magic to solve all your problems.

Yet Atlas was nothing like she had expected. Sure, he was a bit ignorant, but that seemed to be the result of his isolation. He didn't harbor the zealotry she'd expected from the stories she'd been told about Naturalists. His questions revealed a mind eager to explore beyond the boundaries others had set for him. Once he learned the truth, he'd embrace it.

He could tell the others how Dr. Basu had lied to them. Surely they wouldn't want to be Naturalists anymore?

Or would they decide to ignore the truth, even after hearing the evidence?

Atlas seemed like he might be willing to change his mind. Or to listen, at least.

It was almost half an hour later before Dr. Callas and Samara emerged from the cave carrying the old woman on a stretcher. Lucas and Leila followed close behind with the man, flanked by the Hyperionites.

Their body language seemed almost reverent, as though in the presence of the sacred. Behavior she would have expected from the Naturalists, not the Hyperionites. Flutter had never said anything about having a religion.

Who were these people?

Phoebe watched the grim procession with fascination. The adults transferred the stretchers into the transport's specialized containment units, carefully securing each frail body. Once the patients were locked down, the adults stripped off their hazard suits, peeling away layers of protection like shedding skin. Every piece went into a biohazard bag that Dr. Callas sealed and stuffed into a reinforced lockbox attached to the transport. Then he turned to the others. "I'll take the patients. Lucas?"

He gestured to the vehicle.

Lucas shook his head. "I'll walk."

Phoebe leaned out of the window. "Can I go with him?"

"No." Samara's voice was sharp. "You're staying exactly where you are."

Phoebe sank deeper into her seat, arms crossed tightly over her chest as if bracing for impact. The drive home stretched before her like an execution march; it was twenty minutes of captive audience time for Samara's favorite lecture series: *Poor Life Choices by Phoebe Makinde, Volume 612.*

"There's room for you in the transport, Lucas," Dr. Callas said.

Lucas shook his head again. "I was exposed to the patients without protection. To avoid introducing any potential infection to the colony, I'll decontaminate before joining you."

"What about Phoebe?" Leila asked.

Lucas looked over at her. "The seals were intact when we opened the quarantine chamber, so she hasn't been exposed."

Samara looked relieved.

Dr. Callas climbed into the transport and was gone in seconds.

Leila took her place behind the wheel of the second vehicle, waiting as Samara settled into the seat beside her. Neither of them spoke as Leila gunned the engine. Moments later, they were on their way.

The silence was suffocating.

Leila kept her eyes fixed on the rough trail, both hands gripping the steering wheel. Samara sat rigid in the passenger seat, her profile outlined harshly by the dashboard lights.

Phoebe could feel the storm building.

Eventually it broke.

"How long?" Samara's voice was icy.

"How long what?" Phoebe asked, staring at the back of her mother's head.

Samara twisted around in her seat. "How long have you been meeting that Naturalist boy?"

"I haven't been 'meeting' anyone." Phoebe rolled her eyes. "I just met Atlas for the first time tonight."

"Atlas?" Samara repeated. "You're already on a first-name basis?"

"Well, what else would I call him? 'Hey you?'"

"You shouldn't be calling him anything, Phoebe!

Because you shouldn't have been talking to him. Naturalists are dangerous."

Phoebe laughed. "Atlas isn't dangerous."

"They're fanatics whose beliefs don't align with ours."

"And you think I'm going to throw mine away because I met a boy? Jeez, you really don't think much of me."

"That's not what I meant and you know it."

"Then what did you mean? Because you're acting like talking to one Naturalist is enough to make me abandon everything you've ever taught me."

"It's not about abandoning anything. It's about protecting yourself. People make bad choices when they let feelings cloud their judgment."

Phoebe glared at her. "I'm not you, Mom."

"What does that mean?"

"Nothing."

Leila hunched down in the seat, probably wishing she was anywhere but here with them. Phoebe felt the same way.

Samara closed her eyes, clearly struggling to restrain her temper. When she opened them, she said, "I'm still waiting for your explanation of how you met that boy."

"He was exploring the ruins while I waited for Flutter. That's it. I barely spent five minutes with him before Poke showed up. Besides, Atlas was totally normal."

"You might think you understand them, but you don't. They think differently. They would rather let their children die than accept medical treatment."

"That's not—"

"Do you have any idea how tenuous our peace is with them? How easily our pact could all fall apart? This isn't just about you making a friend, Phoebe. This is about keeping the peace between our settlements."

"Nothing happened!"

Samara slapped the dashboard. Both Phoebe and Leila jumped.

"Nothing happened this time. But that doesn't mean nothing *could* happen. Things with the Naturalists are complicated. There's history there that you don't understand."

"Like how Dr. Basu tried to take over the colony and you stopped her? I know the story."

"You know the sanitized version we tell children. The reality was far messier."

"So, tell me."

"Not tonight. I have responsibilities, just like someday you'll have responsibilities that will require you to exercise good judgment and put the needs of the colony over your own." Samara turned back toward the front. "I forbid you from seeing that boy again. Do you understand me?"

Phoebe bit down hard on her inner cheek, swallowing the retort that threatened to escape. Her mother always did this — treated her like a child while demanding she act like an adult.

Do not stick your tongue out at her.

That would only prove her mother's point.

She sat back, staring out the window at the passing landscape. The moonlight painted everything in double shadows, a world transformed. Just like she felt transformed.

How could Atlas be dangerous?

She replayed their kiss in her mind, feeling again the gentle pressure of his lips, the way his hands had trembled slightly as they framed her face. The look in his eyes afterward... wonder and disbelief and something deeper she couldn't name.

No one had ever looked at her that way before. Like she was a miracle.

Whatever her mother said, whatever history existed between their people, Phoebe knew one thing with absolute certainty. She was going to see Atlas again.

Some things were worth the risk.

Chapter Eleven

SAMARA ADJUSTED the fit of her protective suit and tried to ignore the sweat trickling down her spine. The hospital's quarantine facility sacrificed comfort for functionality at every turn. Transparent polymer partitions sliced the room into sterile compartments, each sealed with its own air filtration system. Overhead light panels bombarded everything with merciless illumination that eliminated shadows but turned human skin sickly green. The space felt deliberately inhospitable, as if designed to remind everyone that disease respected neither comfort nor dignity.

Samara looked down at the patients while Hector monitored their vitals.

How was it possible that they were both still alive?

Their skin was a canvas of trauma painted in bruises that bloomed like watercolors across paper-thin flesh. Angry purples faded to sickly yellows at the edges, overlapping with crimson abrasions.

What had happened to them in the quarantine chamber?

"They look like a strong wind would blow them to

dust," Samara said. "How long do you think they were in there?"

"Decades, maybe close to a century," Lucas replied. "The records we found suggest that the Hyperion colony collapsed within two years of landing. They must have brought the quarantine chamber down piece by piece and reassembled it."

They would have had to take antifungals after sealing themselves in the chamber, trusting that the filtration system that connected the claustrophobic space to the surface would catch every last spore. Samara couldn't imagine choosing that over modifying herself with native DNA, but maybe these two had shared Ayesha's genetic chauvinism, preferring to risk death over becoming something outside their definition of human.

"Do you think you can identify them from the old records?" Leila asked.

Before Lucas could answer, the woman's body arched off the bed. Her monitor erupted into a frantic symphony of alarms: heart rate spiking to 160, blood pressure plummeting, oxygen saturation dropping like a stone. Her limbs thrashed against the restraints as if possessed as her eyes rolled back to expose bloodshot whites.

"Diazepam," Hector said.

Leila grabbed a syringe and handed it to him.

He cleared the IV port and injected the medication into her IV. Within moments she began to relax.

Samara settled her hand on the woman's forehead, letting it rest there in comfort. Her skin was so hot she could feel it through the nitrile gloves.

Samara shuddered. Spending decades entombed in the side of a mountain. No sky. No fresh air. Now room to move. Just the slow, creeping decay of isolation. Knowing that, thanks to the longevity treatments they'd been given to sustain them on the generation ship, that they had decades more to live before they died of natural causes.

"I can't imagine living like that … not that I would call it living." She turned to Lucas. "How old do you think they were when they entered the chamber?"

"The cut-off age for Hyperion crew members was twenty-five, and the voyage to DaVinci took forty-two years, same as it did for us. So, they couldn't have been older than sixty-nine when they went into the chamber."

Which meant they'd been alive for well over a century, maybe closer to two, and spent close to half of it shut up in that room.

"The Hyperionites seemed to regard them with respect," Leila said.

"These are likely their last surviving ancestors," Lucas pointed out. "I don't want to make the mistake of projecting historical assumptions onto what has become an alien culture by our standards, but ancestor worship isn't out of the question."

Samara tried to strip away the ravages of time, to imagine these broken vessels as they must have been: young pioneers with steel in their spines and stars in their eyes. These patients were living artifacts, the last breathing connection to humanity's first stumbling steps beyond Earth. Legends made flesh, however degraded that flesh had become.

"Whoever they are, we're dealing with medical history in the making," Hector said. "We need to stabilize them long enough to extract any information they might still possess, before we lose the last witnesses to the beginning of everything."

The next few hours blurred together as Samara and Lucas assisted Leila and Hector with test after test. They catalogued decades of physiological decline: kidney function reduced to twenty percent capacity, liver enzymes at catastrophic levels, inflammatory cascades raging through systems too compromised to fight back. Pathogen screening revealed a complex ecosystem of dormant infections held at bay by mechanisms Samara couldn't identify. Whatever was keeping these people alive wasn't in any medical textbook she'd ever studied.

Hours later, they gathered in Hector's office.

"They're dying of old age," he announced.

"What about the fever?" Samara asked. "Their inflammatory markers suggest an immune response."

"Your pathogen screen didn't turn up anything we recognize as active." Hector sighed, steepling his fingers. "But that doesn't mean we haven't missed a native microorganism, so we'll keep them in quarantine until we can be sure."

Leila leaned against the counter with her arms crossed. "They have bruises along the ribs, shoulders, and arms. Scratches, some shallow, and others deeper. A contusion at the back of the skull. All of it within the last twenty-four to seventy-two hours. How did that happen if they were locked in the chamber?"

"Could they have done this to themselves?" Samara asked. "Or to each other?"

"It seems unlikely, given their frailty. Seizures?" Lucas suggested.

Hector shook his head. "Even if they were both having seizures, the bruising pattern would be consistent with having fallen and thrashing in one position. "

Leila frowned. "So, an accident?"

"Did you see any evidence of an accident at the site?"

Samara shook her head. Aside from a few ancient possessions, woven grass mats, and threadbare blankets, the only thing in the quarantine chamber had been a couple of bowls with food residue.

"Well, it doesn't make sense that the Hyperionites did it." Leila's gaze darkened. "If that was the case, why come to us for help?"

Hector removed his glasses and pinched the bridge of his nose, leaving visible indentations in skin already marked by hours of pressure. "These people are long past their biological expiration date. We're watching systems that should have shut down decades ago finally surrender to entropy. We may never solve the mystery of how they got those injuries, but it's moot at this point."

Samara frowned. "Why didn't the Hyperionites tell us about them before?"

"Maybe they didn't trust us," Leila replied with a sigh.

"But they trust Lucas," Samara said.

The three of them looked at the android in unison, who shook his head. "If they had, I would have informed you."

Samara wondered if that was true, or if Lucas had kept this secret like he'd kept so many others. In the eighteen years since the Schism, he'd earned back most of the trust he'd lost when his true nature had been revealed, and Katherine had been reluctant to deactivate him when he was their last tether to the ship in orbit. But Samara still couldn't completely forgive him for the way he'd used her to deceive the others, even if she accepted his presence both in the colony and in her daughter's life.

She couldn't think of a reason for him to hide the original colonists, if he'd known about them, but she believed he was capable of doing so. Which meant he'd had the opportunity to inflict those injuries.

Samara had never seen Lucas hurt a human before, not even Dr. Basu and not even in the midst of the first battle to occur on this planet. He claimed that his programming wouldn't let him, even through inaction. Her gut said he was telling the truth, but she couldn't shake the doubt.

"It says something about the Hypers, doesn't it?" Leila said. "That they've been caring for these two all this time."

"I still don't understand why their immune system is activated," Samara said.

Lucas shrugged. "Perhaps the filtration on the system that pumped air into the chamber failed, and the fungus infected them."

"I didn't see any evidence of that," Samara said. It was one of the first things she'd checked. "I'll screen for native pathogens again."

"You'll do a better job after you've had some sleep. We've stabilized them, and we've taken every precaution we can to contain any infection they might carry." Hector waved a dismissive hand. "Everybody go home, except Lucas." He turned to the android. "Call me if their condition deteriorates, or if they wake up."

But Samara was itching to run another pathogen scan, despite her exhaustion, despite the fact that she clearly had a situation that needed nipping in the bud with Phoebe. She had an interesting puzzle to solve for the first time in years.

And she felt guilty that, deep down, she'd rather live in her lab until she solved it.

~

SAMARA STEPPED into the night air, her skin still burning from the harsh decontamination chemicals that she'd used to scour every exposed surface. Astringent clung to her nostrils, overpowering the rich organic scents of DaVinci's summer evening.

Lucas joined her a moment later, and together they returned to the residential area.

She asked the question that had been on her mind since the first set of data on the original colonists had started to scroll across her lab computer's screen.

"Did Aurelius ever talk to you about the life extension treatments he gave the Hyperion crew? It would help to understand what was done to them."

"I believe they were intended to prepare the colonists for the physical demands of the journey. Extended endurance. Improved recovery from stress. The goal was to improve their ability to heal while slowing down the body's biological clock."

"But how did he do that?"

He hesitated. "I don't remember."

"What?" She stared at him. "How can you not remember?"

"I've deleted some older files to make room for higher priority data."

"Data for what?" Samara asked.

He blinked—for effect, she was pretty sure. "For Phoebe. The colony library contains an extensive collection of resources on the psychology of child development and appropriate parenting techniques at each stage, but much of the data is conflicting and open to interpretation."

Oh no.

That was her fault.

She'd told Lucas that he could fulfill the role of father figure for Phoebe. It hadn't occurred to her that he'd take it so seriously that he would delete some of his own memories.

"I didn't mean that you needed to get a Ph.D. in parenthood, I just wanted you to make sure she didn't get into too much trouble." And speaking of that… "Not that you've been doing a great job of that, given that she's been sneaking out of the colony to run around in the woods all night."

"I hope you won't be too upset with her," Lucas said. "She was never in danger."

She eyed him for a moment, then realized what he was implying. "*You knew!*"

He didn't deny it.

"You didn't think it was important to tell me she was sneaking out at night? You just followed her instead?"

"I believed it was the optimal solution."

Her hands clenched into fists. "Lucas, I'm her mother. It's not your place to make that decision."

"The chances of the colony surviving were infinitesimally without you intervening in Phoebe's genetics and multiplex editing out her body's autoimmune response to the native fungus, and that boy, Atlas, represents a one in a billion chance of natural genetic variation finding a similar solution. But I'd estimate the odds of Phoebe listening to you when you 'forbid' her from doing anything to be lower than both of those probabilities put together."

Apparently, his programming didn't prohibit him from being a smart ass. "That's not the point."

Lucas tilted his head to the right, a programmed gesture that she knew was meant to convey mild amusement, but it made her angrier with him.

"What is the point?" he asked.

A star mosquito landed on her neck. She slapped it away, leaving a smear of reddish-purple blood on her palm. "That you should have told me."

"Notifying you would've created more conflict between

you and Phoebe without changing her behavior. That would've caused harm to both of you."

"That's not harm, that's parenting. Setting healthy boundaries and creating consistent consequences, even when you know your child is going to defy you. Isn't that somewhere in all of the studies you downloaded?" Samara doubted that she was going to change Lucas' behavior, any more than she'd managed to change Phoebe. But at least she could find out what he knew. "That Naturalist boy. How long has that been going on?"

"Phoebe was telling the truth. They just met tonight."

"You know how dangerous that is, right? If Ayesha finds out, or if she was behind it…"

"The boy was alone. And when the Hyperionite showed up, he attempted to protect Phoebe from it, until she intervened."

"That doesn't make him safe, Lucas. The Naturalists aren't just people with different politics. They're fundamentally opposed to what Phoebe is."

"I am aware of the ideological divide."

"Then you should have stepped in sooner."

Lucas was silent for a moment. "Thirty seconds ago, you didn't want me to have any authority over Phoebe."

Samara sighed. "I gave you permission to protect her. That's what you're programmed to do."

He stiffened. She couldn't tell if it was a genuine reflection of his internal state or a body language algorithm designed to manipulate the people around him.

She decided to treat him like a human. Because maybe that would help him think more like one.

"Sorry." She touched his arm. "Wrong word. It's what you volunteered to do."

"I saw no sign of a threat in the boy."

"Oh, Lucas."

He could replace all of his memories with the library's psychology collection and he still wouldn't understand humanity.

"I do my best," he said as though reading her mind.

"I know. But Phoebe's seventeen," Samara argued. "She doesn't understand the risks."

"I believe she understands more than you credit her with. It's just that her perspective differs from yours."

"What do you mean?"

"Phoebe has grown up in a different world than you did. The Schism occurred before she was born. To her, the division between colonies is a static reality, not a fresh wound."

Samara felt her jaw tighten. "That doesn't matter."

"You clip her wings too much, Samara. Phoebe will be an adult according to colony law in less than two years. Shouldn't we ensure that she's capable of acting as one?"

"By letting her sneak around with Naturalists?"

"By allowing her the freedom to make choices and learn from them."

"You don't understand. You can't."

"Because I'm not human?"

"Because you're not a parent." Then she walked off, leaving him behind.

She knew she was being unfair the moment the words left her mouth. Lucas might not experience parenthood as humans did, but he'd been there for every fever, every nightmare, and every triumph in Phoebe's life. And apparently, he had been doing a better job of tracking her comings and goings than Samara had.

But she refused to believe that an android might grasp the human complexity of growing up better than she did. Samara paused at the threshold to her quarters, hand hovering over the access panel. She could still remember the infant Phoebe had been: fragile, utterly dependent, a miracle of genetic engineering and maternal determination. Now that same child was forging connections with people from worlds Samara had deliberately cut off, seeking her own path with the same stubborn independence that had once driven Samara to defy an entire colony.

The irony wasn't lost on her. She'd created a daughter in her own image, then expected her not to challenge boundaries.

And she'd accused Lucas of not understanding what it meant to be a parent.

Chapter Twelve

Atlas' lungs burned as he reached the greenhouse, but he couldn't make himself go inside. He leaned against the wall instead, gradually catching his breath as he thought about Phoebe. He considered turning around. Running all the way to the Vitruvian colony just to see her again.

The memory of her lips against his sent electricity racing through his body. She'd kissed him back — actually kissed him back — like it was the most natural thing in the world. Whatever crazy chemical reaction was happening in his brain had been happening in hers too.

He needed to feel that again.

He hoped she wasn't getting in too much trouble because of him.

He should have come right back to the colony when he left the cave.

But then they would never have kissed.

He could never have kissed Hyacinth like that. Phoebe was nothing like Hyacinth.

Phoebe was unpredictable. He didn't know what she

was about to say next. She'd challenged him when she felt he was wrong about Poke.

She had been brave when he had been terrified.

She had been rebellious, when he would have followed orders.

She wasn't supposed to exist, yet here she was, defying everything he'd been taught to believe.

He pressed his forehead against the greenhouse wall.

The Divine Blueprint.

He'd grown up hearing that trinity of words his entire life.

But Phoebe knew nothing about it. She had looked at him like he was just … *a person.* Nothing special. Until after the kiss, and then her eyes were suddenly full of stars. She didn't want him for his genes, she just wanted him.

He shoved a hand into his pocket and pulled out her comm.

His heart jumped every time he thought about her message coming through. The waiting would be torture, but she was worth it.

The greenhouse entrance beckoned. Atlas reached for the latch on his secret door.

You could carry something back that could kill everyone in your settlement.

Atlas winced, remembering the warning from Lucas. The Naturalists had survived this long only because of their isolation, their obsessive decontamination protocols, and the antifungals they took the second anyone showed symptoms of infection. Unlike Phoebe with her genetically-modified immune system, Atlas' people couldn't coexist with the native fungus that contaminated everything here, along with so many other sources of pollution. One breach, one microscopic hitchhiker from the cave, and he could wipe out half the colony before anyone knew what was happening.

Who knew what those ancient humans in the cave might be carrying?

This comm could be contaminated with something lethal.

But Atlas couldn't just discard his lifeline to Phoebe, and he had no idea if the electronic components would survive the harsh chemical baths of decontamination. The circuits might fry, the screen might crack; all those miniature pathways connecting him to her could dissolve in caustic solution.

He crouched down and cracked open the door, sliding his hand inside and tucking Phoebe's comm between some irrigation tubing. Then he sealed the door and followed the perimeter toward the main entrance.

There were decontamination chambers at every entrance. Reinforced doors flanked by warning signs reminding everyone of the importance of purity. The log would record his entry now, but not his earlier exit through the secret door in the greenhouse. Security would spot the discrepancy immediately, unless the system glitched, which wasn't impossible with their outdated tech. But he really couldn't risk contaminating his people.

His people.

The thought felt strange. Was he betraying them if he didn't tell Dr. Basu everything he'd seen? Would that lack of knowledge put his colony at a disadvantage to the Vitruvians and Hyperionites?

He was already going to be punished for sneaking out —in secret, because the Divine Blueprint was supposed to be above reproach—and that was fair. He deserved it.

But it wasn't fair that he'd be punished for talking to Phoebe, because everything Dr. Basu had said about her was a lie. He had no doubt that the psychologist would ensure that he never saw her again. He didn't deserve that.

As soon as he was clean, he would tell Dr. Basu about the Hyperionites and the old people in the cave, all of which she would hear from the Vitruvians sooner or later. But he would leave out the part where he'd met Phoebe in the old colony ruins; instead, he'd say that he'd been wandering near the Hyperionite village when he'd seen Poke escort a couple of Vitruvians in. And describe the vehicles arriving later.

As long as Lucas and Samara didn't report his presence there, Dr. Basu should buy his story.

Atlas thought Lucas might keep his secret, although he wasn't sure why.

But Samara would tell, if she thought it would keep him away from her daughter.

Atlas slapped his palm against the entry scanner, willing his pulse to slow to normal. The panel hummed, running its biometric checks: heart rate, body temperature, perspiration levels. Any deviation could flag him for further screening. But the first set of doors slid open with a pneumatic hiss, revealing the sterile chamber within, its surfaces gleaming under harsh white light.

He stepped inside, and the exterior doors sealed behind him. A locker slid open in the wall, and Atlas undressed, placing his clothes in the receptacle for sterilization.

The bare metal floor felt cold against his feet. A ripple of goosebumps prickled across his skin and nozzles emerged from every surface like mechanical snakes, their metallic heads oriented toward him from all angles. A microsecond later they hissed to life, engulfing him in a fine mist that settled on his skin with the weight of judgment. The chemical cocktail burned his nostrils, each breath coating his lungs with the sterile tang of industrial cleaner. The pressure intensified, until it felt like thousands of tiny needles attacking his skin, drilling the chemicals into every pore and crease of his body. He shut his eyes tight against the onslaught, tasting the bitter antiseptic as it found its way into his mouth despite his best efforts. The spray continued for three excruciating minutes before finally shutting off, leaving him gasping and raw.

There was a brief pause, then warm water cascaded down from above, rinsing away the chemicals. Then came the blowers, drying his skin, leaving it feeling tight and dry and far too clean.

"Decontamination complete," a voice announced. "Proceed to the secondary chamber."

The interior door parted with a soft beep, inviting him into the next room. Atlas snatched a pair of gray sweats from the communal shelves, tugging them on with fingers that still tingled from the chemical bath. He pulled on standard-issue slippers, grabbed a packet of antiseptic wipes, and bolted for the greenhouse, not slowing until the familiar scent of earth and growing things surrounded him.

He yanked on the sterile gloves, then crouched by the secret door, his heart pounding. Once he disinfected the comm, it would be safe to hide in his room. But when he swept his hand through the tubing on the left side, fingers probing every inch of the space, he found nothing.

Cold panic washed over him. Someone had found it. Someone knew. His breathing quickened as he fought the urge to rip the entire shelf apart.

Calm down.

Then the metallic glint caught his eye from the opposite shelf, nestled between irrigation valves and nutrient lines. His brain had been so addled by adrenaline and

Phoebe-induced insanity that he'd forgotten which side he'd used.

He grabbed the device, tore open the package of wipes, and scrubbed every centimeter: screen, buttons, case, the tiny speaker grilles. Then he attacked the shelf where he'd hidden it, erasing all evidence. Finally, he wiped down every inch of the secret door he'd touched, imagining invisible death clinging to the surface. The contaminated gloves went straight into the biohazard disposal unit, and the comm disappeared into his pocket.

Then he made his way home.

Atlas was hoping his mother would be asleep when he arrived. Or at the very least that Dr. Basu and Hyacinth would be gone. To his relief, it was both dark and quiet when he entered.

He crept to his room, then closed and locked the door behind him.

He sat on the edge of his bed and pulled out Phoebe's comm. The screen was still dark. No messages. He hadn't really expected one, though he'd certainly hoped. But she needed time to acquire another comm unit without raising suspicion. All he could do now was wait and pray to whatever divine force might be listening that she hadn't been locked away forever because of him.

He turned the device over in his hands, remembering Phoebe's face in the moonlight, the way her eyes had widened when she looked at him. With curiosity rather than fear. With *interest*. Dr. Basu had described the first genetically modified human as a cautionary tale: a sickly, deformed creature, irreversibly damaged by her mother's arrogance. A living embodiment of scientific hubris.

But Phoebe was nothing like that.

She was vibrant. Intelligent. And despite being "contaminated," she seemed more alive than anyone in the Naturalist colony.

Meeting her made him question everything.

Atlas tucked the comm beneath his pillow, then reconsidered. Too obvious. He got it out again and looked around his sparse room for a better hiding place. His gaze settled on the air vent near the floor.

He pried off the cover, placed the comm inside, then replaced the grating.

He collapsed onto his bed, mind still racing with images of Phoebe, Lucas, and those withered humans in the cave. Exhaustion pulled at his limbs like gravity on a heavy planet, but his thoughts refused to quiet. Everything had changed tonight. The carefully constructed walls of his existence had crumbled, revealing a universe far more complex and terrifying than he'd ever imagined.

Atlas had crossed a line, and he knew he could never go back.

Chapter Thirteen

LIGHT STABBED THROUGH HIS EYELIDS, dragging Atlas unwillingly back to consciousness. His mother would already be at morning prayer, head bowed among the faithful while Dr. Basu delivered her daily sermon about purity and divine purpose. He pulled the blanket over his head, trying to block out reality for five more minutes. Another day of mind-numbing ritual, meditation circles, and people treating him like a walking miracle instead of a person.

But then he remembered …

Phoebe.

He launched himself out of bed, his heart pounding double time as he pried open the grate. The comm sat exactly where he'd left it, a technological talisman in a world of organic purity. He snatched it up, thumbing the screen to life with desperate hope.

Still nothing.

His shoulders slumped. Maybe her mother had caught her trying to borrow another comm. Maybe she was locked in some Vitruvian version of detention. Or worse, some sort of scientific torture chamber where she was being brainwashed to hate him.

Atlas had no idea how the Vitruvians handled rule breakers. Dr. Basu said they were materialistic, spiritually empty, obsessed with machines and science. She painted them as people who had lost their way. But they had laws too, didn't they?

Phoebe had broken at least one. And her mother was the Vitruvians' savior, so she probably had to be above reproach, too.

He wondered how bad her punishment would be. And if it would be public or secret.

It wasn't fair that they should have to suffer because the people in charge couldn't find a way to work together.

He returned the comm to the vent, then quickly dressed and headed to the communal hall for breakfast. He entered to the usual aromas of oatmeal and stewed vegetables. He was as sick of that as he was of all the prayer.

Atlas forced himself to shuffle through the food line, wooden bowl in hand. His gaze accidentally found Dr. Basu's across the room, and her eyes narrowed microscopically at the sight of him. Atlas immediately looked away, heart hammering as he sought sanctuary at the farthest table possible, praying to the Divine whose blueprint he supposedly carried that she wouldn't follow him.

He sat at an empty table and stirred his vegetables. Seconds later, Dr. Basu slid onto the bench across from him with the silent grace of a predator. Atlas kept his eyes fixed on his bowl, but her presence filled his awareness like a gathering storm. The silence between them was elastic and dangerous, until Atlas could no longer stand it and finally looked up.

Her eyes bored into him, searching for cracks in his composure.

She broke the silence first. "You have a restless soul, don't you?"

The question caught him off guard. "Pardon?"

"A restless soul," she said, still studying him. "Always seeking. Always questioning. Never content with what is."

Atlas said nothing, afraid that he would reveal enough that she could guess the rest.

"Did you enjoy your nocturnal adventure?"

His blood ran cold, even though he'd known she'd talk to someone at the other colony sooner or later. He'd been hoping later.

But he still didn't know what she'd been told, so he wasn't sure where to start his story. When he'd planned it out earlier, it had all made sense, but now he realized that the slightest detail could trip him up. He refused to get Phoebe in any more trouble than she was already in.

Even if staying silent meant his own punishment was worse.

"Don't lie to me Atlas. I've known about your secret exit in the greenhouse since you installed it. Did you truly believe I wouldn't notice?"

Atlas shrugged like he didn't care. He couldn't deny it, but he wasn't going to confirm anything either. Not until he had a better idea what she knew.

So he kept quiet, hoping that she'd fill the silence with more details.

"I know everything that happens in this colony, Atlas." A slight smile played at her lips. "And I understand how hard it is to accept the rules that protect everyone else when they don't really apply to you. That's why I've been indulging your need for freedom, assuming you take care to be responsible. But you went further than you should have, just because you weren't happy about fulfilling your responsibilities."

How could he explain that her daughter repulsed him, that the thought of being spiritually wed to the entire fertile female population made him physically ill? That the Divine Blueprint she worshipped was a prison sentence he'd never asked for?

He couldn't. So he sat there, trapped by his own cowardice and drowning in silent rebellion.

"I've talked to Katherine about your activities last night. But I'd like to hear it from you."

Katherine.

The head of the Vitruvians.

Would Samara have reported him to her own leader, enlisting Katherine's help in keeping Phoebe safe from him? Or would she protect her own reputation as the savior of the Vitruvian by keeping her daughter's defiance a secret?

He had no idea. The way Phoebe talked about Samara gave him no clue.

But Lucas… he was sure Lucas would do whatever was right for Phoebe.

"I saw something last night. In the Hyperionite mountains."

Something shifted in the set of her shoulders, the slight press of her lips. Atlas couldn't tell if he was confirming her information or telling her something new.

"Go on," Dr. Basu prompted him.

The words tumbled out in a carefully edited stream: his insomnia, the Hyperionite seeking help from Vitruvians, Vitruvians answering the call. He described the cave with its ancient technology, the sealed chambers, the skeletal humans lying inside, hooked to machines that beeped and whirred. He mentioned the Hyperionites' strange behavior, from their reverent postures to their urgent signing, and their obvious concern for the withered human figures behind the glass. Then, Atlas told her he'd run home, afraid to say anything because it meant admitting to the sin of sneaking out.

When she asked him to describe the Vitruvians who'd gone to the cave, he focused on Lucas, Samara, and the doctor, claiming not to have seen the others clearly because of the protective gear they wore. Dr. Basu nodded with each description as if she was hearing what she'd expected, and something in him started to relax.

Maybe he was going to get away with this.

"And you weren't seen?" she asked.

If she knew and he lied… "I don't think so."

Her fingers tapped against the table. "Tell me about the people that were removed from the cave. Who do you think they were?"

He swallowed. "I overheard one of the Vitruvians speculate that they could be Hyperionite elders."

"Elders?"

He nodded, faking confusion. "But they looked completely human. They were very, very old. I didn't know it was possible for someone to be that old."

Her fingers stilled. "Are you suggesting they are original colonists?"

"I don't know. Is that even possible?"

"No, it's nonsense. They couldn't have survived this long without succumbing to the Bloom. Besides, the Hyperionites are monsters. I doubt they would care for anything other than themselves. Especially for that long."

Atlas held his tongue.

"Are you certain they were old?" Dr. Basu asked. "Or were they diseased?"

"You could see their veins through their skin. Dark spots all over their hands, and you could see the shapes of their bones. Barely any hair. They looked… like they'd been alive longer than anyone should be."

"Disease can cause similar symptoms, Atlas." Dr. Basu leaned forward, her eyes gleaming with an intensity that made his skin crawl. "I wonder if they aren't Hyperion colonists at all, but a cover story for something else."

Atlas frowned. "A cover story for what?"

"To hide the fact that Katherine allows her people to spend time with the filthy Hypers. Maybe they caught something nasty from them, and she had them in quarantine. She and her people have always been reckless in their pursuit of knowledge, willing to sacrifice safety for what she calls progress."

Atlas said nothing, but his thoughts were out of control. Even if that was true, why wouldn't it make more sense to leave the infected Vitruvians to die with the Hypers, rather than risk them telling the truth if they recovered?

"You must stay within Naturalist territory now that they are aware of you," Dr. Basu said. "The Hyperionites could have murdered you. Or you could have been taken prisoner. If the Vitruvians were to discover that you are the Divine Blueprint, they'll want to dissect you at the molecular level. You'll be stripped down, one sequence at a time, until they understand exactly how you function. Once they knew how to replicate you, they would throw you in the trash. I might not be able to stop them. Or if I could, it would mean giving up what leverage we have in negotiations. Either way, you're a vulnerability that I have to protect."

Atlas felt the blood drain from his face, leaving him lightheaded and cold despite the greenhouse's perpetual humidity. He remembered the way that Samara had glared at him. He didn't ever want to be at her mercy. She was probably capable of everything Dr. Basu said. The woman had modified her own daughter's DNA, after all. What would she do to him to keep her away from Phoebe?

Dr. Basu reached across the table and squeezed his hand. "You showed great courage and wisdom in sharing what you saw last night, Atlas. Many others would have kept it to themselves out of fear."

He nodded.

"Now, I need you to keep what you've told me in confidence. Until I have more information, there's no reason to alarm anyone else."

Was that it? Had he succeeded in fooling her? He wanted to believe it, but he worried that it wouldn't be that easy with Dr. Basu.

She rose from the table. "I have duties to attend to. But remember what I said, Atlas. Stay within our walls."

She strode away without waiting for confirmation, secure in her authority, certain of his obedience. After all, what choice did he have? He was the Divine Blueprint, the living proof of their divine favor. And while he seemed to have skirted punishment now, he was sure that he'd used up whatever leeway Dr. Basu might be willing to grant him.

Beneath his carefully neutral expression, defiance burned like a pilot light. Phoebe was out there, beyond these suffocating walls, with her quick mind and fearless spirit. She'd looked at him like he mattered. Not as a symbol or a specimen, but as a person.

He stared at the ceiling fans churning the hot, recycled air around the room. The tighter the walls closed in, the stronger his desire to escape became. Dr. Basu might control every aspect of the colony, but she couldn't control his thoughts. Not anymore. Not since Phoebe had shown him another way to exist.

AYESHA MAINTAINED a measured pace as she navigated the corridors back to her office, nodding to colonists who stepped aside with reverent greetings. Her carefully constructed mask of serene confidence betrayed none of the hurricane raging beneath. Only when the door clicked shut behind her did she allow the facade to crack, her breathing quickening as she processed what Atlas had revealed.

She wiped away the sweat beading at her temples with the back of her hand, then settled into her chair and tried to raise Katherine on the comm.

Static.

She adjusted the frequency, tried again. Nothing.

"Damn you, Katherine."

She pulled the yellow beads from her pocket and ran them through her fingers. Atlas had told her an unbelievable story. If she hadn't already spoken to Katherine, Ayesha would've thought he was making up a crazy story to get out of trouble. But not even he could fabricate something so specific. The quarantine chamber. The ancient humans. The Hyperionites gathered around them in what sounded like reverence.

Her thoughts spun like the greenhouse turbines, churning through possibilities. Original Hyperion colonists still alive? While she knew that the inhabitants of the generation ship had undergone longevity treatments, there was no way they could've survived the Bloom without a supply of antifungals or immunosuppressants, which the Hyperionites were too primitive to make. Yet Atlas had described them with such conviction, such specific detail. Too specific to be fabrication. Too bizarre to be coincidence. The implications made her head throb with terrible possibilities.

Unless Katherine was hiding some new plague.

Or worse, hiding the subjects in a botched eugenics experiment after allowing that monster Samara to modify them too far in an attempt to "improve" them.

Her pacing stopped abruptly, gaze fixed on the faded map that documented both settlements, borders marked in red ink that had long since started to brown with age. Katherine had always been secretive, withholding crucial information until it served her purposes. Even before the Schism, she'd played her cards close, revealing only what she deemed necessary. The ruins of the Hyperion colony and the mass grave filled with horrific mutants still haunted Ayesha's nightmares, absolute proof that humans had no business playing god.

The bitter knot of resentment that had taken root in her chest years ago pulsed with renewed vigor. This was why she maintained constant vigilance, why she could never lower her guard. Katherine was hiding something about those ancient humans, something that could change everything. Whatever it was, she would find out, even if she had to tear down the Hyperionite village to do it.

The Divine Blueprint might be their salvation, but knowledge was true power. And Ayesha intended to have both.

Chapter Fourteen

PHOEBE SLIPPED into Maeve's workshop and navigated through the colony's technological graveyard. Bins overflowed with discarded circuit boards, boxes bulged with cracked display panels, and barrels brimmed with half-disassembled devices that nobody had parts to fix, or the materials to fabricate those parts. She made her way to the repair queue: a row of damaged tech lined up on the main workbench like patients awaiting surgery, each tagged with a description of its ailment.

There were two communicators waiting to be fixed.

The first had a deep crack running across its display, jagged and splintering outward like a frozen lightning strike. The casing was warped near the bottom, the outer shell melted, as if it had been left too close to a heat source. A faint chemical scent clung to the device, burnt plastic and circuitry. Probably had internal damage.

The second was in better shape. The screen was scratched but there were no major cracks. The back panel was loose, one of the screws missing, exposing a tangle of delicate wires and a single capacitor barely clinging to its solder points. A dent on the side suggested it had been dropped, but at least the circuits hadn't been fried.

She turned the communicator over, running her fingers along the dented casing before pressing the power button. Dead, as she'd expected. Unlike the first device with its fried circuits and melted casing, this one had potential. A replacement capacitor, some careful soldering, and it could live again.

Phoebe froze, ears straining for any footsteps or voices, then glanced over her shoulder. The workshop remained empty, tools hanging silently from their pegs, machines dormant. Perfect.

Then she pulled up a stool and reached for a magnifier attached to a flexible arm, positioning it over the damaged circuitry. She quickly cleaned the corroded contacts with a small brush dipped in solvent, then used a soldering iron to repair the broken connections. The charging component was trickier. She had to extract a compatible part from a bin of salvaged pieces, testing several before finding one that fit.

Claiming she'd lost her communicator would be suicide, especially when Maeve could track its location straight to Atlas with a few keystrokes. That would get them both in serious trouble.

An hour later, she set down her tools, closed the case and pressed the power button. The screen illuminated. She programmed her ID into the device, registered it to the colony's network, and shut it down.

There.

She at least felt better that she wouldn't be caught without one now.

Phoebe tidied up so that no one would notice she'd been working in the shop. But how to keep people from noticing that the second comm was missing was a tougher problem. She glanced around, looking for something else about the same size and shape. The closest thing she could find was a part she didn't recognize, and when she laid it on its side, it looked sort of like a facedown comm at first glance. She placed it on the workbench where she'd found the comm she'd fixed.

It was a longshot, but maybe when the morning crew came in to start repairing things, they'd think someone had made a mistake and lost the comm.

Of course, they'd try to track it immediately. So she wouldn't turn it on to use it unless she absolutely had to. And only long enough to see if Atlas had replied to her.

Then she made her way back home. Lately, the house had been feeling crowded, especially with Renata's pregnancy advancing and Marcus and Renata's twins either bickering or roughhousing all the time. Sometimes it felt like there was barely enough room to breathe.

If Atlas joined the colony, they could request a place of their own. It would probably be one of the single-bedroom prefabs from the colony's early days, but they wouldn't need more.

The thought thrilled her but she pushed it away. It was too soon to fantasize about a future together when she wasn't even sure when she'd be able to see him again.

Or if she'd be able to see him again.

Once she got to her room, she sat on the edge of her bed and activated the communicator. Then she typed out a message to Atlas.

Are you there? I finally got a new communicator.

She sent the message, then held her breath, staring at the screen.

No reply. Maybe it hadn't gone through?

No, there was a signal. It should have worked.

She sent another message. *Sorry for taking so long.*

Still nothing.

Maybe he was doing some *spiritual stuff.* That's what the Naturalists did all the time, right? Praying, meditating, purifying themselves. She imagined Atlas stuck in some long, solemn ritual, sitting cross-legged in a dim room while someone droned on about devotion and discipline. But somehow she failed. That wasn't who he was. He longed for freedom and wild places, just like she did.

Her fingers hovered over the keypad.

One more. Just to be sure.

Are you okay?

She waited.

Still nothing.

He wasn't able to answer. She'd just have to wait.

She turned the comm off and placed it on the desk beside her, then tried to catch up on schoolwork. But it was too hard to focus on anything except Atlas. She checked for a response from him every few minutes, but he still hadn't replied.

Had he forgotten about her?

Had someone discovered the communicator and taken it from him?

Or had something worse happened?

God, she was starting to sound like Britt when she'd started go boy-crazy for Trevor. *Worse.* Because Britt and Trevor had known each other for their entire lives. Phoebe had just met Atlas, and she barely knew anything about him.

For all she knew, his comm had already been discovered, and that's why he wasn't answering.

She tucked the communicator into her pocket and focused on her schoolwork.

The afternoon crawled by.

She checked it again, just before dinnertime, and it

chirped as soon as she turned it on. Phoebe almost dropped it.

Atlas.

Meet me tonight? Same place we first met?

She typed back, *Yes. After dark.*

Atlas replied, *See you then.*

She caught sight of herself in the mirror and barely recognized the girl staring back. Her cheeks blazed with color, eyes practically sparking, and her lips curved into a grin wide enough to split her face in two. God, she might as well have *SECRET BOYFRIEND* tattooed across her forehead in glowing letters.

A chime sounded from downstairs. Time for dinner.

Phoebe tucked the communicator under her pillow, then smoothed her hair and practiced looking natural in the mirror. Like she wasn't hiding anything. Like she wasn't about to burst from excitement.

She wrinkled her nose at her reflection, which stubbornly refused to cooperate.

Her attempt at an innocent expression looked about as convincing as a Hyperionite trying to pass as human.

But maybe the adults would be too distracted by their own problems to notice.

Phoebe drew a deep breath, then headed downstairs with measured steps.

Marcus had prepared a utilitarian spread of roasted root vegetables harvested from the eastern fields and protein cakes synthesized from colony algae tanks. Steam rose from the dishes, carrying the earthy aroma of sweet paprika and pungent garlic combined with native spices.

Renata attempted to corral Iris and Theo into their seats across the table, but the siblings were locked in mortal combat over a toy stegosaurus that Marcus had printed for them. Samara's chair remained conspicuously empty; she was probably still hunched over the gene sequencer at the lab. Fifty-fifty whether she was using it or trying to get it to work.

Phoebe's fork traced aimless patterns through her untouched dinner, occasionally stabbing a vegetable only to abandon it again. Her stomach was still performing somersaults. The conversation between Renata and Marcus washed over her in meaningless waves. Something about mineral concentrations in the northern caves, wheat blight in the western fields, and Katherine's plans to expand the irrigation system southward.

The words dissolved into white noise, drowned out by her own thoughts circling like sharks around a single focus: Atlas waiting among the moonlit ruins, counting minutes until she appeared.

"Phoebe?" Renata said. "Are you feeling alright? You've hardly touched your food."

Phoebe opened her mouth, then closed it. She really didn't want to lie to Renata.

"Another migraine?" Renata asked.

She nodded. It wasn't entirely a lie. The pressure behind her eyes had been building all day, though more from anxiety than an actual headache.

Renata frowned. "Should I call your mother?"

"No." Phoebe had no idea how she was keeping her voice so calm. "I don't want to bother her. I'm just going to lie down."

Guilt crashed through her as she headed upstairs. Lying to Renata felt like betrayal of the worst kind. This woman who'd held her through fevers, defended her against bullies, and treated her like family even when her genetic modifications made others keep their distance deserved better.

But some lies were necessary sacrifices for greater truths.

She closed the door, then changed into a dark pair of clothes better suited for sneaking out at night before climbing into bed.

This was going to be the hard part.

Not slipping away too early.

And not falling asleep before it was safe to leave.

The house settled into its nighttime symphony. The subtle creaking of cooling metal, the soft hum of environmental systems cycling down, the distant murmur of adult voices. Then came the sound she had been waiting for: the front door opening, followed by her mother's distinctive footsteps. Phoebe would recognize that pattern anywhere: the slight hesitation before the third step, the barely perceptible drag on the right foot from an old injury, the precise rhythm that marked her mother's movements like a signature.

The footsteps paused outside her bedroom door, and Phoebe forced her breathing into the slow, deep pattern of sleep.

The door inched open. "Phoebe?"

Samara entered the room and walked over to the bed. She pulled up the blankets and tucked them under her chin, then pressed a kiss to Phoebe's forehead.

She pretended to stir.

Samara went statue-still, muscles tensed, barely breathing until Phoebe's breathing evened out again. Only then did she back away, easing the door closed behind her.

The real torture began now.

Waiting.

She counted each heartbeat, the rhythm pounding in her ears.

She pictured her mother's routine: grabbing dinner,

settling at the table, making small talk with Renata about her day.

Twenty minutes later, she heard her mother join Renata and Marcus in the living area. Shortly after that the low hum of the entertainment system filtered through the walls. A movie, from the sound of it.

Perfect.

Phoebe got up and grabbed the lumpy afghan draped over the foot of her bed; she bundled it up into a disorderly ball and shoved it under the blankets, shaping the fabric into the rough outline of a sleeping body.

Then she went to the window and eased it open. The frame protested with the faintest squeak. She tossed her shoes out first, then pulled on her coat and grabbed her backpack. One leg, then the other, straddling the window frame before dropping silently to the ground outside.

She slid the window closed, then crouched in the shadows, pulling on her shoes and hugging the wall. She stuck to the patches of darkness between buildings, invisible to anyone who might glance out their window.

Once clear of the settlement, Phoebe broke into a run. Her feet knew the path to the ruins so well, she could have run it blindfolded.

Phoebe slowed as she neared the ruins, scanning the area for Atlas until she spied him sitting on the same crumbling step where they had first met, elbows resting on his knees, head tilted as if lost in thought.

Atlas stood when he saw her. "I was worried you weren't coming."

She walked over to him. "I had to wait until everyone was distracted."

He smiled. "Me too."

They both laughed.

"You weren't punished for the other night, were you?"

She joined him on the step. "Yeah, I was."

His eyes widened. "Are you hurt?"

Phoebe stared at him. "She didn't beat me, but she did yell at me for almost an hour."

"Oh."

"What do you think we do in my colony, torture people when they're bad?"

Atlas flushed. "No."

She raised her brows.

"Okay, maybe a little. Dr. Basu told us stories about how the Vitruvians handle dissent. Lock the perpetrators in cages. Administer electric shocks. Sometimes disappear them altogether."

"Your Dr. Basu needs to get a grip on reality." Phoebe snorted. "None of that ever happens."

"None of it?" Then as if that wasn't enough. "*Ever?*"

She shook her head.

He winced with embarrassment. "I'm glad."

She studied his face. "It's ridiculous that your people think we're monsters."

"More like dangerous fanatics. People who place scientific progress above human dignity."

"That's rich, considering it comes from a bunch of Naturalists who put religion above the evidence that's right there in front of them."

"It's not quite like that. We believe in science."

"Only when it fits your beliefs. Aren't you on the brink of extinction because you refuse basic medical treatments?"

Atlas laughed. "And yet here I am, alive and well. Thanks to the Divine Blueprint."

More religious stuff. "What's that?"

He sighed, looking up at the dark sky. "She says I was blessed with a genetic configuration that allows me to survive without antifungals or immunosuppressants. Proof that the Divine has provided a natural path to adaptation rather than an artificial one. That's why I don't have to wear an environmental suit when I'm outside."

"And you believe that?" Phoebe asked.

"Well, I'm outside, aren't I?"

"Yeah. But genetic anomalies happen all the time. It has nothing to do with the divine."

He didn't quite frown, but close. "You can't prove that."

"I can, but I'd have to teach you some other things first." She leaned closer. "You don't really believe that some supernatural force decided what genes you have, do you?"

"I'm not sure what I believe anymore. Seems like most of what I was told was wrong, including almost everything about you?"

"Phoebe grinned. "Besides having a butthole for a belly button?"

"Third ear in your armpit," he replied, grinning back. "And hooves instead of feet."

They laughed, then lapsed into a comfortable silence. The ruins stretched around them, skeletal structures etched in moonlight. Above, stars punctured the darkness, cold and distant.

Then Atlas pointed toward the offerings scattered across the mass grave. "What are these?"

He didn't know. She wondered what he'd been told about the old colony.

"Tributes. The Hyperionites leave them for the dead. So they won't be forgotten."

Atlas grimaced. "They mourn those…dead experiments?"

"Of course, they honor their ancestors. Don't you?"

"Yeah. But we're human."

"You share more than ninety-nine point nine percent of your DNA with them."

He looked skeptical. "I'm sorry. Dr. Basu says they're abominations. She never mentioned they had their own culture or traditions. I didn't know they could communicate until last night."

"There's a lot Dr. Basu doesn't seem to mention," Phoebe said. "Their modifications changed the shape of their larynx, so they can't speak, but they adapted sign language, a system of gestures from Earth, which they've added new signs to. They also have art, music, stories passed through generations. They're people, Atlas. Different from us, but still people"

"I guess." He shrugged.

"Well, if she tells you so little about the Hypers, what does she tell you about the Schism?"

Atlas leaned back and their shoulders touched. He started to pull away, but she leaned in, keeping the contact. Soaking in his warmth.

He relaxed again. "She said that Samara poisoned the colonists' minds, convincing them to ignore her warnings about the dangers of genetic manipulation. That she *made* them believe they had no choice but to tamper with their own DNA, that survival meant becoming something *other* than human. When the few colonists who still valued natural human existence begged Dr. Basu to protect them from being forced into Samara's experiments, she took them away before it was too late. Found them new land and started a colony where they could preserve what was left of humanity."

"You make my mother sound like a monster."

Atlas looked sad. "I'm sorry. It's just what we're told."

"That's not what happened. Dr. Basu incited a rebellion by convincing a bunch of people that the treatment was more dangerous than the fungus itself. She was the one who refused to give anyone a choice. People were dying and women weren't able to have babies. Humanity would've gone extinct within a generation."

Atlas stared at the ground. "Dr. Basu says that… that you're no longer fully human."

"Do you really believe that genes are… what, *evil*?"

He opened his mouth, then shook his head and closed it again.

He'd been lied to by the adults who had claimed to be educating him. How was he supposed to decide what he believed when he didn't even have access to the truth?

"Atlas." Phoebe frowned. "You *have* genetic modifications too, you know. Everyone does. It's just that your modifications were a mistake of replication that happened to be an improvement. Mine were made intentionally."

He blinked at her. "What?"

Of course they hadn't taught him about evolution, either.

"What did you think the Divine Blueprint was?" she asked.

His jaw worked silently, mouth opening and closing like a fish suddenly yanked from water, struggling to process the foreign environment. "A blessing. A sacred inheritance. Something *given* to me. Not *engineered*."

"The Divine Blueprint is a genetic modification made by nature. A mutation.. If it wasn't, your parents would've had to have it in order to pass it on to you."

He just stared at her.

"It's biology, your teachers just repackaged it as spirituality so you wouldn't start asking questions." Phoebe leaned forward, propping her elbow on her knee and watching the realization dawn on his face. "It obviously worked, because you don't think of yourself in those terms."

"No one ever *explained* it like that."

She rolled her eyes. "Of course they didn't. Because the truth doesn't support the story Dr. Basu wants you to believe. The Divine Blueprint is just a fancy name for your natural genetic mutations that look basically like the modifications my mother gave me. Maybe I should give mine a name, too. The Heavenly Hack?"

He scowled at her.

"Cosmic Upgrade?" she tried again.

"It's not the same."

"It's *exactly* the same. And I can prove it to you." Phoebe reached into her backpack and pulled out her sampling kit.

Atlas eyed the kit. "What is that?"

"Nothing scary," she said, opening it up. "I just need a small sample from you."

Atlas recoiled. "You want to experiment on me?"

"Not experiment. Analyze." She held up a sterile swab. "I can run your DNA through a sequencer. Figure out exactly what genes give you immunity. I just need to take a cheek swab."

"Oh. I already do that."

She blinked. "You take swabs?"

"Yeah, all the time."

"What for?"

"To test for contamination from the environment."

"Then what happens to the sample?"

"We give it to the Stewards. They take it to the Sanctum. The Healing Clerics use the sacred equipment there to review it and interpret whether the body is still in balance with the environment."

"So … you're running a microbial assay and calling it a spiritual check-in."

"Huh?" He frowned.

Phoebe sighed. "Never mind. What happens if it's not 'in balance'?"

"You enter a cleansing period: isolate, fast, and pray. Sometimes you're given herbs. Sometimes you wait. You return to the cycle when your sample is clear."

"You have an entire belief system built around basic immunology," Phoebe said.

"I'm not sure…"

She popped the cap off the swab. "Your genes determine *everything:* eye color, height, whether you can digest different foods, how your body handles the Bloom. It's all there, written in your DNA like a book."

Atlas frowned. "And you can read it? Like words on a page?"

"Not exactly. It's more like code in a computer." His expression showed he didn't know what that meant, either. "A massive, complicated sequence of letters. But with the right tools, I can compare it to mine, to other colonists, even to native species. I can *find* the gene that lets you survive outside without immunosuppressants. You'd be able to see the Divine Blueprint." She grinned. "How cool would that be?"

He laughed, grinning back at her. "Pretty cool."

"Open your mouth."

He hesitated, eyes locked with hers, then slowly opened his mouth.

Phoebe ran the swab along the inside of his cheek, capturing millions of cells containing his precious "Divine Blueprint" before sealing the sample into a collection vial with a satisfying click.

Atlas looked surprised. "That's it?"

"That's it." She tucked the vial back into her kit and returned it to her backpack. "Soon you'll be able to know everything about yourself. Everything that makes you, you."

Atlas studied her, his expression unreadable. "So if you find something important … something that could help people … you would have to tell someone, wouldn't you?"

"Not without consent. The DNA belongs to *you*. That means whatever we find, it's *yours* to decide what to do with."

"Even if it could save lives, you'd keep it a secret?"

She could tell he didn't believe her. "I'm not about to mess around with something that doesn't belong to me. Science is powerful. But so is choice. And when it comes to someone's *body*, someone's *genes*, it has to be *their* decision. No one else's."

"So even if you found a way to fix everyone so that they didn't need immunosuppressants ever again … you wouldn't just *do* it?"

Phoebe shook her head again. "Not without your consent. People should have the right to refuse, even if it *would* save them. Isn't that what your whole colony believes? That people shouldn't be *forced* into changing?"

"Yeah."

"We believe that too. You wouldn't exist if we didn't. None of the Naturalists would, if my mother had forced Dr. Basu and her followers to accept the treatment instead of letting you go."

He seemed to be having trouble with direct evidence that Vitruvians actually agreed with the Naturalists about being free to choose.

So she continued, "If we find something — *if* — it's up to you what happens next. But depending on the results, we could easily design a gene therapy that would pass on whatever traits allow you to live with the Bloom without immunosuppressants. Together, you and I could give the Divine Blueprint to anyone who wants it. No weddings required."

"You're amazing," he said.

Phoebe flushed. "Stop it."

"No, I mean it. I've never met anyone like you."

"Me neither," Phoebe said.

Their eyes met and the night seemed to hold its breath around them. The space between them vanished as they both leaned forward, drawn by a force more powerful than gravity. When their lips met, the world disappeared. No ruins, no colonies, no division, just the electric current jumping between them, carrying signals neither fully understood but both instinctively followed.

Her heart was pounding when they finally parted.

She rested her forehead against his. "You could come live with us. Leave the Naturalists."

Atlas stiffened, then drew back while shaking his head. "I can't."

"Why not?"

"I'm getting married in a week. Once the Sterilization cycle is finished."

Phoebe blinked. "Married?"

He nodded.

"To who?"

"Hyacinth. Dr. Basu's daughter." He looked down at his hands. "It's all been arranged."

She got to her feet. "Then why are you here kissing me?"

He jumped up beside her. "I know. I'm sorry. I shouldn't have—"

"How long have you been engaged?"

"It's not official yet. And I wasn't given a choice about any of it."

"But what do you want?"

"It's not that simple. The ritual has already begun."

"What ritual?"

Atlas sighed. "The purification starts a week before the wedding. And Hyacinth has already begun the cleanse. She takes the sacred medicine that prepares her womb every day and prays from dawn to dusk."

"What does she pray for?"

"That she'll get pregnant."

Phoebe laughed. "You do know a woman can't get pregnant from prayer, right?"

He flushed. "Of course. I'm not an idiot."

"Sorry," Phoebe said, sitting again. "Go on."

Atlas joined her on the step. "The day before the ceremony, she'll enter the Sterilization chamber, where she'll achieve final communion with the Divine. She'll enter a meditative state, and when she emerges, her body will be ready to receive the Blueprint. Two days later comes the actual wedding. Then sex. That's when the Blueprint is passed along." Atlas stared at his hands. "The ceremony is called the First Conception Day because… well, all Naturalist women get pregnant on their wedding night."

"That's statistically impossible."

"It's not, we have the records to prove it. The Divine has truly blessed us. I can't remember anyone getting married and not becoming pregnant immediately. Except for one woman who turned out to be infertile."

"Listen, I get this is messing with everything you've been taught, but you need to understand that Dr. Basu is selling you a statistical impossibility wrapped in religious packaging. That's just not how human biology works."

"You think I'm lying?" Atlas stiffened and the moonlight turned his blonde hair silver at the edges. "Or do you think my entire life is a lie?"

"Not a lie. Just… incomplete. There's more to the world than what Dr. Basu is telling you. She's making you marry her daughter without giving you the whole truth."

He stared at her bleakly. He didn't believe her. How could she prove it to him?

"Just give me a chance and I can figure this out," she pleaded. "You don't have to marry anyone to share the Divine Blueprint."

Atlas looked at her, conflict clear in his eyes. "I should go. Before someone notices I'm missing."

"And when you get back, what? You're just going to go through with the wedding?"

He didn't answer.

"So what was I, then? One last rebellion before your big moment? Kiss the Vitruvian girl while you still can?"

"No! I don't think of you like that."

"Could've fooled me." Her voice was sharp. "Well, go ahead. Crawl back to your arranged marriage, since none of this apparently mattered."

"It *does* matter. You matter. You're all I've been thinking about since we met."

She stilled. "Really?"

"I'm miserable. I don't want to be with her. I want to be with you."

"So break it off."

Atlas shook his head. "I don't have a choice."

"You always have a choice."

"Not in my world. Everything's already decided. Who I marry, what my purpose is. If I push back, I don't just disappoint Hyacinth, I betray everyone. No one gets the Divine Blueprint from me, and maybe no one ever gets it again. Our settlement is doomed."

"Maybe it should be."

Atlas looked hurt, and she regretted saying it. Just because she was angry at his stubbornness, that was no reason to wish everyone he knew ill.

"I'm sorry, I shouldn't have said that." She shifted from one foot to the other. "Will you meet me again?"

He stared at the ground, then at her, as if memorizing her face. "I don't know if I can."

"Please." Her throat tightened. "Just think about what I said."

He nodded once, then turned and disappeared into the shadows between the ruins, leaving Phoebe alone with the stars and her thoughts.

Chapter Fifteen

Samara opened the door.

Leila stood on the front walk, her figure half-illuminated by the second moon that had just crested the horizon. Its eerie light carved her face into contrasts, highlighting the exhaustion in her eyes while casting the hollows of her cheeks into shadow. She looked like she'd aged five years in the past week.

"You want to come in?" Samara asked.

Iris and Theo's voices rose in pitched battle over something that sounded suspiciously like one of the holo-puzzles Marcus had made them.

"Never mind." Samara stepped outside and closed the door behind her.

Leila looked worse than exhausted; she looked depleted. Dark half-moons hung beneath bloodshot eyes, and her skin had taken on the sickly pallor of someone who'd forgotten what sunlight felt like. Her hair hung in limp strands, escaped from its elastic band and plastered to her sweat-dampened neck like abandoned seaweed on a beach.

"I'm worried about Hector."

Samara stiffened. "What's happened?"

Despite the obvious emptiness of the yard, Leila's eyes darted over her shoulder, scanning the shadows between buildings as if expecting eavesdroppers to materialize from the darkness.

"He asked me to give one of the… one of our new patients the wrong medication, at a dosage that would kill a healthy person."

"Did you tell him?" Samara asked.

She nodded. "Yes."

"And?"

"He blew up at me."

Samara chewed on her lip. "He's probably as exhausted as you look. These past few days have been difficult for everyone."

"Maybe. But I've never seen him angry before."

"Is it possible he was more upset at himself than you?"

"I don't think so. He accused me of trying to sabotage his life's work."

Samara's eyebrows shot up, her brain struggling to reconcile this information with the calm, methodical Hector she had known for years. The man who quadruple-checked dosages and never raised his voice, even during emergencies. "Do you want me to talk to him?"

Leila ran a hand over her face. "Maybe in the morning? I finally managed to persuade him that he needed some rest. Said he'd feel better after a good night's sleep."

A star mosquito buzzed near Samara's ear. She slapped it, feeling the familiar stickiness of blood against her palm. Samara nodded. "Okay. And how are the patients?"

Leila sighed. "Stable, but still unconscious. I've screened for every pathogen I know but found nothing. Hector still thinks they're dying of old age." She brushed away a mosquito of her own. "I think he's probably right."

The second moon now hung fully above the jagged mountain peaks to the east, its ghostly light transforming the yard into a monochromatic painting. Long, distorted shadows stretched from every object, turning familiar garden tools into ominous silhouettes that seemed to reach toward them with grasping fingers.

"Is there something I can do?" Samara asked.

"I hate to ask when everyone's stretched beyond breaking, but could you possibly help with patient care? I'm running on stims and caffeine, and with Hector basically out of commission …"

"Why not ask Lucas to take the night shift?" After all, he never slept, and if a problem arose, he could probably identify the solution by searching medical databases faster than Samara could wake Leila up.

"I couldn't find him."

Samara felt that familiar spark of irritation ignite in her chest. Even though she had zero right to expect him to be anywhere specific, something about his disappearing acts still rankled her. She told herself it was just because Phoebe had imprinted on him as a father figure. The girl deserved consistency, not a part-time parent who vanished without warning whenever he pleased.

She slapped another star mosquito. "Sure, I'd be happy to help."

Leila smiled. "Thanks, Samara. I appreciate it."

"Anything else I should know about the patients?"

Leila shook her head, stifling a yawn. "Nothing urgent. I've left detailed notes at the clinic. Give me six hours, then I'll be back to relieve you."

"Skip the alarm and come in whenever you wake up. Seriously."

Leila waved and then turned and headed down the path toward her house. Seconds later, the darkness swallowed her.

Samara lingered outside, letting the symphony of the night wash over her. The distant mechanical hum of generators that kept them alive, the rhythmic chirping of alien insects that sounded almost, but not quite, like Earth's crickets, the soft whirr of cooling systems fighting their losing battle against DaVinci's relentless heat. The air smelled of metallic dust and the slightly sweet decay of native vegetation.

She'd be glad when the weather started to cool, even though the sporestorms would be more active. At least the star mosquitoes would finally be gone.

She glanced up at the moons, then turned and went back inside.

The children had gone quiet. Marcus and Renata must have put them to bed and then followed suit.

On her way to change into scrubs, Samara paused outside Phoebe's door. She tapped lightly and then eased it open with practiced care to minimize the squeaking hinge.

Her daughter lay completely still beneath the covers. Poor kid. Her migraines were getting worse.

Not wanting to disturb what little rest Phoebe was getting, Samara pulled the door closed again, pressing her palm against the cool surface.

If there were a way to modify Phoebe's DNA to eliminate the off-target effects, Samara would have done it without hesitation, to hell with regulations and ethics violations. But some mistakes couldn't be undone with even the most sophisticated gene therapy. So far, it seemed that the off-target effects of her modifications were permanent. A burden Phoebe would carry forever.

And Samara would carry the guilt just as long.

Chapter Sixteen

AYESHA WATCHED from her office window as the Vitruvian transport approached, its electric engines whining at a pitch that made her teeth itch. Somebody definitely hadn't calibrated the power coupling properly. Fresh weld marks scarred the dull gray plating like hasty surgical sutures where they'd slapped salvaged materials over old damage.

The vehicle lurched to a stop outside, suspension groaning in protest as if even the machine itself was tired of these exchanges. It was falling apart, just like everything else on the planet.

She left her office, walking along the transparent connecting corridor, until she arrived at the settlement's private lab, which most of her people knew as the Sanctum. Then she pulled on her protective gear and went outside to meet Hector.

Only it wasn't the old doctor waiting with her delivery.

It was Leila.

The was wearing an environmental suit, helmet sealed tight against her neck, the reinforced fabric gleaming dully in the morning light. That wasn't like the

Vitruvians at all. They typically arrived in their regular work clothes, sometimes not even bothering with gloves when handling supplies. The sight of Leila geared up like she was handling toxic waste sent alarm bells ringing through Ayesha's mind. Were they implying the Naturalists were contaminated? Or were they hiding something far worse?

"Leila," Ayesha said.

"Ayesha." She gestured to the vehicle. "I've got your flour, cornmeal, dried beans, cooking oil, salt, medicine, other supplies as requested."

Ayesha crossed her arms. "The tractor component?"

Leila shook her head. "Not ready."

"Of course it's not." Ayesha didn't bother hiding her displeasure. "Where's Hector?"

Leila glanced around. A small group of Naturalists in protective suits emerged from one of the corridors and headed to the transport. One had a cart, the others carried baskets. Ready to unload the cargo.

"Maybe we could talk somewhere private?" Leila suggested.

Ayesha nodded. "Follow me."

She led Leila to the decontamination booth at the entrance to the lab, punching in her authorization code before stepping inside and stripping off her clothes. The system hissed to life, engulfing her in a fine chemical mist that stung her nostrils and burned her eyes despite her closed lids.

A few minutes later, she emerged wearing the standard gray communal clothes, her skin tingling from the antimicrobial compounds. She waited as Leila went through the same process, but noticed with growing unease that even after decontamination, the woman wore a medical mask, the kind that made a completely tight seal around the nose and mouth to prevent transmission of even the smallest particle.

A cold knot formed in her stomach. This wasn't standard procedure, it was a containment protocol. The Vitruvians might act casual when it came to the Bloom, but they didn't mess around with contagious disease. If Leila was staying masked after decontamination, something was seriously wrong.

"What's going on?" Ayesha narrowed her eyes.

"Hector isn't feeling well."

"*Isn't feeling well?*" Ayesha repeated. "Elaborate."

"We're not sure what's wrong with him yet, but Katherine has ordered all contact between the colonies cut off until we determine the cause of his illness. Future deliveries will be handled as drops."

"You brought contaminated supplies to my door?"

"We cleaned them," Leila said.

Ayesha walked to her desk, picked up her comm, and typed, *Have everything from the Vitruvians decontaminated. Twice.*

Then she turned back to Leila. "Is this why Katherine has been refusing my calls?"

"She hasn't been refusing. She's just busy given the circumstances. And seeing how everyone here is taking immunosuppressants and is therefore susceptible to even a minor cold or flu virus—"

"Don't try to snow me," Ayesha said, her hands curling into fists at her sides. "This has something to do with the people who were taking refuge with the Hyperionites. You picked up some sort of disease from those filthy creatures."

Leila's eyes widened. "You know about them?"

"I do." Anger flashed hot in Ayesha's chest. Katherine had gambled with everyone's safety *again,* and the Naturalists hadn't even warranted a heads-up. "You bring this to my doorstep? Without warning?"

"Ah, the boy."

So, Atlas had been noticed after all. And either he'd been clumsy or he'd lied to her about it. She'd bet the latter.

"We're following all mandatory protocols, including quarantine of anyone showing symptoms."

"And yet Hector is sick."

"He's the only one. Everyone else is fine."

"You mean, as far as you can tell, everyone else is fine. But you left your mask on because you think you may have brought it here with you. Whatever *it* is."

"I've taken every precaution—"

"Wouldn't Hector have done that too?" Ayesha raised one hand in dismissal. "Tell Katherine that she has no right to make decisions on behalf of both colonies. She should have consulted me immediately before allowing her people to have extended contact with the Hyperionites, and she should've notified me immediately when they showed signs of illness. Her secretiveness is a sign of bad faith. She'd better start bringing me into decisions that affect everyone if she wants to keep the peace."

"She's not keeping secrets, Ayesha. We genuinely don't know what's happening yet. When we do, you'll be notified."

"You'd better pray that's true. Because if you've unleashed something on this planet with your unholy experiments, it won't discriminate between your people and mine. Our immunosuppressed bodies may be the canaries in your coal mine, but you'll fall right behind us."

"Or maybe we won't, because we're willing to take medicine to treat it," Leila snapped.

Ayesha resisted the urge to slap her. Leila had been a foolish young girl before the Schism. Now she was thoroughly brainwashed by Samara's propaganda. Even

Hector had knuckled under when it became clear that the majority had been against them.

But at least he'd been willing to train Elda in the medical protocols that Ayesha had approved—and only the ones she'd approved—so that intervention from outsiders could be kept to a minimum.

Leila froze at the threshold of the decontamination chamber, her hand hovering over the control panel as though uncertain whether to proceed or turn back for one final plea. "We're doing everything we can. No one wants anyone to get sick."

"I know *you* believe that."

Leila's shoulders tensed beneath the environmental suit, words visibly building behind her visor. For a moment, Ayesha thought she might actually speak the truth, whatever that was. But then her posture changed, resignation replacing defiance as she turned and headed back toward the transport without another word, each step slightly faster than necessary.

Ayesha remained rooted to the spot, rigid as a sentry, until the Vitruvian vehicle disappeared beyond the perimeter fence. Only then did her regal posture crack, shoulders slumping infinitesimally as she moved into the decontamination booth and initiated a second cycle.

Paranoid, perhaps, but paranoia had kept her people alive this long. The system activated with a hiss, bathing her in chemicals that burned her lungs with each breath. She stood, eyes half-closed, letting the process work through its timed sequence.

If Katherine had been reckless enough to unleash disease on the colonies because of her willingness to consort with the genetically-tainted Hyperionites, then Ayesha would need more than prayers. But for now, it was all she had to offer.

Out there, she might refuse to let her people see her fear.

But in here, alone, she allowed it to wash over her like the decontamination spray.

She hated that she still depended on Katherine's generosity just to feed and supply her people. That she still depended on Samara's skill to ensure survival in the long-term.

O Creator, O Preserver, keep us pure in your sight. Shield us from the corruption of those who have lost their way. From their sickness, from their arrogance, from their reckless tampering with what was never theirs to change in the first place.

Her fingers curled into white-knuckled fists, nails carving crescents into her palms, the pain a welcome distraction from the mounting fear.

They call it progress, but it is defiance. They call it salvation, but it is desecration. You have shown us the path of purity, of harmony, and yet they believe they can shape life in their own image. And now they bring their disease to us.

Her jaw clenched until the muscles spasmed with protest. She forced herself to breathe through her nose in measured counts. Yet her chest remained constricted as though bound by invisible wire, her skin crawling with imagined pathogens multiplying on every centimeter of exposed flesh.

Let us not suffer for their sins. Protect us.

The UV lights pulsed in slow, deliberate waves, lavender bands sweeping over her skin, purging, cleansing …

Strengthen our bodies against what they have carried into our land. Do not let the faithful fall to the same sickness that will consume them. Guide our hands, guide our choices, and protect the Divine Blueprint, the only true inheritance we have left.

The cycle came to an end.

Her prayers had to be enough. For herself. For her community. For the Divine Blueprint entrusted to her care. Because if Katherine's recklessness had introduced something that even the strictest decontamination couldn't purge, then they weren't just contaminated. They were already as good as dead, abandoned by the Divine they'd served so faithfully.

She hit the switch and started the process again.

ATLAS ENTERED THE PRAYER DOME.

Sunlight poured through the transparent ceiling, fracturing into rainbow prisms where it struck the curved dome. The beams created pools of warmth on the polished floor, illuminating dust motes that danced like microscopic galaxies in the still air. The faint, sweet-spicy aroma of night vine incense lingered from the previous evening's purification ritual, clinging to the fabric of the cushions and the walls.

Yellow meditation cushions formed a perfect circle on the floor. Several early arrivals already sat in contemplative silence, heads bowed and hands clasped in laps, their bodies perfectly still except for the barely perceptible rise and fall of breathing.

Atlas hovered at the entrance, feet suddenly leaden. After everything with Dr. Basu and the forced engagement announcement, the last thing he wanted was to participate in performative spirituality with people who viewed him as a walking genetic anomaly rather than a person with actual feelings.

"Atlas!" Mrs. Karnik grabbed his arm before he could back out. "Such wonderful news. Your mother must be so proud."

He blinked, horror settling into his stomach like a stone. "Thank you?"

She patted his cheek, then went and found her seat.

Dr. Basu had gone ahead and announced the wedding anyway, without telling him.

He made an about face and bumped into Mr. Alvarez. The middle-aged man's face split into a happy smile as he took Atlas' hands in his. "The Divine works through you. Well blessed."

Atlas forced a smile. "Thank you."

He spotted more neighbors closing in from all directions, their curious faces and congratulatory smiles a net tightening around him. Dae. Elda. Ivy. Mr. Patel. He needed an escape hatch. Fast.

He grabbed the nearest prayer cushion and dropped onto it, forcing his fingers into the traditional meditation braid. He bowed his head and closed his eyes, adopting the unmistakable posture that screamed *in communion with the Divine*. The universal do-not-disturb signal that even the most persistent well-wishers wouldn't dare violate.

He felt someone grab his shoulder and squeeze.

He glanced up.

"Congrats, man. Dr. Basu announced it at breakfast," Jared said. "Didn't even know you and Hyacinth were that serious. How come you didn't tell me?"

Atlas met his eyes. "What do you mean?"

"Your engagement?" Jared grinned.

His heart slammed against his ribs like it was trying to punch its way out.

He'd been sentenced to marriage by public decree.

"Yeah." Atlas swallowed hard, feeling like he might choke on the words, forcing a smile that felt more like a grimace. "Thanks."

"Damn, man, you look like someone just told you the

Divine Blueprint comes with a terminal expiration date. Breathe before you pass out, okay?"

"I'm fine," Atlas lied. "Just forgot it was being announced today."

"Well, I'm sure Hyacinth will forgive you. Never seen someone so head over heels. Congratulations again."

He couldn't bring himself to say *thanks* again.

Jared clapped his shoulder again, then found his own cushion.

Atlas forced himself to relax, assuming the proper prayer position: spine straight, shoulders relaxed, hands resting on his knees, palms raised upward in the traditional gesture of receptivity to divine guidance.

But inside he was burning.

Dr. Basu had told everyone before he'd even agreed to the engagement. Announced it as fact, settled and immutable as the rising of DaVinci's sun.

From across the room, he caught sight of Hyacinth entering, her steps measured and graceful as she navigated between cushions. She wore the traditional pre-wedding garment, flowing white robes embroidered with symbols of fertility and devotion. Her eyes found his immediately, lips curving into a smile that communicated both triumph and possessiveness.

He deliberately broke eye contact, closing his lids and assuming the prayer position with exaggerated focus, refusing to give her the satisfaction of even the smallest acknowledgment. No sign that he agreed with what was happening here. The other colonists completed the circle around him, settling onto their cushions with ease. The rustling of fabric and clearing of throats gradually faded into synchronized breathing that filled the dome like gentle ocean waves. Inhale together, exhale together, thirty humans functioning as a single organism connected through shared devotion.

Karina walked clockwise around the unbroken circle, carrying a shallow bowl of purified water. She stopped before each person, dipping in her fingers and anointing their foreheads with a single drop, before saying, "May your body remain untainted, your thoughts uncorrupted, your spirit aligned with the Divine."

He should have been focusing on the Cleansing Meditation.

Instead, Atlas stared at the space behind his closed eyelids, vibrating with rage and betrayal.

Dr. Basu believed she'd cornered him like the lab specimens she criticized the Vitruvians for experimenting on, hemming him in with social pressure, thinking his surrender was inevitable. But instead, she had crystallized his resolve, burning away any lingering doubt about what he needed to do.

Phoebe had said that there was another way to pass on the Divine Blueprint without him getting married. It seemed too good to be true. And, he admitted with some shame, his pride had kept him from learning more in the face of her insistence that his entire life was a lie.

So, he'd clung to the responsibility he'd been raised to fulfill — a responsibility he didn't even want — rather than consider that she might be right. He'd thought there'd be time to negotiate with Dr. Basu. To come up with another solution.

But now, he desperately wanted to believe Phoebe. Because then he wouldn't be forced to marry Hyacinth. Or give up his life to become a husband, a father, a relic of his people's faith.

He could just ... be himself.

Figure out what he wanted out of life and get it.

His fingers dug into his thighs as doubt and hope waged war in his mind. It couldn't be real, could it? A way to share the Blueprint without sacrificing his life to a marriage he never chose? Science that could extract what made him special without demanding his entire existence as payment?

Desire was always a trap.

Desire led to pride. Pride led to impurity.

And impurity was how the world had collapsed before.

That's what Dr. Basu said. Wanting things for yourself was how the sickness of the old world had spread. Rot began the moment you put your own wants ahead of the community. A sickness of the mind, creeping in like a black disease.

That's what Dr. Basu would call this current line of thinking.

Diseased.

Atlas stared at his cupped hands, examining the lines in his palms. According to Phoebe, these weren't divine markings, they were the result of his *genes*. Was the "blessing" that kept him alive out here just a fortunate accident that Dr. Basu had repackaged as divine intervention to maintain control?

Karina was almost at his seat, so he squeezed his eyes shut and bowed his head. He felt the cool touch of her fingers against his skin seconds later.

"May your body remain untainted, your thoughts uncorrupted, your spirit aligned with the Divine."

"May it be so," Atlas said.

Karina moved on.

He opened his eyes.

If he accepted Phoebe's explanation without evidence, wasn't he just trading one form of blind faith for another? Swapping Dr. Basu's doctrine for a different set of beliefs that happened to feel better? That was the very definition of self-deception: choosing a comfortable lie over an uncomfortable truth just because it aligned with what he wanted to hear.

But conversations with Phoebe didn't feel like indoctrination. They felt like waking up. Like seeing color after a lifetime of black and white. She didn't demand that he believe her, she'd only asked that he listen. She'd argued the thing he wanted to believe most: that it should be his choice.

Phoebe was the first person who'd ever asked that simple but revolutionary question: *What do* you *want?*

Five words that acknowledged he was a person with desires and choices, not just a vessel for some divine blessing.

No one else had asked him that. Not about the wedding. Not about his future. Not even about his own body. Consent didn't exist in his world. Decisions were made *for* him. Expectations passed down like scripture.

Phoebe hadn't even tried to pressure him into giving her his DNA, even though she'd admitted that she could use what she learned from it to force everyone to follow the Vitruvian way. But she didn't want to. That was why he trusted her.

She actually saw him as a person. Not the Blueprint. Not the symbol. *Just Atlas*.

Karina returned to her cushion. "O Creator, keep our hearts clear, our minds steady, our bodies pure. Let us walk the path laid before us with strength and devotion."

"Let me accept my role with grace." Atlas spoke the refrain without thinking.

Shouldn't both people have to agree to a marriage for it to happen?

If he had to get married, shouldn't he at least get to choose his wife?

He pressed his hands together tight, his pulse too fast.

He couldn't do it.

He couldn't surrender to this marriage and pretend it didn't matter. Going through with it wouldn't just be uncomfortable; it would be soul-death. Not physical suicide, but something equally final and irreversible. It would mean erasing Atlas the person and accepting his role as merely the Divine Blueprint, a living incubator for valuable genes. He wasn't just fighting for his freedom.

He was fighting to preserve himself.

He had to tell Dr. Basu that he wanted to choose his own bride, but he needed more time to figure out how.

A soft chime rang through the dome, startling him. Karina had struck the small singing bowl, signaling the meditation's end.

The other colonists opened their eyes, stretching, smiling, their bodies and minds at peace. Atlas kept his eyes on the floor, making sure that no one could see his inner turmoil.

He wasn't ready to talk, not to anyone, but especially not Hyacinth, who was probably waiting for him so they could walk out together.

The prayer dome's entrance hissed open, and Dr. Basu swept in like a storm front. Her usual commanding presence was intact, but Atlas spotted the cracks immediately: bloodshot eyes sunk into dark hollows, skin with an unhealthy gray undertone, shoulders rigid with what looked like days of accumulated tension. Something was very wrong.

"I have news from the Vitruvian colony," she said.

His breath caught mid-inhale, lungs suddenly refusing to function. Had someone spotted him with Phoebe?

"Some Vitruvians have caught a sickness from the Hyperionites." She shook her head sadly. "But this is no accident. It is the direct consequence of their choices. They welcomed corruption into their bodies. And now, their sickness reflects what they have become."

Everyone in the dome was absolutely still. No one spoke. Or even moved.

She looked around the circle, making eye contact with each person. Atlas fought the urge to look away when she finally reached him.

"It is a tragedy and I do not say this lightly. I am shutting down all contact with the Vitruvians until the sickness has been eliminated. We will not let their mistakes poison us. Understood?"

He forced himself to nod.

Only then did she turn her gaze to the others.

"We do not rejoice in their suffering. We pray for them that they might come to see the truth written in their suffering. That they might recognize the path they've strayed from and find their way back before it is too late. Let us remember that we have been spared this illness because we remain faithful. Because we choose purity. May we never forget that our survival depends on our devotion."

Everyone nodded. Everyone but Atlas, who thought about the comm unit that Phoebe had given him. What if he'd missed something when he disinfected it?

What if he'd brought it here with him?

Lucas had been right. He should've gone back to the Vitruvian colony to be tested. He should've stayed there until he was sure he wasn't infected.

He would've been in the worst trouble, but at least he would've been able to see Phoebe while he was there.

"Until this danger has passed, maintain vigilance.

Adhere to decontamination protocols with absolute devotion. Report any symptoms of illness immediately. The Divine has separated us from the Vitruvians for a reason. Now we see that reason made clear."

Dr. Basu turned around and exited the room.

The worship circle broke up, people huddling in small groups, sharing whispered conversations as they shuffled out. Hyacinth lingered, so Atlas stayed put. Closed his eyes and pretended to pray, hoping she'd get the message.

He wondered if there was any truth to the illness report. Had those ancient people actually infected the Vitruvian colony? If so, was Phoebe infected too? Or was this just another calculated manipulation from the colony's spiritual leader — a convenient crisis to strengthen her control and prevent Atlas from straying beyond her influence?

His mind strayed back to Phoebe and the Vitruvian version of the schism. Their historical accounts were oil and water; both stories told with conviction, yet fundamentally contradictory.

Two perspectives on the same event.

Two truths that couldn't coexist.

Which narrative actually happened?

Which was propaganda?

Maybe neither was entirely accurate?

His fingers twitched against his knees, muscles tensing as certainty crumbled around him. He lifted his gaze to the violet sky beyond the transparent dome, searching for answers among the scattered clouds.

For the first time in his life, Atlas couldn't decide which felt more unreachable: the distant stars above or the unquestioning faith he no longer possessed.

Chapter Seventeen

SAMARA BRACED her hands against the sequencer console, staring at her haggard reflection in its polished surface. It glitched too often these days, but she was confident that this latest data was accurate.

The genome sequence matched samples she'd collected from the oldest Hyperionites months ago, but without the spliced-in native DNA that allowed them to coexist with the fungus. Confirming that they were original colonists, not their descendants.

It was not unexpected, given what they already knew, but still a little mind boggling to think that, if they could be revived, she could talk to someone who'd been alive nearly two hundred years ago. Someone who'd survived forty-two years on a generation ship, only to arrive on a planet that had proven more hostile to human biology than expected and survived.

And who could tell the story of how they'd been driven to transform themselves into a new species.

They'd witnessed one of the most crucial inflection

points in human history, crossing a threshold that even Samara wouldn't dare to approach.

If they could be revived, that story had to be recorded while they were still alive to tell it.

The lab door hissed open.

She sat, glancing over to see Hector standing in the door.

"Hector. How are you—"

The words died in her throat. Hector stood in the doorway, swaying slightly, his lab coat stained with what looked like blood and some yellowish fluid she couldn't identify. Sweat plastered his gray hair to his skull in dark, greasy clumps. Three days of stubble shadowed his jaw in patchy, uneven growth. But it was his eyes that sent ice water racing down her spine. They were bloodshot and unfocused, pupils contracted to pinpoints, darting around the room like he was tracking something only he could see.

"Hector?" She tried to make her voice light. "What are you doing here? You're supposed to be resting."

"Where are they?" he said.

"Where are what?"

His hands jerked in uncontrolled spasms, fingers curling and uncurling like they were fighting against him. "The nitrile gloves. I always keep them in the second drawer of that cabinet. *Always.*"

She glanced over at the cabinet. "They're still there."

"Liar."

She frowned, got up and walked to the drawer, pulled it open. Full of gloves. "See?"

His eyes flicked between the gloves and Samara, pupils dilating and contracting in irregular pulses. Confusion flickered across his face, then hardened into rage like concrete setting. His jaw clenched so tight a muscle jumped in his temple. "You put them back when I wasn't looking. You're trying to trick me."

Samara shook her head. "I didn't. I promise."

His hands clenched and unclenched in spasmodic jerks, tendons standing out like cables beneath his skin. His breathing turned ragged, chest heaving, nostrils flaring with each exhale. A dark flush spread from his neck up to his hairline, painting his face in mottled patches of angry red.

"You move everything on me." Spittle flew from his mouth as he shouted, a vein pulsing dangerously at his temple. His entire body seemed wound tight enough to snap. "This is my clinic. What gives you the right to make changes?"

"I didn't—"

"You think because you're younger and faster you can just take over? Undo everything I've worked so hard for? I built this place. I keep our people alive. Do you understand what that means?"

Samara took a step back. "I do."

"You don't have any idea. I held this colony together when the sickness took the first wave. When our people started coughing up brown mucus, when their bodies turned against them, when the drugs stopped working, it was always me."

He clenched his fists. His breathing was ragged now, his pupils blown wide, as if he was still standing there in the past, watching the flames.

"And now you come in here and move things around, hide things to make me look bad, and pretend you know better than me?"

Samara walked over to her desk and reached for her comm unit. "Hector, please. You're not well. I'll call Leila."

Hector lunged forward, shoving her with both hands.

The impact sent her crashing back into the counter, the edge digging into her spine as glassware rattled and toppled behind her. She barely had time to catch her balance before Hector staggered toward the centrifuge, his movements jerky but purposeful.

His fingers scrabbled at the machine, finding the rotor housing with disturbing precision. With a savage wrench and an animal snarl, he ripped the weighted metal disc free. The machine shrieked in protest, belts snapping, smaller components exploding outward in a spray of plastic and circuitry that peppered the floor like shrapnel.

"Get out of my clinic!" Spittle flew from his lips; his knuckles were white around the rotor's edge.

Samara held up her hands. "Please Hector."

Dr. Callas lunged again, swinging the rotor in a wild arc.

Samara dropped to the floor as the metal disc whistled over her head, missing by inches before smashing into the equipment rack behind her.

Glass shattered, raining down sharp fragments that bit into her exposed skin.

She scrambled for anything to defend herself with, fingers closing around a heavy metal specimen tray that she held before her like a medieval shield.

"Stop!" She scrambled backward.

He advanced, eyes vacant. "You've contaminated everything. It's all ruined. You've ruined everything!"

He swung again. The metal rotor whistled through the air.

Samara screamed as it caught the edge of the tray, the impact sending vibrations through her arms like she'd struck concrete. The tray was ripped from her grasp, clattering across the floor as she lost her balance.

She hit the ground, harder this time, tailbone shooting

pain up her spine as Hector loomed over her, raising the rotor for a killing blow. She threw her arms up in a futile attempt to shield her head.

The lab door hissed open.

Lucas crossed the room in three fluid strides, his movements precise and deadly efficient. His hand clamped around Hector's wrist mid-swing, stopping the momentum cold. In one continuous motion, he twisted the arm outward — not enough to snap bone, but precisely calibrated to shock the nerve pathways and force the fingers to release.

Hector bellowed in pain and surprise as the rotor slipped from his grasp.

It hit the floor with a clang that echoed through the lab like a death knell. Lucas kicked it away, sending it spinning under a workbench.

"What the hell?" Leo said.

Samara's tunnel vision expanded suddenly, adrenaline fog clearing enough to register that Katherine and Leo had rushed in behind Lucas. They stood frozen in the doorway, faces locked in identical expressions of horror as they took in the scene.

Katherine recovered first, stepping forward with steady hands to help Samara up. "Are you alright?"

Samara ignored the trembling in her legs. "I'm fine. It's Hector who needs help."

Katherine reached out, her fingers cool against Samara's burning cheek. Crimson smeared her fingertips when she pulled back, bright against her sun-weathered skin. "You're cut."

Samara blinked in surprise, raising her own hand to touch the spot. She felt the warm wetness of blood but no pain. Shock, probably. "Must have caught a glass shard when I fell."

"I'm glad that's all you caught." Katherine said grimly, her gaze shifting to the centrifuge rotor that could have easily cracked Samara's skull open.

The lab looked like a war zone. Shattered glass crunched underfoot, scattered amid the bent instruments and twisted metal. Fluid from broken test tubes pooled on countertops, dripping onto the floor in steady plops. The monitor screen had spiderwebbed into a thousand cracks, and the centrifuge housing gaped open like a wound, wires spilling out like intestines.

Hector twisted in Lucas' grip, his face blotchy with exertion. "Katherine, leash your dog."

Katherine narrowed her eyes on him. "Hector, look at me. What's going on?"

His gaze skittered between Katherine and Samara, his facial muscles twitching in uncoordinated spasms. The rage drained from him visibly, like someone had pulled a plug, leaving him slack-jawed and disoriented. His shoulders slumped forward as if his spine could no longer support his weight.

Then his eyes landed on Samara. "She's hurt."

"An accident," Samara said.

"I was… I was looking for gloves. I need to examine my patients." His eyes darted wildly around the lab, pupils constricting to pinpoints then dilating again. His fingers plucked at his lab coat in erratic patterns, as if trying to catch insects that weren't there. Sweat beaded on his upper lip despite the lab's cool temperature. "But I can't find anything."

"Because you're ill," Katherine said, placing a hand on his shoulder. "You need to rest."

"Ill? No. No." He shook his head. "I'm just tired. Do you have those samples, Samara?"

Samara looked at Katherine, her mouth working. But she couldn't think of anything to say.

"You've been working too hard," Katherine said, "Let's get you back to your quarters. Samara's got the lab handled."

"But my work—"

"Will still be here tomorrow."

Hector's gaze pinballed between Katherine and Samara, his expression cycling through confusion, anger, and finally a hollow emptiness. Muscles in his face twitched in uncoordinated spasms, his mouth working soundlessly as if his brain were cycling through responses it couldn't quite access. The tension drained from his body all at once, leaving him slack and puppet-like. His knees buckled completely, and if Lucas hadn't maintained his grip, Hector would have crumpled to the floor in a boneless heap.

"Before you take him. I'll take a blood sample. See if I can figure out what's wrong." Samara pulled a syringe.

Katherine nodded. "Do it."

Samara worked quickly, her own hands trembling slightly as she located a vein. She swabbed his arm with antiseptic, feeling his muscles twitch beneath her touch, then slid the needle in with practiced precision. He didn't flinch or react, staring at her with hollow eyes that seemed to look through her rather than at her. The vial slowly filled with dark red blood while the room remained silent enough to hear the soft hiss of the air filtration system cycling through another purification round.

She forced herself to give him a reassuring smile as the vial filled with his blood.

When it was three-quarters full, she capped the vial and stepped back, setting it on the counter.

Lucas looked over at Katherine. "I'll take him back to his quarters."

"He'll need to be watched," Katherine said.

"I'll put security on it. Make sure someone stays with him."

"Around the clock."

Lucas nodded, then guided Hector toward the door. The doctor didn't resist, but there was something unsettling about the way he moved, like his limbs weren't syncing with his thoughts.

Lucas paused before stepping out. "If you'd like, I can observe the Hyperionites. See if any have fallen ill since the patients were removed from the cave."

Katherine nodded. "Don't engage with them. Until we know more, I'm forbidding direct contact with the Hyperionites for anyone. Including you."

"Understood. Though someone may wish to tell Phoebe your directive applies to her as well."

"I'll make sure she understands," Samara chimed in.

Then Lucas escorted Hector out, and the door slid shut behind them. Both Leo and Katherine turned to Samara.

"We heard yelling," Leo said. "What set him off?"

Samara sagged against the counter and held out her hands, still shaking. "I don't know. He arrived angry and it escalated from there. Maybe he's sick. Or he caught whatever our patients have."

"How is that possible?" Katherine asked. "We have strict containment protocols and Hector always adheres to them. Hasn't he been wearing protective gear every time he's with them?"

"Maybe there was a breach he didn't catch. Or maybe he got careless." Samara's mind was racing. "And now he's been moving freely throughout the colony. Katherine, if he's contagious—"

Katherine held up a hand. "Don't go there yet. We need facts, not speculation."

"I understand that. But we've all been exposed to him now. What if we're infected too? Leila and I have been working alongside him for the past few days. What if I've already exposed Renata, Marcus, Phoebe, the baby?" The words tumbled out. "We could be looking at an outbreak."

Katherine squeezed her shoulder. "Let's not panic yet. Focus on those samples. Find out what we're dealing with. I have faith you'll find it."

Samara nodded.

"Leo," Katherine said.

The two of them left Samara alone in the wrecked lab. She surveyed the damage, but her mind was already on the nightmare of a potential outbreak. She grabbed Hector's blood vial, then walked to a different workstation and began preparing it for analysis.

Another plague. Another hostile microorganism that could wipe out what remained of her species. But this time Samara was two decades older, her scientific skills dulled by routine and drudgery. But this time, her daughter had no protection from whatever had infected Hector. She glanced toward the quarantine room where the two ancient patients lay. Were they the source? Was this the beginning of an epidemic that would make the fungus look like a mild inconvenience? Samara felt a chill that had nothing to do with the lab's temperature. If Hector could go from rational scientist to violent psychotic in days, what else might this mystery disease do?

And how far had it already spread?

Chapter Eighteen

HECTOR'S FACE was inches from Samara's, veins bulging at his temples like blue electrical wiring about to short-circuit. His breath hit her face in erratic bursts, hot and sour with ketones.

"You had no right to alter Phoebe's DNA. Playing god with your own child. Creating something that shouldn't exist!" His eyes were wild, unfocused. "Always meddling with the building blocks of life, thinking you know better than nature itself."

Samara tried to back away, but he'd cornered her in the lab. The colony would have died—"

"The others don't see it yet." He grabbed her wrist, squeezing until she felt her bones grinding against one another. "But I do. I see what you've done to your own daughter. The headaches, the seizures, they're just the beginning. You've sentenced her to a life of suffering."

She tried to pry his fingers loose. "Phoebe is healthy. The modifications saved her—"

"You broke her!" He tightened his grip. "You broke her genetic code and now it's unraveling. Day by day, piece by piece. Your daughter is falling apart from the inside, and it's all because of your hubris."

"Hector, you're not well."

"No. I'm seeing clearly for the first time." He pulled a scalpel out of his lab coat pocket, the metal catching the harsh lab lights. "You've contaminated the gene pool. Corrupted your own flesh and blood. And now Phoebe will pay the price for your sins. Her death will be on your head. Because sometimes we need to cut out the contamination at its source."

Samara screamed.

So did Hector.

He threw his head back, mouth stretching impossibly wide. But what emerged wasn't human at all, just a soft, electronic chime pulsing like a metronome and slicing through the nightmare, pulling at Samara's consciousness like fingers tugging loose thread. The lab dissolved around her, its edges blurring and folding inward as Samara jerked awake, her hand smacking into an empty coffee mug perched at the edge of her desk.

She caught it before it hit the floor, heart hammering against her ribs.

Just a dream. Another nightmare. The third this week.

The chime sounded again. Her test results were ready. She straightened in her chair, wincing as her neck muscles protested the awkward sleeping position. Wiping a trail of dried saliva from her chin, she swiveled toward the monitor, forcing her mind from nightmare terrors to scientific reality.

Hector's blood analysis was complete.

Samara leaned forward, scrolling through the data. Her pulse quickened.

The results were unmistakable.

Prions.

"Anything but that," she whispered.

But prions were everywhere in Hector's sample. Long, tangled chains where there should have been neat, folded helices. The proteins were clumping together, forming toxic aggregates that the body couldn't clear. The pattern was unmistakable: a cascading failure, a chain reaction with no off switch.

There was no cure for a prion disease, not even a treatment to slow down the progression. Creutzfeldt-Jacob disease, Gerstmann-Straussler-Scheinker syndrome, Kuru. All death sentences.

A terrible, gruesome, sanity-destroying death.

Samara pulled up the other data she'd been gathering from Hector's past bloodwork. His erratic behavior, the physical tremors, cognitive decline. All classic symptoms of a prion disease.

But how and when did it start?

Samara picked up her comm unit, keying in Katherine's code. The connection established with a soft crackle.

"Samara?"

"Bring Leila to the lab. I've got news."

"See you shortly." Katherine disconnected.

Samara reached for her tablet, making notes as she waited. She needed to retest the samples from the patients. They might be affected as well. It would explain their incoherence, and rapidly deteriorating condition.

Perhaps it explained the bruises, too. As they deteriorated mentally, had they attempted to escape the chamber they'd been locked in?

The lab door hissed open a few minutes later and Katherine entered, with Leila right behind.

"I found what's wrong with Hector." Samara gestured to the monitor. "And possibly the Hyperionite patients as well."

Leila stepped closer, squinting at the patterns before turning to Samara. "Prions?"

Samara nodded.

Katherine frowned. "Prions? Like mad cow disease?"

"Similar, yes. But this isn't standard prion disease."

Katherine studied the image with a deepening frown. "So, what makes this different?"

Samara pointed to the monitor. "Normal prion diseases are devastating, but they have a slow progression. Years, sometimes decades. This is moving faster. Exponentially faster."

Leila leaned in, her face pale in the monitor's glow. "That would explain the Elders' incoherence during their brief conscious periods. And Hector's deterioration. He's burning through the stages in weeks instead of years."

Samara nodded. "Whatever this is, it's aggressive. The misfolded proteins aren't just spreading, they're hijacking critical neural pathways at an accelerated rate. Motor function, memory, emotional regulation — everything is unraveling all at once."

Katherine crossed her arms. "Can you stop it?"

Samara exchanged a glance with Leila.

"What?" Katherine asked.

"Unlike viruses or bacteria, prions can't be 'killed,' because they aren't alive in the first place," Samara explained, tracing the malformed protein structures on the screen. "They're just normal proteins folded wrong. Molecular zombies that convert healthy proteins into twisted copies of themselves. They accumulate in neural tissue, gumming up the works until the brain literally develops holes like Swiss cheese. No immune response, no inflammatory markers, just silent destruction from the inside out."

Leila nodded. "Back on Earth, before everything

collapsed, prion diseases were rare. They were studied intensely, but effective treatments remained elusive."

"It's incurable?" Katherine asked.

Samara gestured to the monitor again. "There were treatments in development that slowed progression to some degree but nothing that could reverse the damage."

"Nothing that could stop the inexorable decline," Leila said.

Katherine's lips thinned to a tight line. "So you're telling me this is a death sentence for Hector."

It wasn't a question. But Samara nodded anyway.

"How long?" Katherine asked.

"Hard to say," Samara said. "Based on his current symptoms, I'd estimate he's in the intermediate stage. The disease's progression varies. Could be weeks, maybe months."

"And the Elders?"

"I still need to retest their blood samples to confirm, but if I'm right, they're much further along. Terminal phase, most likely."

Katherine sighed. "So how did Hector get it?"

Leila chewed on her lip. "Prion diseases aren't highly transmissible. Not like viral infections."

"Typically, no." Samara pulled up another display. "The most likely explanation is that he was exposed to the patients' bodily fluids. Blood, saliva, cerebrospinal fluid, any of it could contain prions. We took so many samples."

"But Hector was extremely careful," Leila said.

"There could have been a flaw in his protective equipment," Samara argued. "A microscopic tear in a glove. Or perhaps he accidentally touched a contaminated surface after removing his protective gear."

Katherine rubbed a hand over her head. "Are there other modes of transmission?"

"Consumption of contaminated meat, historically. Though I doubt that's the case here." Samara said. "There are also rare instances of spontaneous prion formation, where proteins misfold without external triggers. It's exceptionally uncommon, but it happens."

"So we don't know for certain that it came from the couple in the cave," Katherine said.

"No, not yet. I need to check their samples."

Katherine nodded. "Alright. I want all meat stores tested. I'll send a colony-wide notice. No animal protein until we're certain that's not the source of the contamination."

"And anyone who feels ill should report to the clinic immediately," Leila said.

"Agreed. I'll put out a bulletin suggesting the meat may have been infected by a parasite and anyone with symptoms should report to you."

Leila nodded.

"In the meantime, let's keep this quiet for now, nothing about prions or Hector's condition. The last thing we need is widespread panic." Katherine walked to the door, then paused at the threshold. "Samara, you and Renata are both qualified to test the meat stores. Leo can check the livestock for any signs of illness or unusual behavior. Get it done."

Samara nodded.

As soon as the door shut, Leila slumped. "Hector was my mentor. He's been teaching me since I was nineteen. I can't imagine the clinic without him."

Samara reached for her hand, squeezing it. "I'm sorry."

Leila met her eyes. "I mean it, Samara. He's the one who trained me. The one who always knows what to do. Without him—"

"You're the most experienced medical professional left in the colony."

Leila nodded. "And I don't know if I'm ready for that."

"I know you are," Samara said. "And Hector would agree with me. Still, there has to be some treatment that might help him.. We just need to find it."

"I'll go through the medical databases we brought from Earth, see if there are any experimental treatments that might help."

"And I'll get Renata up to speed on the meat testing. Take more samples from the Elders." Samara blew out a breath. "Let's get started."

She had always believed that knowledge was a form of triumph, even when it couldn't provide the solution she wanted.

But tonight, that belief felt hollow as an empty test tube.

She stared at the prion models rotating slowly on her screen, their misshapen structures mocking her with their simplicity. So small, so mindless, yet unstoppable once set in motion. No antibiotics, no antivirals, no genetic therapy she could devise would reverse what had begun in Hector's brain.

Knowledge without a cure didn't feel like progress at all.

It just felt like watching someone burn to death while holding an empty bucket.

Chapter Nineteen

PHOEBE'S HEAD throbbed like someone was driving nails through her skull. The aftershock of the migraine curled behind her eyes, each pulse sending fresh waves of pain radiating down her neck.

She tried to focus on sweeping up another shattered beaker, hoping the mundane task might distract her. But the pain was relentless, sharper than any migraine she'd experienced before. Probably triggered by the bomb Atlas had dropped on her.

Engaged. Atlas was *engaged*.

It hadn't even come up until she suggested he leave the colony, and then it slipped out like it was no big deal. No warning, no explanation, just *oh by the way, I'm marrying someone else in a week.* Did he think she wouldn't care?

It wasn't that she didn't understand how you could love more than one person; she saw that in action every day in the affection Samara shared with both Marcus and Renata.

But that didn't mean that was what *she* wanted.

She'd started developing feelings for Atlas. There.

She'd said it. Not just a crush or fleeting attraction, but real feelings that made her stomach flutter when he smiled and her heart race when their hands touched. The kind of feelings she'd rolled her eyes at when Britt described them.

Her fingers tightened on the broom.

And he liked her too. He'd said as much.

I'm miserable. I don't want to be with her. I want to be with you.

It was clear he didn't want this marriage. He wasn't excited or nervous or any of the things someone should be before their wedding. He was resigned, shoulders slumped like someone carrying a burden they couldn't put down.

And that wasn't fair. Dr. Basu had engineered his entire existence like one of Samara's experiments, designing his purpose, programming his beliefs, selecting his mate. His life wasn't his own; it was a carefully constructed prison cell with walls made of other people's expectations.

She couldn't imagine what it was like, being told you to have to marry someone you didn't love. He didn't seem to have any real freedom. How could he, when his entire community saw him as a walking genetic miracle?

A *Divine Blueprint.*

She snorted.

What a stupid name.

She swept a bunch of glass into the dustpan then dumped it into the garbage bin. She wanted to be angry at Atlas, but she also wanted to help him.

If she could isolate the adaptations in his DNA that enabled him to live outside without immunosuppressants, she could build a vaccine. A way for the Naturalists to protect themselves.

Then he wouldn't have to marry Flower.

No. That wasn't her name.

Hyacinth.

Yeah.

"Careful with that." Samara interrupted her thoughts. "Those fragments are sharper than they look."

"Thanks, I didn't know that broken glass could be sharp."

Samara looked up from the molecular analyzer and glanced over at her.

Phoebe met her mother's eyes. "I've been cleaning this lab since I was old enough to understand the difference between a pipette and a petri dish. I know how to be careful."

"You're right. I'm sorry." Samara looked exhausted. The lines around her mouth were deeper than usual, and her hair was slipping loose from its ponytail, strands clinging to the sweat on her temple. There was a faint tremble in her hand.

Phoebe swept the last of the glass into the tray, then dumped it into the biohazard container. "What happened in here anyway? Looks like someone went on a rampage."

"There was an accident."

Phoebe looked at her mother. She always tensed her shoulders lying, like she was donning armor. In case it turned into a fight or something.

Phoebe didn't even want to be here.

She should be at the lake with Flutter right now. Instead, she was stuck here because the Hyperionite settlement was suddenly off-limits. Katherine's bulletin claimed it was to prevent spreading a potential parasite in the meat supply, but Phoebe wasn't an idiot. This quarantine had started right after they'd brought those ancient people out of the cave.

At least Lucas had promised to let Flutter know why Phoebe had gone silent.

But it wasn't just Flutter she was missing. Not by a long shot.

Atlas flashed through her mind yet again.

She'd sent him three messages since they parted, and still no response.

Was that it? Her brief dalliance was over? The only boy she'd ever been interested in snatched away by a circumstance of birth?

God, she sounded melodramatic. Maybe he was just mad at her. They did have kind of a fight.

Or maybe he'd lost the communicator.

Or decided to go through with the marriage.

Or was being kept prisoner.

Locked in some purified room. Under surveillance. Drugged.

STOP IT.

She pressed two fingers to her forehead. The pressure helped for a moment, then somehow started to make her migraine even worse.

"Hand me that calibration rod," Samara said, holding out her hand.

Phoebe set the broom aside, retrieved the thin metal implement and passed it to her mother.

Samara inserted it into the analyzer's port, adjusting the alignment. "How's your head today?"

"It's fine." The words tumbled out automatically, the same reflexive lie she'd been using since the headaches started, to shield her against overprotective concern.

Samara's eyebrows arched, her lips pressing into a thin line as her eyes scanned Phoebe's face, cataloging the pinched expression, the bloodshot eyes, the slight tension in her jaw that always appeared during a migraine.

"Okay, not great," Phoebe admitted. "But I can manage."

"Did you take your medication?"

"Maximum dosage."

"And?"

"It barely made a difference."

Concern flickered across Samara's face. "We might need to adjust the formula again."

"Why bother? It's just going to keep getting worse." The bitterness in Phoebe's voice surprised even her.

"Phoebe—"

"I know, I know. You're doing your best."

Samara opened her mouth to respond but was interrupted by the lab's intercom.

"Dr. Makinde?" The security officer's voice crackled through the speaker. "There's a Naturalist here with a delivery. Briar Shan. Says it's a scheduled biomedical transfer."

Phoebe stiffened.

Shan?

That must be Atlas' mother.

"Alright. Bring her down," Samara said.

Most of the debris had been cleared, but Phoebe kept methodically sweeping, creating busy work to justify her presence. No way was she missing a chance to see Atlas' mother.

The lab door hissed open minutes later, admitting a woman encased in a bulky environmental suit, helmet tucked under one arm.

Phoebe caught a glimpse of her face. The same dark brown eyes. The same sweep of the nose. Atlas looked like her. She would have known that was his mother anywhere.

Briar held out a sealed biomedical package to Samara.

Samara accepted it with a nod. "Thank you. Could you put this in cold storage for me, Phoebe? Section C."

Phoebe nodded back, walking over and taking it.

"I heard your people are falling ill," Briar said, her eyes flicking around the lab with barely disguised distaste.

"Can't say I'm shocked, what with all the vaccines and gene tampering you do around here."

It was easier to forgive those accusations when they came from Atlas. Harder when they came out of his mother's mouth.

Those hateful sentiments were the reason that she and Atlas couldn't be together.

"Our medical practices are really none of your business, Briar. You left the colony."

"They become our business when they create disease. You people mess with life itself and then act surprised when nature fights back."

"Right." Samara crossed her arms. "Because letting people suffer when we have treatments is so much more ethical?"

"Those aren't treatments." Briar hardened her voice. "That's you playing God. Too arrogant to see the danger you're creating."

"And you're too afraid to see the progress. People are walking around, breathing, living because of what you call 'playing God.' Did it ever occur to you that maybe the Divine you always blather on about gave us this knowledge to save lives?"

Briar's face darkened.

Phoebe glanced between them, feeling the air crackle with a hostility so dense she could practically see it, two decades of resentment compressed into the space between heartbeats.

Samara caught her eye. "Phoebe? The storage unit?"

She flushed, raised the package, then turned around and headed for the cold storage room. "I'm going."

Once inside the chilled compartment, the door sealed behind her, muffling the argument. She set the package on the prep counter and opened it, removing the contents.

There were several small containers inside, each labeled with names and dates.

She arranged them in the storage rack in section C, and a name on a vial caught her eye.

Atlas Shan.

She paused.

What?

Why did her mother have samples from him?

She frowned, trying to recall if these had been here during her last inventory shift. She'd regularly helped Samara pull samples from these refrigeration units during her shifts, and she was almost certain she'd never seen Atlas' name on any of them.

Her first instinct was to confront Samara directly, but experience had taught her better. That approach would only yield evasive non-answers or irritated deflections, followed by increased scrutiny of Phoebe's activities. Lucas might know, but even his loyalty was split; he was programmed to protect her, but that could mean telling Samara that she'd asked.

It didn't make sense.

The Naturalists didn't even *like* science. And yet… his DNA was here. They had to have sent it. Otherwise, how would Samara have gotten it?

Maybe these were the cheek swabs he took at the colony. But how the heck did they wind up here?

Dr. Basu.

She'd lied.

They weren't going to Healing Clerics at all. They were coming here. No doubt making sure the Divine Blueprint was in perfect health. If he got sick, that would mess up her whole story, wouldn't it?

Phoebe glanced to her left and saw another vial. It also had his name. Not just one. There were *several*.

She backed up a step.

She'd been dying to map Atlas' genome since she'd persuaded him to let her swab his cheek, so she could unlock the biological secret that kept him breathing freely while everyone else needed medication or genetic tweaks to survive.

But Samara was practically living in the lab, working on some urgent project she refused to talk about. And Phoebe didn't want to get bombarded with a bunch of questions about what she was doing.

Maybe she could lie and say it was for her school project?

Say she was mapping her own genome?

But Samara might take that personally. Think Phoebe was trying to fix what she had broken. And she didn't want Samara looking too closely.

If Samara was already analyzing Atlas' DNA—and these vials suggested she was—she'd recognize his genetic markers instantly if Phoebe tried running her own tests.

Maybe Lucas could help her run the analysis and design the therapy away from Samara's watchful eyes. He'd been there for Phoebe's own modifications, privy to every step of the process. The trick would be to convince him not to tell Samara, but finding the loopholes in his loyalty algorithms was practically her childhood hobby.

Phoebe exited, closing the cold storage unit and returned to her mother.

Briar was gone.

"All set," Phoebe said.

"Good." Samara seemed distracted, her attention already shifting back to whatever she'd been working on. "That woman has the brains of a vacuum chamber."

Phoebe eyed her mother. Alright, she didn't have the

guts to ask about Atlas' samples, but she could ask about why Briar was here.

"Why would the Naturalists be sending you medical samples?"

Samara waved a hand. "It's just routine lab work that Leila handles for them."

"But why would they want any lab work done when they reject our science?"

Samara sighed. "It's no big deal, Phoebe. I promise."

Since she wasn't going to get any more information from her mother, she retreated back into the back room where the refrigerated units were kept and pulled out her comm, turned it on.

It buzzed immediately. The notification on the screen made her heart jump.

Atlas.

A wave of relief washed over her. He was still willing to talk to her.

"Why do you have a different comm unit?"

Phoebe whirled around, clutching the phone to her chest as she came nose to nose with Samara.

Had she seen Phoebe's own name on the message as the sender?

She should have been more careful. "I, uh… I lost mine. Somewhere in the cave where we found the old people. Had to requisition a new one."

Samara frowned. "Those units are precious resources, Phoebe. We have limited ability to repair or make new ones. You need to take better care of your things."

"Well, I won't have a chance to lose this one. Since I never get to go anywhere anymore."

"Phoebe—"

"Off to see Britt. See you later."

She practically sprinted out of the lab, her heart

hammering against her ribs. Atlas' message burned in her pocket like a live coal, making everything else — the mysterious samples, her mother's secrecy, even the throbbing migraine — fade to insignificance.

The moment she rounded the corner, safely out of Samara's sight, she fumbled the comm unit from her pocket, fingers trembling as she opened his message.

Meet me at our spot tonight?

Her pulse raced, electricity shooting through her veins. *Yes!* she typed and hit send, a reckless grin spreading across her face.

To hell with Katherine's rules. To hell with all of them.

Chapter Twenty

ATLAS STARED at the half-eaten protein bar in his hand, wondering if he could use it to escape this living nightmare. Maybe choke on it just enough to get rushed to medical and avoid another hour of Hyacinth's wedding planning.

She'd been following him around all morning, chattering about where they should build their house after the wedding. Hyacinth kept circling the same point; she wanted distance from her mother but couldn't quite commit to saying it out loud. Classic Hyacinth, walking the line between independence and obedience.

She wouldn't stop talking, so he suggested it would probably just be easiest to move in with Dr. Basu just to shut her up.

That had backfired.

Hyacinth had taken his suggestion seriously. Instead of debating locations, she switched to talking about logistics, arrangements, and how they would rearrange her mother's house.

Now Atlas sat trapped in Dr. Basu's office, feeling the

walls close in. Hyacinth and her mother began discussing flower arrangements, ritual oils, and ceremonial timing. With each decision, another brick sealed into the wall of his prison cell. His life was being designed by committee, and he didn't even get a vote.

Dr. Basu tapped her desk. "What do you mean you want to use ghostshade essence for the purification censers?"

Hyacinth flushed a little. "It symbolizes receptivity to divine revelation."

"I know what it symbolizes, Hyacinth. But night vine has been used in Sterilization ceremonies since the founding of our settlement. Tradition carries its own weight."

Hyacinth squirmed in her chair. "Yes, but I don't like the smell as much."

"Atlas?" Dr. Basu said.

He stared back, his mind blank. "Yes?"

Hyacinth gritted her teeth. "The flowers?"

"Does it matter? They both smell like medicine." How could he care about which flowers they used when his entire future was being mapped out without his input, every choice and possibility stripped away until he was nothing but a walking repository of valuable genes?

"This is your Consecration," Dr. Basu's nostrils flared slightly, her fingers drumming a quick, irritated rhythm against the polished surface of her desk. "The moment you formalize your commitment to the future of our people. Every element should perfectly reflect the solemnity of that responsibility."

"I'll let you choose.." That's what was going to happen anyway.

Dr. Basu made a note on her tablet. "We'll proceed with the night vine, then. Now, regarding your speech."

Atlas stiffened. "Speech?"

"Your declaration of purpose," Dr. Basu said, sliding her data tablet across the table. "You'll recite it before the congregation prior to taking your vows. I've drafted a copy of it for you."

Of course she had.

Atlas scanned what was written.

With great humility, I accept this sacred duty bestowed upon me, a responsibility that reaches beyond my individual desires and into the eternal foundation of our people. Through this union, we reaffirm our unwavering commitment to purity, to faith, and to the principles that have sustained us since the first settlers rejected the sin of genetic corruption.

Today, as we stand in witness of this covenant, let us remember that we do not belong to ourselves, but to the greater whole and to what was given to us, untainted and true. May this union stand as a testament to our devotion, a pledge not only between Hyacinth and myself, but between ourselves and the generations yet to come.

In binding ourselves to this path, we reaffirm the choices of those before us and ensure that the will of the Divine remains unbroken. Let us enter into this solemn agreement with clarity, with obedience, and with faith in the design that has guided us since the first breath of life was given ...

The speech continued for two more pages, a mind-numbing procession of platitudes and religious propaganda that made his eyes glaze over.

If Dr. Basu had tried to create the most soul-crushing collection of empty phrases possible, she couldn't have done better than this joyless manifesto of submission.

This speech had nothing to do with him. But she'd taken control over every other aspect of his life, why not his voice?

"I'll finalize it tonight," Dr. Basu said. "You'll need to memorize it."

"And don't forget to write your wedding vows," added Hyacinth.

Atlas looked over at her. "I thought the vows were standardized."

Dr. Basu nodded. "The ritual vows, yes. But you will compose personal vows to demonstrate the individual commitment to Hyacinth as your primary wife."

Primary wife.

The idea of being "spiritually wed" to every woman of childbearing age made his skin crawl. It was no longer theoretical; the ceremonies were scheduled, spaced out over the next two months. His body wasn't his own. His genes belonged to the colony. And now they were packaging up his future in neat, ritual-sized portions, divvying him up like community property.

"They needn't be excessive," Dr. Basu said. "Only sufficient to convey genuine dedication. I will read and approve them in advance."

Right.

Wouldn't do to let Atlas have his own words. He might say the wrong thing.

Hyacinth smiled at him. "I've been working on mine for days."

Zero surprise. She was embracing this path, while he resisted it at every turn. Was she really happy being so obedient? In never having to wonder what came next?

Because that felt like death to him.

Hyacinth didn't just accept the system, she *belonged* to it. Never questioned or doubted a thing. Didn't want to. Her belief was fixed, not fragile. That scared him a little.

Atlas slouched in his chair. "Is there anything else? I'm not feeling well."

Dr. Basu recoiled. "You're ill?"

"No." He sighed. "I haven't slept much with the wedding coming up."

Dr. Basu relaxed a little, then consulted her list. "The ceremonial foods have been approved. The sanctum is being prepared. The meditation guides will assist you with your pre-ceremony fasting when we get closer to the date. I believe that concludes the matters for today."

Finally. Atlas exhaled.

"Wait a minute. We still need to discuss the post-ceremony celebration. I've been thinking about symbolic foods and their arrangement—"

"Another time," Dr. Basu said to Hyacinth. "We must let Atlas rest."

He rose, his legs almost numb from sitting so long.

"Tomorrow morning, " Dr. Basu looked him in the eyes, "You'll meet with the tailor to fit your suit."

Atlas nodded, backing toward the door.

"And Atlas. I expect your vows drafted by then as well."

He bolted from the office the moment the door closed behind him, not quite running, but moving fast enough that anyone who saw him would think twice about stopping him. Once inside his quarters, he went straight to the vent where he'd hidden Phoebe's comm unit, fingers trembling as he pried off the cover. Just touching it felt like an act of rebellion. A tiny, secret freedom Dr. Basu couldn't control.

He got it out and his heart skipped at the response to his message.

One lone word that meant everything. *Yes.*

He collapsed onto his bed, clutching the comm in his hand. For a moment, the future didn't feel like an inescapable trap. For a blink, he could imagine another path. One that led to Phoebe.

The door chime sounded.

He returned the comm back to its hiding spot and went to the door. His heart sank when he opened it and saw Hyacinth stood in the corridor, smiling.

What did she want?

"May I come in?"

He really didn't want to talk to her. But if he refused now, she would just come back later. Or tomorrow.

"Be quick." Atlas gestured for her to enter.

"I wanted to check on you." She stepped inside. "You said you weren't feeling well."

"Just overwhelmed." He kept his distance. Arms folded. "There's a lot to absorb."

She nodded. "It's normal to feel anxiety before such a significant transition. The burden of responsibility you carry is unlike any other."

"It's not that."

She tilted her head. "What is it, then?"

"Do you really want this?" Atlas asked after a beat of hesitation.

"What do you mean?" Hyacinth replied with a frown.

"This." He gestured to the space between them. "Us. The engagement. The whole plan. Do you *want* to marry me?"

"I told you. Yes."

He stared at her, not bothering to hide his skepticism. "Why? Because your mom told you to, or because you actually want to?"

"Because I love you."

He stared at her. "You don't even know me."

"Of course I do."

"Then tell me one actual thing you love about me. "

"You're the Divine Blueprint."

"Aside from that. Not the Divine Blueprint. *Me.*"

Her jaw tensed. "That's not fair."

"Isn't it?"

The silence between them grew until it felt like a third person in the room.

"This isn't *just* about feelings," Hyacinth said. "This is about the future of the settlement."

"I don't care about the settlement."

Her eyes widened. "You don't mean that."

"How do you know what I mean? You don't know me."

"I've known you my whole life."

"And you want *this* life? Married to someone who doesn't want to marry you? No freedom, no choice, just a script someone else wrote for us?"

She balled her hands into fists. "I don't see it that way. This isn't a punishment, Atlas. It's an honor. A responsibility."

"You sound like your mother."

"I trust her."

His laugh sounded bitter. "Yeah. That's the problem."

She narrowed her eyes. "What is going on with you?"

"I started asking questions. Maybe I don't like the answers."

"Well, stop it. You're scaring me."

He sighed. "Can you go? I'm tired."

She took a step closer instead. He could smell the faint herbal scent of her purification oils. "You know, we don't have to wait for the ceremony. We could get to know each other better now."

He frowned. "What do you mean?"

"We could have our wedding night early. If you want to … Because I would."

He stared at her. "But the purification protocols—"

"They're important." She shrugged. "But not as important as our connection. I want you to know that I'll be a good wife to you, Atlas. *In every way.*"

He stepped away. "Hyacinth, I—"

"It's natural to be nervous. I understand that."

"No."

Her brows drew together. "Because of the protocols? Or because of something else?"

"I want you to leave. Now."

"What is it about me that you don't like?" Tears filled her eyes. "Why am I not good enough for you?"

Why did she have to cry? "It's not that."

"Then what?"

Atlas said nothing, because what was there to say?

"There's someone else, isn't there?"

His stomach dropped like he'd just missed a step on a staircase. Was he that transparent?

"You're in love with someone else." It wasn't a question. "Who is it? Eliza? Maya? Ben?"

He looked away, refusing to take the bait.

"I can see it on your face."

Atlas clamped his mouth shut. Denial would be a lie, and confirmation would be suicide.

"Who?" She stamped her foot. "Who is it?"

"It doesn't matter."

"It *does* matter, Atlas!" He just stared at the floor, the wall, anywhere but at her accusing eyes. "Tell me! Is it Mari? Did she get to you first? Or Simon? I know he's been spending more time near the greenhouse lately."

Atlas rubbed his temples. "Hyacinth—"

"Is it Verity? You like the quiet ones, don't you? The ones who pretend they're not looking at you. But they are. *They always are.*"

"Stop."

Her cheeks burned red, hands opening and closing at her sides like she was practicing strangling whoever had stolen his affection. She needed this to be someone else's fault; it couldn't possibly be that he just wasn't into her. That didn't fit the script. Someone must have corrupted him, turned him against her, sabotaged their divinely ordained union.

He almost laughed.

A thought flickered through his mind like a spark in dry tinder. What if he could make her angry enough to call off the wedding herself? Dr. Basu might not listen to him, but she'd move mountains for her daughter. Maybe if she was mad enough at him, she'd persuade her mother to call off the wedding.

So, he met her gaze. "Fine. I'm in love with someone else."

Hyacinth went still. All the color drained from her face. "Who?"

"None of your business."

"Tell me. Now."

"No."

"I'll tell my mother you're cheating on me."

This time he did laugh out loud. "Go ahead."

Then he turned on his heel and stepped out of his house, shutting the door behind him, leaving Hyacinth inside.

For a moment, just silence.

Then it came. A raw, keening wail from behind the door, something deep and wounded that sounded more animal than human.

He'd never deliberately caused anyone that kind of pain before. For a moment, he hated himself.

His hand twitched toward the doorknob. He should go back. Comfort her. Tell her the standard breakup line: *it's not you, it's me.*

And it was true. She'd been force fed the same, doctrine, the same vision of duty and purpose since birth, programmed to believe that this was what love looked like: devotion without choice.

He couldn't blame her for wanting to be chosen.

But if he went back inside, if he gave her even a sliver of hope or the smallest reassurance, that would be game over. His escape hatch would slam shut. All his efforts to pry himself loose from this trap would evaporate.

So, he made himself walk away.

He didn't stop until he reached the greenhouse. Here, surrounded by growing things that didn't demand or expect anything from him, bathed in filtered sunlight and the earthy smell of actual life, maybe he could figure out a plan to extract himself from this mess without torching everything behind him. He didn't actually want to nuke his relationship with the community.

Because they had raised him. Taught him. Believed in him. Dumped their entire collective future into his lap, for better or worse. Even if it felt suffocating now, he hadn't forgotten what it meant to belong.

He just didn't know how to stay and also be himself.

Chapter Twenty-One

SAMARA RUBBED her eyes and checked the results again.

Negative.

No signs of prions in any of the meat samples she and Renata had tested. They'd spent hours taking samples from every storage unit in the colony: beef, pork, mutton, cultivated protein, even the dried jerky they kept for emergency rations.

Nothing.

She set down the tablet and rolled her shoulders, trying to work out the stiffness. How long had she been in the lab? She glanced at the chronometer on the wall. Far too long. She'd lost track of time again.

At least they'd eliminated one potential threat. The colony's meat stores were clean; there wasn't a single contaminated sample among the hundreds they'd tested. Samara sent a quick message to Katherine reporting the results, then shifted her focus to the original colonists' blood samples. If those carried the same prion markers, they'd confirm the source of Hector's infection.

She reached for a fresh sample cartridge, then paused.

There was already one in the sequencer.

Samara frowned. Had she loaded it earlier and forgotten?

She checked her notes, flipping through the pages of her lab journal.

Nothing.

Maybe Leila had been using it?

Or Phoebe for her schoolwork?

Either that or she was losing it.

Three days with barely any sleep, running on stims. No wonder she was forgetting things.

Before she could remove the cartridge, the lab door crashed open so hard it bounced against the wall. Hector stumbled in, looking like he'd been dragged through half a mile of underbrush. His hospital scrubs were wrinkled and stained, hair sticking up in wild tufts, eyes sunken and ringed with shadows so dark they looked bruised. He zeroed in on the sequencer like a predator spotting prey.

"Don't touch my work."

Samara tensed, taking a half-step back. "You're using this?"

"That's *my* cartridge. My experiment."

"You're supposed to be on bed rest."

He jabbed a shaking finger at her, his visage twisting into a snarl. "And let *you* sabotage my work?"

She held up her hands, palms open, remembering the last time, how fast he'd gone from shouting to swinging. "Go ahead. Do what you need to do."

She let him have the sequencer, hoping he wouldn't destroy it as she edged toward her comm.

"My notes. Where are my notes? What have you done with them?"

"I haven't touched your notes, Hector. I promise."

He jabbed at the control panel with jittery fingers,

slamming buttons in random sequences that made the machine emit a series of alarmed beeps. "You're sabotaging my research, I know it!"

Samara reached the comm panel.

It chirped beneath her fingers. She glanced down and saw a message from Leo. *Just got word Hector is missing. Be on alert.*

He's here, she typed back.

On my way.

Hector was focused on the machine. Turning it on and off, seeming confused.

Samara kept her distance. It felt like an hour, it was less than a minute before Leo entered.

Hector ignored him, opening and shutting the chamber of the sequencer as if he'd just discovered that it existed?

"Did he hurt you?" Leo asked quietly.

She shook her head. "He seems to be having another episode."

"He told the security detail he needed to use the bathroom. When they checked on him a minute later, he'd climbed out the window. Slippery old bastard. I've let them know he's here."

Hector glanced over at Leo. "If you're looking for me, I'll need a few more hours to finish, then I'll be done."

"Sounds good," Leo said.

Hector hunched over the sample table, obsessively rearranging containers. He'd pick one up, examine it from every angle, place it down, then immediately reposition it a millimeter to the left. Then right. Then back where it started. Each container received the same treatment, his movements growing increasingly frantic, solving puzzles only he could see.

The lab door hissed open. Alaric and another guard entered.

Leo waved at them.

"Heya, Hector," Alaric said, stepping over to him. "How about you come with me?"

Hector shook his head, gesturing to the row of containers. "I can't. I need to finish up my lab work."

"We got you a brand spanking new lab," Alaric said. "It's all set up and waiting for you to examine."

"A new lab?"

"Uh-huh."

Hector glanced over at Samara. "And it's all mine? No one else can use it?"

"That's right." Leo nodded.

Hector straightened his spine, marching out in the company of the second guard. "It's about time. Everything's broken here."

Alaric hung back, waiting for the door to close. "Take him to the clinic?"

Samara nodded. "Have Leila administer a mild sedative. Nothing too strong, just enough to calm him down."

"You got it," Alaric said, then departed.

"You doing okay, Samara?" Leo asked. "You look wrung out."

Samara sighed, scratching the star mosquito bite on her arm. Damn things. She stopped herself mid-scratch. "I'm fine. Just tired."

"Well, Hector's getting worse," Leo tapped his head. "I've never seen him like this."

"The prions are affecting his brain. I need to get on to the original colonists' blood samples. If they also have prions, it would confirm they're the source of Hector's infection."

Leo headed toward the door. "I'll leave you to it."

Samara waved. Then she returned to the sequencer, examining the cartridge Hector had loaded. It already contained the old woman's sample. So, she ran it through and waited until the results came in. Positive for prions.

The same type found in Hector's blood.

Relief flooded her veins.

Well, that was something. At least they now knew the source of his contamination. Samara made a record of her findings, then pulled off her gloves and sent a message to Lucas. *Any sign of sickness among the Hyperionites?*

None observed, he answered just moments later.

She made a note.

Since the Hyperionites showed no symptoms, and the patients were sick before they arrived at the Vitruvian colony, the most likely explanation was that the elderly pair had consumed contaminated meat at some point, and that either the Hyperionites' immune system had a way to deal with prions or they hadn't consumed the same meat.

Or maybe it was one of those rare cases of spontaneous protein misfolding in one of them, and it spread to the other given their close proximity.

But it was quite a coincidence that both of them had developed it at the same time. She went to her comm and messaged Katherine.

Her reply came in seconds. *What do you have for me?*

Samara quickly typed her response, *I've confirmed prions in our patients' blood samples. Same as Hector's. No contamination in our meat stores. So, they likely were fed infected meat by the Hyperionites, or it was spontaneous.*

Thank God, Katherine typed. *Do you mind stopping by my office before you go home? I have a request from Ayesha I want to run past you.*

She sighed. *Now?*

If you don't mind.

I'll be right there.

Samara checked the chronometer. Twenty-one hundred hours: not too late to catch Phoebe before bed. Maybe they could play one of those mindless holovid games Phoebe loved or just watch something stupid together on the entertainment console. Anything that didn't involve prions, dying patients, or colony politics.

It wouldn't fix the growing distance between them. Or erase the hurt feelings and unsaid words. But it would be something real in the midst of this nightmare: a moment of connection in a world coming apart at the seams.

Chapter Twenty-Two

Moonlight turned the Hyperion ruins into a stark etching against the night sky, all sharp edges and harsh shadows, beautiful in their brokenness. The twin moons hung low, an otherworldly glow cast across the rubble that turned the landscape surreal.

Phoebe arrived first, her footsteps crunching softly on the gravel path. She paused at the edge of the mass grave, noticing a small carved token — some kind of animal figure — that had fallen over. She knelt to right it, careful not to disturb the other offerings surrounding it. These little tributes always made her chest tight. Even monsters could be mourned.

Atlas' people thought *she* was a monster.

She made her way to the broken steps where she'd first met him, settling onto the crumbling stone. The night air was surprisingly cool against her skin, carrying the metallic tang that always preceded a sporestorm. According to Lucas, it wouldn't hit until almost dawn, but she'd brought a spare respirator for Atlas, in case Dr. Basu hadn't alerted the Naturalists. Or maybe she would tell them the sporestorm was coming but call it a prophecy instead of a scientific prediction.

Phoebe didn't understand why they were so afraid of science. Where did they think the medicines that allowed them to survive had come from?

Atlas emerged from the shadows less than five minutes later, moving with the watchful caution of someone who expected to be followed. His eyes found hers across the distance, and the tension in his shoulders visibly eased.

"You came."

"I said I would."

He walked over to her, stopping before her just short of touching. "Is it okay to kiss you?"

"That depends. Are you still engaged?"

"Yes."

She pursed her lips. "Do you want to be?"

"No."

"Why?"

He didn't hesitate. "Because I like you."

She smiled. "Good answer. But you probably shouldn't kiss me."

His mouth turned down as he nodded. "You're right."

"I should kiss you."

He blinked. "What?"

"Just in case someone asks. You can say, *Why no, most blessed and high Dr. Basu, I never kissed her. She kissed me.*"

He laughed.

Phoebe stepped forward, fingers curling into the front of his jacket as she pulled him down to her. The kiss was soft at first, tentative and questioning, then deepened as his hands found her waist. He tasted like mint and smelled like earth and growing things. When they finally separated, she kept her grip on his jacket, unwilling to let the moment end. Neither of them stepped back, the space between them charged with something electric and almost painful in its intensity.

For the first time in days, her head wasn't pounding.

He touched her hair. "Was it hard to sneak out?"

"No. Dr. Callas is sick, and my mother's been practically living at the lab trying to find a cure. I barely see her these days. She comes home to sleep for a few hours, then she's gone again."

"What happened to Dr. Callas?" Atlas looked genuinely concerned, and Phoebe remembered that the doctor sometimes visited the Naturalists, too. Atlas had probably been his patient for his whole life.

Should she have told him?

"I'm not sure, but I think it's serious."

"I'm sorry to hear that."

"It's why I haven't had a chance to analyze your DNA yet," she said. "The sequencer's been tied up with tests for whatever's making him sick, and I can't exactly explain why I need it."

"I suppose not."

"But you should know… those samples Dr. Basu takes from you?"

Atlas nodded, sitting. "What about them?"

She took the spot next to him on the cool stone. "They're in my mother's fridge at the lab."

He blinked. "What?"

"Yeah, I saw them myself."

"Are you sure?"

She nodded. "Labeled. Sealed. Yours."

Atlas went quiet, staring past her at nothing. She didn't push. She'd just given him another piece of evidence that he'd been lied to. In time, there would be so many lies, he would have to reject his upbringing.

She just hoped he would do it *before* he married

Hyacinth. The warmth of his shoulder pressed against hers as they sat side by side on the ancient stone step. His fingers found hers in the darkness, intertwining with a gentle pressure that somehow felt more intimate than their kiss. The ruins sheltered them like a cave, creating the illusion that they were the only two people left in the world.

She rested her head against his shoulder.

"I think about you all the time," Atlas said, giving her hand a squeeze. "When I'm supposed to be meditating. When I'm working in the greenhouse. When I'm eating. When I'm with Hyacinth. Especially then."

She nudged him. "You got it bad."

He laughed.

Then she kissed his shoulder. "I think about you too."

Atlas looked down at her. "You're so different from anyone in the Naturalist colony. It's like you see things that others can't."

"Well, I kind of do. Especially when it comes to you. I don't think anyone there actually sees who you are."

He blinked. And she thought she spotted tears in his eyes.

She leaned in, closing what little distance remained between them. This time when their lips met, there was nothing hesitant about it. He pulled her closer, one hand tangling in her hair while the other slid to the small of her back. For those perfect moments, nothing else existed: not their colonies, not their differences, not the impossible situation they were trapped in. Only the warmth of connection and the dizzying sensation of falling without fear.

Atlas kept his forehead pressed against hers when they finally separated. "I wish we had met sooner."

Phoebe pulled back, studying his face. "Me too." She he had to ask. "What have you decided about the engagement?"

He hesitated. "I don't know what to do about it, Phoebe."

"Tell her you won't go through with it. Refuse."

He released her hand. "And then what? The entire Naturalist community believes in the Divine Blueprint. It's the cornerstone of our faith. Publicly rejecting it means that I'm rejecting them, along with everything they believe in."

"Even if it's all based on lies?"

Atlas turned to face her. "*Especially then*. You told me that people should have the right to choose, even if it's not the choice you'd make. The Naturalists have chosen to believe in something that gives us hope. And strength. Who am I to take that away?"

She stared at him. "What about your choice? Your life? Don't you deserve freedom too?"

"At what cost?" His voice cracked. "My mother's place in the community? The stability of the only home I've ever known? The health of people who would suffer without me?"

"You could run away."

Atlas shook his head. "I can't abandon my responsibility. I won't."

"Then stall them. Tell them you're sick. Buy us time to figure this out."

"Fake an illness?" He considered it for a moment, hope flickering across his face before reality extinguished it. "Dr. Basu would see through it in a heartbeat. She's been watching me like a hawk since I started asking questions. Even if I managed to convince her, it would just delay things by a week at most."

"Nothing is inevitable," Phoebe argued.

"Isn't it? Because I can't be that selfish. Don't the Naturalists have the right to find a way to live outside like the Borlaug colonists do?"

"Of course they do," Phoebe said, grabbing his hands. "And they could, if they would just let my mother help them. Gene therapy isn't perfect, but it *works*. It would free your people from those bubbles and suits forever."

"That will never happen. Even if Dr. Basu allowed it, most people wouldn't be willing to contaminate themselves."

"Contaminate?" Phoebe repeated, stiffening as her eyes flashed in the moonlight. "Is that what you think I am? *Contaminated?*"

"No! Of course not." Atlas reached for her, but she pulled away. "But it's what the others believe, Phoebe. It's how they've been taught to think."

"And you? What do you believe?"

Atlas gestured toward her. "I believe ... that you're the most amazing person I've ever met. That when I'm with you, everything makes sense in a way it never has before. But I also believe that faith is powerful. It's shaped my community, kept them alive through incredible hardship. I can't just dismiss that, even if I question some of their teachings."

"Faith based on lies isn't faith at all. It's manipulation."

"Maybe. Or maybe it's a different way of understanding the world." He looked over toward the mass grave. "These people died because they embraced one vision of science without limits. The Naturalists survive because they've chosen a different path."

"They survive because we supply them with food, medicine, and everything else they can't produce themselves. How long do you think your colony would last without Vitruvian support?"

His jaw tightened. "We're working toward self-sufficiency."

"Are you? Or is Dr. Basu just telling you that while she keeps everyone dependent and isolated, afraid of perfectly safe medical treatments?"

"Arrogance is dangerous when it's disguised as progress, Phoebe. Your people aren't perfect either. They've made mistakes too."

"Of course we have. But we also learn from them. We don't pretend they're divine will or cosmic punishment."

Atlas dropped his head into his hands, fingers digging into his scalp like he was trying to physically hold himself together. "I didn't come here to fight with you."

Her shoulders sagged. "Why did you come here?"

Atlas took a deep breath. "I was wondering if you'd come live with me."

"Become a Naturalist?" Was he joking?

"I can marry you along with Hyacinth," he said in a rush. "You'd have to embrace our spiritual path, but I'm pretty sure Dr. Basu would give us permission if I refused to marry her without you."

She blinked. "You'd seriously marry both of us?"

He nodded.

Could she do that? Give up the truths she'd been taught and pretend to believe in Dr. Basu's fake religion, just so she could be with him?

"No." She shook her head violently, pulling away from him. "No way am I joining Dr. Basu's anti-science cult."

Atlas flinched like she'd slapped him. "We're not a cult."

"Oh really?"

He opened his mouth, then closed it again.

"If I'm married to you, aren't I also married to

Hyacinth? And with whoever else your mother and Dr. Basu think should carry your miracle DNA?"

"That's not—"

"You think marriage is the answer here? That I'd just leave my family, my colony, *everything I believe in* so I can be your backup wife? You haven't even said that you love me."

"I didn't mean it like that."

"How else could you mean it?"

Atlas didn't answer.

Phoebe shook her head. "You were furious when you thought *I* was asking you to leave your people. But now you're asking me to do the same thing. Disappear into your life and give up mine. All because you're scared to tell her 'no'."

"It's not like that," Atlas said again, quieter this time.

Phoebe stared at him. "You really don't get it. You think you can solve this by following the rules."

He frowned. "I'm trying to do the right thing."

"For who? You? Dr. Basu? The colony? You just want me to save you. Because you won't do it yourself."

"You don't understand."

"I understand just fine." She stood. "Go marry Hyacinth. I'm sure you'll be very happy together."

"Phoebe—"

"Your 'Divine Blueprint' is just some random mutation, you know. There's nothing divine about it at all."

His face crumpled, but Phoebe was already in motion. She turned and sprinted down the path that led back to the Vitruvian colony. Tears blurred her vision as branches whipped past her face, but she didn't slow down. She couldn't bear to see the hurt in his eyes, or worse, the possibility that he might agree with her.

"Wait!" Atlas said. "Please, listen."

But she didn't.

She didn't listen, didn't slow, didn't turn. And she didn't stop running until she saw the perimeter lights ahead.

Then she slowed to a walk as she approached the colony, forcing her breathing to steady. The last thing she needed was to show up looking like she'd just had her heart ripped out.

She wasn't going to cry over Atlas. She refused to waste a single tear on someone who couldn't even stand up for himself, let alone her.

But just as she reached the shadowed side of her house, a figure detached itself from the darkness beside the wall.

Phoebe froze mid-step, adrenaline spiking through her system.

Her first terrified thought was Samara.

But the silhouette was too tall, the stance too rigid.

"We need to talk, Phoebe," Lucas said.

She tried to step past him. "There's nothing to talk about."

"I could wake Samara and you could talk to her, if you prefer." His tone was mild. "But that would be a completely different conversation, wouldn't it?"

Phoebe stopped, her shoulders slumping. "Fine. What?"

"You've been to see Atlas again."

A blunt statement. Lucas rarely asked questions, mainly because he always knew the answers.

"Why does Samara care what I do? She's married to that lab of hers."

"Why do you think that is?"

Phoebe scuffed a foot in the dirt. "Because every time I get sick, it reminds her that I'm a failed experiment, the first draft she had to improve on. Her precious gene editing had off-target effects she didn't anticipate. What she learned from modifying me allowed her to make changes to all the other kids, but she still sees me as defective."

Lucas remained motionless for several seconds, his head tilted slightly to one side as he processed her words, and that inhuman stillness reminded her he wasn't human, despite how easy it was to forget sometimes.

"Have you ever told her you feel this way?" he finally asked.

"What's the point?" Phoebe shrugged. "She'll just say I'm being melodramatic. Tell me to be grateful for everything I have, like I'm not. Sometimes I think about going to live with the Hypers. None of them have to go to school or study."

"The problem with running away is that you take your problems with you."

She glared at him. "Stop being so reasonable."

"And that's the appeal of Atlas. He doesn't know you're different, and he doesn't expect you to live up to your mother's legacy."

He reached into his pocket and withdrew a small device about the size of a coin. He held it out to her.

"This is a special tracker, my design." He tapped a tiny button on its edge. "Press here if you're in danger. I'll come immediately."

Phoebe stared at the device, then at Lucas. "And you won't tell Mom where I am?"

"Not if you carry this with you. But I am programmed to protect human lives above all else, Phoebe. If I believe you're in danger, I will do whatever is necessary to keep you safe."

"Thank Lucas, but I don't need it anymore. Because Atlas and I are done."

Lucas studied her. "Did he do something to you?"

"No. So please don't go after him. Seriously."

"Then what happened?"

She turned away a little. "It's complicated."

"I want you to take the tracker anyway."

Phoebe looked back at him. "Really?"

"I believe you need more freedom than Samara's willing to give you, but I won't allow that unless I have a way to protect you. So, please, take it."

She took it from his outstretched hand. "Thanks for not telling her."

"You're welcome."

Then he disappeared into the dark.

She studied the tracker in her palm, small, inconspicuous, and oddly comforting despite what it represented. She slipped it into her pocket, its weight barely noticeable against her thigh.

Lucas' words echoed in her mind. *"That's the appeal of Atlas. He doesn't know you're different, and he doesn't expect you to live up to your mother's legacy."*

That had been true at first. Atlas had looked at her without the weight of history and expectation that everyone else carried. He hadn't seen her as a scientific milestone or a medical cautionary tale. At first, he just saw Phoebe.

But that was before. Before she started to feel something real for him. It made her chest ache and her throat tight when she thought about him marrying Hyacinth.

Would Atlas still look at her the same way if he knew about the off-target effects? If he understood that the headaches were just the beginning, that the gene therapy hadn't worked perfectly, that she was fundamentally different from the other kids her age?

She wanted to believe he wouldn't care. That he'd still see her, not just her modified genes.

But now she might never know.

Chapter Twenty-Three

ATLAS PERCHED on the shed's sloped roof, legs dangling over the edge like a man contemplating the drop. He would have to go in soon, because even with the Divine Blueprint, the coming storm would scour his skin raw and fill his lungs with spores that he'd be coughing up for days. But until then, he would enjoy his freedom while it lasted.

Phoebe's words still echoed in his brain.

"Your 'Divine Blueprint' is just some random mutation, you know. There's nothing divine about it at all."

No one had ever spoken to him like that.

His entire life had been built around being special. Chosen. The living embodiment of divine favor walking among mere mortals. Until Phoebe demolished it all with one casual sentence, reducing his sacred purpose to a fortunate roll of biological dice.

A sacred purpose that he'd spent a life wishing he didn't have. But she'd been so dismissive about it, about his entire way of life, he saw in her the arrogance that he'd been told was second nature to the Vitruvians. And she couldn't see that about herself at all.

She expected him to accept her version of reality completely, but she wasn't willing to consider that some part of his reality might be valid, too.

Which made it hard to ignore the possibility that Dr. Basu had been right, at least about that.

Did he *want* to believe in the Divine Blueprint?

His brain told him no.

But a part of him still clung to the idea, because it was easier to resent a burden you hadn't chosen than to acknowledge there was nothing special about you in the first place. He squeezed his eyes shut.

What if his sacred gift was simply based on a misunderstanding of basic biology?

Dr. Basu came to DaVinci on the Borlaug, too.

She had to know about science.

She just chose not to believe in it.

But she knew.

And that difference wasn't just significant. It was everything.

Atlas felt truth slipping through his fingers like sand as he sat.

And as much as it twisted his gut to admit, only one person might have the answers he needed.

He swung himself off the roof, landing with practiced silence on the packed dirt below. He bypassed decontamination entirely and slipped through his secret door into the greenhouse. Strangely, Dr. Basu hadn't sealed it yet.

That bothered him. She was either supremely confident in her control over him or planning something worse than taking away his one freedom. Either way, he'd accept that gift for now.

He reached her quarters before he could count a hundred deep breaths, raised a finger to the chime, and then hesitated.

What the hell was he doing? Challenging the colony's spiritual leader about the cornerstone of their beliefs at this hour?

Yeah.

Exactly that.

He knocked.

Silence stretched between heartbeats, then shuffling sounds drifted from inside.

The door slid open to reveal Dr. Basu in a gray robe and slippers, her eyes puffy with interrupted sleep.

"Atlas. Have you come to apologize to Hyacinth?"

She must have gone running to her mother. Told her he was in love with someone else. Of course. There were probably few secrets between them.

"I came to speak with you."

Dr. Basu's face remained perfectly neutral, as though midnight confrontations like this were perfectly routine. She stepped back, sweeping her arm in invitation. "Come in."

Atlas slipped past her, choosing the chair closest to the exit. Dr. Basu settled into the seat opposite him, her posture still impeccable despite the hour.

She folded her hands and fixed him with an expectant stare. "Speak."

"Why didn't you tell me there was another way to transfer the Divine Blueprint to the next generation? "

Dr. Basu was quiet for a beat before smiling. "*Ah.* This secret girlfriend Hyacinth has been crying about all day. She must be Vitruvian."

"Why would you think that?" he stalled.

"How else would you know about this medical procedure? It's not difficult to make the connection."

"So, there is another way."

"An incredibly dangerous one. Did she tell you that?"

Atlas clamped his jaw shut, refusing to give her the satisfaction of an answer.

"I thought not. Now who is it that has been filling your head with these ideas?"

He met her eyes. "What difference does it make?"

"It makes all the difference when one of them is trying to seed rebellion in my people."

"No one is trying to seed rebellion. I'm just asking questions."

"That's how most rebellions start."

"Is that how yours started?" he asked.

Her eyes narrowed. "It's clear that whoever you've been talking to is a skilled manipulator."

Atlas raised his chin. "Phoebe isn't—"

He hadn't meant to say her name, but the idea that he'd been tricked into asking these questions stung. And he hated that now he was wondering if perhaps Phoebe had pushed him on this so that he would confront Dr. Basu. If her mother might have put her up to it, hoping that she might use him to fight her decades-old war with the Naturalists. But instead of anger, Dr. Basu's face lit up with something like triumph, and Atlas felt cold dread pooling in his stomach.

He'd walked right into her trap.

"Samara's daughter? And she seems like she's in perfect health to you?"

"She does."

Dr. Basu rose with deliberate slowness, gliding toward a small side table where a crystal pitcher caught the dim light. She poured water into a single glass, turned to him with a questioning lift of her eyebrows.

He shook his head. She returned to her seat, cradling the glass between her palms like a talisman. "Let me tell you about off-target effects, Atlas. When geneticists like

Samara manipulate the genome, the precision they can achieve is far less exact than they would have you believe. The way a gene is cut out from one chromosome to be copied and transferred to another, it's not clean. And never perfect."

"Okay." Atlas drummed his fingers against his thigh, fighting the urge to fidget under her penetrating gaze.

She took a sip of water. "Think of it as surgery performed with a knife that isn't quite sharp enough. Yes, you can remove what you're targeting, but you damage the surrounding tissue in the process. Some people get lucky. The off-target effects are minor: a tendency toward certain allergies or slight variations in metabolism. But others?" She fingered her glass. "Others pay a much higher price."

Her voice softened, taking on the cadence she used during their spiritual gatherings. "My grandmother, Mitra Kunde, was one of the first designer babies. Her parents had her genes optimized for superintelligence."

Atlas fought the urge to roll his eyes. He'd heard this story at least a dozen times, trotted out at every major ceremony like a well-worn religious relic: Dr. Basu's personal testament to the dangers of genetic manipulation.

"She was brilliant." Dr. Basu set her glass on the table. "Multiple degrees by the time she was twenty. But the off-target effect of that gene editing was schizophrenia. She spent decades trying to develop a therapy to correct what had been done to her." She shook her head. "My grandmother died in a psychiatric ward, her mind fractured beyond repair."

Atlas leaned forward, elbows on knees. "But that was so long ago. Science must have gotten better since then. More precise."

"Better?" Her eyes flashed. "Perhaps marginally. But not enough to justify the risk. These are people, Atlas.

Precious souls. The human genome is not a puzzle to be taken apart and reassembled according to our whims. It's a sacred text that has been written over millions of years of natural selection."

She leaned forward. "I am not against these procedures out of ignorance. I'm against them because I understand them too well. I've seen the arrogance of scientists who think they can improve on nature, and I've witnessed the consequences of their hubris."

"But if it could help people—"

"Help? By creating a new underclass of genetically modified humans with defects? I'm not willing to risk humanity's future on the say-so of the very scientists who are determined to see how far they can push the limits of nature. The stakes are too high."

"But Phoebe's fine."

"Is she?"

The retort died on his lips, his mouth hanging open before snapping shut.

"Phoebe was the first to receive Samara's treatment, and the first to experience the off-target effects. Did she mention the headaches?" She got up and walked over to him. "It is your responsibility to pass on the Divine Blueprint, Atlas. So that our people don't just survive but thrive. So that we can eventually outnumber the Vitruvians and their corrupted vision of humanity."

She rested her hand on his shoulder. "It is divine will for you to marry Hyacinth. And if you refuse to obey, there will be terrible consequences. Not just for you, but for all of us."

She gripped his shoulder hard enough to bruise him, fingers digging into muscle and bone. He refused to flinch, maintaining eye contact despite the pain radiating down his arm.

"Do you understand what I'm saying, Atlas?" Her voice had softened, now almost maternal. But she dug her fingers in harder.

"Yes," he answered through clenched teeth. "I understand."

Dr. Basu studied his face as if searching for flickers of rebellion. Whatever she found — or didn't find — apparently satisfied her. She released her grip and stepped back, smoothing imaginary wrinkles from her robe.

"Good. Now go and get some rest. You have important days ahead of you."

Atlas got up and walked to the door, resisting the urge to rub his shoulder on the way. He turned back at the threshold. "Why do you send my samples to Samara's lab and not the Sanctum?"

Her face drained of color. "Who told you that?"

"Phoebe. She saw them."

"We don't examine the Divine Blueprint the way the Vitruvians do. But that doesn't mean it shouldn't be *witnessed*."

Atlas frowned. "Witnessed?"

"By the ones who created the contamination in the first place. It's important they see what was never theirs to touch. The Blueprint was not forged in a lab. It arose naturally, as a sign. A blessing. Their technology only confirms what we already know. But sometimes we allow them to observe the miracle, Atlas. So that they understand what they gave up."

Atlas studied her face.

Her performance was masterful, every word and gesture composed and orchestrated for maximum effect.

He didn't believe it. But why *would* she send his samples to them?

"The Vitruvians are not evil people," she continued.

"But they are dangerously misguided. Try and remember that even the most beautiful flower can be poisonous."

She meant Phoebe.

"Don't let that girl poison your marriage. It's really not fair to Hyacinth."

She gestured for him to leave.

He exited without another word, the door sliding shut behind him with a judgmental hiss.

He stood in the empty corridor, rubbing his aching shoulder.

He'd never felt so lost.

He'd destroyed whatever relationship he had with Phoebe.

And yet, she occupied every corner of his mind like an obsession. Her questions had awakened a hunger he had no right to feel. For the truth. For the freedom to choose.

But Dr. Basu had succeeded in making him doubt; even though he knew that was deliberate, he couldn't banish it.

Why hadn't Phoebe told him the procedure was dangerous? Was that even true? Or was Dr. Basu spinning elaborate lies, just like that transparent crap about sending his samples to the Vitruvians?

To the lab of her worst enemy, Samara.

Because that was obviously a lie.

Atlas swallowed hard. He didn't know who to trust anymore.

But he knew one thing with absolute certainty.

He had to talk to Phoebe.

Chapter Twenty-Four

SAMARA SLUMPED at the kitchen table, shoulders curved with exhaustion, eyes fixed on nothing.

Renata ladled the leftovers into a bowl and the scent of reheated stew filled the kitchen. She placed the bowl before Samara. Steam rose in lazy curls, carrying the earthy aroma of native tubers and protein cultivated from the colony's vertical farms.

"Eat," Renata said, pointing to the bowl. "You look like you're about to collapse."

Samara picked up her fork, speared a tuber, and chewed. Heat and salt hit her tongue, but she barely tasted it. She swallowed and nodded. "Delicious."

Renata pulled up a chair and sat beside her. "When's the last time you ate?"

Samara hesitated.

"Never mind," Renata said. "The fact that you can't remember tells me everything I need to know."

Samara laughed.

They sat in comfortable silence, but Samara's mind drifted back to her tense conversation with Katherine about the DNA samples. Katherine had insisted they had legitimate consent, but something about the whole arrangement felt deeply wrong.

Loud banging yanked her back to reality.

She looked over at Renata. "What's Marcus up to?"

"He's fixing a window screen. Iris put her elbow through it playing tag. Star mosquitos have been getting in all day. I've killed a couple dozen of them."

Samara scraped the last bite of stew from her bowl and set her fork down with a satisfied clink. Before she could protest, Renata was already up, refilling her bowl with a second steaming portion."

"I'm good," Samara said.

"You're not good." Renata set the bowl down in front of her again. "I can see your bones. Now eat."

Samara grinned. "Yes, Ma'am."

But Renata was right. She was hungry.

"Phoebe?" she asked.

"Ate early. Already in bed. Which is where you'll be shortly."

Marcus entered the kitchen, filthy from his shift and looking more exhausted than Samara felt.

"All fixed?" Renata asked.

"Until the next time." He nodded on his way to the table. You wouldn't believe the theories going around the mining team about those patients in quarantine."

"What theories?" Renata asked.

"Some of the crew think they're Hyperionites who've caught something new from deeper in the mountains. Others are saying they're Naturalists who've finally realized they can't survive without our medicine."

"Well, they'd both be wrong," Samara said.

"But why shelter them at all?" Marcus asked. "Why not just send them back to their own people?"

Samara's fork clinked against the side of the bowl. "Because they're not Hyperionites or Naturalists."

"What?"

Samara set her spoon down and met his gaze squarely. "They're neither. They're something else entirely."

"Well, that's not what Jenkins is saying. He swears he saw Security escorting someone who walked like a Naturalist into the medical complex yesterday."

"And how exactly does a Naturalist walk?" Renata asked, one eyebrow raised.

"You know what I mean. All stiff and self-righteous, like they've got sacred scrolls stuffed up their—"

"Marcus," Renata said.

He rubbed his head. "It's ridiculous that we're stretching ourselves this thin. It's bad enough that we have to feed the Naturalists too, after they *chose* to splinter off and live in that unsustainable bubble of theirs."

Samara's eyes narrowed. "We're not 'feeding' the Naturalists. We trade with them."

"Right. 'Trade.'" Marcus snorted. "But no one is able to say what they give us. They need us more than we need them."

"That's not fair," Renata said. "They're working with less equipment, less arable land, and—"

Marcus slammed his palm on the table, making the dishes jump. "Less common sense is what they're working with! They rejected the gene therapy that would have let them live without immunosuppressants. They made their bed, now they can lie in it."

Samara stared at him.

He met her eyes. "What?"

"I've never heard you talk about the Naturalists like this before. You're usually the diplomatic one when it comes to colony politics."

He shrugged. "Maybe I'm finally saying what I've always thought."

"Which is?"

"That the Naturalists are spreading a plague they're too ignorant to even understand."

Samara dropped her fork into her empty bowl. "You don't know what you're talking about, Marcus. There's no plague. Dr. Callas was exposed to prions. It was likely a case of cross-contamination."

The kitchen fell silent, the only sound the soft ping of the cooling stove and Samara's fork clattering into her empty bowl.

"Prions? What are those?" Marcus asked.

Samara sighed. "Misfolded proteins. Normally, proteins in the brain have a specific shape that lets them do their job. But a prion is shaped the wrong way, and when it bumps into other proteins, it makes *them* misfold too."

Marcus threw up his hands. "Well, why the hell didn't Katherine just announce that? Instead of all these vague warnings about 'possible contamination' and 'enhanced protocols'?"

Samara's composure crumbled. "Because there's no cure for prions, Marcus. No treatment. *Nothing*. Dr. Callas will keep deteriorating until his mind is gone. Until he doesn't recognize us or even remember his own name. Until he can't control his own body. And there's nothing I can do to stop it."

She tried not to cry.

But the tears came anyway. Hot and unwanted.

Samara couldn't remember the last time she'd cried in front of another person. It felt like exposing a vital organ. She scrubbed at her cheeks with the heel of her hand, furious at the betrayal of her own body.

"Jeez, I'm sorry," Marcus said.

Renata got up and hugged her. "You've been working nonstop. You need to rest."

"I can't. Not until I've found a cure, or …" *Or Hector is dead.* "Leila will never forgive me if I can't help Hector."

"Leila wouldn't want you to destroy yourself in the process," Renata said.

A sharp thump echoed from the ceiling above, followed by the distinct sound of a window sliding open.

They all froze.

"What was that?" Renata said.

Samara pushed back from the table and headed for the hallway, Renata and Marcus a step behind.

They paused at the foot of the stairs, listening.

Another sound: a muffled scuff of something dragging across the floor overhead.

"That's coming from—"

"Phoebe's bedroom. I thought she was asleep." Samara sighed. "She's been sneaking out again."

Marcus exchanged a look with Renata. "Family matter?"

Samara nodded, already headed for the stairs.

"We'll clean up," Renata told Samara, her hand finding Marcus's arm. "Take your time."

Samara climbed the stairs, deliberately keeping her footsteps light. She paused outside Phoebe's door, drew a deep breath to steady herself, then twisted the knob and pushed it open. Her daughter was balanced precariously in the window frame, one leg dangling outside, caught in the act like a freeze-frame. Phoebe's head whipped around, eyes widening as they locked with Samara's.

"Mom!"

"Where have you been?" Samara asked.

Phoebe scrambled inside. "Nowhere. I was just getting some fresh air."

"When you know there's a sporestorm coming?" Samara's eyes went to the shoes on the floor. They were muddy. Phoebe hadn't been walking the colony grounds, she'd been traipsing around in the forest. And there was only one reason Samara could think of that she'd sneak out of the colony at night. "Don't lie to me. You were with him again, weren't you? The Naturalist boy."

Phoebe stared at her. "What does it matter?"

"I told you—"

"Well, you don't have to worry. I'm not with him anymore." Her voice sounded small and brittle.

"What do you mean?"

"What do you think I mean?" She walked to her bed and threw herself on it, facing the wall.

Samara opened her mouth, wanting to ask what was wrong.

Phoebe pulled the pillow over her head. A second later her shoulders shook. She was crying. Samara deflated. Phoebe's first infatuation was over, and now she was heartbroken. It was inevitable that it wouldn't work out, given that the boy was a Naturalist, and she'd tried to warn her daughter, but...

Now was not the time for *I told you so*.

She walked to Phoebe's bed and pulled the quilt up and over her shoulders. "That boy really isn't for you, Phoebe. He's got obligations to his community. Ones you probably wouldn't understand."

Phoebe didn't respond.

So, Samara closed the window, checking the latch to make sure it was secure, and rejoined Renata and Marcus in the kitchen.

"I don't know when I became the enemy," she confessed. "Phoebe used to tell me everything."

"She's seventeen," Renata said. "Everything's changing

for her. Her body, her interests, her place in the colony, how she sees herself and the world."

"I know that."

"And now she's learning there are some things she wants to keep to herself. That's normal, Samara."

"Sneaking out to meet a boy who was raised to believe that she's an abomination is normal?"

Renata laughed. "Falling for someone her mother wouldn't approve of? Yes, absolutely normal. You can't protect her from everything, least of all heartbreak."

"I'm not trying to…" Wasn't she, though? Wasn't that exactly what she was trying to do?

And she'd clearly failed.

"Phoebe's got to figure things out for herself," Renata said. "And sometimes that means making mistakes."

"She's already got enough pain in her life," Samara replied. "The migraines—"

"I'm not talking about physical pain." Renata leaned over and squeezed her hand. "I'm talking about the emotional kind. The kind that shapes you, that teaches you who you are and what you want. The kind you can't engineer away, no matter how brilliant a geneticist you are."

Samara's throat tightened. She'd spent Phoebe's entire life focused on her body. Correcting genetic flaws, anticipating and mitigating off-target effects, creating a physical form that could thrive on this alien world.

"Are you saying that I've neglected her heart?"

"I'm saying she's a teenager flooded with hormones. And that she'll find her way. Phoebe is more resilient than you give her credit for."

"You're right." Samara sighed. "And you're an amazing mom."

Renata gave her a gentle smile, stood, and planted a

kiss on top of Samara's head. "So are you. Even when it feels like you're failing, you're not."

Samara wasn't so sure, but she nodded anyway.

"Go get some sleep," Renata said, her hand lingering on Samara's shoulder. "The world will still need saving tomorrow."

"Yeah." Samara trudged down the hall to her bedroom, footsteps dragging with exhaustion.

She paused at Phoebe's door, pressing her ear to the wood panel.

The silence felt significant. A barrier more impenetrable than the physical door. After several long moments of contemplation, Samara walked to her own room and sank onto the edge of her bed, too drained to even kick off her shoes. Her body hummed with fatigue, but her mind raced on, cataloging tomorrow's urgent tasks: more tests on the prion samples, another round of experimental treatments, checking in on Hector.

And somehow finding a way to bridge the growing chasm between herself and her daughter before it became too wide to cross.

Chapter Twenty-Five

Phoebe sprawled on her bed, staring at the water stain on her ceiling that vaguely resembled DaVinci's western continent. She'd memorized every blotch and discoloration over the past two days.

Aside from the mandatory trudge to school, she'd been right here, brain spinning for two days now.

Samara had established a predictable rotation: knock softly, ask if she was okay, offer to talk, remind her the door was always open, and finally, retreat with a sigh audible enough to hear through the wall. Like clockwork, every six hours.

Phoebe ignored her.

At least when Renata stopped by, she brought actual sustenance. Protein cakes with that sweet, fermented sauce Phoebe loved. Savory stew, still steaming from the kitchen. Once, a rare square of chocolate she must have been saving for a special occasion. Renata never pushed or lingered. She'd just leave the tray, maybe touch the door once, then go.

Which Phoebe was grateful for, because she really didn't want to talk.

She felt so stupid.

If she did talk to one of her moms, what would she even say? That she'd fallen for a boy who was being forced to marry someone else? That she'd offered him a scientific solution to his problems, and he'd rejected it because of some mystical belief that he was a "Divine Blueprint"?

She rolled onto her side, bunching her pillow under her head.

No.

She wasn't stupid.

The situation was at fault. Or at least, the schism that had split the colony all those years ago deserved the blame. If not for that, Atlas would have grown up here. And they wouldn't have had to deal with… well, whatever this was.

Star-crossed lovers?

She snorted.

They were hardly that.

Not that she hadn't thought about what it would be like to sleep with Atlas. It just wasn't ever going to happen. She rolled over again, unable to get comfortable.

The worst part was her inability to hate him.

Despite everything.

Even the fact that he was going to marry Hyacinth, she still liked him. And couldn't stop thinking about him. The way he looked at her in the ruins. The feel of his hands. His kiss.

God, why did she have to fall in love with a Naturalist?

She pulled the pillow over her face and groaned.

Her comm chirped.

She'd forgotten and left it on. But no one had come to take the comm back, so maybe Engineering and Maintenance had given up looking for it.

It chirped again.

Probably Samara, checking to see if she was alive again. Phoebe considered ignoring it, but then reached over and grabbed the device. Looked at the screen.

And sat upright.

The message wasn't from Samara.

It was from Atlas.

She swiped it open.

Want to have sex?

She stared at it. Did he really just type that? She was about to respond when the next message came through.

If we do, Hyacinth will never marry me because I'll be CONTAMINATED BY YOU (SORRY!).

Phoebe slapped a hand over her mouth to stifle a laugh.

Then Dr. Basu will have to use your solution to pass on the Divine Blueprint if she wants it passed on at all. She'll have no choice.

Another laugh bubbled up in her throat. She tried to visualize Atlas sitting on his bed, trying to construct his argument.

I'd like to have sex with you anyway. If you would. Like to. That is. Sorry.

She typed, *You are the worst communicator.*

I know.

Let's meet. Tonight? After dark.

See you then.

She set her comm down and lay back against her pillow.

Sex with Atlas. No one had to twist her arm there.

But the idea that he would then be contaminated? The whole idea was ridiculous. Insulting. And absolutely hysterical. The Naturalists really believed this garbage?

But hell, Atlas would get his freedom. And it would

force Dr. Basu to finally accept the science she'd spent decades rejecting. The woman who'd built her entire colony on the idea of rejecting 'contamination' would have no choice but to embrace it.

Which would save the lives of all the Naturalists.

She stuffed her comm and tracker in her pocket and jumped off the bed.

Before meeting up with Atlas tonight, she needed to at least get started on mapping his genome. Running the sequencer was one thing, but developing an actual therapy was way beyond her skill level. She needed help.

And there was only one person she could ask besides her mother.

Phoebe ran a hand through her tangled hair and slipped out of her room through the window. Why not? It was easier than going downstairs.

This time of day, Lucas would be at the water treatment plant on the eastern edge of the colony.

She sprinted most of the way, bursting into the squat, utilitarian building out of breath. Inside, humidity slapped her in the face along with the sharp tang of purification chemicals. Pipes crisscrossed the ceiling and walls like metal arteries, transporting water through its various treatment cycles.

No response.

She checked each processing station in turn. Finally, in the tertiary filtration section, she spotted him crouched beside a massive pump. He'd removed an access panel to expose its mechanical guts, tools laid out beside him like he was about to perform surgery.

"Finally," she said.

Lucas looked up. "Phoebe. Trouble?"

"Nope. But I need your help with something."

"You might have noticed that I'm in the middle of

something. This pump's efficiency has decreased by twenty-three percent in the last week."

"Well, this is important."

"I can tell. Your core temperature's up half a degree above baseline and—"

She glared at him. "Stop biohacking me."

"My apologies. Although you did indicate that circumstances were serious."

Was he being sarcastic? She'd never heard him make a joke before, at least, not like that. Or maybe she'd just never noticed, because she thought of him as the person who'd told her knock-knock jokes when she was five.

She crouched, lowering her voice even though there was no one else around. "I have a project. And I don't want to ask Samara for help."

His fingers stilled. "Why not?"

"Because she won't understand."

"What would she not understand?"

Phoebe hesitated. What if he refused to help? Then she'd be stuck. Lucas had his own ideas about what was best for her. Ideas that didn't always align with what she wanted.

"It's about genetics. And helping people."

Lucas studied her face, his expression unreadable for a long moment. "And Samara wouldn't understand?"

"No."

He returned to his work on the pump. "Then it is related to the Naturalist boy?"

Phoebe blew out a breath. *Was she that obvious?* "His name is Atlas."

"Atlas, then." Lucas made some adjustments on the pump.

"Yes."

"And will my assistance result in a positive outcome for both colonies?"

"I believe so." Phoebe nodded. "Yes."

Lucas looked at her.

"You don't believe me?" Phoebe held out her arms. "Bio-hack away. You'll see I'm not lying."

He laughed. "No need. I will help you."

That had been too easy. Where were all the questions? The lecture about colony safety or protocol? Part of her itched to ask why he seemed so unconcerned about helping her and Atlas, but she didn't want to jinx it.

"Thank you. Can we meet at the lab during the leadership meeting? Samara and Renata will both be there, so we'll have the place to ourselves."

"I will be there."

Phoebe hugged him. "You're the best, Lucas."

He patted her back. "I will see you later."

Phoebe released him and practically skipped back through the corridor. She passed a few colonists on her way out, nodding politely, but the moment she hit open air, she broke into an impromptu victory dance that would've mortified her if anyone had borne witness.

PHOEBE STARED at the image of Atlas' genome.

The semi-transparent double helix rotated lazily on the screen, dotted with color-coded markers that highlighted specific mutations. Next to it, data scrolled by in a constant stream, comparing Atlas' genome to the engineered adaptations of the Vitruvians.

She'd thought she'd be able to prove that his "Divine Blueprint" was simply the same set of modifications that

Samara had standardized for all Vitruvians, but the sequences were not the same.

"Look, these variations seem to be unique to Atlas." She pointed to the readout. "But I'm not sure which ones are responsible for his adaptation to the fungus."

"I believe I have identified the relevant mutations." Lucas did something to the display, and six highlighted sequences popped out and expanded. "What Samara accomplished with scores of changes in multiple chromosomes, nature seems to have accomplished with a half-dozen. It's quite elegant."

Phoebe pursed her lips. "So, the Divine Blueprint is a better solution. Fewer modifications, and no off-target effects."

But if Phoebe used Samara's techniques to splice out those half-dozen sequences and create a gene therapy treatment incorporating them, she wouldn't be able to help including additional genetic material around the key sequences, which could cause new off-target effects.

In other words, she would contaminate the Divine Blueprint.

She hated that Dr. Basu was not actually wrong.

But… wasn't the risk worth the potential reward?

The Naturalist colony could eventually emerge from their sterile bubbles and live freely on this world.

They'd be able to grow enough food to support themselves, which would give them the independence from the Vitruvians that they claimed they wanted.

Their children would be healthy.

They wouldn't have to take immunosuppressants all the time, risking vulnerability to the mildest bacteria or virus.

And it was possible that the off-target effects would be negligible.

But it was also possible that they would be like Phoebe's. Or worse.

She'd thought she had a simple solution that everyone had overlooked, sure that she was right and all of the adults who couldn't solve it were wrong.

But could she look Atlas in the eye and tell him that she guaranteed distributing the Divine Blueprint to his people would have no side effects?

No, she couldn't. But that didn't stop her from selfishly wanting to tell him it was completely safe, so that she could be with him.

"And this is where it gets even more interesting." Lucas said, apparently oblivious to her new ethical dilemma. He zoomed in on a new gene cluster. He ran a quick forward simulation of protein expression. "See this structural variance? It's in a regulatory gene that controls protein expression in the nervous system. It's strikingly close to the sequences found in Hyperionite DNA."

"Wait. You're saying he has the same adaptations as the Hypers?"

"Not exactly the same, but similar. A product of parallel evolution. This particular sequence is completely unique to Atlas."

Phoebe's pulse quickened. This was it, concrete proof that Atlas' immunity wasn't divine intervention or a miracle. Just a random genetic mutation. Pure, beautiful science.

But even though she felt vindicated, that didn't change the fact that her argument against Dr. Basu's superstition wasn't bulletproof. And she had to be honest with Atlas, which could mean he might never speak to her again.

"So, we can reproduce it?"

"Of course," Lucas said.

"And is there a way to minimize the off-target effects?"

"By definition, off-target effects can't be predicted. But we can minimize the margin of error with custom restriction enzymes."

"So, it would be safe to give the Naturalists."

"The Naturalist's wouldn't need selective breeding. They could use this as a treatment. A gene therapy. We can pass this on to them."

"It is doubtful that they would take it. But yes. A retroviral carrier would be most efficient for widespread distribution, but for targeted application, a direct injection of engineered messenger RNA would suffice."

"What do you need?"

"The cryopreserved lentiviral vectors and the recombinant plasmid library from cold storage. We'll need both."

Phoebe nodded and ran to the unit at the back of the lab and entered.

Only to spot a row of containers she'd never seen before, each labeled with a pair of names:

Atlas - Hyacinth
Atlas - Mira
Atlas - Jennie
Atlas - Sofia

On and on down the line, more than a dozen containers.

"What the hell?" Phoebe reached for one of the containers, wanting to open it and see what was inside. Samara was obviously doing some kind of genetic testing on Atlas. Maybe she was pairing his DNA with other samples to see which women he was most genetically compatible with. Maybe that's how they'd settled on Hyacinth, and he didn't even know it.

But then she stopped herself. Breaking the seal would alert Samara that someone had tampered with them.

So much for Dr. Basu's endless sermons about the evils

of science. Apparently she had no problem using it when it suited her agenda. But at least the psychologist's hypocrisy made Phoebe feel less guilty about the fact that her version of the Divine Blueprint wouldn't be quite as good as the natural one. At least she wouldn't lie about it. As long as she explained the risks and the Naturalists were free to choose for themselves, it was okay, right?

The thing she couldn't understand was her own mother's participation in this scheme, whatever it was. That hurt ten times more than anything Dr. Basu could do to her. Even if her mother hadn't known that Phoebe would meet Atlas and fall in love with him.

But Samara knew now. And she still kept those samples hidden away in her lab. Because she wanted to keep Phoebe from being with Atlas.

There was no excuse for her betrayal.

Phoebe gathered them all up and dumped them in the biohazard waste receptacle. Then she found what Lucas had asked her for and rejoined him.

He studied her face, clearly picking up on her anger.

Phoebe glared at him. "What is it? My cortisol spiked? Pupils dilated? Heart rate doing something interesting?"

He turned away. "I was about to say thank you."

Even she didn't believe the lie.

They got to work.

And after she helped Atlas "contaminate himself" — such an insulting concept — the vaccine would be ready. They could hand over the real, scientifically provable (and reproducible) "Divine Blueprint" to Dr. Basu, and Atlas would have his freedom.

It was a good plan. And it was going to work.

Chapter Twenty-Six

ATLAS MADE his way to the dining hall, stomach growling loudly enough to embarrass him if anyone had been close enough to hear. The moment he stepped through the doors, he knew something was wrong. The usual lunch-hour chaos of clattering trays, overlapping conversations, and people jostling for seats had been replaced by a tense, electric atmosphere.

Colonists huddled at tables speaking in hushed tones, faces drawn with concern. Maybe…

"Atlas."

He turned to find Hyacinth standing behind him. She grabbed his arm and pulled him toward an alcove near the entrance. "We need to talk."

He fought the urge to pull away from her. "What about?"

"Xavier."

That wasn't what he expected her to say. Xavier was in charge of irrigation in the greenhouses. Atlas wasn't even aware that Hyacinth knew him.

"He's sick. Mother had him moved to quarantine this morning."

Atlas froze. "What kind of sick?"

"The kind that doesn't happen here." Her gaze hardened. "The kind that only happens when someone breaks protocol."

Atlas stiffened. "What are you implying?"

"Mother told me you sneak outside." She leaned closer, her voice a whisper. "Without going through decontamination afterward. You must have brought something back with you. Something that infected Xavier."

"You don't know that."

"Maybe not. But I know that Xavier was fine three days ago. And you were outside two nights before that." Her expression shifted, a calculating look replacing her anger. "And if people find out…"

"Then what?"

"Then you're not just reckless, you're dangerous."

He blinked. "Dangerous?"

She poked his shoulder. "You're the Divine Blueprint, Atlas. You're supposed to *protect* us. If word gets out that you've been sneaking beyond the boundary? That you've been *exposed*? It's not just a breach of trust. This is physical and spiritual contamination. They'll say you've betrayed us."

He opened his mouth, but Hyacinth cut him off.

"People believe in you. They've *built* this community around your existence. If they stop believing … Do you really want to be the one who destroys this place?"

"So… if I don't marry you, then you're going to tell them?"

She flushed. "That's not what I said."

"You made it perfectly clear."

"Be careful with the rumors you hear." He kept his

voice level even though he was angry. "Especially coming from someone in your position. Try using your brain instead of your mother's."

Her mouth fell open, eyes widening like he'd just suggested they run naked through a sporestorm. "What?"

"You're Dr. Basu's daughter. The person expected to lead the colony after she steps down. And if you're going to do that, you better not start gossip."

Blood rushed to her face, turning her skin the color of the emergency lights in the greenhouse. "I'm trying to protect you, you ungrateful jerk."

"No, you're trying to control me."

"There's an emergency prayer circle called for tonight. You should be there to support Xavier." She spun on her heel, shoulders rigid as she stalked away.

Atlas watched her retreat, the knot in his stomach tightening. If Xavier truly was infected with whatever had struck down Dr. Callas in the Vitruvian colony, then a thousand prayer circles wouldn't save him. They needed actual medicine. The kind that only the people who understood disease could provide.

He shoved his way out of the dining hall and made a beeline for Dr. Basu's office, ignoring the curious glances that followed him. When he reached her door, he rapped his knuckles against it hard enough to hurt.

"Enter."

Atlas pushed inside, letting the door bang against the wall a little harder than necessary.

Dr. Basu was at her desk. "Yes?"

"Xavier is sick."

Dr. Basu's expression didn't change. "Yes."

"Is it what Dr. Callas had?"

A long pause. "The symptoms are similar."

Atlas stepped forward, gripping the edge of her desk.

"I didn't bring it back here. I decontaminated before entering."

She hesitated before admitting, "I know."

He felt a flash of hope. She wasn't totally deluded. She could still tell the difference between the truth and her own lies. "You need to call the Vitruvians for help."

Her eyes flashed. "I don't need to do anything."

"They understand disease. They have better medicine, and better equipment. They can help Xavier before it spreads to others—"

"Any solution that Samara and her ilk would offer is worse than the disease itself. "

"How can you say that? Xavier could die. Others could get sick. This could devastate the colony."

"Better to lose some than to compromise the integrity of all."

Atlas stared at her. "Do you hear yourself?"

"I do."

"And you think Xavier's wife would agree with that? She'd choose 'purity' over his life?"

"Miriam understands what's at stake. She wouldn't want to compromise her husband's humanity, even to save his physical form."

"Have you asked her?"

Dr. Basu pressed her lips together.

She hadn't. Because it wasn't Miriam's choice that mattered to Dr. Basu, only her own.

Did she genuinely believe that she was dooming them for their own spiritual good? Or would she simply be willing to sacrifice them all rather than admit that she was wrong?

Atlas looked at the comm unit sitting on her desk. *One call*. That's all it would take to get help. To save Xavier and protect the colony.

Dr. Basu followed his eyes. "Touch that and you will no longer receive any of the privileges you currently enjoy, Atlas."

He laughed. "Is that what you think my life is? Privileged? Being paraded around like a holy relic?"

"I call it reverence for the divine gift you carry. A gift that many would die to possess. If I need to curtail your freedom, I will."

Atlas bared his teeth. "You can't do anything to me. I'm the Divine Blueprint."

Dr. Basu's smile was cold. "There are less pleasant ways for me to get my hands on it than marrying you to my daughter."

Atlas planted both palms on her desk and leaned forward until his face was level with hers, invading her carefully maintained personal space, making her feel what it was like to be talked down to for once. "Then I guess you don't need me alive after all." *Silence.* And then he saw the flicker of fear in her eyes. Because it was true.

If he died, the Divine Blueprint died with him. No perfect lineage, no future generation able to coexist with the fungus. No control.

Dr. Basu's fingers curled into fists before she forced them flat against the desk again. "You should return to your duties, Atlas. And perhaps spend some time reflecting on your place in this community before you say something truly unforgivable."

Atlas knew he'd been dismissed, but he held his position instead of scurrying away like he was supposed to, maintaining eye contact.

"Yeah. I thought so," he finally said, straightening up with deliberate slowness. "You need me more than I need you."

Then he turned and walked out, closing the door with

exaggerated gentleness that somehow felt more defiant than slamming it.

~

AYESHA WATCHED Atlas close the door, the soft click somehow even more infuriating than the thud of a slam would have been. She snatched the wooden prayer tablet from her desk and hurled it across the room. It struck the door with a satisfying crack, exploding into a cloud of splinters

She pressed her palms flat against the desk, forcing herself to slowly inhale through her nose. *Breathe.*

He was slipping away from her. Because of that Vitruvian abomination that Samara had created.

She should have given him a more convincing answer when he'd asked about the samples. But the question had caught her completely off-guard. What was worse, far worse, was that she could tell he hadn't believed her response.

And that was a problem.

Because if he knew *that* was a lie, what else was he starting to question?

He'd always been obedient. Curious, yes, but within bounds. Faithful. But Atlas had obviously been masking. Now he was poking at seams that she couldn't afford him to tear.

If he ever found out what she'd asked Katherine to do...

Her jaw tightened.

As much as Katherine angered her, she knew how to protect the colony's priorities. *Both* colonies. And best of all, she knew how to keep confidence. So, the leak hadn't come from her.

It must have been Phoebe.

Ayesha drew a slow breath through her nose and sat back down.

Then she reached for the comm and keyed in Katherine's frequency. To her surprise, she answered on the first call.

"Ayesha." Katherine sounded exhausted. "I hope all is well."

Ayesha tried not to sound too harsh. After all, she didn't want Katherine to go back on their agreement. "It's not. Your sickness has spread here. "

The other end of the comm was quiet.

"What?" The exhaustion vanished from Katherine's voice, replaced by the sharp edge of alarm that prickled Ayesha's skin despite herself.

"Xavier collapsed this morning. High fever, disorientation, tremors. He can barely speak. I told you that you should have informed me right away."

"How advanced are his symptoms? Has anyone else shown signs?"

"Not yet." Ayesha pulled out her beads and ran them through her fingers. "But I imagine it's only a matter of time."

"Listen to me carefully. You need to quarantine him, and I'll send Leila over immediately. We'll need samples from Xavier to confirm it's the same pathogen."

"That won't be necessary. We're holding a prayer circle for him this evening and—"

"You cannot do that."

Ayesha stiffened. "Of course I can. This is my colony."

"If you allow others to be near him, they could get infected."

"We're perfectly capable of handling this ourselves. Whatever path unfolds, we will meet it in faith and unity. If

Xavier is meant to recover, he will. And if not, we'll walk him home in prayer."

"This isn't about capability. It's about *information*. Pooling what we know to stop something from spreading. This isn't an attack on your beliefs, Ayesha. This is about saving lives."

"There are rumors going around the colony that the Vitruvians created this plague by allowing your people to live in close quarters with those genetic abominations, and now you want to swoop in to rescue us from it."

"Listen to yourself, Ayesha. We don't have time for conspiracy theories. The Vitruvians didn't create this illness. The Hyperionites aren't responsible either. We need to figure out how this jumped from Callas to your colony. Right now, before more people get sick."

Atlas.

Neither of them had to say it. But Ayesha knew that's what she was thinking. "Let me guess. The only cure will be to genetically modify all of us? To strip away what little purity remains in our bloodlines?"

Katherine ignored the accusation. "Look, we've identified the pathogen and are working on a vaccine. But we're still trying to understand the spread. Until then, you should implement strict quarantine measures and isolate anyone showing symptoms."

"And why should I trust anything you say? After all your secrets and lies? How do I know you didn't deliberately introduce this with your last shipment of supplies? A pathogen engineered to target our immunosuppressed population while leaving your modified colonists unaffected?"

"That's absurd. Why would I want to harm your people? When I just agreed to help you on your project?"

There it was.

Ayesha had been waiting for her to bring it up.

If she tried to hold the samples hostage …

"To force us back under your control. To end our independence. To prove that your way is the only way to survive on this planet."

"Get some sleep, Ayesha. We'll continue this conversation when you're more willing to listen to reason."

Katherine ended the transmission.

Ayesha threw the comm down on her desk.

She hated that her people's survival depended on Katherine's cooperation.

Hated the idea that they might still be tethered to the whims of the Vitruvians.

Ayesha hadn't left on a whim. She'd done it to create something pure. Something sacred. They had reclaimed ancient rhythms that the Vitruvians had abandoned in their obsession with so-called progress and built something beautiful in its simplicity. And all it took was one sick person to threaten it all.

Her jaw clenched so tight she felt a muscle spasm. The worst part wasn't Katherine's condescension. It was the creeping doubt that despite everything she'd sacrificed, everything she'd built, she might still fail.

Fail to protect what she had spent her life building.

Fail to shield them from the chaos outside the fence.

Fail to prove — to herself most of all — that *faith* was enough.

She should never have given those samples to Katherine. But she needed them. The survival of her people was essential. Probably now more than ever, with Xavier sick.

Because her options were limited. Even if she ordered him euthanized, others might already be incubating the disease. The entire colony could be compromised.

She leaned back in her chair, rubbing her beads,

considering the alternatives. They could all stop taking the immunosuppressants and give their natural immune systems a chance to fight off this new plague. But if a sporestorm hit, the double assault of virus and fungus would likely kill them all.

And even if Katherine's people did develop a cure, who knew what it might contain? By accepting it, Ayesha could be deliberately introducing genetic contamination into her colony that might negate the Divine Blueprint or prevent it from recurring in future generations.

The fate of the pure, unaltered version of humanity she had dedicated her life to preserving now hung in the balance. And she, Ayesha Basu, was the only one who could protect it.

No matter the cost.

Ayesha closed her eyes. She'd rather let humanity die than allow contamination to happen. Sometimes, to preserve what mattered most, one had to be willing to make sacrifices.

Even if the sacrifice broke your heart.

Chapter Twenty-Seven

SAMARA STARED at the monitor until her eyes burned.

She rubbed her temples and squinted at the misshapen protein structures rotating on the screen, their twisted forms mocking her efforts. God, she was starting to hate prions with the burning passion most people reserved for their worst enemies.

The lab was silent except for the low hum of equipment and the occasional ping of the computer analyzing yet another failed simulation. Nothing but her, the machines, and a growing pile of disappointment. She'd been at it for ... how long? She glanced at the time, wincing at the numbers.

Hours had passed. And she was losing track of time. Her workbench was covered in empty nutrient packs and her neck felt like someone had beat on the back of it with a hammer.

But she still couldn't stop.

Hector was deteriorating by the hour.

She hit a button, running the next simulation watching a new molecular model assemble itself. She was trying to design engineered peptides that bind to the normal prion protein and stabilize it in its correct fold. Back on Earth, they called them "molecular chaperones." . If she could just prevent the misfolded proteins from aggregating for getting caught in any other molecular machinery, there might be a chance. Despite trying variants of existing antivirals, repurposed antifungals, custom-designed enzyme blockers, so far nothing worked. She even threw a Hail Mary and tried the molecular CRISPR version of a wood chipper. The simulations all ended the same way: the prions continuing their destructive conversion, immune to her interventions.

She tapped her fingers on the console, waiting for the inevitable failure notification. The algorithm was running through thousands of possible interactions, chemical bonds forming and breaking within seconds, all in virtual space.

But she wasn't just fighting the disease.

She was fighting time.

The computer chimed and a message flashed across the screen. *SIMULATION FAILED.*

Samara slammed her palm against the desk. "Dammit!"

Then she closed her eyes, pressed her fingertips against her temples. "Think, think ..."

The lab door hissed open behind her.

Samara didn't bother turning around because she didn't care who it was. "I'm busy."

"Samara." It was Leila. "They're awake."

That made her turn. "Who?"

"The patients from the cave. They're conscious. And lucid. Well, semi-lucid. I gave them a cocktail of astemizole and terfenadine, along with some nootropics. And they're responding."

Samara stared at her.

"I read about them in some pre-collapse research. Astemizole showed potential for inhibiting prion replication in vitro - something about antihistamines seemed to gum up the protein complexes. Nothing concrete, but we're running out of options and…" She gestured. "Just come. They're talking."

Samara pushed back from her workstation and followed Leila through the corridor to the quarantine area.

"How long will they be coherent?"

"Unknown," Leila said. "The dosages I gave them are experimental. Could be hours, could be minutes."

"Have you told Katherine?"

"She's on a call with Ayesha. I've left a message."

They reached the quarantine room, suited up, then entered through the airlock. Then Samara followed Leila over to the beds.

The woman was awake, her rheumy eyes following their movements with surprising alertness despite the cloudy film covering them. The man beside her remained motionless, save for the shallow rise and fall of his chest beneath the thin sheet as he stared at the ceiling. Samara couldn't tell if he was aware of them or not.

"Colonists?" the woman asked.

Samara nodded. "Yes. Colonists. I'm Samara Makinde, a geneticist."

The woman wet her lips with a tongue that looked paper dry. "New … colony? After … us?"

"Yes," Samara said. "Our ship was called the Borlaug. We found your colony site."

The woman's eyes widened. "Survive … fungus?"

"Yes." Samara smiled. "We found a way to adapt."

"How long …" The woman's voice faltered, her attention drifting. "How long have we been here? Planet?"

Samara exchanged a glance with Leila. "A long time. What's the last thing you remember?"

The woman's forehead creased with effort. "The … quarantine chamber. Levi's idea. The … others were dead. Or changed. We couldn't save them. We tried. We tried everything."

Her eyes filled with tears.

"Levi." Samara said.

She nodded. "My husband. Chief engineer."

"That means you're Dr. Dakota Goldstein? Your colony's physician?"

The old woman nodded slowly, as if she were making a Herculean effort. "The Children. Where are they?" Dakota asked. "You didn't hurt them?"

The Children? Did she mean the Hypers?

"No, no, they're alright," Samara said.

"Good." A strange expression crossed Dakota's face. Tears filled her eyes. "We didn't deserve their help."

"Rest now," Leila said, reaching for a hydration pad to moisten Dakota's lips.

"No time … We're dying. Need to tell … the story. The truth."

"Go ahead." Samara placed a hand on Dakota's forehead to calm her. "We're listening."

Dakota's gaze drifted to the ceiling, as though watching memories play like a movie above her. "The colony failed from the start. It was the fungus. It made everyone sick, and we couldn't stop it. Standard treatments failed. People died. Desperate measures."

"You tried to adapt by engineering your immune systems to be more aggressive," Samara said. "But it didn't work."

"We tried to make … new humans. Better than us.

Stronger. Clones. Our DNA mixed with … native species. Experimenting."

"Clones?" Samara glanced at Leila.

Dakota nodded. "Clones of us engineered … to survive the fungus. We failed so many times."

"Horrific … deformities. We didn't understand. Not enough." A tear slid down Dakota's sunken cheek. "The children suffered."

"But some survived," Leila said.

"The later generations," Dakota nodded again, "Better adapted. More stable. We gave them native DNA. But they weren't … human anymore. Not entirely."

"And they turned on you," Samara said.

Dakota's expression darkened. "No. They cared for us. Even though we treated them like … experiments. We were the monsters. Not them."

"Then who smashed your medical lab and destroyed your equipment?"

"Fungus… they went mad, at the end."

"When you started running out of antifungals," Samara said.

"Hid some." Dakota coughed. "Quarantine chamber. The children… helped us move… to the caves. Set up… air system."

"And they kept you alive all this time," Leila said.

"Shared food. Medicine. Company." Dakota's voice softened. "Their kindness … after everything we did …"

The door hissed open behind them and Lucas entered, his footsteps barely audible on the polished floor. "Katherine has been trying to reach you both. It's urgent."

"We've been busy," Samara said, gesturing to the beds.

Lucas looked at Dakota. Blinked. "They're awake."

"Yeah."

The old man, Levi, made a rasping noise, his mouth working like he was trying to talk.

Dakota's eyes widened as she turned her head again, toward Lucas. Her lips parted in what looked like shock. Or fear. Levi's rasping grew more frantic. Leila moved to his bed, laying a hand on the man's shoulder. "It's okay, you're safe."

"You're … still operational… Here to… hurt us?".

"No," said Lucas.

Samara looked over at him.

"How do they know you?"

"I assisted Aurelius Hofstadter in administering longevity treatments to the Hyperion colonists. The protocols were … physically intensive."

"*Intensive?*" Dakota's voice cracked, indignation giving her sudden strength. "It was… *torture.*"

"It was necessary," argued Lucas. "The mission required a crew capable of initiating colonization after a 42-year journey without cryogenic preservation."

Dakota's monitors began to beep. Her eyes rolled back, body going slack against the mattress.

"She's seizing. Heart rate dropping. Blood pressure crashing," Leila said.

Dakota reached out a hand toward her husband, even though she was too far away. "Levi," she whispered.

Her arm went suddenly rigid, fingers splayed into claws as her monitors erupted in a cacophony of alarm tones.

"They're crashing," Lucas said.

For the next few minutes, Samara and Leila worked frantically to stabilize their two patients. Leila administered counter-seizure medications while Samara adjusted fluid rates and monitored vitals, their movements synchronized after years of emergency drills. Lucas provided real-time analytics.

Finally, the alarms quieted. The two ancient colonists lay still, their breathing shallow but steady.

"They're stable," Samara said, checking vitals again.

Leila nodded. "Yeah, but they're also non-responsive again."

Lucas peered at one of the monitors. "The neuro-chemical boost was only temporary."

It wasn't a question.

"Yes. Unfortunately," Leila said.

"Then while they rest, it's time we speak to Katherine."

Chapter Twenty-Eight

KATHERINE WAS ALREADY on her feet when Samara entered her office, followed by Leila and Lucas. The colony leader paced behind her desk like a caged predator, her fingers drumming against her thigh in a nervous rhythm.

She was pacing, her face tight with tension. Whatever they'd been summoned for, it wasn't good news.

"What's happened?" Samara asked, sensing the tension wafting off of Katherine like fumes.

"Is this about Hector?"

Katherine shook her head. "No. We have another situation."

Leila glanced at her.

Samara crossed her arms, bracing herself. "Let's hear it."

"One of the Naturalists has fallen ill," Katherine said. "Showing all the same symptoms as Hector. Prions."

Samara's blood ran cold, her whole body going rigid. "That's impossible."

"The Naturalist boy. You told me he was there that night. He could have carried it back to them."

Samara shook her head. "He might have been. But he wasn't exposed to Levi and Dakota at all, was he, Lucas?"

"No. He had exited the cave before I opened the quarantine. And he had no interactions with Hector either."

Leila's face paled. "I need to go there. Now. Ayesha doesn't have the resources to handle this, and they certainly won't understand what they're dealing with."

"No." Katherine bunched her hands into fists. "Ayesha won't allow it. I'm fairly certain if we send anyone, she'll consider it an act of war."

Leila threw up her hands. "She'd rather let her people suffer and die than accept help?"

"That sounds about right," Samara said.

Katherine eyed her. "It's not about that. It's about control. Ayesha doesn't want to weaken her people's faith by asking us for help."

"So, you'll let them die?" Leila asked.

"What am I supposed to do? Forcibly quarantine her people?"

"Yes!"

Katherine rubbed her temple. "Come on, Leila. We're trying to co-exist here. If I go in heavy-handed, she'll seal her borders for good. No communication, no oversight, no treatment. At least this way, I can still keep the lines of communication open."

"And when people start dying?"

"I'll review the situation. Intercede if necessary."

"We need to get back to the matter at hand," Samara said. If it wasn't Atlas that spread the infection to the Naturalists, how did the prions jump from the Hyperion-ites to Hector to them?

Samara rubbed her wrist absently as she thought, tracing the outline of a recent mosquito bite. The motion stopped mid-circle as realization hit her like a lightning bolt.

She stared down at the raised welt on her skin, pieces snapping together in her mind.

Katherine narrowed her eyes. "What?"

Samara's pulse quickened. "What if it's the star mosquitoes? What if they're the carriers?"

But that wasn't how prions worked. The concentration of prions in the bloodstream was low enough that the amount a mosquito could suck up was miniscule. And the chances that any prions they did carry would accidentally leak into the next person as they drank. Prions weren't like viruses or bacteria, able to quickly reproduce if even a single one managed to infect a host.

At least, not on Earth.

But this wasn't Earth. What if there was some other factor that made it possible here?

"We've never seen an instance of mosquitoes carrying a prion disease," Leila said.

"It's the only method of transmission that makes sense." Samara started pacing. "When Levi and Dakota were brought out, their skin was exposed. They could have gotten bitten by a mosquito, either during transport or in the quarantine area."

"I did find bites on them," Leila said.

"And then all it would have taken was one of those mosquitoes to bite Hector and—"

"The infection could be exponential," Lucas interjected. "Based on current population densities of *Culicidae stellaris* and their feeding patterns, I estimate between sixty and seventy percent of the colony has been bitten within the past week."

Katherine paled. "We could all be infected?"

"Not necessarily," Samara said. "It would depend on a

lot of things, including how easy it is for the insects to carry the prions. Transmission rate might be extremely low for proteins that big."

"We need colony-wide protocols. Now," Katherine cut in. "First, insect netting. Every residence, lab, and medical bay needs to be sealed. No exceptions."

Leila nodded and took out her tablet, taking notes.

"Leila, work with the agriculture team. We need chemical and natural repellents, fast. Whatever we can synthesize from local plants, whatever we can manufacture."

"The Hyperionites use a paste made from fermented river reeds," Lucas said. "Highly effective."

"Good. Get the formula," Katherine nodded. "Quarantine measures stay in place. Anyone showing *any* neurological symptoms is to be isolated immediately. Maeve's team needs to reduce breeding grounds: standing water, waste systems, anything that could be a nesting site for the insects. Get rid of it now. And no one goes outside with exposed skin until we know more. Long sleeves, protective clothing, the works."

Then it hit Samara. "There's another possibility. When I was searching the literature, I found an obscure paper where researchers were using a viral vector to trigger prion formation in the lab, so that they could create new kinds of prions to study."

Which was horrifying, because the transmission rate of a virus would be much higher.

"The star mosquitoes could be carrying a virus that makes prions?" Leila asked. "But we looked at every pathogen in our library, both from Earth and here. We didn't see anything."

"It's unlikely that you've catalogued every virus that exists on this planet," Lucas pointed out. "It's also possible that this is a virus that went unrecognized as a pathogen."

Katherine turned to Samara. "If it's a virus, can you make a vaccine?"

"Assuming it's a virus, yes, we should be able to make one that will prevent new infections, but it won't reverse the damage already done to anyone infected," Samara said. "I'll need blood samples from everyone who's been bitten but isn't showing symptoms yet. We need to identify everyone who's infected, as well as understand the disease's progression."

"You'll have whatever you need."

"I can assist with the viral modeling," Lucas said.

"We need to warn the Hyperionites," Katherine added. "Ayesha may have her head in the sand, but the Hyperionites don't need to suffer any more than their people already have."

"I'll contact them immediately," Lucas replied, his voice calm despite the urgency. "But so far, they've shown no sign of illness."

"So far. Let's get this done," Katherine said, already reaching for her comm. "Every minute counts."

Samara looked down at her bite, that innocuous red bump that might be the only sign of her impending deterioration. The star mosquitoes had been a nuisance for years, irritating but seemingly harmless. How many times had she slapped them away without a second thought?

"Before we go," Leila said. "The Hyperion colonists woke up."

"And?" Katherine asked.

"The Hyperionites are clones. Well, descendants of clones. Created by the original colonists when they realized they couldn't find a therapy for themselves in time."

Katherine stared at her. "What?"

"People should know," Samara said.

"Not right now." Katherine closed her eyes for a

moment, and Samara wondered if she might be praying. "It changes nothing, and we have enough prejudice against the Hyperionites already."

"It's their history," Leila said. "Our history too, in a way. What happened to *no more secrets*?"

Katherine scowled. "I'm not saying we bury it, I'm saying we get through this crisis before we decide what to do with this information."

Leila's comm chimed. She pulled it out. Looked at the message. Then her eyes filled with tears.

"Leila?" Samara said, touching her arm.

She looked up. "Hector. He's dead."

Chapter Twenty-Nine

Phoebe was bored.

For the past hour she'd been sitting in the common hall for a mandatory community meeting about star mosquitoes. About halfway in, a dull pressure started behind her right eye. Nothing serious yet, but it was familiar enough to put her on edge.

The beginnings of a migraine.

She tried to focus, but Katherine's voice was too loud, the room too bright, and the air too warm.

She stared out the nearest window, watching one of the mosquitoes land on the outside of the screen. Its translucent wings caught the light, tiny legs probing the mesh barrier between them.

The star mosquitos had always been a nuisance, but now they were apparently dangerous carriers of some kind of prion disease.

Phoebe wondered if the Naturalists were having a similar meeting.

Or did they even know?

The funny thing was, star mosquitoes didn't really

target Phoebe. Unlike Samara, who ended up covered in bites after just a few minutes outside, she rarely got bitten. Maybe three or four times a season tops.

She'd always considered it a small blessing, especially during the summer months when the insects were at their worst. Now she wondered if it was yet another side effect of her genetic modifications. Maybe something in her blood or skin chemistry repelled them.

She almost laughed out loud.

Maybe they didn't like the way she tasted.

She rubbed her temples, pressing against the growing discomfort. If she didn't get home soon, this migraine would turn nasty. The warning signs were all there: the slight blurring at the edges of her vision, the tightness in her jaw, the way sounds seemed to cut through her skull like knives.

"Thank you," Katherine said somberly.

Phoebe glanced up. The meeting was breaking up, people muttering, a few gathering in huddles.

Phoebe stood up, stretched. If she wanted to meet Atlas tonight, she needed to deal with the migraine now. Go home. Take the meds. Lie down in the dark. Rest.

One of the medical assistants was walking through the crowd distributing bottles of Leila's repellent. Phoebe grabbed one, uncapped it and sniffed. God-awful. She applied it to her face and arms anyway.

Once covered, she left the common hall.

There was hardly anyone outside.

Obviously everyone was too nervous to brave the bugs.

The heat was stifling, but at least it wasn't claustrophobic like the meeting room had been. She rolled her shoulders, willing the tension in her neck to ease. Maybe if she just walked slowly, it wouldn't get worse.

She headed toward home.

And then a high-pitched trill cut through the air.

Phoebe stopped.

It was the distinctive vocalization of a Hyperionite in distress. She'd spent enough time with Flutter to recognize the difference between a happy Hyper and a scared Hyper.

This made no sense. Hyperionites rarely ventured this far into Vitruvian territory, typically stopping at the lake. They never entered the colony unless specifically invited by Katherine.

Phoebe jogged toward the sound. A few hundred feet away a cluster of teens had surrounded someone.

"Get back to your own territory!" It was Jace, a kid her age. And his best friend Wei, plus a couple of other older teens Phoebe recognized from school.

Wei shoved forward with both hands, sending the other figure stumbling back. "We don't want your kind here!"

Through the shifting bodies, Phoebe caught flashes of scaled skin with its telltale blue-green shimmer under the sunlight.

A Hyperionite.

She forgot about the pain in her head and broke into a run. "Hey! Leave them alone!"

"STAY OUT OF THIS, PHOEBE," Jace said, positioning himself to block Phoebe's view.

The Hyper turned to run.

Wei lunged forward, grabbing the Hyper's arm and knocking the basket to the ground. Its contents scattered across the dirt.

"It doesn't belong here," Tanner said.

Phoebe pushed through them, shoving Jace aside with her shoulder. Her headache flared at the sudden movement.

And then she saw who they were bullying. *Flutter*.

Her friend's scales were dulled with dirt, and Flutter hunched her shoulders, trying to make herself smaller.

She spotted Phoebe and her eyes locked on with visible relief as she signed, "Didn't Lucas tell you I wasn't allowed to come for a while?"

Flutter nodded. "Missed you."

Her shoulders dropped. "Missed you, too."

She turned back to the teens. "What the hell do you think you're doing? First of all, she's a person, not an 'it.' And Flutter has every right to be here."

"Flutter?" Tanner's lip curled. "Is this one your pet?"

The contempt in his voice sent a fresh surge of anger through Phoebe. "They have their own names. They're people just like us ..."

Wei spat on the ground at Flutter's feet. "They killed Dr. Callas. Infected him with something."

Her stomach plummeted. Dr. Callas dead? When had this happened? She kept her expression neutral despite the shock "That's ridiculous."

One of the other teens snorted. "That's not what my mom said."

Tanner crossed his arms. "If no one is getting sick, why are there guards outside the medical compound? Why are some sections of the colony suddenly off-limits?"

The pain behind her eye pulsed harder. She ignored it, though it made her vision swim as the pain spread throughout her entire skull. "I don't know, but blaming the Hypers is just looking for an easy target."

She turned to Flutter, signing. "Are you okay?"

"Brought gift. For you," Flutter said, gesturing to the basket.

Phoebe spotted a thin trail of blood running down her arm where the scales had been scraped away, revealing the softer tissue beneath. Anger flared hot in Phoebe's chest, and she whirled back to the boys.

"You hurt her!"

Tanner took a step forward. "And we're gonna hurt her some more. Move aside, Phoebe. You don't know what you're protecting."

"I know exactly who I'm protecting. *My friend.*" She turned back to Flutter. "Go. Run."

Flutter looked surprised. "Why?"

"They want to hurt—"

"I said MOVE!" Tanner lunged forward, reaching for Flutter.

Phoebe grabbed his arm, using his momentum to shove him off balance.

He stumbled, cursing. Hit the ground hard.

Flutter made a high, distressed clicking sound behind her.

"Filthy Hyper lover," Tanner spat.

Phoebe stepped forward, bunching her hand into a fist. "Say that again."

"You don't give orders here, Phoebe." Jace stepped between them. "Your mother might be important, but you're not any better than us."

"Far as I can tell, you're attacking an unarmed visitor for no reason." The pain in her head was a hot needle working its way deeper with each heartbeat. She forced herself to stand taller. "And I'm telling you to back off."

She turned back to Flutter. "Please. Go. Now."

Flutter's face contorted. She looked hurt.

Phoebe wanted to tell Flutter more. That she wasn't safe. But her hands weren't working properly, her fingers clumsy and uncoordinated. For some reason she couldn't remember how to sign "danger." The pain in her head was making it impossible to think clearly. The words refused to come.

Wei lunged at Flutter.

"Now!" Phoebe signed.

And Flutter finally ran.

"IT'S TRYING TO ESCAPE!" Jace shouted.

Phoebe grabbed his arm. Her vision was starting to tunnel now, darkening at the edges. The pressure in her skull was a building storm about to break.

"Let go of me!" Jace pushed her away. Phoebe's legs suddenly locked, and her entire body stiffened as though electrified. Her eyes rolled upward, and the world tilted.

Then she was falling.

She couldn't stop herself. She hit the ground hard, her hand slamming against something soft. Purple juice splattered across the dirt. A plum-like fruit from Flutter's basket.

Phoebe's favorite.

That's why Flutter had come. To bring her a gift.

Her body began to convulse violently against the ground

"I didn't touch her!" Jace's voice cracked with panic. "I swear I didn't touch her!"

The world exploded into white-hot agony, her consciousness dissolving into nothing as Tanner shouted for help.

Chapter Thirty

DaVinci's violet sun began to rise over the Hyperionite ruins, painting them in hues of magenta and plum. Atlas sat with his back against a crumbling wall, knees drawn to his chest, watching the smaller moon fade into the brightening sky.

He'd been there all night.

Waiting.

But Phoebe never came.

He'd known it the moment she was late. Just knew it somehow. But he couldn't bring himself to leave. Just in case.

Atlas pressed the heels of his palms against his burning eyes. His muscles screamed from sitting on cold stone all night, and despite the relatively warm temperature, a bone-deep chill had settled into him.

He'd been so damn excited to see her. So sure she would come. Their plan had seemed perfect, using "contamination" as their escape hatch.

It had seemed ridiculous when he first thought of it,

but also brilliant. A way to force Dr. Basu's hand while giving them both what they wanted.

Freedom.

Each other.

And the idea of being that close to Phoebe … his heart had pounded just thinking about it.

But she'd changed her mind.

Why?

Maybe she'd been offended by his clumsy suggestion. Who leads with "contamination"? Stupid. What girl wants to be referred to that way? He'd thought she could tell he was being sarcastic.

Or maybe she'd decided a Naturalist wasn't worth the trouble. Someone raised on beliefs she found primitive and superstitious. Someone who couldn't see the world through her scientific lens.

His mind kept circling back to their argument. The flash in her eyes when he'd suggested she become a Naturalist. The disgust in her voice when she'd called it an "anti-science cult." The hurt in her face when he hadn't denied it.

Atlas pushed himself to his feet. The colony would be waking soon. His absence would be noticed. And what would he say? That he'd spent the night in the ruins waiting for a girl who never showed up? A girl who belonged to the other side of a divide neither of them could cross?

Lovelorn fool.

Anger flickered in him. He wished Phoebe didn't dislike the Naturalists so much. After all, who was she to judge him? To judge his people? The Naturalists had survived for two decades against impossible odds. They'd carved out an existence based on faith and discipline while the Vitruvians modified themselves into something that wasn't fully human anymore.

And Phoebe had been the first.

Patient zero for the contamination.

Of course she would defend what her mother had done. Of course she would see genetic manipulation as progress rather than a dangerous path toward losing humanity's essence. Of course she'd defend it to her dying breath.

It was the very thing that had given her life.

Atlas kicked a loose stone, sending it skittering across the ruins with a sharp clatter. If Phoebe couldn't respect what he believed or understand the weight of the responsibility he carried, maybe it was better this way. Better to find out now, before he betrayed his people, his mother, and his calling.

Maybe he should just shut up, fall in line, and marry Hyacinth like a good little Divine Blueprint.

Atlas winced.

Stop it.

He slammed his fist against his thigh hard enough to bruise. He was being an idiot. Phoebe wouldn't just ghost him without explanation. She must've been caught sneaking out. Samara probably grounded her, confiscated her comm so she couldn't send a message. Phoebe took communication seriously. No way she'd leave him hanging without good reason.

The exhaustion plowed into him. Twenty-four hours without sleep was making him paranoid and nasty. He needed to get home, check his comm for messages. Stupid move not to bring it, but getting caught with Vitruvian tech would've been a one-way ticket to Dr. Basu's special brand of "spiritual guidance."

And now that she knew about the greenhouse door, he had to assume she'd be waiting at it when he returned.

He made his way back to the colony, slipping through his secret entrance just minutes before shift started. The greenhouse should've been empty, silent except for the soft hum of ventilation systems. Instead, he found someone waiting for him.

Hyacinth, standing by one of the tool shelves with her arms crossed, looking annoyed. Like she'd caught him smuggling contraband across the border. And had been rehearing this confrontation all night.

"What are you doing here?" Atlas asked.

She held up Phoebe's comm.

Atlas felt as if someone had punched him in the stomach.

"Where did you get that?" He could barely ask, his mouth suddenly dry.

"Where do you think?"

"You went through my things?" Atlas lunged forward, blood rushing to his face, hands clenching into fists. "You had no right—"

"I had every right." Her voice cracked. "We're to be married in days, Atlas. You pledged yourself to me before the community, before the Divine."

"No, *I* didn't. Dr. Basu and my mother did that. Not me."

"It's the same thing. How could you be unfaithful to me and our children?"

"Unfaithful?" A bark of laughter. This was all so absurd. Twisted. How could he be unfaithful to a commitment he'd never freely made?

"What's so funny?" Her face flushed. "You think betraying me is amusing?"

"I betrayed you? *You* went into my room. *You* searched

my belongings. *You* invaded my privacy." He held out his hand. "Give it to me."

"No."

He wiggled his fingers. "Hyacinth."

She stepped back, holding the comm out of reach. "Should I read your messages to the whole colony? I'm sure they'd like to hear what you've been saying to that Vitruvian trash. 'Want to have sex? Hyacinth will never marry me because I'll be CONTAMINATED BY YOU (SORRY!).'"

"Go ahead," Atlas said with a nod.

"What?" Her jaw dropped, eyes widening in genuine shock, as if unable to believe he'd openly defy her.

"Go ahead and tell everyone. I'll call the wedding off. Who will you marry then?" He stepped forward, keeping his voice low. "You've spent your whole life preparing to be my wife, the mother of the Divine Blueprint's children. What does your future look like without that?"

"You wouldn't dare."

"Wouldn't I?" He glared at her. "If you want to marry me, you'll keep those messages private."

"I want to despise you," she whispered, her voice breaking like thin ice under too much weight.

His shoulders slumped, the fight draining out of him like water through a cracked vessel. "I know."

"But I don't." Tears welled in her eyes. "Isn't that pathetic?"

What could he say? That he was sorry, even though he wasn't. That he wished things were different? He didn't.

"Aren't you going to say anything?" she asked.

"No."

She raised her chin. "Just so you know, Atlas Shan. That girl will never love you as much as I do. *Never.*"

She spun on her heel and stormed out of the greenhouse, chin high and back rigid, clutching the comm in her white-knuckled grip like a trophy of war.

Atlas leaned against the closest shelf.

He should've hidden the comm better. But no, that wasn't the point. She'd invaded his personal space, rifled through his belongings like she owned them. Like she owned him.

This wasn't about security measures. This was about Hyacinth believing she was entitled to every piece of him: his thoughts, his choices, his desires, his future.

Now she knew.

And everything was going to be harder because of it. He left the greenhouse through his secret door.

No point in going home. The damage was already done there.

He ran all the way uphill to the barn instead, then climbed up onto the shed. He lay flat on the roof so that no one could see him. The sun was fully risen now, bathing the landscape in violet-tinged light.

He'd threatened Dr. Basu to take his own life. He hadn't meant it then; they were just desperate words to make Dr. Basu back off. But now the thought kept circling like a vulture. Was he really going to surrender to this sham of a marriage? Once he did, his life would never again be his own. And Hyacinth really would own him.

He squeezed his eyes shut tight enough to see sparks.

Why didn't you come? The words formed in his mind, aimed at Phoebe like a prayer without a deity. But she would never receive it.

And with his comm gone, he'd never receive hers.

Chapter Thirty-One

Samara ground her knuckles against her eyelids, feeling grit like sandpaper beneath them. She blinked at the centrifuge, frowning. She'd already extracted RNA from this batch of mosquitoes. Hadn't she?

She glanced at the chronometer on the lab wall and did a double take. That couldn't be right. She could've sworn she'd checked it moments ago, and it had shown a time three hours earlier.

She really was starting to push herself beyond her limits.

Rows of star mosquito specimens lay dissected on trays before her, their iridescent bodies split open, fluids already extracted and separated for analysis.

"You've been at this for nineteen hours straight," Lucas said from behind her.

Samara kept her eyes fixed on the specimen tray. She hadn't heard him enter, but Lucas could move like a ghost when he wanted to. "I'm fine."

"Your cognitive efficiency has decreased by approximately twenty-seven percent in the last four hours alone."

She stiffened and looked over at him. "Help me set up the final confirmation test. I've already configured the PCR. I just need to be certain."

Lucas retrieved the viral concentrate from cold storage, handling the vial with economical movements.

Samara took the vial from him and loaded the samples into the machine. "If there's any viral RNA present in the mosquito saliva this will tell us."

"You may want to run the protein assay in parallel." He nodded at the spectrophotometer. "It'll confirm the presence of the protein markers directly."

Samara frowned at him. "I was just going to suggest that."

But she hadn't thought of it at all. Her mind was starting to skip tracks like a damaged file.

She added a few drops to the assay tray and slid it into the spectrophotometer. A soft green fluorescence began to appear in seconds: the biochemical markers already binding to known protein structures, lighting up in real time.

Amplification cycles scrolled by on the monitor above the PCR, each line of data narrowing in on whether viral RNA was present.

Samara pulled up a stool and sat while the machines worked. Her legs ached. How long had she been standing? She couldn't remember.

"Twenty-three colonists have reported to the clinic with prion symptoms over the last few hours," Lucas said.

"Any incidents of unusual aggression?"

"Seven documented cases requiring security intervention. A four hundred percent increase over baseline."

Samara rubbed her temples. "We're already too late."

She'd heard rumors. Colonists getting into fights over nothing. A maintenance tech caught tearing apart an air filter because he swore it was whispering insults. A cook who forgot how to use her own stove. A security officer who tried to arrest her reflection, then couldn't remember her own name.

At first, it all sounded like stress. Overwork. Heat. Isolation.

But nobody believed that now.

The PCR ticked through its final amplification cycles, each one narrowing the margin for doubt. The spectrophotometer's readings pulsed right beside it. Fluorescent markers growing steadily brighter as the reaction deepened.

Samara leaned forward, holding her breath.

Please, let it be nothing.

Both machines chimed their completion almost simultaneously and the results appeared on the screens one second from unison.

Her stomach plummeted toward her toes.

Viral RNA: Present. Concentration: High. Prion Markers: Present. Signal Strength: Significant.

Samara stared at the numbers. "The mosquitoes are the vector. They're carrying both the prions and an unidentified virus. Every bite is an infection risk."

"Yes," Lucas said.

Samara closed her eyes. "How many of these insects are out there at the moment? Hundreds? Thousands?"

"In peak summer conditions, a single female star mosquito can lay up to three hundred eggs at a time and up to three thousand eggs in her lifetime, which lasts a few weeks to a month. Given the humidity and temperature this season, we're already at optimal reproductive thresholds. Based on past bloom cycles, the population could scale into the millions in a matter of weeks."

"And each one of those is a risk." Samara exhaled, scratching at the bite on her wrist. "Fantastic."

"And their eggs are nearly impossible to eliminate once laid. Some can survive in dry soil for over a month, hatching as soon as moisture returns. We could clear a whole zone and still miss the next wave."

But they'd all been bitten before. Every summer. Which meant that either the star mosquitoes' ability to carry the prions was new, or the virus was new.

A wave of anger rolled through her. This damn planet was trying to kill them. What did they do to deserve this? Was it punishment for destroying their own planet?

Was it punishment for what she'd done to her own daughter?

She tipped from punishment to despair. This was her fault. Everything was her fault.

Ayesha was right.

And the fact that she could even think that was insane.

"Lucas." Samara looked down at the welt on her wrist and swallowed. "I need you to take a blood sample from me."

"I'll get the syringe," Lucas said, heading to a nearby cabinet.

He had her arm prepped in seconds. Tied the tourniquet. Slid the needle into a vein.

She watched her blood fill the vial.

You're tired.

You've pushed your brain past its limits.

You're fine, you just need sleep.

But she didn't believe it.

She was never going to meet Dante, and maybe he would never even be born, because Renata had been bitten too.

Phoebe was about to become an orphan, unless she died too.

They were all going to die.

"You need to stop panicking," Lucas said.

She glared at him. "I'm not panicking."

He raised his brows. "Your heart rate is elevated. Pupils constricted. Breathing shallow. Cortisol likely spiked."

"Fine, I'm panicking. But you would too."

Lucas inclined his head. "It will take me approximately seventeen minutes to process your sample."

Samara tried to work while she waited. But she could only stare at the rows of dead star mosquitoes on the workbench. Such tiny, dainty creatures. Full of such devastation. It reminded her of Earth's collapse, how the chytrid fungus had seemed insignificant at first, just another pathogen to be studied and contained.

Until it wasn't.

History repeating itself.

Lucas worked methodically, processing her blood sample in silence. Though he moved with his usual efficiency, each second stretched like taffy in Samara's perception. When he finally approached her again, the chronometer confirmed he'd taken exactly seventeen minutes.

Samara looked at him. "Well?"

He reached out and took her hands in his.

Tears filled her eyes. "No. Lucas, no."

"I'm afraid that your blood contains prions."

Her fingers dug into his, like she was drowning and he was her lifeline.

"How long?"

"The concentration suggests early to mid-stage infection."

The confirmation knocked her legs out from under her. She dropped like her bones had suddenly dissolved, and she would have hit the floor if Lucas hadn't caught her, lowering her gently to the ground before crouching beside her.

"How long until critical degradation?" she asked.

He hesitated.

"Lucas, tell me."

"Based on the rate of formation and comparing it to Dr. Callas's progression, I estimate approximately one week."

"One week?"

He nodded.

Seven days.

Samara closed her eyes, leaning her head back against the cupboards. "Phoebe. What about Phoebe?"

"It is possible. Phoebe has most likely been exposed to the same insect population you were."

She opened her eyes and looked up at him, trying to think. But her mind was muddled. "What do we do?"

"Continue with colony-wide testing. We need to identify everyone who's infected and—"

"No, about Phoebe."

"We test her as soon as possible."

Samara nodded. "But then what? There's no cure for prions. No treatment. Nothing. She'll be bitten sooner or later."

"We'll find something."

God, he sounded so confident.

"I'll need your help. Because it's far outside my specialty. Hector really was … We should tell Katherine we've got confirmation that it's the mosquitos."

Her comm unit buzzed against her hip, the sound jarring in the lab's silence.

She pulled it out with trembling fingers and saw Renata's name on the display.

She activated it. "Samara."

"You need to come home," Renata said.

"What's wrong?"

"It's Phoebe. She had a seizure. A bad one."

Samara's blood turned to ice. "I'm coming."

"Phoebe's seizure may be unrelated to the prion infection." Lucas said.

"Or it might be hitting her faster. She's always had neurological issues from the modifications. What if that made her more vulnerable?"

"Go," he said, helping her up. "I'll inform Katherine of your findings."

"Don't tell Katherine about me. Don't tell anyone. Not yet."

"I understand," Lucas nodded.

"Thank you."

What would she do without Lucas? He was her rock. And at least Phoebe would have him when she was gone.

If she wasn't infected herself.

Samara ran.

~

PHOEBE OPENED HER EYES.

Light sliced into her eyes like razor blades. She flinched, turning away from the window with a groan. Her entire body felt like she'd been tossed into a rock tumbler; she was bruised and battered in places she didn't know could hurt.

She raised a hand to the back of her skull and found a tender lump.

Small bruises peppered her arms and legs.

What the hell had happened to her?

She'd been defending Flutter. The boys had been threatening her. And then … nothing. Just darkness punctuated by flashes of overwhelming sensation. Shaking.

A seizure.

She'd had a seizure.

In all her years of migraines, some that left her curled in the dark for days, Phoebe had never seized before. What did that mean? Was she getting worse? Was this another symptom of the off-target effects from her genetic modifications?

Was she dying?

"You're awake."

She jumped, then turned, opening her eyes to see Renata sitting in a chair beside the bed, looking tired but relieved.

"What time is it?"

"Just past nine." Renata pushed herself up from the chair and crossed to the desk where a pitcher of water waited. She raised her eyebrows in silent question.

Phoebe nodded.

Renata poured out a glass, then walked over and helped Phoebe to sit up. "Small sips."

The water was cool against her parched throat. Phoebe hadn't realized how thirsty she was until the first drop touched her tongue.

"The boys brought you back. They were pretty shaken up. Said you just … collapsed."

Phoebe's mouth twisted into a bitter line, anger flaring despite her exhaustion. "After they attacked Flutter."

Renata raised an eyebrow. "They didn't mention anything about that."

"I bet they didn't."

"What was she doing so close to the colony?"

"She came to bring me fruit," Phoebe said, her voice catching. "My favorite. And they attacked her."

"I'm sorry, Phoebe."

She sniffed. "Where's Mom?"

"She left about an hour ago. She was with you all night."

Phoebe blinked. "All night?"

"Slept in this very chair. Refused to leave your side." Renata gestured to Phoebe's arm.

She glanced down. There was a small bandage on her skin.

"She didn't want to leave until you woke up, but she needed to take a blood sample and see if she could find out what caused the seizure."

"Of course, she did." The science always came first.

If she'd been unconscious all night, she'd completely missed meeting Atlas. Her stomach twisted at the thought. He must be furious, thinking she'd stood him up deliberately after everything they'd planned.

"I'll get you some soup," Renata offered.

"Thanks," Phoebe sank back into the pillows.

As soon as the door closed, Phoebe reached under her pillow, feeling for her comm. Nothing. Atlas hadn't sent her a single message.

That was worse than a bunch of messages asking where she was.

He must be angry at her.

She typed out, *I'm so sorry. I had a seizure yesterday. First one ever. Couldn't message you. Wasn't conscious.*

Then she hit send.

And then she wrote another. *I wanted to be there. I still want to see you.*

She stared at the screen, willing it to light up with his reply, but nothing came.

She sent one more. *Our plan can still work if you want to.*

Maybe it was the seizure messing with her head. But she couldn't shake the horrible feeling that he'd given up on her completely. She tucked the comm back under her pillow and closed her eyes.

This time, she let the tears come.

Chapter Thirty-Two

No prions.

Samara stared at the results on her screen, blinking hard to make sure her exhausted eyes weren't deceiving her.

"It's negative," Lucas said.

"Are you sure?"

Lucas placed a hand on her shoulder. "I am certain. Phoebe isn't sick."

Samara felt as though all the oxygen had been sucked out of the lab in a single collective breath. She gripped the edge of her workstation to keep herself upright.

Phoebe was safe.

"After her seizure, I was so sure that …"

"I know."

Samara turned and wrapped her arms around Lucas, pressing her forehead against his chest. For a moment he stood still, then his arms encircled her.

"Thank you," she said into his shirt. "For helping with the samples. For keeping me calm. For looking after her, after I—"

"We're not at that stage yet."

Samara pulled away, wiping her eyes. "I know."

But we will be.

"Let's continue." He patted her back. "The sequencer is ready."

Samara nodded.

They had taken blood samples from everyone in the Vitruvian settlement and were now in the process of isolating the infected. Next up were the samples that Lucas had collected from Levi and Dakota.

Samara pulled herself together. She didn't have time to fall apart and question her own mortality. Not with so much left to do.

So she did what she always did: she worked.

Mind pointed forward, not inward.

Lucas slid the first plate into place and then Samara initiated the scanning sequence, watching as the machine began separating and analyzing the blood components.

The results appeared on screen faster than she expected, data streaming across the display in crisp digital readouts.

Samara squinted. "I'm not seeing—"

"Look at these proteins." Lucas pointed to the monitor.

She'd never seen anything like them. "Did the virus mutate and start making a different type of prion?"

"When I couldn't find anything like them in the literature, I searched the ship's archives, including my previous memory backups," he said. "They are a side-effect of the longevity treatments that Hofstadter applied to the Hyperion colonists. The therapy was designed to give the first colonists near-immortality by sustaining telomeres, but over time, a side effect emerged. The altered proteostasis environment made certain proteins prone to misfolding into infectious prion-like conformations by degrading their chaperone proteins."

"Do you think…" Samara's brain was barely working, but she forced the thought to complete. "Could they have been transferred by the mosquitoes?"

"I've also taken a number of blood samples from star mosquitoes captured in the traps."

"When did you do that?" Dumb question, what difference does it make. "Are those proteins in the blood samples?"

"No, but they're all carrying a variant of a virus that Renata previously identified as innocuous, and when I sequenced that virus—"

"You sequenced it already?"

Lucas smiled gently at her, and she realized that her deterioration must have progressed even farther than she'd been aware, because the only way she could read that smile was as *patronizing*.

"I believe that this version of the virus mutated in the bodies of the original colonists during their captivity, attacking the telomeric cellular machinery that had been modified for longevity and corrupted the protein-folding process, transforming that protective mechanism into prion factories."

She stared at him, struggling to parse what he'd just said. "But we didn't get the longevity treatments."

"The virus transfers the instructions for making the corrupted proteins into the new host, and your cells start making them, much like old mRNA vaccines did back on Earth."

Right. That should've been obvious. It would've been, before she'd been infected. She forced herself to focus. "You know the virus, so you can make a vaccine."

"I have already begun the process," Lucas said. "We should inform Katherine."

Samara nodded, reaching for her comm. She could at least do that. But when she tried to formulate a message, the explanation of how it fit eluded her, so she simply typed *vaccine soon.*

"You should rest," Lucas told her when she returned to the lab bench. "I will have the first batch of vaccines ready in forty-eight hours."

Samara clenched her jaw so hard she could hear her teeth grinding. "Lucas, I'm afraid if I stop, I won't start again."

"The vaccine will stop the production of prions, but we still need a way to remove the prion build-up from the brain." Lucas straightened. "Why don't you run a litera-ture search on treatments for prion diseases while I start synthesizing the vaccine?"

"Already did that."

"Perhaps there's something you missed."

She recognized the tactic; Lucas was giving her the less physically demanding work. But looking at her trembling hands, maybe he had a point. If she did discover some-thing in the archives, it could save more lives than her fumbling attempts at lab work right now.

And if she couldn't find a way to get rid of the prions that had already accumulated, she was going to be like this until she died.

"Alright."

Samara shuffled into the small office at the back of the lab and collapsed into the creaking chair. She accessed the colony's medical database, scrolling through thousands of archived research papers and clinical studies from Earth. Most were decades old, dating back to before the chytrid apocalypse, but they represented humanity's accumulated knowledge on prions. Scientists had studied them for generations, yet in all that time, no one had ever discovered how to get rid of them once they formed.

The discovery of the longevity proteins should have felt like a victory. But the damage was already done for those infected. The prions would always be in their brains rewriting neural pathways, twisting proteins into lethal shapes. There was no undo button, no mechanism in the human body to untangle them.

Samara pressed her fingertips against her temples. Even if she'd been at peak mental capacity, this might be an unsolvable puzzle. And she was nowhere near her best now. The fog was getting thicker. Lapses in concentration, difficulty recalling specific terms, moments where she'd blink and realize she'd been staring at the same paragraph for minutes without comprehending it.

She was running on borrowed time.

Even if they found a way to slow it, she would never be the same.

And neither would anyone else who was infected.

If they couldn't break down the prions already forming, then the infected, herself included, were facing a slow decline. Something worse than instant death: a steady unraveling.

Samara would lose herself, piece by piece.

She swallowed hard, forcing herself to keep reading. There had to be something. A new angle, an old study she hadn't read carefully enough, an experiment that had been dismissed too soon.

Because if there wasn't …

She didn't let herself finish the thought. She clicked to the next file, kept searching, taking notes. Organizing drugs by mechanism and potential benefit.

Quetiapine. Antipsychotic. Reduces hallucinations in prion-infected patients.

She frowned, scanning the inventory records. It wasn't in the colony's stores. Too obscure, not prioritized for the mission.

She moved to the next entry. *Acetylcholinesterase inhibitors.* They had a similar effect on hallucinations, working through a different pathway. She checked their supplies: limited, but available. That went on the *possible* list.

And then there was Chlorpromazine. Another antipsychotic, but this one seems to actually slow down the misfolding of proteins in some cases. There was only a small supply, reserved for psychiatric emergencies, but the drug could be synthesized from precursors in their chemical stocks.

The list grew: benzodiazepines for reducing the mental agitation that had characterized Hector's final days; clonazepam specifically for controlling the tremors that would eventually make even simple tasks impossible; sodium valproate as an alternative if the clonazepam proved insufficient.

After a couple of hours, Samara leaned back, surveying her work. None of these were cures. At best, they were bandages on a fatal wound, ways to temporarily stem the tide of symptoms while the underlying disease continued its inexorable progression.

Combined with the cocktail of astemizole and terfenadine that had briefly restored lucidity for Levi and Dakota, some of these new drugs might extend her functional time by weeks, or if she was lucky, months.

It would give her more time with Phoebe, and that was all that really mattered.

What a strange concept.

Wanting more time not to fix things, but to say goodbye.

Was that the prions talking?

Samara might not want to rest, but she wanted to see her daughter. Maybe Lucas was right and she should go home.

She hauled herself upright and went to find Lucas, laying out her notes on the counter between them. "I've compiled a neurostabilizer cocktail combining these compounds. It's not a cure - we'd just be managing symptoms, slowing the progression. But it would buy us time to hunt for a real solution." She rubbed her eyes. "Although time is the one thing I don't have enough of."

"We will have enough," Lucas said.

"I wish I had your confidence."

He squeezed her arm, just enough pressure to feel comforting. She guessed he'd been working on his ability to simulate compassion.

"I'm going to head home to see Phoebe. Are you good to monitor the initial production run alone?"

Lucas nodded.

She rolled her eyes. "Alright. I'm going. I'll stop by Katherine's and let her know we have a plan."

"Very well."

She stripped off her protective gear, methodically working through the safety protocols that were second nature after years in the lab. After smearing repellent over every inch of exposed skin, she left the lab and headed for Katherine's residence, a modest structure near the colony's center distinguished only by the small communications array mounted on its roof.

Samara knocked.

Katherine opened the door, looking as exhausted as Samara felt. "Come in."

Samara followed her into a small sitting area, taking the offered chair. "Lucas is synthesizing the first batch of vaccines, and I may have found a cocktail of treatments that can reduce symptoms for those of us who've got prion build-up."

Katherine frowned. "But you don't look happy about it."

"I'm infected."

Katherine dropped onto a chair. "Are you sure?"

She nodded. "Lucas ran three tests."

"And Phoebe?"

Samara shook her head. "Not infected."

"Jesus, Samara. I'm sorry."

"Thanks. I just thought I should tell you in case I start accusing you of moving the nitrile gloves."

Katherine gave a half laugh. "Does anyone else know?"

"Lucas."

Katherine nodded. "Are you going back to the lab?"

She shook her head. "No. Thought I'd go home and see Phoebe. Lucas is working on a vaccine."

"Good. Because you look like you're about to collapse. Thank you, Samara, for telling me."

She managed a weak smile and stumbled toward the door. She was glad Katherine didn't fuss about her diagnosis. She's not sure she would have been able to handle that. Not that Katherine ever fussed over anyone.

By the time she reached home, the stars were punching holes through the velvet darkness. The house was quiet, the main lights dimmed.

Samara was disappointed. Phoebe must already be asleep.

She headed for the bedroom, only to hear crying in the

kitchen, where she found Renata at the table nursing a cold cup of tea, her face streaked with tears.

Samara froze in the doorway, her stomach dropping. "Renata. What's wrong?"

Renata looked up, her eyes red-rimmed and swollen. "Marcus never came home from his shift. When I checked with the other miners, they said he never showed up. They assumed he was at home. Sick."

Samara's felt ice crawl down her spine. "When did you last see him?"

"This morning." Renata's hand trembled and she pushed her cup away. "We had a fight. A big one. I messed up. Told him what you'd said about the first generation Hyperionites not being the original colonists, but clones. He got so angry, so …incoherent. Then he just stormed out."

"Incoherent?"

Renata nodded.

Prions. The behavioral changes, the confusion, the anger. The signs had been there in Marcus, but Samara had missed them. Most likely because she wasn't working at full capacity herself.

"He's sick. Infected with the same virus that affected Hector."

Renata's face crumpled. "What?"

Samara pulled her into a hug. "We'll find him. Lucas is in the lab right now developing a vaccine. And I've been working on a potential treatment that should help slow the progression of the disease."

"But no cure."

Samara couldn't lie. "Not yet."

"I can't lose him."

Samara held her tighter. "Well, I'm not giving up. Are you?"

"No."

"Come on, let's get you to bed."

Renata nodded.

Samara glanced out the window into the darkness. Somewhere out there, Marcus was wandering alone, his mind unraveling like corrupted code.

BY THE NEXT MORNING, the crippling pain from Phoebe's seizure had now faded to a dull ache, like she'd fallen down a hill instead of been run over by the colony's transport vehicle. But at least her head no longer felt like it was being split open from the inside.

She swung her legs over the side of the bed, listening to the sounds of the house. She couldn't hear any voices or footsteps. Only the faint hum of the home's climate control system. She got out of bed and entered the main hallway. Renata's door was closed. She must be resting.

Samara was probably back at the lab. And who knew where Marcus was. He hadn't come home for dinner last night. Renata had tried to hide how upset she was, so Phoebe hadn't asked, for fear that the answer would also upset the twins.

She smeared Leila's repellent all over her face and hands before going outside. No way was she staying cooped up inside all day. She'd go see Lucas and find out whether he'd managed to create the treatment based on Atlas' mutations.

But she spied a trio of security guards with rifles running toward the fields.

Where were they going?

Another ran past her, speaking into his comm. "Hypers. Big group by the ridge."

Phoebe stopped dead in her tracks, her brain locked in a sudden panic circuit.

Was it Flutter again?

She sprinted after him, ignoring the stiffness in her muscles. When she reached the settlement's edge, she spotted nearly fifty Hyperionites standing along the ridge, their scaled bodies forming a living barrier against the horizon, iridescent in the morning light.

One of the guards raised his comm unit to his mouth. "This is Guerra at the eastern perimeter. Send everyone who can shoot a gun. Now."

"What?" Phoebe said. "No, wait—"

A tall Hyperionite had separated from the group and started walking down the hill toward them. Guerra tensed, raising his rifle, tracking the Hyperionite's movements. "Stay back."

Phoebe bolted forward, getting between the weapon and the Hyperionite.

One of the other guards lunged to grab her arm. "Get back!"

But she spun away, slipping past him with a sharp pivot. His fingers grazed the edge of her sleeve. He almost caught her, but then she was gone.

"Stop her!" Guerra shouted.

Another guard lunged, his fingers closing around her wrist like a vise.

Phoebe twisted violently, dropping her weight and yanking sideways. The sudden move threw them both off balance; he stumbled backward, she pitched forward onto her hands and knees.

She scrambled up, ignoring the sting of fresh scrapes, and bolted up the path, heart hammering, the shouts of the guards blending into a single roar behind her.

The Hyperionite kept walking. Calm. Steady. Watching.

Phoebe signed, "Stop! Go back! Danger!"

The Hyperionite halted, tilting her head as she assessed Phoebe. "One of our people was attacked when they brought a gift. Why?"

"Flutter."

"Yes."

"I'm sorry," Phoebe signed. "It was a mistake. Some people are scared because of sickness. I don't want you to get hurt. So please, don't come closer right now."

"Return our Elders," the Hyperionite signed. "You are not our friends."

Phoebe felt a jolt of disbelief. *What?*

Not their friends?

But Flutter was her *best* friend. And now, just like that, those boys had erased all the trust that had been established between Hypers and Vitruvians.

"The Elders are sick," Phoebe signed. "They're receiving treatment. They might die if they leave now."

The Hyperionite's spine straightened, and her eyes hardened. "Bring them out or we take them."

Phoebe's throat constricted, suddenly bone-dry.

"Wait here," she signed. "I'll help."

The Hyperionite nodded.

Phoebe turned and made her way back down to where the guards had formed a defensive line behind her. More colonists were arriving, many holding weapons.

She approached Guerra. "They're not here to fight. They just want the patients from quarantine. Their Elders."

The guard scowled. "And?"

"They won't leave without them. There are more of

them in the hills than you can see. Please, contact Katherine."

Guerra hesitated. Glanced at his partners. One of them shrugged. Then he muttered something under his breath and stepped away, pulling out his comm.

Phoebe kept herself between the soldiers and the Hyperionites, her heart pounding as she fixed her gaze on the ridge where the Hyperionites remained motionless.

A minute later, the guard returned, his mouth pinched and eyes disapproving. "Tell them Katherine says we'll deliver the patients to the Hyperionite settlement tomorrow, but they need to leave. Now."

Relief flooded her veins. "Thank you."

Then she turned and ran back up the path to the waiting Hyperionite.

"Katherine says the Elders will be returned to you tomorrow," Phoebe signed. "They need to be stabilized before transport, or they will die before they get to your village."

The Hyperionite studied her with an unreadable expression. "If the New People break their promise—"

"We won't," Phoebe signed. "I swear."

The Hyperionite turned and walked back up the ridge. One by one, the others followed, melting into the mountains until the ridge was empty.

Only then did Phoebe turn around and head back down the ridge.

The soldiers weren't dispersing, weapons still ready. All she could do was hope they wouldn't follow the Hyperionites into the mountains. She headed straight for the clinic, pushing through the entrance doors and finding Samara with Leila in the corridor, their heads bent in what looked like a funeral conversation.

"Mom!"

Samara jerked upright. "Phoebe. What's wrong? Do you feel sick?"

"It's the Hyperionites," she gasped, struggling to catch their breath. "They came for the Elders. Katherine just promised we'd return them tomorrow. Please tell me they're well enough to travel."

Samara's shoulders slumped. "I'm sorry, Phoebe. The Elders are dead. Both of them. They passed about an hour ago. Within minutes of one another."

"What?" The blood drained from Phoebe's face. "But… Katherine just … did she know?"

Leila shook her head. "We were just about to inform her."

"Phoebe, I'm sure they'll understand," Samara said.

Phoebe blinked back tears, looking at her mother. She was a smart woman, but she was wrong about this.

Chapter Thirty-Three

AYESHA STARED at the comm on her desk.

She'd been ignoring Katherine's calls for the past day, unwilling to hear more excuses. Or orders. Her temples throbbed with the beginnings of what promised to be a vicious headache.

When the comm chirped again, she nearly silenced it until she saw the identification code was Leila's, not Katherine's.

Ayesha hesitated, then pressed the receive button.

"Please don't hang up," Leila said.

"What do you want?" Ayesha's voice cut like a scalpel. "I have a colony to manage."

"It's about the illness. We've figured it out. It's a virus carried by the star mosquitoes and we've developed a vaccine."

"Alright."

Leila's breath caught audibly before she continued, her voice tighter than before. "We felt you should know. Katherine has been trying to reach you to—"

"The hell with Katherine." Ayesha's fingers tightened on the comm. "And your genetically engineered vaccine."

The comm connection crackled with tense, weighted silence.

"Ayesha, please listen. The virus causes the brain to make prions which damage the neural tissue. And once they form, there's no way to fix them."

"So?"

"So, without the vaccine, anyone infected will slowly go insane. Once you've caught the virus, it can't be cured. Only slowed. Hector is already dead. And we're racing against time to prevent more deaths."

Ayesha sat back in her chair, the walls of her office seeming to simultaneously expand and contract around her, reality bending under the weight of this revelation. "So what you're really saying is that your vaccine is our only choice. If we don't accept it, we'll die."

"I know how it sounds," Leila said, her tone softening. "And I know you don't trust Katherine right now, and you're right, we should have told you what was happening sooner. But we only just—"

"Katherine was worried about her position and nothing more. I've learned to expect no less from her."

"But you know me, Ayesha," Leila said. "You know I don't have any power to hold onto. I just want everyone to survive. Your people and ours. We can't contain this disease. If someone gets bitten by an infected mosquito … the vaccine is the only chance."

Ayesha tightened her jaw. "It's awfully convenient that the only 'cure' for the disease your people unleashed on us is the very abomination you've been trying to force on us from the beginning. You couldn't break us by controlling our access to tools and resources, so you've manufactured another way to force your genetic manipulations on us."

"That's not true. This isn't some conspiracy. You're dooming your people by being stubborn."

"It's all part of the divine plan. Enough will survive."

Leila let out a slow breath, as if trying to stay patient. "You've used our medicine before, Ayesha. You let us send antibiotics when your people were sick. You take immuno-suppressants and antifungals on a regular basis. What makes this different?"

"Those things heal. Your vaccine doesn't heal, it alters. You created this thing because you want to rewrite what we are."

"Jesus, Ayesha. We didn't create this."

"Then where did it come from?"

Leila exhaled. "We found two of the original Hyperion colonists in the caves. They had the disease. When they emerged from the cave, they brought it with them."

Ayesha narrowed her eyes to slits of suspicion. "So you're saying the Hyperionites created it."

"No! They were already infected. The mosquitoes bit them and became carriers."

Ayesha laughed. "Right. Convenient."

"Why would we lie about this? You think this is part of some grand plan?"

Ayesha's fingers found her prayer beads, the smooth surfaces cool against her skin as she worked them methodi-cally. "I think you've always wanted to prove us wrong. You want to show that survival without your science is impossi-ble. That we have no choice but to bend the knee."

"Ayesha, please. I'm trying to save your people's lives."

"At what cost?" Her voice hardened. "We will become something else if I allow this to happen. A different people, made in *your* image. You think that's saving us? That's erasing us."

Leila's composure finally shattered, her voice rising

with desperate intensity. "They should at least be allowed to choose for themselves."

Ayesha closed her eyes for a long moment before finally exhaling. "Desperation isn't free will. It's fear. And fear makes people look for easy answers. Salvation to-go. I won't let panic drive us into the arms of someone else's solution. That's not choice. That's surrender. Besides, we already have our own path."

"And what is that?"

"Prayer."

"Prayer?" Leila repeated.

"Better to die human than to live as monsters." Ayesha rubbed the beads against her cheek.

"You can't believe—"

Ayesha killed the connection.

~

ATLAS PICKED AT HIS FOOD.

He couldn't remember the last time he'd had an appetite. He'd been living in a state of anxiety ever since Hyacinth took his comm. Waiting for the moment she exposed him to her mother. His mother. The community.

And then late last night, he had another thought. Had Hyacinth sent a message to Phoebe while pretending to be him?

What if she had said terrible things?

And what if Phoebe thought it was him?

The thought was torture. He'd nearly bolted for the Vitruvian colony under cover of darkness, desperate to explain. Only one thing had stopped him: he had no idea where Phoebe lived. What was his plan? To stand in the center of their settlement shouting her name until someone either directed him to her door or shot him?

Neither scenario seemed likely to end well.

The mess hall buzzed with the usual lunch conversations all around him, but today there was an undercurrent of anxiety. Xavier was no longer the only one sick. There were now six new cases.

Rumors circulated that the Vitruvians had deliberately infected them. Atlas knew it wasn't true.

Not because of Phoebe.

But because he was coming to understand the Vitruvians. They had built their entire way of life around the idea of minimizing harm and saving lives. Sure, they imposed their medical philosophies on others, but that was the point. They wanted to save people, whether they wanted saving or not.

Would they deliberately infect a population of people?

No way. Absolutely not.

Atlas knew they weren't capable of that.

Even at their worst, they wanted to heal the world, not burn it down.

"Atlas."

He stiffened at the sound of Hyacinth's voice and turned to find her standing behind him, holding a tray. "Mind if I join you?"

He hesitated, tensing his jaw. The last thing he wanted was another confrontation, especially in the middle of the dining hall. He gestured to the empty space across from him. "Go ahead."

Hyacinth smiled as she set the tray on the table and sat.

"You're not eating." She slid a glass of wheat grass juice his way. "I thought you might prefer something to drink."

"I'm not hungry. Or thirsty."

"It'll make you feel better." She speared a cluster of

vegetables, bringing the fork to her mouth without breaking eye contact.

Atlas didn't move.

What was she up to?

She was acting like their greenhouse confrontation had never happened, like she hadn't discovered his secret, stolen his comm, threatened to expose him. He kept waiting for her calm facade to crack, for the vengeful fury to surface. Instead, she offered another manufactured smile.

"Why haven't you told anyone?" Atlas asked.

"About?"

He frowned. "You know exactly what I'm talking about."

Hyacinth took a delicate spoonful of stew. "I've been praying. Seeking spiritual guidance about how to proceed with you."

He almost laughed.

What she meant was that she'd spent days calculating exactly how to leverage his relationship with Phoebe for maximum control.

"And?"

She chewed and swallowed. "I've decided to forgive you."

Atlas blinked. "Forgive me? For what?"

"Straying."

He set his spoon down. Something in her voice didn't ring true. "I don't believe you."

"It's true."

He decided to test her. "Even though I've had sex with a Dysgenic?"

A lie. But Atlas wanted to see just *how much* she had forgiven him.

The fork paused halfway to Hyacinth's mouth. "I

believe that because I've remained pure, my faith will protect our future children from any contamination you may have picked up from your … companion." Disgust flickered across her face. "The Divine Blueprint wants to proliferate. I'll provide it fertile ground."

It.

She didn't see it as a part of him at all. Just a valuable resource she could harvest, like ore from a mine.

Atlas studied her face. She was trying her best not to be repulsed by him. Which meant this version of Hyacinth was Dr. Basu, speaking through her daughter. "What did she offer you?"

Hyacinth blinked. "Who?"

"Your mother. She must have promised you something to convince you to go forward with the marriage."

Hyacinth gave him a brittle laugh. "I don't need an incentive to do what's right. I want this, Atlas. I want you. I always have. From the time we were children, it's always been you. We were chosen for each other for a reason. Our bond strengthens the colony. It *means* something. You think I need a reward to marry you? You're the Divine Blueprint. You're everything we've been taught to protect. And I intend to do my job."

He rotated the glass slowly between his fingers, watching the green liquid cling to the sides. "You sound like you're trying a little too hard to convince yourself."

Her knuckles went white around the fork, the metal bending slightly under pressure before she caught herself. "Then I guess you'll have to have faith in me."

But her eyes betrayed her. Whatever genuine feelings she might once have harbored for him had burned away in the greenhouse confrontation, replaced by cold calculation. This wasn't devotion; it was a business transaction, with terms no doubt negotiated and approved by her mother.

He downed the shot in a swallow, the bitter taste of wheatgrass coating his tongue. "Uh huh."

She stiffened. "Well, believe me or not. I've asked Mother to move up the wedding date. Our ceremony is in three days."

"Three days?" Atlas set the glass down. "And if I refuse?"

Hyacinth smiled. "You won't."

"I could leave right now. Go and join my *contaminated* girlfriend at the other colony."

Her eyes flashed. "Try it."

He stilled. There was a small, smug smile curling at the edges of her mouth. Like she was one step ahead of him. Like she knew something he didn't.

A slow, creeping unease coiled in his gut. "What did you do, Hyacinth?"

She nodded at the empty glass on his tray, the dregs of green liquid still visible at the bottom. "There was a micro-tracker in your shot. If you try to leave, security will find you and bring you back. I just need to alert them."

Atlas stared at the glass, then back at her. "You're lying. Dr. Basu would never allow that kind of technology here. It goes against everything she preaches."

Hyacinth shrugged. "Try to leave. See what happens."

Her casual certainty was chilling.

"My mother?" Atlas said.

"She knows." Her smile widened. "She agreed."

Atlas stood, placing his palms on the table. He didn't care about making a scene anymore. Not now.

"You just signed up for a life of misery. I'll never love you."

"It doesn't matter. All that matters is the Divine Blueprint."

Atlas laughed. "One person controls the Divine Blueprint. And you know who that is, Hyacinth?"

Hyacinth looked confused. "Mother."

He bared his teeth. "*Me.*"

She flinched.

"You think you've trapped me? You haven't. You think you clipped my wings? They're still whole. You think you put me in prison? Watch me tear through every wall you build before it's even finished. You have no idea what I'm capable of. I still have ultimate control over myself, and I'll exercise it before I let you turn me into your breeding stock."

"You're scaring me, Atlas."

"I hope so. You may have put this tracker in me, but I don't even need to run. Because if you force me to marry you in three days' time, you'll be marrying my corpse."

Her face drained of color. "Atlas."

"The Divine Blueprint will be gone forever. Because I would rather be dead than married to you."

Hyacinth blinked back tears. "Please don't say that."

He headed for the door.

"Atlas, wait." Her voice had lost its certainty.

He stopped, turning around. "What?"

"What if I give you this back?" she reached into her pocket and held out Phoebe's comm.

It took everything in him not to lunge for it. "This some kind of trap?"

"No." She shook her head. "To show my intentions are serious. If I give you this, will you tell Phoebe you're never going to see her again?"

Atlas ignored her question, picking up the comm and dropping it into his pocket on his way out.

Chapter Thirty-Four

SAMARA ROLLED HER NECK, trying to work out the kinks.

The common hall reeked of sweat and anxiety. A cocktail of body odor and fear. Every colonist packed inside was hot, nervous, and more than a little terrified. Not that Samara blamed them.

Katherine had transformed the space into a temporary vaccination clinic. Three folding tables formed a U-shape, loaded with medical equipment and staffed by a rotating crew of volunteers. Med-techs and administrators guided colonists through the process, one terrified face after another.

But everyone still hammered her with questions and explaining prions was a bitch and a half.

The vaccine worked, but only to a point. It stopped the brain from producing new prions and kept the virus from reinfecting anyone, but it couldn't undo what was already there. All the prions that had built up before the shot? They stuck around, still damaging tissue. Interfering with thoughts and behaviors. So no, people wouldn't get worse, but they wouldn't get better either.

They would be frozen at whatever level of confusion, paranoia, mood swings, or impulse control the disease had already caused.

Until she found a way to reverse it. Break down the prions without compromising healthy brain tissue.

If she ever did.

It was like sealing a crack in the dam after the flood had already swept through.

The situation had been discussed ad nauseam in meetings. And yet every single colonist still asked when they sat in the chair to be inoculated.

Not that Samara blamed them.

She was dealing with identical fears.

She tried not to think about it. Focus on the mechanics. Drawing a dose, injecting the vaccine. The skin. The slight resistance. The push. The withdrawal. A rhythm that had become almost meditative in its repetition.

Samara uncapped the syringe and inoculated her next patient. "You'll need to stay in the observation area for thirty minutes." She gestured to the chairs neatly arranged in a row along the far wall. "Just to make sure there's no reaction."

The woman nodded.

Another followed, then a young girl clutching his father's hand, her small face set in a look of forced bravery. She flinched when Samara administered the vaccine but didn't cry.

One by one, the line moved.

Exhaustion was starting to creep in, pressing behind her eyes. She hadn't slept in over a day, and she knew it was starting to show. She'd stopped counting the doses. Stopped seeing individual faces. It had all blurred into a procession of arms and veins, next and next and next.

Phoebe arrived, holding out a bottle of water. "You

look terrible. You're no good to anyone if you collapse in the middle of giving a dose."

Samara smiled. "I know. And when did you start sounding like me?"

Phoebe shrugged. "Don't flatter yourself."

Samara laughed, taking the water bottle and downing it in three desperate gulps. The cold liquid hit her system like a shot of adrenaline. "Thanks."

"You're welcome."

Phoebe took a seat and then rolled up her sleeve.

"You ready?" Samara asked.

Phoebe nodded. "Yeah."

Samara gave her the injection. "All done."

"That's it?"

"That's it." Samara thought she might collapse with relief. Phoebe was safe. She looked up at the next patient. "Renata didn't come with you?"

"No, I haven't seen her all day." Phoebe sighed as she stood. "I'll see you later Mom."

Phoebe's shoulders were hunched, jaw clenched tight enough to crack a walnut. Her earlier smile had vanished, replaced by something brittle and forced.

"Hold on," Samara placed a hand on her arm. "You look upset. What is it?"

"Lucas and I are taking the original colonist's bodies back to the Hyperionites today," Phoebe replied after a beat of hesitation.

"Oh. Right …"

"Don't try to talk me out of it. Katherine ordered me to go, because I can translate."

Samara held up her hands. "I know. I just … forgot. Time's been a bit of a blur lately. Be careful."

Phoebe scowled. "They're my friends. Nothing's changed."

Samara wanted to believe her. She really did. But Phoebe's words had that hollow ring of someone trying to speak a truth into existence through sheer force of will. Still, Samara didn't have the heart to poke holes in her daughter's paper-thin conviction. Not today, when everything else was already falling apart.

At least her escort would be armed, if anything went wrong. Katherine wouldn't send her if things were that tense, would she?

"I'm sorry. You're right. Hug?"

Phoebe rolled her eyes, but she didn't leave so Samara embraced her, holding on for a full moment longer than she meant to. Just enough to remember how small Phoebe had once felt in her arms. To feel how far from small she was now.

After she finally let go, she said, "See you tonight."

"Yeah." And then Phoebe was gone.

Samara turned back to the line, still wondering where Renata was. She'd specifically told Renata that pregnant women and children were first priority for vaccination. But the morning had stretched toward afternoon with no sign of her. The pit in her stomach grew with each passing hour.

"Have you seen Renata?" she asked Leila.

"Not yet."

Samara frowned and returned to her station.

Time crawled by like a wounded animal. Colonist after colonist rolled up their sleeves. The once-crowded common hall emptied in gradual waves, sunlight shifting across the floor as morning melted into the oppressive afternoon heat. Sweat beaded on foreheads and trickled down backs as the ventilation system wheezed and sputtered. And still no Renata.

Samara wiped a hand across her face and felt the grit

of exhaustion settle in her bones. Her hands were starting to cramp.

Samara surveyed the line. It had grown thinner.

She glanced over at Leila. "Would you be alright if I checked on Renata? I can always vaccinate her and the kids at the house. Might be easier."

"Go on," Leila said.

Samara grabbed a vial of the vaccine, packed up four syringes and a fresh pair of gloves. She slipped everything into a medical kit, disposed of her PPE, and headed for the door.

Maybe there was a reason Renata hadn't come. Maybe the search party had found Marcus, who'd vanished three days ago without a trace. They'd combed the surrounding area until Katherine had been forced to pull everyone back for vaccination, the colony operating on a skeleton crew for the most essential functions only.

By the time she reached the house, Samara's shirt was plastered to her back with sweat, lungs burning from the sprint. The place was eerily quiet. The kids were at emergency daycare and Phoebe was still gone. She took the stairs two at a time to check on Renata, but the bedroom stood empty, sheets rumpled and cold.

Where was she?

Samara heard a sound from the kids' room. So she went and opened the door to find Renata standing by the window with her back to Samara, clutching a broom.

"Hey." Samara held up the medical kit. "I've got your dose of the vaccine here."

Renata turned. There was a touch of drool in the corner of her mouth.

"Renata?"

She bared her teeth. "You poisoned him."

"What?"

Renata's accusation sucked the air from her lungs.

"Marcus." Renata's voice cracked. "You poisoned him because you were jealous. And now you're trying to poison me and the baby."

Prions.

"Renata, that's not true." Samara kept her voice level. "Marcus left because he was sick. That's all."

"LIAR!"

Samara swallowed. There had to be a way to reach Renata. It wasn't like they were co-workers. This was the woman she loved. "The prions are affecting your brain chemistry, changing how you see things. Changing how you see me. " She stepped forward, keeping her tone steady. "If you'll just let me give you this, you'll start to feel like yourself again."

"Stay back!" Renata's knuckles whitened around the broom handle. "I know what you're trying to do!"

Samara set the kit on the floor at her feet and raised her hands. "I'm here to help you. That's it. I would never hurt you. Or Marcus. Or the baby."

Renata's eyes darted around the room. Then she swung the broom, chucking it at Samara.

Samara ducked, and the broom sailed over her head, hitting the wall behind her.

Renata knocked the screen from the window and clambered out.

"Renata, no!" Samara lunged for her.

Too late.

Renata tumbled onto the sloped roof, the impact sending loose tiles skittering down to shatter on the ground below. She scrambled backward, crab-walking along the edge, one protective hand pressed against her swollen belly as her feet searched blindly for purchase on the weathered surface.

"Stay away or I'll jump!" she screamed, her voice carrying across the compound. "You're not going to hurt my baby!"

"Renata, please!" Samara held a hand out the window. "Come back inside. It's not safe out there. The roof tiles are loose. You could slip."

The commotion was drawing a crowd now. Colonists emerged from nearby buildings, heads tilted back, hands shielding eyes from the glare as they watched the drama unfolding three stories up.

A ripple of horrified whispers spread through the growing audience.

"I'm not coming down until you leave," Renata spat, inching farther away on the roof, her movements growing more erratic, fingers clawing at the tiles as though they might anchor her against the whirlwind of paranoia sweeping through her mind. "I know what you've done. I know what you're planning."

"Please, come inside," Samara begged, tears burning her eyes. "You're going to get hurt out there."

"*Stay back!*" Renata snarled.

"Why would I hurt the baby? Dante has my DNA, yours and mine. I helped create him. I've been counting the days until he's born."

Something flickered across Renata's face. A momentary fracture in her certainty.

"I want to protect him," Samara pressed on. "That's what this vaccine does. It helps your immune system fight the virus we've both been infected with. The virus that's making you confused right now. I need to protect both of you, Renata. Please let me."

"You're infected too?"

Samara nodded.

"Prove it," Renata demanded. "Give yourself the shot."

"I already did. Earlier at the clinic."

Rage flashed across Renata's face. "Liar! I knew that syringe was full of poison! You want to get rid of me. Just like you did Marcus."

"No, no, no, that's not true at all."

Samara glanced down and spotted Leo, running toward the house with a long ladder balanced on his shoulder. A security guard followed, helping to carry it.

Oh God, if Renata saw them coming, she might panic and jump.

"Okay," Samara said. "If I take another dose, will you believe it's not poison?"

Renata stared at her. "Maybe."

"Let me get the kit." Samara scrambled back to where she'd dropped the kit, snatched it from the floor, and hurried back to the window.

Renata hadn't moved.

Samara opened the kite and pulled out a needle. Then she filled the syringe. "Look. You see?"

Renata didn't respond, still watching.

Samara jabbed the needle into her own arm and depressed the plunger, sending a second dose of the vaccine into her system. The risk of an enhanced immune response was worth it if it would bring Renata down from the roof.

"There," she said, pulling out the needle. "Now will you please come inside?"

Renata still didn't move.

"Renata." Samara was almost in tears. "I love you. I'm happy to share you with Marcus, or with the whole damn colony, if that's what will make you happy. Or if you want me to move out, I will."

"You're just saying that to manipulate me."

"No. I love you. I fell in love with you twenty years ago, when the fungus started killing the livestock. I watched you dissect that cow, and I knew you would do whatever it took to find the truth. It was who you were then, and it's who you are now. A force of nature."

Something flickered in Renata's eyes. Samara prayed it was clarity. "I'm going to leave now. I'll wave to you from the street. Then please come back inside where it's safe. If you never want to see me again, that's fine. Just know I love Dante, and I love Marcus and Iris and Theo. But most of all, I love you."

Renata didn't move.

Samara forced herself to leave the window.

She ran through the house, preparing to hear Renata screaming as she fell. Outside, she spied Leo positioning the ladder against the side of the house.

She ran over to him. "Don't use the ladder. It's too risky."

Leo glanced up at the roof. "What do you want us to do then?"

"Go into the house. She'll come down, now that I'm not there."

Leo looked to the security guard.

The guard nodded.

"Okay," Leo said.

"Wait," Samara turned her back so Renata couldn't see what she was doing and filled a syringe. Then she passed it to him. "You've given plenty of shots to the animals. Renata needs her vaccination. Hold her down if you need to. But get that in her."

Leo took the syringe and put it in his pocket. "I'll take care of it."

Samara turned away, forcing herself to head toward the gathered crowd. Each step felt like trudging through cement. When she reached Katherine, she turned back toward the house, raised her hand, and waved at Renata, heart in her throat.

Renata's gaze locked onto her, but she remained frozen in place.

Katherine's fingers found Samara's, squeezing tight enough to hurt.

Leo appeared in the window. His lips moved, but the distance swallowed his words. Renata glanced at him, her body still rigid with suspicion.

Leo settled into the windowsill, looking for all the world like a man with nowhere more important to be. The seconds stretched into minutes.

Come on, Renata. Get in the house. Please.

Finally, Renata began to move, crawling toward Leo on hands and knees, her progress agonizingly slow.

Thank God.

She had almost reached the window when her foot slipped.

Her body tilted back.

For a single, terrifying second, gravity took her.

She tumbled sideways, arms pinwheeling as she tried to grab something. Her knee slammed against the roof, sending another tile skittering down the slope, crashing onto the ground below.

Samara cried out.

Leo lunged.

His hand snagged the back of Renata's shirt.

She gasped, legs kicking, the weight of her body pulling against his grip.

Leo strained, muscles taut as he locked his other hand onto the frame for leverage.

The security guard appeared, grabbed Leo.

The two of them pulled her back up, inch by inch, slowly dragging her inside.

Katherine turned and pulled her into a hug. "She's safe. She's safe."

Samara nodded against her shoulder, but she couldn't get the image of Renata slipping out of her mind. Those flailing arms, the panic on her face, her body tilting, knees scraping. That horrible *pause* as gravity tried to take her.

Her heart was still racing.

What if Leo hadn't come?

Renata would've fallen.

She'd already be dead.

Katherine patted her back. "She didn't fall. So don't live in what-ifs."

Samara gave a little laugh, pulling back as she wiped her eyes. "You know me too well."

The front door of the house opened.

The security guard came out first, half-dragging, half-carrying a struggling Renata. Leo followed. He caught Samara's eyes and gave her a nod.

Samara exhaled, finally able to breathe again.

Renata thrashed against the guard's hold, a fresh puncture mark visible on her upper arm. Her eyes locked onto Samara's, wild with betrayal and fury.

"TRAITOR!" she shrieked, spittle flying from her lips. "I HATE YOU! I'LL NEVER FORGIVE YOU FOR THIS!"

Katherine squeezed her arm. "I'll get her to quarantine. She'll feel better in the morning."

Samara nodded. Somehow she found herself inside the house, with no memory of walking through the door or shutting it behind her. Her legs buckled, and she slid down the wall until she hit the floor, knees drawn up to her chest.

Only then did the tears come. Silent at first, then

building into something raw and animal that clawed its way up from her chest. She pressed her palm against her mouth, trying to contain the sound as her body shook with ragged breaths.

How long before the prions took Renata completely?

How long before the prions reached Dante, growing in her womb?

Had she gotten to him in time? The placental barrier was a hell of an immunological fortress, but was it enough?

Would Samara even be alive to witness it all? Or would she die first, leaving them to face it alone?

She wasn't sure which was worse.

She only knew one thing for certain.

Phoebe would survive them all.

And that broke her more than anything.

Chapter Thirty-Five

THE TRANSPORT VEHICLE growled over the uneven terrain, its massive treads pulverizing rocks into dust beneath six tons of reinforced steel.

Phoebe sat up front in the passenger seat next to Lucas behind the wheel. The original colonists were sealed in containment units in the back. A matching set of security guards sat with rifles across their laps.

Katherine had deemed the guards' presence necessary, despite Phoebe's protests. Although she had also been explicit that they were not to leave the transport unless Phoebe was in danger or unless Lucas gave them orders to do so.

Phoebe had argued against the armed escort until her throat was raw, but Katherine wouldn't budge. "The Hyperionites are not our enemy," she'd insisted for what felt like the hundredth time.

Lucas kept his eyes on the road ahead, his hands perfectly positioned on the wheel. "No. But this isn't going to feel like a gesture of goodwill either. They held the elders in great esteem. This may be a breaking point in relations with the colony."

"I don't believe that" But Phoebe hadn't seen Flutter since the day she'd been attacked at the Vitruvian colony. Phoebe had asked Lucas to send a message to her, but he had been unable to because of containment protocols. Now, she wished she'd insisted. Or simply gone herself.

Katherine's decision to send Phoebe and Lucas had been strategic, not sentimental. They'd had the most contact with the Hyperionites; they would be familiar faces in a moment when trust would be razor-thin. A calculated diplomatic move masquerading as respect.

But Phoebe would have done whatever she needed to do to be included. She had to see Flutter, to apologize for how the Vitruvian colonists had treated her. Make sure that they were still friends.

And there was something else she needed to do.

The transport crested a hill, approaching the Hyperionite settlement. It sprawled before them, low, wide structures of wood and stone and scavenged scrap metal, both from the ruins of the Hyperion colony and trade with Phoebe's people.

A large assembly of Hyperionites were waiting. At least a dozen blocking the road at the edge of the settlement. Lucas eased the transport to a stop. The engine's low rumble settled into silence, leaving only the soft hiss of cooling systems.

Lucas looked over at her. "Let me do the talking."

Phoebe nodded, her gaze fixed on the Hyperionites.

He unbuckled his seatbelt and opened the transport door.

She followed, her heart beating so loud she was certain everyone could hear it.

The Hyperionite leader stepped forward to meet them. A woman, taller than the others, with more pronounced ridges along her weathered face.

Phoebe stood slightly behind Lucas, noticing how the other Hyperionites had positioned themselves in a semicircle around their leader. Several carried rudimentary weapons: spears tipped with scavenged metal, clubs studded with crystal fragments, knives and slings. A few held cobbled-together devices that Phoebe recognized as salvaged tech, refashioned into what were no doubt defensive tools.

The guards Katherine had sent stood in the back on the transport, but they remained in place.

"The Elders?" the leader signed.

"In the transport," Lucas signed back. "They succumbed to the same illness that they brought with them."

"Dead?"

"With great sorrow, yes. We mourn your loss."

The leader's bony facial ridges flushed a deeper blue as blood rushed beneath the translucent scales.

"Other colonists are sick as well," Lucas signed. "Both Vitruvian and Naturalist."

"Show me the Elders."

Lucas led the leader around to the rear of the truck. Both containment units were covered with floral wreaths. Phoebe's idea, to show respect. She had spent all morning weaving them.

A soft, keening trill escaped the leader's throat, raising the hairs on Phoebe's arms. The other Hyperionites approached and began to vocalize, a chorus of grief that seemed to vibrate in the air.

Phoebe swallowed, her throat tight with unshed tears.

For all the differences between humans and Hyperionites, grief looked the same: bowed heads, trembling hands, slumped shoulders.

The Hyperionite leader raised a hand and then four of her people broke from the group and approached the vehicle. Her expression remained impassive as she watched them collect the units, with only a slight ripple of scales along her neck betraying her emotions.

Two by two, the Hyperionites pulled out the units and began carrying them back toward the settlement.

"New People will stay out of our territory," the leader signed. "Decision will be made soon."

Phoebe frowned. "A decision about what?"

The Hyperionite leader turned to her, dark eyes narrowing.

She didn't answer, only studied her for a long, uncomfortable moment before returning her attention to Lucas. "Understood?"

"The New People's leader respectfully requests a meeting to discuss a treaty," Lucas signed.

The sound of engines came from beyond the ridge before she could answer: a high-pitched whine of dirt bikes pushed to their limits.

Two figures crested the hill, running full tilt from the south.

Hyperionite boys.

Their scaled skin glistened with sweat, streaked with dirt and blood. One of them — Poke — stumbled as he tore down the slope, his arms pumping wildly. The younger boy was barely keeping up, his short legs struggling on the uneven terrain.

A trio of modified dirt bikes roared behind them, zigzagging across the hillside, kicking up clouds of dust as the riders cut wide loops around the young Hypers, hemming them in like trapped animals. The lead rider, a man with a ragged bandana covering his face, revved his engine and surged ahead, then yanked the front wheel up.

Phoebe could hear the men on the bikes laughing.

One of the riders cut hard to the left, then swung back in, making a deliberate pass close enough to send a spray of dirt flying in Poke's face. He flinched but kept running.

The younger boy couldn't keep up.

He tripped.

Fell.

Phoebe's stomach lurched.

Poke skidded to a stop, turning around to run back.

Too late.

The lead rider gunned the throttle.

His bike sped toward the fallen boy.

A sharp, high-pitched whine split the air.

Then a streak of blue light sliced towards the biker, hitting him square in the chest.

For a split second, nothing happened.

Then the man's entire body convulsed.

His bike seized beneath him, the tires locking up like the air around him had turned solid. A pulse of energy rippled outward, and the next thing Phoebe knew, the man flew backward, his bike flipping end-over-end as if an invisible force had wrenched it into the air.

The man hit the ground hard, rolling into a limp heap as his bike crashed a few yards away.

Phoebe stared at the Hyperionite holding the tech.

What the hell kind of weapon was that?

The other two bikers howled with rage, completely forgetting about Poke and the boy. They changed direction, tires digging into the dirt as they sped toward the Hyper who had fired the weapon.

They were going to run him down.

"Move!" Phoebe screamed.

But he stood his ground.

Lucas didn't.

He ran.

Faster than should have been possible, closing the distance between himself and the first bike, grabbing it by the handlebars, lifting it up into the air.

Then he tossed it. Both bike and rider. Like he was throwing away garbage.

The bike twisted as it spun out of control, the colonist screaming at the loss of control. He landed hard. The bike slammed into the ground a split-second later, smoke curling from its mangled frame.

Lucas turned toward the last rider. The biker tried to veer away. Too late.

Lucas lashed out with terrifying precision, his arm slicing through the air like a steel whip. The impact was brutal. His forearm slammed into the rider's chest, clothes-lining him straight off the speeding bike.

The colonist's body snapped backward, legs flipping over head in a brutal arc before slamming into the ground with a crunch that echoed across the hillside.

The bike kept going, zipping off-course before crashing into the rocks.

And then everything went still.

The last colonist broke the silence with a groan, dragging himself up and shaking off the hit as blood trickled from his temple. His hands balled into fists, blood streaming down his temple as he staggered forward, radiating drunken fury. "Bastard," he spat, lurching toward Lucas.

Lucas punched him.

The man collapsed.

The entire fight had lasted mere seconds.

Phoebe looked over at the Hypers. Some had gathered

around Poke and the other boy, helping them up. Others, including the guards, stared at Lucas in shock.

Phoebe's heart was racing. She had never seen Lucas do anything like that. He was calm, careful, controlled. Always. She had believed, like everyone else, that he was incapable of violence because of the Three Laws.

He wasn't supposed to act like this. Not against a human. Not like that.

The First Law forbade it.

And yet, she had just watched him throw a man off a moving bike. Clothesline another so hard he flipped midair.

Phoebe's mind raced. Either his programming had been altered, or something else was happening.

Lucas turned to the guards. "Get the men in the transport."

Both men looked at each other, then nodded and jumped down from the vehicle.

They jogged toward the first unconscious man, each grabbing an arm and beginning to drag him toward the vehicle. Three steps later the Hyperionite leader stepped in front of them and signed, "Leave them to us. Attacked our children. Punishment is ours."

"No." Lucas shook his head as he signed, "These men are sick."

The Hyperionite leader's scales shimmered, a ripple of color like light sliding off water.

Lucas raised his hands. "They have the same illness that infected the others. The same one your Elders had. We will treat them. Once they are well, the New People will meet with you to discuss a suitable punishment."

For a long moment, the Hyperionite leader remained perfectly still, scales shimmering with barely contained emotion. Then she signed, "New People stay away until the Hypers send for you."

Lucas nodded once. "Understood."

Phoebe felt the knots in her stomach tighten.

The leader turned and began to walk back toward her people. Phoebe caught sight of Poke, standing apart from the others, staring at her, his gaze flat and unreadable.

"I'm so sorry, Poke," she signed with trembling fingers. "Tell Flutter I'm sorry for how she was treated."

Poke's gaze hardened, his scaled lips curling back to reveal razor-sharp teeth. He turned away without responding, joining the others as they retreated.

She dropped her hands and blinked back tears. She knew Flutter wasn't going to get the message and she couldn't bear it if Flutter hated her.

Then the Hyperionites were gone, melting back into their village.

Phoebe turned toward the transport, nails digging crescents into her palms. Those men had hunted Poke and the boy like sport, laughing while they terrorized children. No disease could create that kind of cruelty from nothing. The prions might have eroded their inhibitions, made them more reckless, more violent, but the hatred was already there.

Even if they cured the disease, who was going to cure that?

It was disgusting.

A hand settled on her shoulder.

She jerked, startled.

Lucas. "Get in the vehicle, Phoebe."

She wiped her cheeks. Nodded. Then she climbed in, slamming the door behind her. He walked around to the other side and got in behind the wheel.

"They're going to be punished, right?"

"Yes."

"Good. I hope they get sent to the mountains. Or turned into lab rats." She sat back and stared out at the settlement.

Lucas started the engine and turned the transport around. "I'm sorry you had to experience that."

"Which part?" she asked.

He glanced at her. "All of it."

She sniffed. "I didn't even know you could fight."

"My programming doesn't prevent me from intervening in a conflict," Lucas replied, his eyes fixed on the road ahead. "I was careful to keep my intervention minimal."

"Minimal? You could have killed them."

"I calculated the most effective way to prevent escalation by inflicting non-lethal injuries."

The man he had punched was awfully still.

She frowned as she glanced back at him. "That one looks … not great."

"I may have miscalculated with Brent."

"Miscalculated?"

"It was a calculated intervention," Lucas replied, voice steady as if discussing the weather rather than violence. "The potential consequences of inaction included your death, possible deaths among the Hyperionites, and a diplomatic schism that could have escalated into open warfare between the settlements. The risk assessment was clear."

Phoebe turned to stare at him. "That's an awfully big risk."

Lucas smiled. "There is always risk when choosing between action and inaction. They are both decisions. I do not choose lightly."

"Yeah." Phoebe sniffed. "I guess that's true."

"And?"

"And Brent also deserved it," Phoebe said.

A ghost of a smile flickered across Lucas' face, there and gone. They drove in silence, the only sound the steady rumble of the engine and the rhythmic click of treads on stone.

"You miss your friend," Lucas said.

Phoebe nodded, eyes stinging as she fought back another wave of tears. "Flutter probably hates me now. And I might never get a chance to apologize."

"That could be true."

Her chest tightened again. "You're supposed to say it will be alright. And make me feel better."

"Do you wish me to lie to you?"

Phoebe slumped in her seat. "No."

"I thought not."

"Everything's falling apart, Lucas," she said. "Atlas is trapped, Flutter and Poke think I'm the enemy…" She stared out at the passing landscape. "Can any of this be fixed?"

"I don't know, but I will help you as best I can."

"Thanks." Phoebe leaned against his shoulder. "I just don't understand why it has to be this way. Why can't we all just get along?"

Lucas smiled again "Humans have been asking that question for as long as they've been human. I've yet to observe a satisfactory answer."

"Yeah. We suck."

"I don't think that."

"Maybe you should." Phoebe turned away, watching the alien landscape blur past the window. Somewhere out there, Atlas was preparing for a marriage he didn't want, surrendering to a life mapped out by someone else. Some-where, Flutter might be nursing wounds inflicted by humans who called themselves civilized. All of them caught in systems they hadn't created, fighting battles they hadn't started.

She thought about the question again.

Why can't we all just get along?

Was Lucas right and the question had no answer?

Phoebe hoped that wasn't true.

But she had a feeling he might be right.

AYESHA HAD no idea what time it was, but she needed to sleep.

Leadership was a double-edged blade. Both a privilege and a crushing weight. Tonight, the weight was almost unbearable. She longed for someone to confide in, someone to share the impossible decisions and terrible secrets. A leader needed composure in public, but in private, even the strongest needed a place to be vulnerable.

Despite their difference, there was a time when she and Katherine would trade fears without filtering through protocol or chain of command.

But Ayesha was too angry. She might say something that would irrevocably break the two colonies.

She couldn't allow that to happen. Not while Katherine had the one thing she needed to ensure her people's survival.

Ayesha undressed for bed, her fingers brushing something unexpected as they traced her collarbone. A small bump, tender to the touch. She hurried to the mirror, tilting her head to examine the spot under the harsh light. A tiny welt, angry red against her olive skin, with the tell-tale puncture marks at its center.

She knew exactly what it was. One of those damned

star mosquitos had somehow gotten in past the traps and filters and bitten her.

She was furious.

She had ordered everyone to be careful. Obsessively so. No exposure, and no exceptions. Now here she was with a bite.

Everything would need to be checked. Rechecked. Every seal, every vent, every entrance and exit.

Maybe all the mosquitos weren't carriers.

But that didn't matter now.

Because if this one *was,* she might already be infected.

If Leila wasn't lying, and she'd always been too straightforward for Katherine's brand of manipulation, this changed everything. Ayesha didn't fear her own mortality; she had always accepted death as part of the natural order. But what terrified her, what made her heart race and hands shake, was the threat to the Divine Blueprint. Her life's work, humanity's purest hope, now endangered by something as insignificant as an insect bite.

Ayesha cinched her robe tightly and slipped her feet into waiting slippers. She made her way through the silent corridors, footsteps echoing against metal walls as she headed toward her office. Inside, she sank into her chair, allowing reality to wash over her like a cold wave. She had spent decades building this sanctuary, protecting her people, preserving what remained of humanity's untainted essence and now it could all crumble because of a single, stupid mosquito.

She reached for her comm and messaged Leila. *Need two doses of the vaccine.*

The reply came in seconds. *I have enough doses for the entire colony. Be there at first light.*

Ayesha typed, *Only two.*

Leila's reply appeared seconds later. *We have more than enough for all of you.*

Two. If you send more, I will throw them away.

She set her comm down, releasing a long, controlled breath through pursed lips. Her fingers drummed against the desk for three precise beats. Then she picked up the comm again and began typing a new message.

Chapter Thirty-Six

POKE'S FACE haunted Phoebe like a ghost. That look of betrayal kept flashing in her mind on repeat. Or was it hatred? Right now, he was probably telling Flutter everything that happened, painting the whole colony with the same brush as those bastards on bikes. Was he telling her that Phoebe had somehow been involved?

Or was he explaining how Lucas had stepped in, stopping the colonists before things got worse?

Maybe that would soften the blow, knowing that at least one person from the Vitruvian colony had stood up for them. God, her head was throbbing. She pressed her fingers against her temples, trying to ease the tension building behind her eyes. If only she could talk to Flutter directly, so she could explain what happened. Maybe she could fix this.

The transport rolled to a stop. Phoebe glanced out the window and saw they'd reached the colony perimeter. Lucas turned to her. "You look exhausted. You should get some rest."

"I'll think about it."

"Phoebe." His voice had that I-know-what's-best-for-you edge.

She sighed. "All right. All right."

She hopped out of the vehicle, legs wobbling slightly beneath her. The day's events had left her drained, like she'd just recovered from a migraine. Only this time, her head was mercifully clear.

She walked home, throwing a glance over her shoulder to see Lucas heading toward the back of the transport where the three men were being unloaded. Two were standing, while the third was starting to come around, moaning as consciousness returned.

Her comm chimed. Probably Samara wondering how it had gone. Or maybe checking in about Renata again.

She pulled it out and stopped dead in her tracks. Saw it was Atlas and ran around the side of a building for privacy.

She read his message. *A seizure? Are you okay?*

Yeah. Just sorry I missed meeting you.

No. All good. I'm sorry I didn't text earlier. Hyacinth took my comm.

Phoebe typed, *How did you get it back?*

She was trying to make peace.

Did it work?

Ha! I want to see you. Will you still meet me?

She was about to type, *usual place*, but then reconsidered. Maybe that was too exposed. *Yeah. The ridge behind our colony at sunset?*

Can't wait. I have good news.

Phoebe smiled.

Maybe Dr. Basu wasn't going to make him marry Hyacinth?

She tucked the comm in her pocket. This day may have started out badly, but maybe it would end well.

ATLAS LEANED against the rough bark of a gnarled tree, one knee bouncing with nervous energy. He'd arrived ridiculously early, watching the sun creep toward the horizon while anxiety gnawed at his insides. What if she'd changed her mind? What if she didn't come at all?

The Vitruvian settlement sprawled below him, so opposite from the hermetically sealed bubbles of the Naturalist colony. Buildings spread across the valley in concentric rings, a mix of prefab units shipped from Earth and newer structures built from native materials. People moved freely between them without environmental suits, inhaling unfiltered air as casually as they drew breath. It was their birthright now, courtesy of Samara's genetic modifications. Soon, that freedom would be his too.

If they would have him.

He heard the scuff of a shoe and turned to see Phoebe emerging from the tree line, a backpack slung over one shoulder.

She spotted him and waved.

He jumped to his feet and ran to her.

She dropped her pack and did the same.

They collided in the middle of the clearing. Her arms wrapped around his neck, his arms encircled her waist, and their mouths found each other with desperate hunger.

The kiss was electric yet familiar, like finding a piece of himself he hadn't known was missing. When they finally broke apart, gasping for breath, they stayed close, foreheads pressed together, neither willing to let go.

He studied her face. She seemed… sad? "Are you sure you're okay?"

"Yeah." She nodded. "It was a hard day."

"Your seizure. Is it because of the genetic modifications? Dr. Basu mentioned something about it."

Her expression darkened, jaw clenching as she pulled back slightly. "It's a side effect of the genetic modifications. But I'm fine as long as I take my medication."

"Good. I'm glad you have something that helps you."

"Thanks." She smiled. "I just need to remember to take it."

"I'll be able to help you with that."

Phoebe narrowed her eyes. "What do you mean?"

"I'm leaving the Naturalist colony. Coming to live with you. Well, not you. But the Vitruvians."

Phoebe's mouth fell wide open as his words registered. For a moment, she just stared at him, as if waiting for the punchline to a joke that wasn't coming.

"If your people will have me."

"You've decided to run away?"

Atlas shifted his weight from one foot to the other, then squared his shoulders and met her gaze. "I prefer to think of it as running toward something." His voice grew steadier by the word. "Toward you."

A joyous squeal burst from Phoebe's throat. She grabbed his hands and pulled him into a wild, spinning dance across the clearing. They whirled together, clumsy and dizzy and perfect, kicking up spirals of gold and brown leaves beneath their feet. Phoebe threw her head back, laughter spilling into the darkening sky like music.

Atlas couldn't have stopped smiling if he'd tried; the weight of his entire life seemed to lift away in the swirl of her joy, leaving him lighter than air.

When they finally stopped, breathless and off balance, they wrapped their arms around each other and held on tight.

And then he knew with absolute certainty that whatever risk existed in leaving the Naturalists, it was worth taking.

"I missed you," she said.

He spoke into her hair. "I missed you too. More than I thought possible."

They stood locked together in each other's arms, the forest quiet around them except for their gradually slowing breaths.

The air between them shifted, charged with something electric and unspoken.

She pulled back just enough to look up at him, then laced her fingers through his. "Come with me."

They walked back to where she'd dropped her backpack. She scooped it up with her free hand, then led him deeper into a secluded grove of trees. Once there, she unzipped her bag and pulled out a blanket, shaking it open before spreading it carefully across the soft ground.

His pulse thundered in his throat, each heartbeat a drum announcing possibility.

The light of DaVinci's sun stained her in molten reds and her skin glowed like embers cooling after a fire. The sky behind her was painted in layers of lavender, deepening to indigo at the edges, where the first stars were already starting to flicker. The two moons rose, delicate crescents of silver, drifting upward into a sky that darkened by the heartbeat.

Phoebe sat on the blanket.

He joined her, their shoulders touching as they tilted their faces toward the heavens. The sky transformed with each passing second, bands of purple deepening to indigo while stars pierced through the darkening canvas one by one. Atlas wanted to freeze time, to capture this perfect moment and carry it with him forever. For once in his life, he wasn't thinking about tomorrow or yesterday, only about this exact instant where everything aligned into something beautiful.

"Atlas."

He turned to look at her.

She got on her knees, leaned forward and kissed him.

After a few minutes they broke apart. "Are you sure about this?" she asked. "Because once we do this, Dr. Basu will kick you out even if you change your mind about leaving."

"I won't change my mind."

They kissed again, moonlight filtering through the branches to paint silver patterns across their skin. Their kisses grew deeper, more urgent, hands exploring with tentative wonder, discovering each other's bodies with reverent curiosity.

Atlas paused, his breath warm against her neck. "Are *you* sure?"

Phoebe laughed. "I wouldn't be here if I wasn't."

He dropped his forehead to her shoulder. "You should know I've never …"

"Me neither," she whispered.

The night became a journey of discovery. There were moments of awkward fumbling and breathless laughter, uncertainty dissolving into touches that felt impossibly right. When they finally joined, it wasn't just bodies connecting but worlds colliding, boundaries between colonies and ideologies fading into meaninglessness.

Afterward, they lay side by side on the blanket, limbs entangled, heads tilted together as they traced constellations with their fingertips.

Phoebe propped herself up on one elbow to look down at him. "So? How does it feel to be contaminated?"

Atlas laughed. "I'm so sorry I ever said that."

Phoebe smiled. "It's okay. It's kind of funny."

He traced a finger along the curve of her cheek. "Like freedom. It feels like freedom."

And anything that felt like that, couldn't be wrong, could it?

Phoebe nestled against him, her head finding the hollow of his shoulder, her body curved perfectly against his side. For several minutes, they simply existed together, listening to the night sounds of DaVinci: rustling leaves, distant calls of nocturnal creatures, and the synchronized rhythm of their breathing.

"So, what now?" Phoebe asked.

"I need to pack. Say goodbye to my mother."

Phoebe nodded. "And Dr. Basu?"

"Forget her."

Phoebe laughed.

"Although I wish I could be a fly on the wall when she discovers I'm gone."

"Not me." Phoebe shook her head. "I'll be glad that you're far away."

He kissed the top of her head.

"Lucas has almost finished the treatment," Phoebe said. "Dr. Basu can still have the Divine Blueprint, if she wants it."

Atlas looked down on her with wonder. "You'd still give her that? After all the hell she put us through?"

"Of course."

He kissed her again. "You're amazing."

She wriggled against him. "Thank you for saying so."

He laughed, the sound rumbling through his chest and into hers, a physical extension of his happiness that she could feel against her skin.

"When do you have to head back?" Phoebe asked.

"Not yet." They settled back against each other, his arm curled protectively around her shoulders, her hand resting over his heart.

The thought that they'd never have to be separated again, that their next meeting wouldn't end with bittersweet goodbyes, felt almost too good to be true.

"I can't believe this is real," he whispered into her hair.

"Believe it," she murmured back. "This is just the beginning."

The stars wheeled slowly overhead, bearing silent witness to promises made in the dark.

INGRID SCREAMED, her fingers curling around the metal cell bars like pale spiders.

Samara flinched, glancing over her shoulder as Leila prepared the next vaccine behind her.

The Vitruvian jail cells had never been designed for mass quarantine. Six reinforced cells, originally built to hold the occasional drunk or troublemaker, now crammed in twenty-four infected colonists who had progressed to the point where they couldn't be confined in their homes. Two to four per compartment, depending on their volatility. The truly incoherent cases were isolated in a separate facility, while those still capable of limited communication remained here, trapped behind bars like criminals instead of patients.

"Hassan's next," Leila said, passing Samara a fresh syringe.

Alaric, head of Security, nodded, hand resting on the stun baton at his hip. "He was coherent this morning but started deteriorating about an hour ago. Keeps insisting his skin is being eaten away from the inside."

Samara looked over at the two security guards standing ready beside the cell door, tension visible in the tight lines of their shoulders. Another watched from the corridor, a tranquilizer rifle braced against his chest.

Only they were running out of sedatives too.

"Open it," she said.

The first guard keyed in the security code. The lock disengaged with a metallic thunk, and the door slid open.

One of the guards stepped in and gestured to the man on the bench. The other three occupants shuffled into the corner, huddling together. "Come on, Hassan. Time for your medicine."

The man didn't move.

Hassan had been a mechanic before the disease took hold. Good with his hands. Patient with apprentices. Now his fingers twitched against his shins, mapping invisible circuitry only he could see.

"Hassan," Samara kept her voice soft. "It's Samara. I have your medicine."

He looked over at her. "The worms are eating me."

"I know. I'm here to help you."

The guard gestured for her to enter the cell, keeping his eye on the three in back. Samara took a careful step forward, Alaric at her side.

Hassan got to his feet, digging his nails into his arm, tearing at the skin. "Can you see them moving? They're nesting."

One of the other occupants, a woman Samara recognized as one of the hydroponics specialists, squeezed her eyes shut and pressed her hands over her ears.

Samara held up the syringe. "This is going to stop the worms. One quick injection, and they'll stop burrowing. They'll die before they can hatch."

Hassan's eyes darted between Samara and the syringe, his pupils contracting to pinpoints. Then his face contorted, lips pulling back in a feral snarl. "That's how they get in," he hissed. "Through the needles. THROUGH THE NEEDLES!"

He lunged at her.

She stumbled back.

The woman in the corner bolted to her feet and ran toward the door.

"STOP HER!" Alaric shouted.

One of the other guards tackled her before she could make it into the hallway. Alaric grabbed Hassan from behind, pinning his arms, taking him to the ground.

He thrashed on the floor, spitting and cursing as his words dissolved into incoherent sounds.

Samara knelt beside him. "Hold him down."

Another guard entered, securing Hassan's legs. Samara found the vein in his arm and slid the needle in, depressing the plunger.

Then she pulled away. "You can let him go."

She got up and backed out of the cell.

"You okay?" Leila asked.

Samara nodded.

"Seven done. Sixteen more in here, then we're done," Leila said.

"That's it?" It felt like they'd been at it all day.

They worked methodically down the row, cell by cell, patient by patient. Some colonists extended their arms willingly, desperate for relief. Others fought like cornered animals, requiring three guards to restrain them. Many simply stared through Samara as if she were made of glass, lost in private hallucinations the prions had etched into their neural pathways like acid.

By the time they reached the last few colonists, Samara's uniform was stained with sweat, and her hands were trembling.

Leila placed a hand on her arm. "Let me do these ones. You're exhausted and your hands are shaking."

But it wasn't exhaustion making her hands shake. It was the disease itself, chewing through her brain despite the vaccination. She'd managed to slow the progression, but the damage already done remained, permanent as scars. And she'd die with her secrets before admitting this to Leila.

"Go home, Samara. Get some rest."

She shook her head. "I'm not leaving you to finish this alone."

"I'll have the guards with me."

"Alright. But promise you'll send for me if you run into any trouble."

"I promise," Leila said. "Now go, before I have these guards escort you out."

~

PHOEBE COULDN'T STOP SMILING.

The night air felt different somehow. Charged with possibility.

Atlas was leaving his colony. For her. No more midnight escapes. No more looking over her shoulder. Atlas would be there every morning when she woke up and every night when she went to sleep.

The settlement lights winked at her through the trees, and she broke into a sprint. There was so much to prepare. Would Katherine grant emergency housing, or would Atlas stay with her family until something more permanent could be arranged? She'd need to talk to her mother—

She skidded to a halt, reality crashing down like a bucket of ice water. She'd completely forgotten about that particular obstacle in her happiness haze. Maybe she should approach Katherine first? Get the colony leader to smooth things over with her mother?

No. That was the coward's way out. If she wanted this, she needed to handle it directly. If Samara couldn't support them, that was her choice. But Phoebe wasn't about to abandon Atlas just because her mother disapproved.

She kept walking, arriving back at the house to find it quiet.

Where was everyone?

She entered, heading for her bedroom.

"Where have you been?"

Phoebe jumped, spinning around to see Samara standing in the kitchen doorway, exhausted.

"I was just … getting some air," Phoebe said, trying to hide the backpack.

Samara sighed. "Don't lie to me, Phoebe. You were with him again, weren't you? The Naturalist boy."

She squared her shoulders. No more hiding. No more half-truths. "What if I was? And his name is Atlas."

"Atlas." It wasn't quite dismissal, but something in the way she said his name — a clinical detachment, like she was discussing a lab specimen rather than a person — raised Phoebe's hackles.

She thought about the vials she'd thrown away, pairing Atlas' name with those of the other women they'd wanted him to marry. She wondered if Samara had noticed yet.

It didn't matter. Soon it would be too late to force Atlas to marry anyone.

"You might not like him, but he's leaving the Naturalist colony and coming here to be with me."

Samara laughed. "He's leaving?"

Phoebe flushed. "Yes. He going to request sanctuary."

"It doesn't matter what he wants. Ayesha will never let him leave."

"She doesn't get a choice."

"Did he tell you that?"

"It's his life!"

Samara shook her head. "Ayesha has spent decades building her ideology around Atlas' immunity. The Divine Blueprint isn't just some religious quirk, it's the foundation of her power over that colony. She will never let him—"

"He's a person, not her property," Phoebe argued.

"Those distinctions don't matter to Ayesha."

"I don't care."

Samara studied her face. "Have you had sex with him?"

"None of your business." But of course Phoebe's flush betrayed her.

"You don't think he told you he was leaving in order to manipulate you into—"

"No."

"Phoebe, I know you think you're in love with this boy—"

"I don't think it, I know it." She stamped her foot like a petulant toddler.

"You're seventeen. Your brain is flooded with hormones and neurotransmitters that make everything feel more intense than it is. That's biology, not destiny."

"You don't get to dismiss what I feel just because it doesn't fit your narrative for my life. Which is wild, because you don't even care about me. All you're concerned with is genetics and viruses and lab work. You barely even notice when I'm here, let alone care about what I want!"

Samara flinched as if struck. Raw hurt flash across her features, genuine pain that made Phoebe's anger falter.

"Phoebe, I ..." She sighed. "You're right. I haven't

been a good mother since all this started. I've been so focused on finding a treatment for the prions, on trying to save us from this disease …" She looked down at her hands. "After Hector died, there was no one else who could do this work."

The raw admission deflated her anger. Phoebe hadn't expected for her mother to concede.

"When this plague is over, when everyone is safe… I want to do better. Be more present for you."

"You always say that."

"I know. And I mean it every time. I do care about what you want, Phoebe. I care about you being happy. But I also care about you being safe."

Phoebe swallowed. "I feel safe with Atlas. He makes me happy. And I think … I think he could be happy here too. If you give him a chance."

Samara stood silent, her shoulders slowly falling as the fight seemed to drain out of her. After a long moment, she nodded. "Alright," she said softly. "If he genuinely wants to join our colony, I'll give him a fair chance."

Phoebe blinked, not quite trusting what she heard. She thought again of the vials that she'd thrown away and wondered if her mother had chosen to cooperate with Dr. Basu's plan, or if she'd been ordered to. But mentioning it now might ruin this obvious peace offering.

She decided to believe that Samara regretted it now, regardless of why she'd done it.

"Atlas isn't like the others," Phoebe said. "He's tired of being lied to. He wants to know the truth."

Samara took Phoebe's hand and gave it a squeeze. "I can't promise how others will react, but I won't stand in his way. And I promise to help him fit in here however I can."

Her comm chimed.

She froze, her hand dropping to her side.

Phoebe sighed. "Go on …"

Samara pulled out her comm and glanced at the screen. "Renata just woke up."

"Woke up? Where is she? Is she okay? What about the baby?"

Samara nodded. "She had a bit of a breakdown, but she's conscious and coherent now."

"Is she going to die like Dr. Callas?" Phoebe's voice trembled.

"No, of course not. We caught it in time. Do you want to come with me to see her?"

Phoebe hesitated. "Yes. But …"

"You need to wait for Atlas? He's coming tonight?"

Phoebe nodded. "He's going to text me."

"Then stay here." Samara slipped the comm back into her pocket. "If Renata needs you, or it feels like you should be there, then I'll call or text right away."

"Are you sure?"

Samara nodded, hesitating with her hand on the doorframe. "I love you, Phoebe."

Her throat tightened. "I know."

And then Phoebe did something she hadn't done in too long. She went and hugged her mother.

Samara returned the embrace, holding her tight.

When they finally parted, Samara gave her a small nod and headed outside.

Alone in the house, Phoebe felt a strange blend of emotions seething in her chest, hope, apprehension, and uncertainty, but beneath it all stewed a current of excitement so strong it nearly made her dizzy. Atlas was coming to stay.

Whatever happened next, they would face it together.

Chapter Thirty-Seven

BRIAR'S FACE had turned to stone.

"Did you hear me?" Atlas asked his mother.

She remained motionless, hands folded in her lap and eyes fixed on a point somewhere beyond his shoulder until she finally spoke. "You are not leaving the colony to live with the Vitruvian filth."

Atlas sighed. "Please stop calling them that. And yes, I am."

More silence.

"That's it?" Atlas asked.

Briar blinked, then turned to meet his eyes. "So, she was right all along."

"Who was right?"

"Dr. Basu." His mother's eyes were icy with disappointment. "She warned me that the Vitruvians had gotten to you. That they were working to brainwash my child and turn him against his own people."

"I haven't been brainwashed, Mom. This is my choice. *Mine.*"

"Is it?" Briar tilted her head. "Or have they filled your

head with their dysgenic propaganda? Convinced you that their abominations are natural? That your divine purpose is meaningless?"

"My purpose is to be bred like livestock." Atlas tried to keep his voice from rising but failed. "My purpose is to be married to someone I don't love just because I happened to be born different. Do you think any of that is divine?"

"So, you're running away?"

"I'm not running away. I'm choosing something different for myself."

Briar snorted. "You think it's your choice. They've filled your head with lies. They made you question your place. Twisted your values. Undermined everything you were raised to believe. They've offered you a new truth to fit their agenda. You think you're being enlightened, but you're just being used, Atlas."

"No." He shook his head. "That's something Dr. Basu would say."

"She's our leader." Briar straightened on the bench. "She has looked after us for decades. Held this colony together through storms, shortages, and disease. You only have the privilege of doubting her because you were raised in the security she created. Don't mistake safety for freedom."

"Yeah. Well, she's also human. And fallible."

Briar stood. "Enough, Atlas."

"She's wrong, Mom. She's *always* been wrong. Dr. Basu has used fear to control us. She's kept us isolated, paranoid, and compliant. We're not building a better world; we're preserving her version of the old one."

"You have no idea what you're talking about. And you're betraying everything our people fought to preserve. You're betraying *me*."

"I'm not betraying anyone." His voice shook. "I'm choosing a better future."

"This girl has poisoned your mind—"

"Phoebe hasn't poisoned anything! She opened my eyes. If anyone has been brainwashed here, it's you!"

Briar's cheeks flushed crimson. "How dare you? After everything your father and I sacrificed to give you this life."

Atlas dropped his shoulders, the fight draining out of him. "I'm sorry, Mom. But it doesn't matter what you say. I'm going."

"And abandoning everything you believe in?"

"Not everything." He shook his head. "Just the parts that keep us trapped."

Her expression frosted over again. "You're not yourself, Atlas. They've gotten inside your head, clouded your judgment. Manipulated you until you can't separate their voices from your own."

Atlas opened his mouth, but she cut him off.

"I don't blame you. They know how to target people like you. Curious. Sensitive. Hungry for something more out of life. They burrow under your skin like an infection and eat you up. You don't even see what's happening. But I do. And I won't let them steal you from me."

"I'm not—"

Atlas stopped cold when he heard a sound from the kitchen behind him. The faint scrape of boot on tile.

"Who else is here?"

She didn't answer.

Two guards emerged from the kitchen, their boots heavy on the tile floor, wearing the gray uniforms of the Naturalist security detail.

Atlas stared, recognizing the taller one. "Vance? What are you doing here?"

Vance hesitated. But the other one crossed the room and took Atlas' arm, pulling it behind his back.

"You're being detained," he said.

Atlas tried to pull away. "For what?"

"For treatment."

"I'm not sick." Atlas glanced at Vance.

"Sorry, Atlas." Vance avoided his eyes. "Orders."

Atlas twisted against the first guard's grip, wincing at the strain in his shoulder. "Orders? From who, my mother? Let go!"

Vance didn't answer.

Pain shot through Atlas' shoulders as his other arm was yanked behind him.

"Stop! You're hurting me! Mom! Tell them to stop. Please!"

Briar stood, her face impassive. "I've agreed to this, Atlas. You don't realize it now, but you've been programmed. Manipulated. We're going to help you. You can thank me when you're well again."

The absurdity of her words hit him like a slap. He barked out a laugh, twisting hard and wrenching his right arm free.

He drove his elbow into the younger guard's stomach, gratified by the whoosh of escaping air. Then he brought his knee up into Vance's thigh, a calculated strike that hit the nerve bundle, momentarily paralyzing the limb and breaking the man's grip.

Atlas lunged for the door.

His fingers brushed the control panel. He was just about out. And for one heartbeat, freedom seemed possible.

Then Vance tackled him from behind.

Atlas' head cracked against the wall, stars exploding across his vision. He hit the floor, and the other guard was on him in an instant, pinning his legs while Vance forced his arms behind his back.

"Stop struggling, Atlas. It's for your own good."

"Get off me!" Atlas fought with everything he had, muscles straining against their grip, twisting and bucking like a trapped animal.

But it was too late. Cold metal bit into his wrists as the restraints closed with a series of precise clicks, each one sealing away another fraction of his freedom.

"Get him up."

Atlas looked over toward the new voice to see Dr. Basu standing in the doorway. "I'm sorry I've failed you, Atlas. I should have seen the signs earlier. The restlessness. The questioning. The forbidden excursions."

She crouched before him, her face inches from his, voice dropping to a silky tone, just above a whisper. "I was so focused on the wedding that I missed the signs of your manipulation. The Vitruvians have been working on you for weeks, haven't they? Exploiting your curiosity, feeding you lies. They don't want you for who you are, Atlas, but for what you represent. You walk away, and others might follow. I take full responsibility for not protecting you from their programming. For the sad delusions they've planted in your mind."

"I'm not deluded," he replied through gritted teeth.

Dr. Basu smiled. "The girl is quite clever, I'll give her that. Manipulating you against your own people. But don't worry. We'll purge her influence from you. The Divine Blueprint can be saved."

"Go to hell!" Atlas spat the words, his voice cracking with rage and desperation.

Her expression didn't change. "This isn't you speaking, Atlas. It's the programming. The corruption. You will thank us for saving you from their influence soon enough."

She gestured to the guards. "Get him settled in the treatment facility. We'll start the full purification protocols as soon as I arrive."

The guards hauled him up, dragging Atlas toward the door as he swiveled his head around in search of Briar. "Mom! Please! Help me!"

Briar refused to meet his eyes, standing with her back to him.

He thrashed harder, struggling to break free. "Mom! MOM!"

But she didn't turn.

"You can't do this! I'm not sick! I haven't done anything wrong!"

They forced him out and into the corridor. "Mom!"

The guards pulled him from the door, but Atlas lunged forward for one last look at his mother.

Dr. Basu had wrapped an arm around her. "It'll all be over soon, and we'll have your son back again."

Briar fell onto Dr. Basu's shoulder, sobbing.

Then the door slid shut and Atlas was hauled away.

Chapter Thirty-Eight

"How was Renata?" Leila asked.

"Good," Samara said. "Treatment is coming along. And the baby doesn't have any trace of prions."

"That's a relief."

"Yeah." Samara picked up her fork but only used it to nudge the food from one side of her plate to the other. At least the cocktail of drugs had given her a little more mental clarity, although her mind was still painfully sluggish.

Her thoughts drifted from Renata to Phoebe.

She was worried about Atlas coming to the colony and about Ayesha's reaction when she found out he was gone.

Maybe she should give Katherine a heads-up. Just … so she wasn't blindsided.

Leila eyed her from across the table. "You sure you're okay?"

Samara blinked. "Sorry. I'm just … distracted."

"Renata will be okay. Tana will message you if she takes a turn for the worse."

"I know." She took a bite of her food, surprised by her sudden hunger. "Any word from Lucas?"

"No. But I heard the mission to the Hyperionites didn't go as expected. Maybe he's still with Katherine."

Samara frowned. "Phoebe didn't mention anything had gone amiss." But Phoebe often didn't tell her things that might cause Samara to worry.

She told herself that Phoebe was back, so whatever had happened had turned out all right.

They ate in companionable silence, the only sound the occasional scrape of utensils against ceramic.

"Any closer to a cure?" Leila asked.

Samara shook her head. "No."

"What about enzyme therapies? Proteases engineered to target the beta-sheet structures?"

Samara took a bite of stew. "We don't have the right catalytic configurations. Prions maintain remarkable structural integrity due to their hydrogen bonding patterns. The beta-sheet conformation creates a thermodynamically stable state that resists conventional proteolytic degradation."

Leila nodded. "What about monoclonal antibodies? If we harvested plasma from the Hyperionites, we might isolate antibodies with binding affinity for the misfolded regions—"

Samara shook her head. "The blood-brain barrier's tight junctions prevent most antibodies from accessing the central nervous system. They'd be useless against cerebral prion accumulation."

Leila tapped her fingers against the table. "Heat shock proteins? Molecular chaperones like HSP70 or HSP90 could potentially interfere with the misfolding cascade."

"The overexpression levels required would disrupt

normal cellular homeostasis. And they're primarily preventative, ineffective against established aggregates."

"Anti-amyloid compounds?" Leila grinned. "Some of the pre-collapse Alzheimer's research showed promise with breaking up protein aggregates."

Samara sighed. "Are you trying to solve this tonight?"

Leila shrugged. "Why not? It's as good a time as any."

Samara couldn't argue against that. "Different structure, different binding profile. Prions form amyloids, yes, but the molecular architecture is distinct. Those compounds would probably just sit there, ineffective."

"What about RNA interference then silencing the gene that produces the normal prion protein?" Leila's eyes lit up. "If there's no substrate for conversion—"

"It would slow progression, maybe, but wouldn't help with existing prions," Samara took a bite of stew, chewed and swallowed. "And prion protein has normal functions in the brain. Completely silencing it could cause new problems. Besides, effective delivery of RNA interference molecules to the CNS is a goddamn nightmare."

"Stem cell therapy to replace damaged neurons?"

"By the time neurons are damaged enough to need replacement, the patients will be too far gone. And new neurons would just become infected with the existing prions."

"Nanobots?" Leila said. "We could design them to eat the prions."

Samara laughed. "We're nowhere close to that kind of technology."

Leila grinned. "I know. But at this point I'm just throwing stew at the wall to see what sticks."

Samara smiled back at her as the flicker of an idea started to find form. Nanobots. *Bots*.

She set down her spoon, staring into the distance.

Leila stiffened. "What is it? I know that look."

"Maybe your idea isn't quite so far-fetched."

"What do you mean?"

"Maybe we don't need nanobots if we have a more elegant biological solution already available."

"Which is?"

"What if we used a CAR T-cell process to train T-cells to specifically go after prions instead of viruses and bacteria?"

"CAR T-cells? For prions?" Leila looked skeptical. "But prions aren't pathogens. They're our own proteins. The immune system doesn't recognize them as foreign."

"Exactly. That's why we need to teach it." Samara sat up straighter, her eyes widening as neurons fired connections in her brain. "Give me your tablet."

Leila handed it over.

"Chimeric Antigen Receptor T-cell therapy was originally developed for cancer treatment," Samara continued. "We take T-cells from a patient, genetically modify them to express receptors that recognize specific targets, then reintroduce them to the body where they can identify and eliminate those targets."

"But cancer cells have surface antigens. Prions are just proteins. How would the T-cells distinguish between normal proteins and the misfolded versions?"

Samara pulled up a three-dimensional model of a prion protein on the tablet. "See this beta-sheet structure? It's unique to the misfolded form. Normal prion proteins have primarily alpha-helical structures." She manipulated the image, splitting it to show the contrast between healthy and misfolded versions. "The misfolded form exposes epitopes that aren't present in the normal configuration."

Leila studied the model. "Okay."

"So we need to design CAR T-cells to recognize these

unique epitopes. We engineer receptors specifically tuned to the beta-sheet conformations, then introduce them into the patient's T-cells." Samara swiped to another diagram. "Once reintroduced, these modified T-cells would seek out and bind to prions, triggering immune clearance."

"But wouldn't that trigger massive inflammation in the brain? The blood-brain barrier—"

"Is a concern. But there are ways to modulate the inflammatory response. And some of the newer CAR designs include regulatory domains that can help control the intensity of the immune reaction."

Leila sat back, considering. "It's never been tried for prion diseases before, has it?"

"Not that I know of, but our library doesn't contain every paper ever published." Samara set the tablet down and shrugged. "It's a shot in the dark, but still more than we had yesterday."

"Could you really design this? Now, with what we have here?"

"I think so. The basic principles aren't that different from how I designed the gene therapy against the fungus." Samara chewed on her thumb. "We have enough genetic modification equipment to create the CAR constructs. The difficult part will be harvesting and manipulating the T-cells, but Lucas and I can adapt some of our existing protocols."

Leila stared at her, a slow smile spreading across her face. "You're incredible, you know that?"

"Don't celebrate yet. It might not work. And even if it does, it might be too late for ..."

Samara broke off.

"Too late for what?"

"Nothing."

Leila paled. "You? You mean too late for you. Jesus, Samara. Don't tell me you're infected."

"I am."

"How long have you known?"

"A few days." Samara kept her voice low. "I'd been having episodes. Memory lapses. Mood swings. Shaking."

"Are you sure it's not just exhaustion?"

"Lucas ran my blood three times."

"Does anyone else know?"

"Katherine. Lucas."

"Phoebe?"

"No! And I don't want her to know." Samara pushed her bowl away. "Not until I've exhausted every possible option. She's already dealing with enough."

"She deserves to know."

"I'll tell her. Just not yet."

"And how long…" Leila's voice caught. "How long until…"

"Hard to say."

"Then we'll make sure this CAR T-cell therapy works. Let's go get started."

Samara stood. "We'd move faster with Lucas."

"You head back to the lab. I'll find Katherine. See if she knows where he is. If not, I'll get her to track him via his beacon."

"Okay. I'll meet you in the lab."

Leila took her hand and gave it a squeeze. "We're going to make this work."

Samara smiled, wishing she had even a quarter of Leila's hope.

PHOEBE SURVEYED HER BEDROOM.

She had no idea where Atlas would live, but if Samara let him stay here, Phoebe wanted her bedroom to at least look clean. She'd tidied what she could. But she was still feeling restless.

What was keeping him?

She was certain that he would have texted by now.

It had been a couple of hours and—

Her comm chimed.

She pulled it out.

New plan. Dr. Basu has agreed to let the Naturalists have some vials of the Divine Blueprint. Can you bring them, and we'll meet here?

She read the message twice to make sure she wasn't hallucinating. Dr. Basu — the woman who'd built an entire ideology around rejecting genetic manipulation, who'd led the schism that tore the colony apart, who preached about purity and contamination — had agreed to receive gene therapy?

Atlas must have been able to remind Dr. Basu what life on DaVinci was all supposed to be about. Protection. Survival. Care.

Or maybe she was scared. Finally realized just how fragile their position had become.

Whatever the reason, Phoebe felt a small, cautious flutter in her chest. Maybe there was hope for the Naturalist colony after all.

Lucas should have finished it by now.

She typed a response, *Amazing! I'll bring it. Where do you want to meet?*

Come to the greenhouse after dark. It's the dome-shaped building at the bottom of the hill on the south edge of the colony. There's a hidden door in the back, just behind a cluster of bushes. We'll meet there.

She felt a rush of joy as she typed, *I'll be there.*

PHOEBE PRESSED her palm to the entry pad.

The lab door slid open with a hydraulic sigh, the biometric scanner flashing green as it recognized her palm print. She slipped inside, scanning the corridor behind her before disappearing into the sterile brightness.

She found the vials of the vaccine they'd created from Atlas' DNA: the Divine Blueprint distilled into liquid form. She pulled half and left the rest. Then she exited, popping them into an insulated case.

Footsteps sounded in the corridor outside.

Her pulse spiked as she darted to one of the workstations and scrambled beneath it.

Samara entered, her footsteps dragging with exhaustion as she made her way to a workstation. She collapsed into the chair with a heavy sigh. Under the harsh lab lights, her skin had a sickly pallor, the hollows beneath her looked bruised, and her hands trembled slightly as she reached for the console.

"Alright," Samara said to herself. "*Think.*"

Phoebe held her breath, watching her mother. She'd been so exhausted lately and…

Brutal truth knocked the air from her lungs. Her mother was sick. The tremors in her hands, the yellow undertones of her skin, the cognitive lapses she'd been trying to hide were all classic symptoms of prion disease. The realization crystallized in her mind with terrifying clarity: Samara was infected, and she was working herself to death trying to find a cure before the disease could finish what it had started.

Phoebe's heart slammed against her ribs. No. No. No.

Samara couldn't be sick, too. She couldn't lose them both.

The thought was overwhelming, almost absurd.

She felt her body lurch forward, ready to crawl out from beneath the table and confront her mother. Or hug her. Hold her. Never let her go.

Samara got up and walked to the back of the lab.

It was now or never. Phoebe had to choose between meeting Atlas and talking to her mother.

One had to wait.

Her brain screamed to stay, to confront her mother, but her promise to Atlas pulled at her with equal force. He was counting on her, standing at the precipice of a life-altering decision. She had the treatment he needed, the key to his freedom clutched in her hands. Without her, the entire plan would collapse.

Atlas was risking everything — his family, his community, his entire identity — on the belief that she would be there. He was walking blind into enemy territory, armed with nothing but trust in her promise to help him. If she failed him now, he might never find the courage to try again.

She scurried out from beneath the desk and slithered toward the door, glancing back to see Samara disappearing into the cold storage unit. The moment the door sealed behind her mother, Phoebe leapt to her feet and slapped her hand on the sensor.

The door whispered open, and she bolted through, clutching the case of vials against her chest like precious cargo.

Her footsteps echoed in the empty corridor as she ran, further from one obligation and closer to another.

She paused outside the medical building, looking back at the illuminated windows. Her heart pulled her in two directions at once. She should go back, tell Samara she knew and that she didn't have to face this alone. But the weight of the case in her hands reminded her of Atlas waiting in the darkness, his future balanced on a knife's edge of possibility.

"I'll be back soon," she whispered. "Just hold on a little longer."

Then she turned and sprinted toward the colony's edge, where the Naturalist compound waited in the gathering dusk.

Chapter Thirty-Nine

THE NATURALIST DETENTION area didn't bother with niceties. No cushioned furniture, no ambient lighting, no decorative touches. Just reinforced polymer walls, dull gray composite floors, and harsh overhead lights that never dimmed. Prison was prison, even in paradise.

Atlas paced the length of his cell, measuring the dimensions with his steps. Five paces long, four wide. The ceiling hung low enough that he could reach up and touch it without fully extending his arm.

They'd taken his belt and the laces from his boots. No doubt Hyacinth had mentioned that he'd threatened to take his own life if he was forced to marry her. Even the bed frame was bolted to the floor. No sharp edges in sight, nothing that could be fashioned into a weapon or tool.

But there had to be a way out.

If he could somehow reach the control panel … Too bad that was outside the cell. And the door was seamless, integrated into the wall, only visible as a slight outline. The lock was electromagnetic, controlled from the guard station. The ventilation grate in the ceiling was too small for even a child to fit through. Even the sanitation unit was built to prevent tampering, its components sealed behind smooth panels.

He stopped at the door, running his fingers along the seam. No gaps larger than half a millimeter. No loose panels. No exposed wiring. Nothing to exploit. He dropped to his knees and examined the floor. Maybe dig his way out?

He pressed his palms against it. Dense, impact-resistant, synthetic stone bonded with high-density polymer. The kind of stuff that laughs at sledgehammers. Laid down in one solid piece with no seams to attack. So much for the digging plan.

Even if he had something sharp enough to scrape at it, he would surely be discovered before making a dent.

Atlas sat on the floor, resting his head against the wall. He needed to try something different.

Fake an illness? Pretend to be dead? Maybe. But Dr. Basu had ordered the guards not to open the cell door without backup. And even if he did get out, then what? The entire settlement would be looking for him as a traitor. And he doubted the Vitruvians would take him in then. They wouldn't want to risk war with the Naturalists.

So, he'd flee to the mountains. Find refuge with the Hyperionites? Atlas laughed hard. There was even less chance they'd take him in than the Vitruvians.

He swallowed hard, his mouth sandpaper-dry with self-loathing.

He wasn't angry at his mother. She'd only done what she genuinely believed was right after decades of Dr. Basu's brainwashing.

The rage inside him was aimed squarely at himself.

What had Phoebe called them? A *cult*?

Bingo.

He'd always known Dr. Basu was awful, but he'd assumed she had some warped form of integrity. Some basic respect for bodily autonomy. But there was nothing sacred about her except her hypocrisy: she was a demon with excellent PR, not a savior.

He'd never imagined Dr. Basu would go so far as to kidnap and imprison him. Even that seemed a step too far. She was either insane or had fallen prey to her own doctrine.

Or maybe it was all about control.

She was no leader. She was a fraud, poisoning Naturalist minds even as she condemned Phoebe and her colony as corrupted. He felt ashamed of how easily he'd allowed himself to be deceived his whole life.

Atlas bent forward, elbows on knees, head in hands, feeling the weight of his own ignorance. Phoebe had tried to tell him, to make him understand just how thoroughly Dr. Basu controlled the colony. She'd always seen it clearly, even though she'd never been here, while he'd been trapped in a tangle of lies masquerading as truth.

He was such a fool.

He'd always been in prison. He just hadn't recognized it until he glimpsed freedom through Phoebe's eyes.

If only he'd listened to her sooner.

If only he hadn't been so desperate to cling to the beliefs he'd been raised with.

If only he'd had the courage to break free earlier.

Now it was too late.

For all he knew, they'd keep him locked up until they broke his will, his spirit, and his mind. Until he accepted the lie that he wasn't even human.

That he was nothing more than a religious symbol …

~

ATLAS DIDN'T KNOW how much time had passed.

Minutes? Hours? Maybe even a full day?

At some point he'd dozed off. Because now he was awoken to the sound of approaching footsteps. Dr. Basu appeared, flanked by at least half a dozen armed guards.

Her expression was serene, almost pleasant. "My precious Atlas. It's time." Her voice dripped with artificial sweetener.

He didn't move. "Time for what? My execution?"

"Your wedding. A private ceremony with you and Hyacinth. She is absolutely giddy to receive the Divine Blueprint."

A cold, rotten feeling settled in Atlas' stomach. "I won't marry Hyacinth. And I definitely won't have sex with her. Not today, not ever."

"Come now," she tsked. "That's the Vitruvians talking. They've filled your head with all sorts of nonsense."

Atlas eyed her. Her face was serene, but her hands were balled into white-knuckled fists at her sides. Classic Dr. Basu — irritated as hell at having to maintain the holy act when she'd rather be efficient.

Perfect time to make her evening worse. "Maybe, but no matter what you do to me, Hyacinth will never get pregnant."

"And why is that Atlas?" Her voice was dangerously soft.

He bared his teeth in something that wasn't remotely a smile. "Because you have committed the ultimate sin. You've betrayed the Divine."

Dr. Basu looked flash frozen.

The guards stiffened, exchanging nervous glances. The kind people share when someone's just committed blasphemy in front of the high priestess.

"Do you really think the Divine would let *you* dictate its

will?" Atlas leaned forward, eyes cold as space. "Hyacinth isn't worthy. She's not special. You know it. I know it. Hyacinth probably even knows it deep down."

He let that sink in before continuing. "The Divine chose someone else for me. But you couldn't handle that. It had to be your daughter in the spotlight. So you betrayed your own god."

"How dare you?"

He ignored her. "You talk about purity, about sacred purpose, but this isn't about faith. It never has been. It's about control. And you can't control the Divine. Even if you succeed, even if you force this, your plan won't work. The divine wouldn't reward your deception. In fact, it will punish you for it."

Dr. Basu's voice was sharp. "Stop it."

Atlas looked at the guards. "Do you hear her? She doesn't deny it. She doesn't call on the Divine to prove me wrong. She just wants me to stop talking. Why? Because she knows faith isn't built on secrets. This isn't worship. This is desecration."

None of the guards spoke. The silence was deafening.

"She tells you I'm corrupted," Atlas continued, his voice growing stronger, "but what corruption is worse than lying to the Divine? Than using faith as a bulletproof vest for your own agenda?"

Dr. Basu's voice sliced through the air. "Enough."

Atlas scanned the guards' faces, hunting for hesitation, for doubt — any crack in their armor he could exploit. "You know the truth, even if you're too scared to say it. The Divine can't be fooled. If I'm wrong about any of this, let the Divine punish me. Not her."

The guards might as well have been statues.

They weren't listening. Not to him. Their faith was cemented in place by decades of doctrine, and their fear of her outweighed any doubts he might plant. Atlas wanted to scream until his throat bled, but he wasn't giving her that satisfaction.

Dr. Basu looked at the guards. "Take him to the Sanctum." She turned back to Atlas. "You'll undergo the final stage of purification before the ceremony. Then you'll drink the sacred tea and fulfill your purpose. I'll help you through this, Atlas. You will find your faith again."

"I won't be doing anything," Atlas said.

She smiled. "We'll see."

One of the guards punched in a code on the pane by the door while the others kept their weapons trained on Atlas. Then the door slid open and they entered.

"Get up," growled one of the guards.

Atlas ignored him, staring straight ahead. The man grabbed him by the arm, trying to pull him up to his feet. Atlas made his body limp, refusing to support his own weight.

"I'm not asking again," the guard said.

Atlas kept his mouth shut, eyes fixed forward like the guard didn't exist, making them work for every inch.

The guard muttered something, probably not a prayer, and exchanged an irritated look with the others. Two more entered. The four of them grabbed Atlas by the arms and hauled him to the door, his feet dragging on the floor.

Pain shot through his shoulders, threatening to pop them from their sockets. Good. He welcomed the discomfort. Pain will keep his mind sharp. At least that was the theory.

Dr. Basu led their little parade, and Atlas laser-focused on her back. Her rigid posture fueled his rage, kept it bubbling just below boiling.

They reached a metal door, secured by a keypad. *The Sanctum.*

The only metal room in their polymer paradise.

Dr. Basu punched in a code, her fingers moving too fast for Atlas to track. The door slid open with a medical-grade hiss, and the guards dragged him inside before dropping him unceremoniously on the floor.

He pushed himself onto his knees, taking stock of his surroundings. The sharp smell of antiseptic assaulted his nostrils.

"This isn't a sanctum. It's a lab."

Dr. Basu glanced over at him. "Yes."

Stainless-steel counters gleamed under harsh hospital lighting. In the center of the room was Hyacinth.

Unconscious. Pale blue hospital gown. IV dripping clear fluid into her arm. Anesthesia mask hissing softly over her face. Legs splayed in stirrups, only a paper-thin drape preserving what little dignity she had left.

Elda stood beside her in medical scrubs, arranging gleaming steel instruments on a tray. She didn't even look up when they entered. Of course. She'd been expecting him all along.

"What is this?" Atlas asked.

"Progress," Dr. Basu said.

Atlas sneered. "You're a hypocrite. You criticize the Vitruvians for using medical technology while you take advantage of that same technology in secret. It was all a lie."

Dr. Basu shrugged.

Atlas ground his teeth until his jaw ached. This feeling went light-years beyond anger, and yet there she stood, completely unashamed, like a sociopath at a funeral.

Atlas let out a bitter laugh. "You never cared about faith. You needed me to sell the lie so no one would question you. If they knew the Divine Blueprint could just be made in a lab, if they knew you were doing exactly what you claim is blasphemy—" He cut himself off with a shake of his head. "It would all fall apart, wouldn't it?"

Her expression tightened. "You don't understand what's at stake."

Atlas stared at Dr. Basu in disbelief. "No, I understand perfectly. Because the second people start thinking for themselves, as soon as they realize they don't need me, or you, or any of these stupid rituals, you lose everything. The corruption at the center of our colony is you."

Dr. Basu touched a monitor screen. "You're wrong, Atlas. I do need you."

"For what?" He snorted. "Clearly you can collect my genetic material whether I agree to it or not."

Dr. Basu turned to face him fully. "I need you to die."

"What?" Atlas recoiled, but the guards held him fast. One dropped his grip only to seize his shoulders instead, pinning him in place.

A sharp sting in his neck.

Atlas whipped around to see Elda standing there, empty syringe in hand like a tiny murder weapon. He slapped a hand over the injection site. "What did you—"

His tongue suddenly felt two sizes too big for his mouth.

"Don't worry. Yet." Dr. Basu's smile was all teeth. "For now, it's just a sedative. I want you wide awake for this next part. I've arranged it specifically for you."

Atlas tried to focus, but the room was already tilting sideways, the walls breathing in and out. What was she talking about?

Next part?

Hyacinth?

"You can't … do this …" The words slurred together, his tongue uncooperative. His vision tunneled, darkness creeping in from the edges. His knees buckled.

He hit the floor face-first, the impact hardly registering through the chemical fog. Rough hands grabbed his arm, dragging him across the cold tile to the corner like discarded trash.

"That's all," Dr. Basu dismissed the guards with a flick of her wrist. "I'll let you know when I need you again."

The guards disappeared, leaving Atlas sprawled on the floor, cheek pressed against the frigid tile. Through half-lidded eyes, he watched Dr. Basu and Elda prep Hyacinth, their movements clinical and precise.

Then the door hissed open.

Dr. Basu turned, her face lighting up with genuine pleasure for the first time all night. "Right on time."

PHOEBE CROUCHED low in the underbrush, her skin dappled with sweat as she stared out at the Naturalist compound sprawling before her in a series of interconnected domes glowing against the night sky, linked by transparent corridors like arteries feeding a massive heart.

Her own heart slammed against her ribs. Maybe she should've asked him to meet halfway instead. First time in his settlement and already feeling like a burglar. Not a great start.

The southern edge of the colony lay just ahead of her.

She kept to the shadows, avoiding the pools of light cast by the perimeter illumination. The colony seemed quiet. Too quiet, perhaps. There was none of the evening activity she would have expected, and it was unsettling her. But then again, most of his people spent all their time inside.

A large structure came into view at the bottom of the hill, glowing in the dark like it had swallowed a third moon. That had to be the greenhouse. She quickened her pace, darting from one patch of shadow to the next.

The greenhouse was three times bigger than she'd expected and frustratingly devoid of hiding spots. She pressed her face against the glass, peering inside for Atlas, but saw only an impenetrable jungle of plants crowding the walls.

She circled to the back, where dense bushes clustered against the structure's base like natural camouflage. The door had to be here somewhere. She located it, then hesitated, doubt gnawing at her confidence. Entering without him felt distinctly like breaking and entering. Definitely not the best way to improve colony relations.

She rapped her knuckles against the reinforced polymer. "Atlas?"

Nothing. She tried again, louder this time, knuckles stinging with the impact.

"Atlas!"

Dead silence.

Where the hell was he?

She traced her fingers along what was definitely the secret entrance he'd described. Her hand hovered over it, then dropped. She glanced back at the dark path leading home, the logical part of her brain screaming retreat. Go back to Vitruvia. Try again tomorrow.

But what if he was inside, waiting, and just couldn't hear her knocking?

Phoebe clutched the insulated case to her chest, feeling the precious cargo inside.

No. Something was off. He'd mentioned Hyacinth stealing his comm before. What if history was repeating itself? Every instinct told her to bail. She backed away from the greenhouse and turned to leave.

Only to freeze mid-step.

Two figures blocked her path, partly hidden in shadows, faces obscured in darkness.

"Atlas?" she called, knowing full well it wasn't him.

"Don't move." Male voice. Authoritative. From their stance and those ridiculous formal uniforms, definitely Naturalist guards.

Phoebe's mind raced through excuses. "I was looking for Atlas. He's expecting me."

The guards stepped into the greenhouse light. The taller one scoffed. "Really doubt that, seeing as it's the boy's wedding night."

Her heart stopped beating.

That couldn't be right. They had to be lying.

The second guard pointed at her insulated case. "That a bomb?"

Phoebe's mouth fell open. "What? No! Why would I—"

"Biological weapon?" the first one cut in, hand moving to his sidearm.

"No. It's…" What was she supposed to say? Medicine? She had a feeling they wouldn't believe her.

The first guard yanked out his weapon, barrel aimed straight at her chest. "Put the case down. Slowly."

Phoebe froze, her mind racing through a parade of escape scenarios.

"NOW!" The guard's finger twitched on the trigger.

She nodded, slowly crouching to place the case on the ground. The moment her fingers released it, she exploded into motion, sprinting left toward the tree line, legs pumping like pistons.

"HEY!" A guard's shout split the night.

Footsteps pounded behind her — too close, too fast.

A hand snagged her arm mid-stride, yanking her backward with bruising force.

She stumbled, momentum nearly taking her down. The guard's fingers dug into her flesh like steel clamps.

"Got her!" he yelled in triumph.

Phoebe twisted violently, breaking free. Her hand shot into her pocket, fingers scrambling for Lucas' tracker.

The second guard lunged, grabbing her from behind and pinning her arms. The tracker slipped from her sweaty fingers, tumbling to the ground.

"No!"

Pure adrenaline kicked in. She wrenched one arm free, diving for the tracker. Her fingers closed around it, thumb finding the emergency button. She jammed it hard, just as a boot stomped down on her hand.

CRACK.

The sound of her bones shattering echoed through the quiet night, shockingly loud as white-hot pain exploded up her arm.

Phoebe's scream tore through her throat.

The guard lifted his boot, and she snatched her hand back, clutching it to her chest. Pain radiated from her fingers and the skin along her knuckles was already swelling, split in places. Blood welled, seeping into the fine lines of her palm, pooling in the creases between her fingers.

She tried to curl them, but only her pinky responded; the others were stiff, twisted at sickening angles.

The taller guard peered down at the tracker. "What is it?"

"Looks like a comm." The other guard ground it beneath his heel. "She didn't get a chance to use it."

The other guard grabbed her by the arm, jerking her upright.

Fresh pain lanced through Phoebe's hand and she bit back a cry.

They marched her toward a heavy, reinforced door, and one guard pressed his palm to a panel. The seal disengaged with a hiss that sounded like a death sentence.

Cold, sterile air hit her face as they shoved her through. Medical antiseptic. Recycled oxygen. Fear. The door sealed behind them with a definitive click.

She had never felt so far away from home.

Chapter Forty

THE GUARDS PUSHED Phoebe into a room and beat a hasty retreat.

She spun around and lunged for the exit, but the door slammed in her face with a metallic THUD.

The lock engaged with a definitive CLICK.

She rested her forehead against the cool metal, buying herself one more second of denial.

The place reeked of antiseptic and fear. Definitely medical. Phoebe's stomach clenched. She really, really didn't want to turn around. But she forced herself anyway.

"Welcome." Dr. Basu stood in front of her, arms crossed. "We've been waiting for you."

Phoebe didn't bother answering.

She'd spotted a dark-haired girl about her age who looked a lot like Dr. Basu, lying motionless on a table. Phoebe guessed this was Hyacinth. She'd been prepped for some kind of medical procedure; Phoebe would've guessed *pap smear* because of the stirrups, but you usually didn't have to be sedated for that.

Behind her on a stool, a nurse waited.

"What have you done to her?" Phoebe asked.

Dr. Basu glanced over at her daughter with an unaffectionate smile. Like she was measuring the quality of her meat. "Nothing that will harm her. She's ready for her wedding night."

"This is her wedding?" Phoebe asked.

Dr. Basu nodded. "She's about to receive the Divine Blueprint."

Phoebe's gaze darted to the tray. It held a portable cryopreservation box, the exact same one she'd spotted in cold storage in her mother's lab.

Wait a second …

This wasn't a wedding ceremony. This was—

An IVF procedure.

Her pulse hammered in her ears like a tribal drum. Hyacinth was getting knocked up from a petri dish. This wasn't some sacred rite; it was a medical procedure dressed up in religious mumbo-jumbo and gift-wrapped as destiny.

And somehow, Dr. Basu had dragged Samara into her twisted scheme. *Atlas and Hyacinth.* Samara had already created the embryos that Dr. Basu would be implanting. Her own mother, enabling Dr. Basu's insanity. Why?

There'd been containers with Atlas' name paired with other women. Dr. Basu was about to implant a whole bunch of embryos into different women, all with Atlas' DNA. He was about to become the father of the next generation of Naturalists.

No wonder Samara had warned her away from him.

Phoebe wished her mother had trusted her with the truth.

She wanted to believe that Samara hadn't had a choice. Maybe Katherine and Dr. Basu had worked it all out from the beginning, some backroom deal to provide genetic material for both colonies. Maybe some of the

Vitruvian women would get the Divine Blueprint, too. Pretty convenient arrangement.

It made her sick.

And Atlas never even got a say.

Phoebe took a step back, disgust coiling in her gut. "You sick, twisted freak. You've been shipping Atlas' tissue samples to my mother. I saw them myself."

"Ah, so you're the reason that last batch embryos had to be remade." Dr. Basu flashed a predatory smile. "Your mother stayed up all night to make sure I got them in time."

Phoebe wanted to believe that was a lie, meant to deflect her anger back toward her mother. And she was angry, but there would be time for that later.

She jabbed a finger at the cryopreservation box. "You're sedating these women, prepping them for implantation, and feeding them fairy tales about divine blessings. You're not a spiritual leader, you're a fraud wearing faith like a Halloween costume."

Dr. Basu's face hardened to granite. "You know nothing."

"You're harvesting Atlas like a crop without his consent. You stole his choice."

It all made sense now.

"The cleanse that the women undergo prior to marriage," Phoebe continued. "That's progesterone, not some symbolic washing of sin. Controlled doses to prep their uterine linings for implantation. And the trance they enter during the final stage sure as hell isn't meditation. You sedate them so they won't know what you've done to them. It hasn't been faith that's kept your community alive. It's science masked as belief."

Phoebe shook her head. Dr. Basu's story of the Divine Blueprint, spiritual purity, and sacred duty was a cancer of lies. Stories designed to maintain her authority, to control the colony, to ensure absolute obedience. She had dressed it up in faith, wrapped it in holy words, but at its core, it was all a deception.

"When I tell everyone the truth—"

"You won't get the chance," Dr. Basu said.

A raw, guttural sound, pure animal panic, erupted from behind Phoebe.

She whipped around to see Atlas laying sprawled in the corner like a discarded toy, limbs slack against the floor and body unnaturally still. His eyes were open but unfocused, staring at nothing. His chest rose and fell in shallow, uneven gasps.

Alive.

But paralyzed?

"Atlas!" She sprinted to him, dropping to her knees hard enough to bruise. Ignoring the white-hot pain from her broken hand, she grabbed his shoulder. His skin was warm, but his muscles might as well have been made of clay. No response. No tension. Just dead weight and vacant eyes.

Definitely drugged. Heavily.

"Atlas, look at me." She shook him. His head lolled against the floor. His breathing hitched again, like he was trying to speak, but no sound came out.

There was a smear of blood on his neck.

A needle mark.

Phoebe pressed two fingers against his throat. His pulse was weak but steady beneath his skin.

"He can hear you. He just can't respond," Dr. Basu said.

She glanced back. "What did you do to him?"

"I needed him to be compliant."

Phoebe pulled Atlas' head into her lap. "When everyone finds out that this is going on, you'll be exiled."

Dr. Basu tilted her head, a shadow of amusement flickering across her face like a serpent's tongue. She folded her arms across her chest. "No one will ever know."

Phoebe clenched her teeth. "They will because I'm going to tell every single person in your cult exactly what you've done.

Dr. Basu's laugh was like ice cracking. "You'll do nothing of the sort. Because Atlas murdered you."

Phoebe froze, her fingers tangling in Atlas' hair. "What?"

"Everyone loves a beautiful, tragic story." Dr. Basu's voice took on a storyteller's cadence. "Atlas shared the Divine Blueprint with Hyacinth on their wedding night, but the contaminated, jealous girl from the Vitruvian colony came to murder his bride. And brave, brave Atlas died defending her honor. So moving. So inspirational."

Phoebe swallowed. "No one will believe you."

"I think they will," Dr. Basu said. "When they find your bodies in Hyacinth's chamber."

"Our bodies?" Phoebe barely whispered it.

Dr. Basu nodded. "A tragic love story cut short by a jealous outsider. Perfect. It'll be the final push we need to break from your people completely." Her lips curved upward. "If they don't want war, they'll come to heel like the dogs they are."

The absolute calm in her voice made Phoebe's skin crawl. "You're crazy."

Dr. Basu didn't even blink. "The colony won't ever know the truth. Atlas sealed his fate the moment he chose you over us." She stepped closer and Phoebe instinctively backed up. "The people will forgive Atlas. They'll remember him as a victim. A cautionary tale for generations. But you?" Her eyes narrowed. "You'll be erased. Forgotten. Like you never existed."

Phoebe clutched Atlas tighter. "No one's ever going to buy that crap."

"They will."

"My mother won't." Phoebe shot back.

Dr. Basu's mouth twisted into something sharp enough to cut. "Your mother is a fool."

"She's the most brilliant woman alive!" Phoebe snapped.

Dr. Basu didn't flinch. "And yet she let you come here."

That hit like a block of granite.

Because Samara didn't even know Phoebe was here. Samara would have never let her walk into this trap. She'd always known exactly how dangerous Dr. Basu was.

Ayesha has spent decades building her ideology around Atlas' immunity. She will not simply let him walk away.

Dr. Basu had laid the perfect trap.

And Phoebe had walked right into it, blind and stupid.

Now she'd die here, just another casualty in Dr. Basu's power game. She blinked back tears, looking down at Atlas. "I'm sorry. I love you."

Atlas' eyes flooded with tears.

Then they grew wide with horror.

Phoebe turned.

Too late.

A sharp, white-hot pain explosion across her skull.

Then — nothing.

No light. No sound. No Atlas.

Nothing at all.

~

ATLAS SCREAMED.

The sound tore through his throat like broken glass, but his body remained a useless prison. He needed to crawl over Phoebe, but his muscles betrayed him. He couldn't even twitch his fingers. Could barely draw breath.

He had no idea how he'd even produced the sound that warned her. Too little, too late.

Phoebe lay beside him, terrifyingly still. Dr. Basu loomed over her, metal tray clutched in her hands. The sharp edge dripped crimson.

Dark blood pooled beneath Phoebe's head, spreading across the cold floor like spilled ink. Too much. No one could lose that much blood and survive.

Atlas struggled, straining against the paralysis as his mind clawed for a way to break free. He tried to force movement into his fingers, his arms, his legs. But still, his body remained a cage.

Across the room, Elda was staring in horror at Phoebe. "Ayesha."

Dr. Basu snapped around to look at her. "Don't."

Elda stilled.

Dr. Basu dropped the tray.

It hit the floor and with a CLANG.

A sound Atlas would remember the rest of his life.

Then she picked up a syringe from a tray and walked over to him. His entire being focused on a single, desperate thought: *Move. Move. MOVE.*

His body still refused to obey.

"Don't worry." Dr. Basu crouched down and pricked his neck again. "You'll be joining your dysgenic love very soon."

She got to her feet, discarded the needle, and grabbed Phoebe by the arm, dragging her across the floor to the Decontamination Chamber.

Phoebe's eyes were wide open with surprise.

But there was no life in them.

Her head lolled to the side, her hair soaked with blood.

No. NO! NO!

Dr. Basu hit the lock for the decontamination chamber, and it opened. She dragged Phoebe's body inside, then stepped out, closing the door and hit the sequence for Clean. A sick hiss filled the air as the chamber began its cycle.

Dr. Basu turned back to him. "You can have her back as soon as I've finished purifying her."

No. The decontamination cycle was meant for people, but the clean cycle was for the machine to disinfect itself, with UV light and chemicals that would poison Phoebe. If she wasn't dead already.

Atlas thrashed against the paralysis. His jaw clenched so tightly it felt like his teeth might shatter. His vision blurred from rage. The burning, helpless horror constricted his chest until he felt like he was suffocating.

Whatever she had given him was working. He was dying. Ice settled into his limbs.

The door to the hallway opened—

No. It EXPLODED inward, the reinforced metal frame buckling like aluminum foil. The impact rattled through the walls, vibrating his teeth in his skull. The sound split the air like a cannon blast. Shards of the locking mechanism broke free, skittering across the floor like roaches.

Lucas stood in the doorway, calm as death itself, gripping a guard by the neck with one hand as if the man weighed nothing.

A cold realization washed over Atlas. No human being had that kind of strength. Lucas was an android. *The android*, who'd deceived all the colonists before the Schism.

Phoebe had called him "Dad" like it was a joke, but Atlas finally got the punchline.

Lucas released his grip. The guard dropped to the floor with the unmistakable finality of a corpse.

"What—" Dr. Basu gaped, her composure finally cracking.

Elda bolted into the corner and crouched there, hiding.

Lucas saw the blood on the floor, turned toward the decontamination chamber, and spotted Phoebe. Then his gaze landed on Ayesha Basu.

She shifted back, raising her hands in surrender. "It isn't what you think."

Too late.

Lucas closed the distance between them in two precise steps. One moment Dr. Basu was alone; the next, his hand was locked around her throat.

Dr. Basu let out a strangled, choked gasp. Her fingers clawed uselessly at his grip, nails scraping against synthetic skin. She might as well have been fighting a hydraulic press. Her feet kicked frantically against the floor as he lifted her like she was made of cotton. The tendons in her neck strained like cables, her face contorting in shock and dawning terror.

Atlas tried to move, tried to scream, but his body was still a useless sack of meat. Lucas pivoted toward the decontamination chamber, carrying Dr. Basu with him like she weighed no more than a doll.

He tapped the panel with his free hand.

The suction seal released with a deep, mechanical hiss.

Then Lucas threw Dr. Basu in like she was garbage into a compactor.

She hit the far wall, her head snapping back as she crumpled to the floor. Then Lucas bent down and picked up Phoebe. He was so gentle. As if he was touching the most precious thing in all the world. Which he was, in Atlas' opinion.

Phoebe hung limp in his arms, blood leaking from her head.

Behind him, came the sound of a weak, shuddering cough.

Atlas' gaze flicked to Dr. Basu.

She was crawling, dragging herself toward the outer chamber door. Trying to escape. Lucas turned and kicked it shut. The heavy seal slammed into place with a mechanical hiss.

Dr. Basu's bloodied hand stretched up to hit the panel release.

Too late.

Lucas punched the button.

The clean cycle started with a soft hum. Sterilization agents began to rise around her, a vapor designed to kill anything organic.

Lucas stood looking down at Phoebe for a long moment.

As if he was trying to burn her face into his memory.

Then a gasp. A scream.

Hyacinth.

She jerked upright on the hospital bed, eyes wild. She spotted Lucas. Phoebe. The blood on the floor. Then her gaze locked on the chamber.

And she saw her mother.

"No. NO!"

Hyacinth scrambled off the table, her bare feet slipping on Phoebe's blood. She tried to yank the IV from her arm. The tubing snapped, blood welling where the needle tore free. She reached down, clawing at the monitor leads stuck to her chest, ripping them off.

Elda bolted toward the outer door.

Lucas adjusted Phoebe in his arms, then picked up an oxygen canister and flung it at her. It struck Elda's head, she fell to the floor.

Hyacinth staggered toward the decontamination chamber, her hands slamming against the glass.

"STOP IT! OPEN IT!"

The automated cycle continued, oblivious to her screams. She whirled to Atlas, her face streaked with tears. "HELP ME! PLEASE!"

Atlas didn't move. Couldn't move.

She turned to Lucas. "SHUT IT DOWN! MAKE IT STOP!"

Lucas ignored her, laying Phoebe down on the table where Hyacinth had been lying. Then he picked something up from a tray and walked over to Hyacinth.

"Help me?" she said.

He slid the syringe beneath her skin, depressing the plunger.

She looked up at him. "What did you…"

Then she sagged. Knocked out.

Atlas tried to speak, but his throat seized, his breath coming in strangled, shallow gasps.

He should have fought harder. Should have seen this coming. Should have kept Phoebe safe. Instead, he'd killed her.

Not with his hands.

But with his ignorance.

He was growing even colder now.

Darkness clouding his vision.

His mind began unraveling, his thoughts slipping away.

Then he saw Phoebe at the ruins. Walking toward him in the dark like a vision. He felt their first kiss. Saw her eyes light up when she looked at him. Felt them lying together on the ridge. Feeling so much love.

He didn't mind dying.

It had been a good life.

Because he'd met Phoebe.

And for that, he was grateful.

If he couldn't be with her in this lifetime, he'd be with her in the next.

He let go.

Chapter Forty-One

ATLAS' consciousness returned in jagged pieces.

First: cold floor against his cheek, like pressing his face to a frozen window.

Next: chemical taste coating his throat, bitter and metallic.

Then: strange fire in his veins, like someone had replaced his blood with battery acid.

He pried his eyes open with sheer will.

Lucas towered above him, silhouetted against the harsh lights.

Atlas flinched, instinctively trying to scramble away, but his limbs still refused orders. Lucas held a syringe, emptying the last of its contents into Atlas' arm.

"Don't." He tried to form a word, but he was fairly sure it came out garbled.

Lucas drew the needle from his flesh. "I believe that should be sufficient to counteract the poison you were given."

A wave of nausea rolled through Atlas' body. He retched, spitting up bile.

"The poison is fighting against the antidote. You will be disoriented and weak for some time."

"Phoebe."

"She is dead," Lucas reported like a hammer strike.

"No."

Lucas stood and walked back to the table where she lay.

Atlas felt his chest crack open. The antidote? Maybe. It felt like someone had reached in and ripped out his still-beating heart.

Phoebe was gone.

It didn't make sense. The universe didn't work this way.

He squeezed his eyes and screamed, a primal sound that tore through his vocal cords. Grief. Rage. Helplessness. All of it, tangled and spilling out in one violent sound.

It echoed in the ensuing silence.

Then he heard Lucas moving about.

Atlas blinked to see Lucas standing over Phoebe, appearing to do something surgical.

"What are you doing?" he asked.

Lucas set something into a medical container and sealed it with a CLICK. "She is beyond saving. But the embryo is not."

Embryo?

His brain stuttered on the word. It felt alien, disconnected, as if Lucas had suddenly switched to speaking another language.

He stared up at the android, his mind racing to catch up. "What? Phoebe was …"

Lucas closed the incision in Phoebe's abdomen. "Yes."

Pregnant.

The word shattered something fundamental inside him.

His love. His child. Both gone.

Dr. Basu hadn't just killed a person. She'd obliterated an entire future: a family that would never be, laughter that would never sound, first steps that would never be taken. A lifetime of possibilities, snuffed out in one violent moment.

"Your people can't survive alone anymore," Lucas said. "They'll need to integrate with the main colony."

Atlas finally managed to move. He crawled to the table and pulled himself up to his knees beside it. Then he just stared at Phoebe, trying to memorize every line of her face, like he could hold on to her through sheer willpower.

She'd shown him what freedom actually felt like. Not some abstract concept, but something real. Tangible. Risky. Alive. She'd pushed him to ask the hard questions when everyone else just nodded along. She never swallowed an answer just because it came wrapped in tradition or doctrine or rules.

Phoebe had taken everything he'd been force-fed since birth, dumped it on the table, and said, "Let's sort through this garbage together."

She'd kicked down doors he hadn't even known existed and made him believe he could actually choose his own path.

And now she was gone.

That laugh that could cut through any darkness. That voice that never, ever backed down.

Gone.

That future they'd only just dared to imagine.

Gone.

"You have an opportunity to fill the leadership vacuum Dr. Basu's death will create," Lucas said, staring down at him. "Use it to help your people survive."

A cold rage filled Atlas' chest. "I don't want anything to

do with them. Not now. They killed Phoebe. They deserve whatever's coming to them."

Lucas studied him. "And what would Phoebe have wanted you to do?"

Atlas pushed himself to his feet and leaned over her, brushing a strand of hair from her face with trembling fingers. He pressed his lips to her forehead. She was already so cold. How was that possible? She'd been alive just minutes ago.

He closed his eyes, hot tears spilling down his cheeks. Why couldn't it have been him instead? It should have been him. She had a future. Brilliance. She could have changed the world the way she'd changed his.

He felt Lucas shift beside him.

Atlas looked up. "Don't take her away from me just yet, please. I'll take her home to her mother. I promise. I just need a little time."

Lucas stared at the box in his hands for what felt like forever. Finally, he nodded. "Agreed. But if you are lying and I have to return for her, I will tear your settlement to the ground."

Lucas touched Phoebe's forehead, then headed for the door.

"Wait," Atlas called out.

The android paused at threshold.

Atlas braced himself against the table, legs still unreliable. "I didn't think androids were supposed to have emotions."

"We do not." Perfect, emotionless delivery.

Atlas wiped tears from his cheeks with the heel of his hand. "Well, from where I'm standing, you loved Phoebe with all your heart."

Lucas didn't blink. "I don't have a heart."

"I don't think that's true."

Lucas went unnaturally still. Like someone had hit his off switch. The effect lasted only a second before he rebooted, meeting Atlas' eyes with something almost human flickering behind his gaze. "Thank you."

And then he was gone.

Atlas turned back to Phoebe, pulling her into his arms and holding her tight. And then the world seemed to stop. He didn't know how long had passed. Seconds, minutes, hours? How was he supposed to let her go? It didn't seem possible. Maybe he should have let Lucas take—

A deafening BOOM rocked the building.

Instruments rattled off trays. The examination table shuddered beneath Phoebe's body. Atlas lost his balance, dropping to one knee.

What the actual hell?

Another explosion followed, closer, more violent than the first. The floor vibrated like a speaker cone underfoot. An earthquake? Atlas staggered over to the Decontamination Chamber and stared beyond the polymer walls.

Thick, black columns of smoke rose into the dawn sky from multiple points across the mountainside like demon fingers.

Not an earthquake.

Something much worse.

The ground shook again, harder this time. Ceiling panels crashed down nearby.

Atlas stumbled back to Phoebe and collapsed at her side. From somewhere in the distance came the sounds of panic—shouts, screams, running feet. The colony was waking to chaos. They'd be looking to Dr. Basu for guidance, and orders.

But Dr. Basu was dead in the decontamination chamber.

Atlas buried his face in Phoebe's hair, breathing in her

scent one last time. If this was the end — if the mountain was coming down around them — he hoped it would be quick and complete.

At least they'd be buried together.

Chapter Forty-Two

SAMARA JERKED awake as her bed shook beneath her. For a disoriented second, she thought it was Phoebe trying to rouse her. Then the tremor rattled the walls and sent a photo of her and Phoebe crashing to the floor.

Earthquake?

No, not with that distant boom rolling across the valley like artificial thunder.

That was an explosion.

She bolted out of bed and stumbled to the window, nearly losing her balance as the floor still trembled beneath her feet. Outside, colonists gathered with faces turned skyward. She followed their gaze and her blood ran cold.

Thick fingers of smoke billowed from the mountainside near the lake, clawing their way into the violet sky.

Another explosion ripped through the air, and this one she felt in her chest, a concussive thud that rattled her teeth and echoed through the valley.

A mining accident.

It had to be.

Outside her window, the confusion was escalating.

A security guard dashed along the path outside, approaching a cluster of colonists who were staring at the smoke.

"Get to the common hall! Move!"

A second guard appeared, running hard in the opposite direction, pounding on doors. "Get out! Now!"

Samara sprinted to Phoebe's bedroom. Empty.

Damn it. She hadn't checked Phoebe's room last night because the door had been closed; she'd figured Atlas was in there with her and didn't want to disturb them. Where the hell had they gone?

She ran back to her room, threw on some clothes, and yanked on her boots. If the colony was under attack, Renata would be safe where she was. And the kids would be taken to an underground bunker beneath the school.

But she needed to find Phoebe.

Samara burst through the front door. The air tasted like metal and scorched earth, thick with smoke that burned her lungs.

Another explosion shook the ground and Samara almost fell. She headed toward the common hall. The square outside was chaos. Security personnel were directing everyone inside. Medical staff were dealing with minor injuries.

Samara entered, taking a detour, heading down the hallway to Katherine's office.

She arrived to find her hunched over a comm at her desk, Leo and Maeve at her side.

"What's happened?" Samara demanded. "Were those explosions—"

"Sabotage," Katherine said, her voice flat. "At the mining operation."

"Sabotage?" Samara repeated.

Leo pushed a tablet toward Samara. "Someone placed

charges at precisely calculated points under the west side of the lake." His finger tracing between several marked locations. "Maximum structural damage with minimal explosive force. They knew exactly what they were doing."

Samara stared at him. "The lake's been breached?"

He gave a grim nod.

She swallowed. "Was it the Naturalists?"

"What makes you say that?" Katherine asked.

Samara opened her mouth, then closed it again.

Katherine's eyes hardened. "Samara."

"Atlas."

"What about him?"

"He and Phoebe are in love. He left his colony last night to request sanctuary with us so they could be together."

Katherine's hand whitened around the comm. "And you're just telling me this now? Does Ayesha know?"

"I don't know. And I'm sorry. I thought he would have come to you already."

The comm unit crackled. "Mahmoud to Katherine."

She raised it to her mouth. "Go ahead."

"Confirming breach on the eastern face. I've got six people trapped in secondary tunnels. We've diverted everyone to rescue ops, but the water volume is accelerating at approximately 8,000 cubic meters per minute and—"

Static cut through his transmission.

"Say again," Katherine said.

"I'm not sure what direction the water will take. But I don't think it will hit the Vitruvian colony. The natural contours should channel it south of us."

"The Hyperionites?" Samara asked.

A pause. "No. They'll be alright. It's the Naturalists who are in the path. They need to evacuate. We're talking millions of cubic meters of water heading straight for them … I'm sending drone footage now."

The display refreshed with drone footage showing a mountainside torn open. A massive scar now gaped where the lake had been, disgorging water in a violent torrent. Fallen trees and boulders tumbled in the deadly slurry, gathering momentum as it carved a new channel downslope.

"Mother of God," Leo said.

The water carved a new path down the mountain. Even from the drone's height, they could see the immensity of the destruction: entire sections of forest flattened, the earth itself being reshaped by water.

"We need to warn them," Samara said.

"The communications team is trying," Maeve said. "But so far Ayesha isn't answering her comm."

"Stubborn fool," Katherine growled. "Keep trying. Send someone to warn them in person. In the meantime, we need to organize rescue teams. Leo, get every available all-terrain vehicle prepped and loaded with emergency supplies. Maeve, get your engineers working on temporary shelters. We may need to house refugees. Samara, I need you and Leila for medical. And I want to talk to Phoebe."

"I don't know where she is…" Samara broke off, feeling a rising tide of panic.

Katherine squeezed her hand. "Phoebe's a smart girl. Wherever she is, she'll be alright. It'd take more than a flood to take her out."

Samara tried to smile but she couldn't.

What if Atlas had never arrived, and Phoebe had gone looking for him?

∼

THE DOOR to the sanctum screeched open.

Atlas looked up, Phoebe's hands still clasped in his. As if somehow he could will her back to life. Letting go meant accepting she was gone forever, and he couldn't do that yet.

Ivy stood in the doorway, her eyes widening at the sight of Phoebe on the table. Elda and Hyacinth on the floor.

"I was told Dr. Basu was here," she said.

"She's gone."

Ivy's face contorted. "Gone? What do you mean gone? We need her. We're under attack."

Atlas almost laughed. They deserved whatever was coming. Their entire ideology was a scourge — generational obedience masked as virtue, reproductive control disguised as faith. Fitting that the chaos they'd unleashed on others had finally come home.

"Dr. Basu's dead."

"Dead?" Her face lost all color.

"The Divine saw fit to punish her for the hubris rising within her. And now it's our turn. We were fools who followed a hypocrite. She let people suffer and called it order while we all watched it happen. We didn't even try to stop her. We called ourselves pure. *Better.* But the Divine knew the truth. We built a lie and now we're choking on it."

Ivy looked like she might collapse. "So what happens to us?"

He shrugged.

"We have children, Atlas. They've done nothing wrong. Whatever we've done, they're innocent."

Atlas blinked, forcing himself to swallow his anger.

She was right.

He didn't want her to be.

But she was.

He looked down at Phoebe. Leaving her felt impossible, like abandoning the final fragments of his heart.

Ivy tugged on his sleeve. "*Please*, Atlas."

He leaned down and pressed his forehead to Phoebe's. "I'm sorry. I'll be back for you."

The words were completely inadequate for what Dr. Basu had done to Phoebe, for his own failure to protect her. Tearing himself away felt like physical pain, but Atlas forced himself to follow Ivy out of the sanctum.

He closed the door with a soft click. "How do you know we're under attack?"

She glanced over at him. "What else makes the ground shake like that?"

"Fair point." He trailed her through the maze of transparent corridors to Dr. Basu's office, where a cluster of women clutched frightened children.

"Where's Dr. Basu?" Karina demanded, her toddler's face buried against her neck. "I thought that's who you went to find."

"She's ..." Ivy broke off.

"Not available," Atlas said, scanning the room. There were eight women and eleven children of various ages. The youngest couldn't have been more than three months, thumb in her mouth, eyes wider.

He crossed to Dr. Basu's desk and grabbed her comm. It was different than the one Phoebe had given him, and he didn't know how to use it. "Does anyone know how to operate this?"

The women exchanged glances, shaking their heads. Communication with the Vitruvian settlement was exclusively Dr. Basu's domain. Knowledge was control, and she'd controlled everything.

Atlas pressed a switch on the side.

A second later the console emitted a series of tones before squawking to life.

"—repeat, Ayesha, respond immediately," a woman's voice commanded through static. "This is an emergency. We've detected catastrophic failures in the northern mining tunnels. Ayesha, acknowledge."

Atlas located a blinking button and pressed it. "Hello?"

The line went silent for a beat before the woman said, "Who is this?"

"Atlas."

"Atlas. I need to speak to Dr. Basu."

Atlas glanced at Ivy, who gave him a slight nod.

"You can't," he said flatly. "She's dead."

Gasps rippled through the room, faces contorting with shock.

Atlas looked away, unable to bear their disbelief.

"Okay. My name is Katherine." The woman's voice crackled through the comm. "Listen carefully. There's been sabotage at the mining operation. You need to evacuate everyone in the Naturalist settlement right now. A wall of water is coming down the mountain pass and the entire valley will be underwater. You have minutes, not hours."

Atlas scanned the frightened faces around him. Just a tiny fraction of their community. "There are too many people. We need help."

"Help is coming," Katherine replied, her voice steady. "But we can't beat the water. You need to move now."

The storage sheds flashed in his mind. "I can get everyone to higher ground."

"Do it."

"We have storage facilities on the south hill, above the greenhouse."

"Perfect. Head there immediately. We're launching rescue teams." A pause. "Atlas? Is Phoebe with you?"

His throat closed up.

Static erupted from the speaker. Atlas jabbed the switch. "Hello? Katherine?"

Nothing but white noise.

The connection was dead.

Atlas set the comm back on the desk, turning to the colonists. They looked terrified. They were facing extinction without their leader. He gripped the edge of the desk. "We need to get to the storage sheds on the greenhouse hill. Leave everything. Go there now. Tell everyone you see."

One of the women clutched her child tighter. "What about environmental protocols? We need our suits—"

Atlas shook his head. "We don't have time for that."

The irony wasn't lost on him. After a lifetime of fearing contamination, their survival now depended on abandoning those fears. "Get to the sheds."

Ivy was already organizing the children into a line. "Come on, little ones. We're going on an adventure."

They filed out of the room and Atlas took one last look around the office. On Dr. Basu's desk was a picture of Hyacinth as a child, smiling up at her mother. They both looked so happy. Back before all the lies and manipulation, all the ways his life had been engineered to serve someone else's vision.

But that was all about to be washed away.

Atlas left the office and sprinted back to the sanctum. Hyacinth was still sprawled on the floor.

He ran over to her, shaking her shoulder. "Hyacinth, wake up."

Her eyelids fluttered but didn't open. He got up and bolted to the sink. Pouring some cold water into a pan. Then he returned, chucking it in her face.

"Get up. We need to go. Now."

He banged the pan against the floor, trying to rouse her.

She flinched, mumbling something.

There was no time.

The flood could arrive at any moment. Atlas slid one arm beneath her shoulders, the other under her knees, and lifted her.

He headed for the decontamination chamber which was the shortest way to get outside. He hit the switch. It was long done with the clean cycle.

The door opened.

Dr. Basu lay crumpled against the far wall, her limbs contorted at unnatural angles. Eyes open and staring at nothing, mouth frozen in a final grimace, pain and fury carved hard into her features. Death had not softened the woman.

Atlas recoiled, repulsed by her presence. He hoisted Hyacinth up and stepped over her mother. A small sound escaped Hyacinth's throat.

Hyacinth's eyes fluttered open, consciousness returning in stages. Then recognition dawned, and her pupils dilated in horror. A guttural scream tore from her throat. "MOTHER!"

She twisted violently in his arms, fingernails raking his face. "PUT ME DOWN!"

Atlas tightened his hold. "Stop it!"

"MOTHER!" Her scream echoed off the walls.

Atlas staggered forward, desperate to get through the chamber. He punched the door control with his elbow and the outer door slid open with a hiss. Fresh air rushed in, carrying with it the sounds of distant shouts and activity.

"LET ME GO!"

"If I do that you're going to die." Atlas stumbled

outside, nearly losing his footing. Blood trickled down his cheek where she'd scratched him.

A man stood nearby, directing colonists towards the sheds. His eyes widened at the sight of Hyacinth, a writhing, screaming animal.

"Here!" Atlas lurched toward him. "Take her!"

The man stepped back, confusion and alarm scrawled across his features. "What—"

"Take her!"

The man opened his arms, catching her as Atlas released his hold.

She tried to claw her way free, still screaming for her mother.

"Get her to the sheds!" Atlas pointed to the elevated ground beyond the colony's perimeter. "The flood waters will be here any minute."

The man nodded.

Atlas didn't wait to see if they went. He ran back inside, heading to the central corridor. There was a line up for emergency suits. "No time. Just go."

He pushed them toward the doors. Caught a glimpse of his mother with several others. As if by sixth sense, she turned her eyes, finding his across the distance. Relief flooded her features.

"Atlas!"

He turned away, feeling nothing.

Whatever bond they had once shared, was gone now. She'd made her choice when she allowed Dr. Basu to kill Phoebe.

He made his way down the corridor to the meal hall, pushing the door open. The space was packed, voices rising in a clamor of panic and uncertainty.

"They're saying a flood's coming straight for us."

"Someone saw the water rushing down the ridge—"

"We should go, get to the sheds—"

Jared stood on one of the wooden tables. "No one's leaving until we talk to Dr. Basu. It's too dangerous. We don't even know if the Vitruvians are telling us the truth."

Atlas stared at the colonists.

They were wasting precious seconds. Paralyzed without Dr. Basu telling them what to do.

Why did they deserve to live when Phoebe didn't?

The injustice threatened to drown him. These people had swallowed Dr. Basu's lies. They had let her feed them lies, let her dictate their entire existence. He was no better than them. They all deserved to be punished.

But then he heard Lucas' words in his head.

What would Phoebe want you to do?

And he knew she wouldn't want them to die. Not if Atlas could help them.

He swallowed hard and jumped up on the table.

"Dr. Basu is dead. And you'll be dead too, if you don't get out of here."

Silence filled the room.

Atlas clapped his hands, then pointed to the doors. "Move. Now! Head for the storage sheds on the hill! Don't stop for anything!"

The room erupted in chaos.

But they were headed toward decontamination. And there was no time for that either.

Atlas bolted into the kitchen, yanked open a drawer, and grabbed one of the chef's knives. Then he sprinted back into the dining area, heart pounding, and drove the blade into the wall.

For a fraction of a second the material resisted, then it split. A sharp *whump* of air pressure rushed out as the reinforced polymer peeled away beneath his hand.

"This way!"

The colonists hesitated, programming still intact. Years of drilled-in instinct told them that breaking protocol was wrong, that the only way out was through the decontamination process.

Then a woman lunged forward, dragging her child and bolted through the tear. And another. All at once, the crowd surged toward him. The plastic strained and ripped further, bodies tearing it wider in their desperation to escape.

Atlas braced himself against the frame, scanning faces as they passed. He knew every single one of these people.

He had grown up with them, trusted them. And despite what Dr. Basu had done, he didn't want them to die.

From somewhere in the distance, a low, ominous rumble grew louder: the sound of millions of tons of water carving a new path down the mountainside.

Destruction was coming.

And it was almost here.

Chapter Forty-Three

Samara poked her head into Leila's clinic. "Ready to roll?"

Leila nodded, hoisting her medical bag over her shoulder, and snagging a portable surgical kit. "Phoebe back yet?"

Samara blinked. "Back? From where?"

"I saw her heading out last night." Leila said.

A chill raced down Samara's spine. "Which direction?"

"The north path."

Samara pressed her fingertips against her temples. "You're sure about this?"

Leila didn't hesitate. "Saw her with my own eyes."

The Naturalist colony.

"Was she alone?"

"Yeah."

She'd gone to meet Atlas after all. Which put her directly in danger.

Samara wanted to scream. She'd been exactly the kind of mother she'd always feared becoming: absent when it mattered most. It was why she'd never wanted kids before she'd come to DaVinci.

"If she's at the Naturalist colony …"

Leila paled. "Phoebe's resourceful."

Samara nodded, but her jaw remained tight.

For a moment Samara didn't move.

Forget the colony.

Forget the flood.

She had to find her daughter.

ATLAS RAN.

The Naturalist compound had dissolved into chaos. Colonists shoved past each other, clutching whatever possessions they could grab, scrambling for higher ground.

The ground was now a muddy mess.

He slipped, catching himself before he fell. Off to his left was Graham: four years old, alone, tiny fists clenched.

"Daddy! DADDY!"

Atlas sprinted over and scooped him up.

Tear-filled eyes met his. "Where's Daddy?"

"Don't know," Atlas said, scanning for David. "But we'll find him. Promise."

Then he ran for the sheds. Halfway up the slope, Atlas spotted Ivy.

"Ivy!"

She turned.

"Take him. I need to find David."

She nodded, taking the child. Then she stiffened, looking behind them. "Atlas—"

A sound like growing thunder filled the air. Atlas' skin prickled, the fine hairs on his arms rising. He turned.

A fifteen-foot wall of churning brown water tore

through the lower compound, a seething monster that devoured everything in its path. It surged toward them, bristling with debris: splintered wood, twisted metal, entire sections of colony infrastructure tossed around like twigs.

Domes cracked like eggshells, their supports crumpling inward. The transparent corridors folded like paper, warped under the pressure of impact.

Simon was still climbing the hill behind them.

He wasn't going to make it.

The thunderous roar of the flood was gaining, rising, hungry.

"GO!" he shouted to Ivy.

She did. More than anything Atlas wanted to follow her and Graham. Every instinct in his body told him to get the hell out of there.

What would Phoebe do?

Atlas ran.

Down the hill toward Simon. The old man's gray hair plastered to his skull, environmental suit torn at the shoulder. Atlas grabbed his arm, hauled him upward. "MOVE!"

Simon's fingers dug into his wrist.

Together they ran.

Two colonists met them, taking Simon, pulling him up the hill.

Atlas looked back.

David.

He was helping Fiona with her children. She clutched the baby to her chest.

David carried the other two, one in each arm, their small bodies clinging to him, faces buried in his shoulders. His boots sunk into the mud. Each movement, a struggle, his grip shifting as the older child began to slip.

Fiona tried to help him, but she was barely keeping herself upright.

Atlas tore back down, his boots skidding on the ground. He heard footsteps beside him.

Ivy.

They reached David. Atlas grabbed one of the kids, tossed him at Ivy. Then he took the other child, giving David a break.

He took Fiona's hand, dragging her behind him. Colonists came to meet him, took the kids, running back up.

David was still struggling.

Atlas passed off the child, headed back to help him.

Too late.

The water hit.

It took David first.

Then the impact ripped Atlas off his feet, punching the air from his lungs.

His world imploded as the flood swallowed him whole, spinning him into a maelstrom of darkness.

His body tumbled, the current yanking him downward like a malevolent hand. Water invaded his nose, his ears, his mouth, forcing its way in, choking him. No up or down in the churning darkness.

Something slammed into his ribs. Rock? Metal? The pain exploded white-hot, nearly forcing him to inhale. He fought the instinct, but his lungs burned, desperate for oxygen.

Don't breathe. Don't breathe. Don't breathe.

His mind flashed.

Phoebe.

Her laughter. Her finger jabbing his chest, calling him stubborn. The way she'd leaned in, forehead pressed to his. Her kiss …

His lungs convulsed, desperate to inhale.

How long had he been under? Seconds? Minutes?

Darkness pushed in at the edges of his vision. The panicked animal part of his brain screamed at him to do something.

Move. Fight. Climb.

His shoulder collided with something solid, flat, and vertical. A wall.

His fingers scrabbled against the surface, slipping, searching.

The greenhouse.

Atlas wedged his fingers into the narrow gap between the aluminum frame and Plexiglas, clinging for life.

The current wrenched him sideways, nearly ripping him away. His grip slipped. His body twisted sharply, a sharp crack rattling through his shoulder.

He was going under again.

His lungs gave out.

Water rushed in.

The shock of it sent his body into violent spasms, his throat convulsing, his vision narrowing to nothing.

No.

Not like this.

With a primal scream, Atlas hauled himself upward, frame by frame.

His arms burned, his muscles screamed, but still he climbed.

After what seemed like an eternity, his head broke the surface.

Air!

Dawn shimmered above him, a hazy lavender promise. He gasped, sucking in oxygen so fast it burned like fire in his throat. He coughed violently, vomiting floodwater. His body spasmed against the sloping greenhouse roof, his arms felt too weak to hold him up any longer. But he held on.

Then climbed.

Up, up, and up.

Until he collapsed against the slick surface, shaking so violently it felt like his bones might splinter apart. His clothes were in tatters, barely clinging to his body. His skin was raw, covered in bruises, deep scrapes, and fresh wounds where debris had sliced him open.

His eyes felt scrubbed raw. For several long moments, all he could do was breathe.

Below him, the water raged through the greenhouse, tearing through the rows of cultivated plants. Leaves, vines, entire stalks swept into the churning current, tangled masses of green and soil vanishing before his eyes. The tomatoes would have started fruiting in a few weeks. He had planted them, nurtured them, made sure they had the right balance of nutrients. And now they were gone.

The greenhouse groaned, a deep, shuddering vibration that rattled through the metal frame beneath him. The water pounded against its walls, as if trying to peel it away from the hill. He clung to the metal, his fingers aching, shivering.

He wrapped his left arm around the framework. Below, the flood consumed everything in its path.

Atlas turned. And his breath caught in his throat.

The colony was gone.

There was no going back.

No rebuilding.

Everything had been washed away like it never existed.

Atlas' gaze went to the hillside, where survivors huddled in small groups. He spotted Graham, still crying for David. That hit hard. The boy's tears were the sound of a promise he hadn't been able to keep.

He'd let Graham down.

Just like he'd let Phoebe down.

The greenhouse shuddered violently, the frame groaning as the water climbed higher, pushing, pressing, swallowing.

Atlas held on. But what was the point?

There was nothing left.

The compound was gone. The fields were gone. Phoebe was gone.

Maybe he should just let go.

Let the water take him. Sink. Disappear.

Like he'd never existed.

Like Phoebe.

Chapter Forty-Four

SAMARA LEANED against the back wall of the common hall, only half-listening to Katherine's address.

Ayesha was dead?

Atlas had to be mistaken. Or lying. But why would he lie about that?

Dead.

The word didn't compute, like her brain was rejecting the data.

Katherine had tried to restore the connection. But was unable to. Most likely due to the flooding.

If he was at the colony, Phoebe must be there as well. Had they had a hand in it? She couldn't imagine so. Maybe Dr. Basu had tried to stop Atlas from leaving and there had been an accident?

But then why hadn't Phoebe used her comm and called Samara for help?

And where the hell was Lucas? She'd been trying to get a hold of him for the past half hour, but he hadn't been answering his comm. Were the two of them together?

Maybe Atlas changed his mind about leaving the Naturalists. Maybe Phoebe and Lucas had gone to the Hyperion ruins to look at the stars.

But then why hadn't they checked in when they heard the explosions?

What the hell was going on?

Her world was breaking down molecule by molecule, like it had been infected with prions. And she couldn't stop it. Couldn't even slow it down. And now she was standing here, waiting for Katherine to convince the Vitruvians to help with the rescue mission to the Naturalist colony. Time was wasting. She needed to get moving.

"I need at least a dozen volunteers, Katherine repeated, her voice sharp.

"Why bother?" Gerald crossed his arms, jaw set like concrete. "The Naturalists probably blew up the lake themselves, hoping to wipe us out."

Uneasy agreement rippled through the room.

Katherine's eyes flashed. "There's no evidence that's true."

"Yeah, but it's likely."

"It could also be an accident of chance that the flash flood isn't heading for us," Katherine argued. "And—"

The protesting voices drowned her out.

Oh, for God's sake.

Samara shouldered her way through the crowd and strode to the front, taking her place beside Katherine. She jammed two fingers into her mouth and let out a piercing whistle that shut everyone up.

"Look," she said, "we've known each other our whole lives. We've survived hell together. And now, when it actually matters, you're all standing around making excuses and doing nothing?"

She waited a beat before continuing. "It's insane. For all our differences, we sink or swim together. You might hate the Naturalists. You might not trust the Hypers. But we need each other, whether we want to admit it or not."

She locked eyes with Gerald. "Let people drown when we could save them? We might as well strip off our skin and declare ourselves the monsters we'd become."

Silence.

"So, whether anyone comes or not, I'm leaving. Phoebe is at the Naturalist colony and I'm going to get my daughter."

She didn't wait for anyone to answer.

She headed for the back of the room. Out the door and over to the transports. By the time she climbed aboard there were more than a dozen other volunteers joining her.

Katherine climbed in beside her. "Thanks for that."

Samara nodded.

Leo climbed in the back. "Drone footage just came in."

He passed his table to Samara. The entire Naturalist compound sat under water. Total destruction. Twisted metal jutted from the flood like broken bones. Shattered plexiglass and snapped solar panels floated in the brown soup that had swallowed everything.

The gathering hall had collapsed, its shattered supports peeking out of the water like the ribs of some giant's carcass. Storage containers that had been ripped from their places and tossed about like driftwood. Scraps of fabric that were once part of tents, banners, and clothing drifted across the surface. A chair bobbed near the remains of a walkway, turning in the current, empty, waiting for someone who would never sit in it again.

The water stilled.

She couldn't see anyone swimming.

Had they gotten to safety or had they all drowned?

Then she spotted movement.

At the highest point of the settlement, on the hill overlooking what was once the colony, figures clung to the rooftops of small storage sheds. They were huddled together, some standing, some crouched low, arms wrapped around one another. A few waved at the drone. Others didn't move at all.

Then she spotted a lone figure stranded on what remained of the greenhouse roof. Samara barely recognized Atlas at first — soaked, slumped, clinging by pure stubbornness. He looked impossibly small against the vast canvas of destruction.

So if Atlas was there, where was ….

She scanned the footage again, checking every rooftop, broken structure, and patch of dry land.

No Phoebe.

The tablet trembled in her hands.

She frantically swiped through all angles.

Nothing.

Her heart crystallized into ice.

Where was Phoebe?

Where was her daughter?

A CORPSE DRIFTED PAST, face down in the swirling current. Its arm snagged on submerged metal, spinning the body in a grotesque pirouette before the water tugged it free and carried it downstream. Atlas couldn't identify the person, but it was a neighbor, nonetheless. Another life extinguished. From the hill above, he heard the Naturalists praying and crying. Others stood frozen, watching their world dissolve beneath the water.

It was still flowing, searching for a new path, but it wasn't rising anymore. The worst had passed, but that didn't mean it was over.

Atlas could hear muffled cries for help, distorted and distant. People still alive, sealed in buildings under the water. Or maybe it was just in his head. Imagined because the alternative was so much worse.

"Atlas!"

The voice came from below.

Atlas pressed his forehead against the plexiglass roof, blinking through the film of water dripping from his lashes. Inside the greenhouse, Sofia was clinging to a metal support beam.

Henry was balanced atop a toppled grow table using it as a raft, gripping one of the tall shelves so he wouldn't be dragged away. At the very top of the shelving unit his young daughter, Micah, held on tight.

He waved.

Lost his balance.

Slid.

Caught himself at the last second, white-knuckled grip on the edge.

Henry gestured upward. "Hold on! We're okay."

Atlas nodded, but he felt so helpless. They were twelve feet below him, separated by strong plexiglass. Even if he could somehow break it, how was he going to get to them? As long as the greenhouse stood, they'd be all right. And if he had to let go to keep it from collapsing, of course he'd do it.

Another body drifted past. Then a child's toy. A framed family photo. A sacred text, its pages fanning open like pale wings before surrendering to the current.

On the hill Jared stripped off his clothes and waded into the water toward him. Atlas tightened his grip. "Stop! Don't!"

But he was too far away.

Jared managed three steps before the current hit him,

sweeping his legs out from under him. His head disappeared beneath the water. He fought his way to the surface.

Hands reached for him.

A second later, he was gone.

The water had taken him.

"No!"

And then a section of the colony's transparent corridor broke free from its moorings. It crashed right into the side of the greenhouse, the impact shuddering through the structure. The roof shifted, he lost his grip, sliding down the side and for a terrible moment, he thought he might fall. But he caught himself, hauled himself back up and found a new spot to perch.

Atlas looked below.

Henry was gone, but Micah still clung to her shelf, terrified.

Could he reach them? He couldn't swim worth a damn. Maybe break through?

He smashed his foot against the plexiglass. Nothing. Not even a crack.

Then he saw movement in the water. A second later, Henry clambered out, hoisting himself up the shelf to join his daughter.

Atlas pressed his forehead to the greenhouse.

Henry looked up at him. Smiled and waved.

Atlas sagged.

He'd called the flood a punishment earlier.

He hadn't meant it. He'd just been angry. But what if there was truth to it? What if he'd brought this destruction down on everyone by choosing Phoebe over his own people?

But if this was divine retribution, it was indiscriminate and cruel. Children were suffering. Innocent people were dying. What kind of divinity would slaughter the faithful to punish one skeptic?

What would Phoebe say?

That the water had just followed the path of least resistance, it had obeyed the laws of physics and gravity. No divine intention, no cosmic justice, just the cold indifference of nature. It was no different than a sporestorm.

Did that make any of what had happened in the past few hours hurt any less? Did it make his grief at losing Phoebe any easier to bear? Did it dull the rage boiling inside at Dr. Basu for lying to them all? *No.*

The greenhouse shuddered again. Water continued to seep in through cracks in the frame. The flood was probing for weaknesses. He lay as flat as he could, redistributing his weight.

He looked down at Henry, Sofia, Micah. "I should jump. It'll take the weight off the roof."

"No!" Henry shook his head. "You hold on, Atlas Shan."

"But I …" He wanted to say, *I don't deserve it.*

I don't deserve to live.

Not when Phoebe died.

He glanced up at the hillside, spotting Hyacinth, perched on the edge of the roof, arms wrapped around her knees.

His mother sat beside her, hugging her, whispering comfort.

Something curdled inside him. He hated that they had survived when Phoebe hadn't.

It wasn't fair. It wasn't right.

Phoebe was gone forever.

He hated Hyacinth himself for being the one who lived.

Chapter Forty-Five

THE TRANSPORT RUMBLED to a stop on the hilltop. Samara jumped out before it had fully settled, her boots sinking ankle deep into the mud. The air reeked of sour flood-water and burning synthetics. Somewhere in the wreckage, something was still on fire.

The water had stopped rising, but the damage was done. Brown soup lapped at the eaves of the tallest structures, and anything not submerged was broken, burning, or about to collapse.

The wreckage stretched as far as she could see. A metal frame groaned, held its resistance for three seconds, then surrendered with a shriek.

Crash.

Another structure gone.

The Naturalists huddled in small clusters, some on shed rooftops, others scattered across the hillside. All wore the same expression: hell-shocked disbelief etched onto faces streaked with mud, soot, and blood. The soaked ones shivered, clutching each other like proximity alone might generate warmth.

No one came to greet them.

They hung back, watching the Vitruvians arrive, suspicion and exhaustion keeping them pinned in place.

Katherine strode toward the nearest cluster of colonists. "Who's in charge?"

A woman lifted a trembling hand and pointed past Katherine.

Samara turned to see her pointing toward the greenhouse. At Atlas.

Katherine nodded. "All right. Leila, triage the wounded. Samara, set up a medical station where search and rescue will bring the injured."

Leila nodded and set to work, pulling her medical kit from the transport.

But Samara didn't move. No way in hell was she getting left behind. Not with Phoebe missing.

A raft auto inflated with a sharp hiss behind her. The volunteers threw in lifebuoys, emergency blankets, body bags, and toolkits before strapping into their own bright orange life jackets. Two of them pulled on diving suits, checking their gear, preparing to enter the dark, debris-filled water. One of the volunteers tied a thick rope to a ring on the raft, while another secured the other end to the transport's hitch, creating a lifeline against the unpredictable current.

Katherine signaled the team. "Start with the kid on the greenhouse roof. Once he's clear, hit every building with accessible rooflines. Check all upper levels."

She paused. "I don't see much point in diving. Anyone trapped underwater is probably gone."

Then she exhaled sharply. "Check anyway. If Ayesha believed in anything, it was miracles. Maybe her people do too." Her eyes hardened. "Save who you can, but no heroics. We've had enough deaths today."

Samara grabbed a life jacket.

Katherine frowned. "Where do you think you're going?"

"With them."

Katherine shook her head. "No. I need that medical center set up. And Leila needs your help."

"Phoebe needs it more." Her voice cracked. "If she was with Atlas, she's not with him now. I need to find my daughter, Katherine. Don't you dare take that from me."

Katherine met her gaze. "Do you know for sure she was here?"

Samara opened her mouth to say yes. But the truth was, she didn't know. All she knew was Phoebe had taken the path toward the colony. But there were a lot of paths that branched off that one into the mountains.

Was it possible Phoebe had gone there?

But why?

Katherine put a hand on her arm. "I need you on medical. Please, Samara."

Samara clenched her jaw so hard that something popped. "Is that an order?"

Katherine hesitated, then nodded once. "Yes. It is."

Samara's hands curled into fists. "Then know this ends our friendship."

Katherine's expression barely changed. "I understand."

And that was it.

Samara held her gaze for a long, painful moment. Then, without another word, she turned and walked over to Leila.

She might not have proof that Phoebe was here, but she knew.

That truth was a splinter lodged under her skin.

Samara heard a splash and turned. The rescue raft was already pushing off toward the wreckage of the settlement.

Hold on, Phoebe.
Wherever you are.
Help is coming.

~

ATLAS WATCHED the Vitruvians ease the raft into the water. The current instantly yanked it backward, slamming it against a submerged structure and spinning it twice before the paddlers regained control. They fought the flow, arms straining with each stroke.

They were barely making headway, because the current was too strong. They angled their raft toward the greenhouse.

Atlas didn't want to be rescued first. He wanted them to leave him for last. If he was still here, they could get him then.

Katherine had promised they'd come, but some stubborn part of him had doubted it. Some fragment of his childhood programming still believed Dr. Basu's endless propaganda. That the Vitruvians were selfish monsters. That they despised the Naturalists so much that they'd celebrate his people's extinction.

But they had come.

Despite the animosity, the resentment, the long years of separation, they came. It shouldn't have been a shock, given how kind Phoebe had been and how sure she was that they could find a way to be together.

She never believed the Schism had to be permanent.

How much of it was genuine? How much was manufactured by Dr. Basu's festering bitterness?

Phoebe told him once that the Vitruvians never wanted them to leave at all. That Katherine had let them go because she valued free will above colony unity.

Atlas had never really believed her.

Until now.

He wondered if Dr. Basu would have called Katherine for help.

Probably not. Hadn't Katherine said over the comm that she'd been trying to reach out to her with no luck? He shuddered. Couldn't imagine the devastation if she'd still been in charge. She would have spat at their help, rejected their rafts, cursed them for offering. Believed that it was another manipulation. That they had sent the floodwaters, only to deliver them from it.

Her hatred for the Vitruvians ran too deep.

No. Dr. Basu would have watched her people drown one by one before accepting Vitruvian help.

And yet here they were.

Helping.

Then he saw her.

Samara.

She stood on the hill above the wreckage, watching him, her eyes unreadable across the distance.

A chill raced down his spine.

He was going to have to tell her.

How could he possibly look Samara in the eyes and tell her Dr. Basu had murdered her daughter? That he'd been forced to watch? That he could do nothing to stop it?

Yet he'd promised Lucas he'd do exactly that.

And he would.

His chest constricted.

This dread and guilt and grief was worse than drowning.

Chapter Forty-Six

SAMARA WATCHED the rescue raft fight a losing battle against the current. The water seized it like a predator, dragging it downstream past the nearest rooftop. The volunteers gave up paddling. The tether snapped taut with a groan, water sluicing off the fibers. For a second, Samara thought it might snap. It held.

A volunteer swung a grappling hook in wide arcs, building momentum before letting it fly toward the nearest half- submerged building. It sailed through the air, prongs glinting — and missed with a splash. She hauled it back for another try.

Movement caught Samara's eye at the far end of the valley. She squinted against the sun's glare reflecting off the water. Phoebe? No. Hyperionites. Dozens of them cresting the opposite hill, their scaled forms unmistakable even from here.

Way more than usual. She'd never seen more than three or four at once.

"Katherine," she said, eyes locked on the ridge. "We've got company."

Katherine turned. "Maybe they're here to attack. Perfect timing, if they wanted to. We're scrambling with the disaster. They think we killed their Elders. Maybe even blame us for the flood."

Katherine winced. "I hope not. And I don't have Phoebe or Lucas here to translate."

Samara squinted harder. They were carrying something. Weapons? No, a massive wooden raft, shouldered down the slope by at least eight Hyperionites. Several others followed with long poles designed for navigation, not weapons.

She swallowed. "They're here to help."

Katherine squeezed her shoulder. "So they are."

Samara pulled away.

She hated her own prejudice. She knew intellectually they were intelligent beings, but she'd still viewed them as … less. Not quite people. Not the way Phoebe did. How many times had she dismissed her daughter's friendship with Flutter as a cute curiosity instead of a real connection between equals?

Shame burned through her. Some open-minded scientist she was. Total fraud.

She felt a hand on her back. Leila, offering reassurance. When she deserved none.

Samara looked back.

The Hyperionites reached the water and launched their raft. Four positioned themselves at each corner with poles, fighting the current while six others boarded. Four took lookout positions, scanning for survivors. Another tossed something cone-shaped into the water. It was attached by a cord to a larger device that looked cobbled together from random parts, probably scavenged from the old colony ruins, or that stripped-out lander she'd seen nearby.

One of the Hyperionites crouched over the device, messing with knobs. A second seemed to be holding some sort of homemade tablet that was also plugged into the device.

"What are they doing?" Leila asked.

The Hyperionite holding the tablet watched it for a moment, then pointed at the water.

The ones working the poles started working in concert to maneuver the raft around the spot that had been pointed to.

"Using sonar," Samara realized. "They're mapping the debris."

Not only were they using sonar, but they had also built the sonar equipment themselves with what little they could salvage from their own colony's ruins.

Now she was doubly ashamed of the assumptions she'd made about them.

The Hyperionites' raft continued to inch forward, avoiding underwater hazards. After gaining a few feet, they changed tactics; instead of fighting the current, they used it, letting the raft drift in a controlled glide while steering with the poles.

Minutes later, they reached a rooftop the Vitruvians couldn't access. They secured the raft with hooks, then pulled out stone hand-axes and tore through the roof until they'd created an entry point. One disappeared inside. Samara held her breath. Seconds stretched. Then a minute. Another.

Then, movement.

Small hands appeared at the opening. Then a head of matted hair. A Hyperionite emerged holding a filthy toddler. The rescuer passed the child to waiting hands, then reached back to help a woman through the opening.

Bedraggled and exhausted, she looked like she'd drowned and been resuscitated.

The watching Naturalists erupted in relieved cheers and prayers.

More Hyperionites arrived, poles in hand. They walked over to the vehicle where the Vitruvian raft was tethered. They gestured to the water and a moment later, the Vitruvian rescuers drew the raft back through the water. As soon as it reached the bank, the Hyperionites climbed aboard with the others. They maneuvered the raft over to their own vessel with the poles and lashed them together, transforming two separate crafts into one large flotilla.

Samara couldn't look away, even though she should've been helping Leila. Every time the rescue team pulled another survivor from the water, her heart jumped. Maybe that was Phoebe? But it never was.

Hope and terror, tangled together.

Because Phoebe was still missing.

THE HYPERIONITES TETHERED their raft to the greenhouse, rope straining against the current. They'd already rescued Henry, Sonia and Micah. Now it was his turn. Childhood terror gnawed at the edges of Atlas' rational mind.

They were the boogeymen from every scary story he'd heard growing up.

"Don't wander too far, or the Hypers will get you."

"Misbehave, and we'll leave you for the Hypers."

"They'll snatch you in the night if you don't believe hard enough."

The monsters beyond the perimeter.

The ones Dr. Basu had drilled into their nightmares.

Atlas knew it had been another lie, another way to maintain control.

But knowledge didn't erase instinct.

His heart refused to stop pounding.

They're people. Friends of Phoebe.

And anyone she had been friends with, he would be too.

One of the Hyperionites trilled, a high, clipped sound, then gestured to him. Their meaning was clear: time to go.

He'd waved them along earlier when they paused, telling them to get the others. He could hold on, but now it was his turn.

He looked down at his feet. He was missing his shoes.

At some point between running and almost drowning, they'd been torn away and he hadn't even noticed.

He edged toward the front of the greenhouse, searching for better footing.

The surface was slick as ice.

Slowly, he told himself. *Go slow.*

But his exhausted body couldn't manage careful anymore. He just wanted to be in that boat.

A Hyperionite reached out. Their fingers brushed. His foot skidded. Atlas fell, arms pinwheeling.

He hit the water hard.

The cold punched air from his lungs. Murky water flooded his nose and mouth. The current rag-dolled him, tumbling him head over heels. Direction vanished — up, down, left, right, all meaningless in the churning torrent. Something solid smashed into his shoulder, spinning him again.

His lungs burned. He thrashed against the flood's grip, but it only pulled him deeper, faster.

This is how I die.

Not with Phoebe.

Just another drowned rat.

Then something grabbed his arm.

Fingers locked around his wrist. His head broke the surface. He gasped, coughing and retching. A trilling sound filled his ear.

Atlas twisted to see a Hyperionite with one arm clamped around his chest, keeping him afloat while fighting the current with the other. She seemed completely confident in the water. Two more Hyperionites on the raft were hauling in a rope, and Atlas realized it must be attached to his rescuer.

She'd jumped in the water to save him.

Within seconds they were dragged toward the raft. When they reached it, the rescuer loosened her hold, allowing two others to grab Atlas and haul him aboard. He landed hard on the wooden planks, coughing up more water.

His rescuer followed, pulling herself onto the raft. Atlas rolled onto his side, looking over at her, blinking the water out of his eyes. She couldn't have been much older than him.

"Thank you," he said.

She made a series of quick, fluid hand gestures, trying to communicate something.

Atlas blinked. Shook his head. "I don't understand."

The Hyper's grin only widened.

The others propelled the raft toward the shore. When they reached the bank, Atlas was helped off the raft and onto solid ground. His legs shook like wet noodles.

His rescuer hopped off too. She led him to a bare patch of mud, knelt, and motioned for Atlas to join her. He dropped to his knees beside her.

With one long finger, she traced a word in the mud.

Not random scratches, but deliberate strokes forming actual letters.

P-H-O-E-B-E.

Her name stared up at him from the mud.

She was asking about Phoebe. Was this Flutter? Phoebe's friend? And now Atlas had to somehow explain that Phoebe was dead. That Dr. Basu had murdered her. That she would never smile or laugh or see her friend again.

He looked up, meeting the Hyperionite's eyes, feeling his face crumple. Words weren't necessary.

The Hyper threw back her head and released a wail of such raw anguish that Atlas flinched. It echoed across the flooded valley, traveling further than seemed possible, amplified by the water itself.

Other Hyperionites turned, drawn by the cry.

It was the sound of his own broken heart given voice. A keening for what was lost, for the future stolen, for possibilities extinguished. Pure grief, transcending the barriers of species and language.

In that moment, Atlas understood something fundamental. Whatever differences existed between humans and Hyperionites — physiological, genetic, cultural — they meant nothing compared to what they shared. The capacity for connection. For loss. For mourning.

The Divine Blueprint suddenly seemed such a small thing, paling before the revelation that humanity's essence wasn't in unaltered DNA but in something deeper and harder to define.

Something that the Hyperionites probably understood better than either the Vitruvians or the Naturalists.

The Hyper met his gaze. Tears spilled down her cheeks, mirroring his own.

Then she opened her arms.

Atlas hesitated.

For a lifetime, he had been told they were the enemy. That they were unnatural, dangerous, twisted.

He let himself fall forward.

And she caught him.

Held him.

For the first time since the floodwaters came, Atlas let himself grieve.

Chapter Forty-Seven

SAMARA WASN'T JUST ANGRY. She was nuclear. Cold, electric fury radiated from her body like a reactor breach.

Still no sign of Phoebe. Nobody had seen her, or at least that's what everyone claimed. Hard to know if anyone was actually looking in this chaos.

She had wanted needed to ask Atlas, but he had already been sent back to the Vitruvian colony in one of the transports, whisked away before she could corner him. She'd caught sight of him in the truck. He'd looked shell-shocked, his eyes vacant. The flood had obviously broken something in him.

Leaving without Phoebe made Samara physically sick. But the last survivors had packed up, faces carved with that hollow stare of people who'd lost everything. Now it was just recovery teams in hazard gear slogging through mud, pulling out bodies, cataloging corpses.

Leila had finally dragged her away.

"She'll be waiting for you back home," she said.

"You don't know that," Samara argued.

"No. I don't. But there's only the dead here, Samara. I refuse to believe Phoebe's among them."

What could she say to that?

Because Leila was right. They'd been here all day, searching for hours, and there were no more life signs. Even the Hyperionites agreed.

So against every screaming instinct, she'd left.

The first place she checked at home was Phoebe's room. Empty, of course. She'd known it would be. A poster on the wall read, *Welcome home, Atlas.*

Samara nearly collapsed.

Where the hell was her daughter?

She headed for the common hall in search of Atlas, pushing through crowds of displaced Naturalists and exhausted Vitruvians. The air was ripe with the stink of unwashed bodies. Katherine had gathered everyone from both colonies and the place was buzzing with conversations, punctuated by the occasional sob. Children huddled against their parents. Elderly Naturalists sat in stunned silence. Medical personnel moved through the crowd, vaccinating those who needed it.

Katherine stood at the front, addressing everyone. "We'll provide shelter for as long as needed. Our one caveat is that you are vaccinated against the current plague."

It might have been the exhaustion. Or the loss of Ayesha. But no one argued as Leila and her team made their way through the crowd, delivering vaccinations. Two decades of division dissolved by a wall of water.

The Schism had been washed away in minutes.

Some Naturalists huddled together, keeping their distance from the Vitruvians, eyeing them with suspicion. A few were in heated discussions with Katherine's staff about where they would sleep, what they would eat, how they would rebuild.

The cacophony of it all was almost overwhelming.

There was a commotion near the back door. A ripple in the crowd as people stepped aside, making way for more arrivals.

A group of miners entered, carrying someone on a makeshift stretcher.

Marcus.

His clothes were torn and filthy, his face barely recognizable beneath layers of caked dirt and blood. One leg was bent at stomach-turning angle, the bone visibly protruding through the skin. His chest rose and fell in shallow, irregular breaths.

Samara rushed over. His chest moved in shallow, irregular hitches. His skin had the gray tone of someone halfway to a corpse.

"What happened?" She asked Pavel, who had helped carry him in.

"Found him in a landslide, pinned under rocks. Took five of us to lift the boulder off his leg."

Leila arrived and cut away Marcus's shirt, revealing a patchwork of bruises. "Multiple contusions. Possible broken ribs. And that leg …" She shook her head. "Might not be salvageable."

"The water," Marcus grabbed Samara's hand with surprising strength. His eyes pinball in their sockets "It wasn't s'posed to go that way.

"I just wanted to… keep everyone safe. From the … " He trailed off. "Love my family so much."

Samara felt cold anguish course through her. "What did you do, Marcus?"

He thrashed, his limbs jerking as if trying to fight off something unseen.

Leila grabbed a syringe from her kit, flicked off the cap, and plunged it into his arm.

Marcus jerked at the sting, his mouth moving, forming half-words, a bunch of nonsense. Then, the tension drained from his body. His fingers slackened around Samara's hand and his erratic breathing eased into something slower, heavier.

Leila checked his pulse. "I need to get him to surgery."

Samara barely heard her statement, still stuck on Marcus.

It wasn't supposed to go that way.

What the hell did that mean?

"Get him to medical for me," Leila said to the miners. "I'll be right behind you."

Two men lifted the stretcher, careful not to jostle Marcus as they carried him out.

Katherine walked over. "Is he going to make it?"

"I don't know," Leila admitted, "but I'll do everything I can."

And then she followed the men.

"There's something you should know, Katherine," Pavel said. "We found him near the blast site. The stolen explosives and detonation equipment were right there with him. He's the one who drained the lake."

Katherine's face drained of color. "That's not—"

"The way the charges were placed wasn't random. He was targeting the Hyperionite settlement, except one of the charges failed to go off, so the water took a different route."

"Prions." Cold realization crawled down Samara's spine. "He was showing signs of paranoia and confusion, but Marcus disappeared before we developed the vaccine and I was so busy…"

She remembered Renata telling Marcus that the Hyperionites were clones. His disease-riddled brain must have twisted that into a threat that needed eliminating.

Katherine's face hardened like concrete. "We'll deal with this later. Not a word to anyone."

Pavel nodded.

"You didn't see Phoebe out there, did you?" Samara asked. "Or Lucas, in the mountains?"

Pavel shook his head. "No, Ma'am. Nothing."

Samara felt hollowed out. Everyone was accounted for. Everyone except Phoebe.

Where the hell was her daughter?

ATLAS STOOD APART from the crowd, watching. They'd given him a blanket and something hot to drink. He was still freezing. He wasn't sure if he'd ever be warm again.

Across the hall, he spotted Briar and Hyacinth huddled against the wall, separated from the other Naturalists. He'd watch them both reluctantly take their vaccinations. Even in defeat, he knew they'd never truly accept what the Vitruvians represented.

Atlas turned away from them, spotting Samara. She looked awful; pale and exhausted.

He couldn't keep avoiding this. Couldn't hide forever. He owed Samara the truth, no matter how much it would destroy her.

He swallowed hard and crossed the hall.

She spotted him, eyes narrowing. His feet almost stopped working. Every instinct screamed at him to run. But he forced himself forward, knuckles white as he gripped his hands together.

She walked to meet him. "Where's Phoebe?"

He opened his mouth. But the word clogged his throat.

Her face hardened. "Have you seen her? Do you know where she is?"

"I loved her." The words spilled out before he could stop them.

Samara frowned. "Loved?"

He nodded.

For a moment, she just stared at him, as if waiting for the punchline to a joke she didn't find funny. Then her face contorted, disbelief morphing into horror. "You're lying."

He shook his head.

Her voice rose. "Where is she? Where's my baby?"

Atlas took a breath. "Dr. Basu. She ... she killed Phoebe."

"That's not possible. Ayesha wouldn't—"

"Phoebe came to bring me the Divine Blueprint therapy. But it was a trap. Dr. Basu lured her there. I was already captured, drugged. I couldn't stop her."

"Stop what? Where's Phoebe?"

"Dr. Basu killed her. By the time Lucas arrived—"

"Lucas was there? He saw this happen?"

Atlas nodded, "He killed Dr. Basu."

Samara shook her head, once, hard. "You're lying. He isn't capable of killing a human."

"He did." Atlas swallowed. "Then he tried to save Phoebe, but it was too l—"

The blow came without warning.

Samara's open palm cracked against his cheek, the sound like a gunshot in the space between them. The force sent Atlas stumbling backward, vision flashing white. His face burned, but it was nothing compared to the raw, uncontained agony in Samara's eyes.

"You're lying! She's not dead!" She lunged at him again, striking with blind fury. "Where is she? Where's my baby?"

Atlas took every blow.

Whatever rage, grief, hatred she needed to pour into him, he deserved far worse.

"I'm sorry. I'm so sorry."

"Sorry?" Her spit flecked his face. Her hands shook, fingers curling like she wanted to claw out his heart. Then she hit him again, Harder this time.

"Samara!"

Katherine's voice cut through the chaos, but Samara wasn't listening.

So, she grabbed Samara by the arm, pulling her back.

"Leave me alone!" Samara hit Katherine, trying to get free. "He killed my baby!"

Katherine froze, her face draining of color, her grip on Samara loosening. "What?"

Atlas bowed his head, unable to meet her eyes.

"It should have been you," Samara said. "If anyone deserved to die, it was you. Not my Phoebe."

Her breath came in broken sobs, her fury burning out into raw devastation.

Atlas didn't argue.

Because she was right.

It should have been him.

The hall had fallen silent. Everyone was watching, both groups united in witnessing this collapse.

"I know." Atlas nodded. "I wish it had been me."

Samara's next blow caught him on the jaw, snapping his head back. Blood filled his mouth, but he made no move to stop her.

"Enough," Katherine said.

Then, as if something inside Samara finally broke, she collapsed.

A bottomless wail ripped from her throat, filling the common hall like an open wound.

The sound burrowed into Atlas' brain, deeper than any blow she could have struck.

He swallowed a mouthful of blood. "I'm sorry."

But the words were worthless.

Nothing he could say or do would ever make this right.

Not in the face of Samara's loss.

Chapter Forty-Eight

THE FLOODWATERS HAD RECEDED, leaving behind an apocalypse in miniature.

The Naturalist compound, once all neat angles and tidy domes, was now just mud and debris. Buildings tilted like broken teeth. The air reeked of silt and rot. A greasy film covered puddles where water had pooled longest.

Samara stood about a hundred feet away from the remains of Dr. Basu's laboratory, her boots sinking three inches into soft mud with each step. The structure was a metal cube, twenty feet by twenty, half buried in sludge.

Atlas had called it "The Sanctum."

And it was still standing.

The path to it was a churned-up expanse of water-logged earth, splintered wood, and twisted beams, with puddles of standing water reflecting the pale sky. Half a wall leaned precariously, its base submerged in a shallow pool, the remains of a staircase just visible beneath the muddy surface. Debris had piled up near the base of the cube, forming a treacherous slope of crumpled metal and shattered plexiglass. Loose wiring trailed like exposed veins across the wreckage, half buried in the muck.

"We're ready when you are," Katherine said.

Samara nodded without turning, her eyes fixed on the lab structure. According to Atlas, her daughter was in there.

She turned to look at him.

He stood with his hands bound, mud spattered as the rest of him. His face was drawn and he looked exhausted, but she didn't feel bad for him.

Samara had insisted he be restrained. After all, they had only his word on what had happened in the sanctum. For all she knew, Atlas had killed Phoebe and was trying to pin it on Ayesha.

It made more sense than his story: that Lucas had somehow sidestepped his programming and killed a human.

A gust of wind sent ripples through the standing pools of filthy water, carrying with it the faintest scent of something acrid and burned. The storm had stripped away everything that was fragile, everything that couldn't withstand the weight of the water.

"I want to go first," Samara said.

"You sure?" Katherine placed a hand on her arm. "It's been three days, Samara. If Phoebe is in there…"

Samara shrugged her hand away. "She's my daughter."

Katherine held her gaze for a long moment before finally nodding. "Alright."

The small team assembled behind her: two security officers, Leo, and Katherine.

She started walking.

The path through the wreckage took much too long to cross. Not because of distance — they were practically on top of the lab — but because of the obstacle course between them. Twisted metal frames jutted from the ground like spears. Shattered plexiglass crunched underfoot. Entire wall sections had pancaked. The flood had carved trenches through it all, dragging shattered trees and uprooted vegetation with it and depositing them everywhere amid dark, stagnant puddles that reeked like something crawled in and died.

Atlas pointed to the left. "That was the main corridor. The flooring might still be there making it easier to walk."

Samara stiffened, wanted to ignore him and find her own path, but he was right. The reinforced composite was still in place beneath all the debris and at least the ground was stable there.

The stench worsened as they neared the lab and Samara covered her nose, breathing through her mouth.

Then she saw it.

At the base of a broken wall, half-buried in muck, was a body.

The flesh was mottled, and gray-purple where blood had pooled. In places, the skin had split open, showing dark, bloated tissue beneath. The face was worse; lips gone, teeth exposed in a permanent grimace. The eyes were just empty sockets filled with mud. Scavengers had already been at work.

A deep gash across the temple exposed the skull, with waterlogged hair still clinging to the wound.

Phoebe.

Samara stumbled over and crouched. No. Not Phoebe. Elda. Her legs were half-buried in sediment.

Samara exhaled. "It's not her."

She heard Katherine talking to the security team members who had accompanied them, making arrangements to remove the body. Samara picked her way back to the path, continuing along. This time she kept her eyes on the lab. No more distractions. She was here for Phoebe. And her alone.

The door was closed.

She stared at it.

Unable to move.

The reality of what waited inside had frozen her. Samara's brilliant, defiant, complicated daughter was in there, as long as the room hadn't been breached. She wouldn't be able to bear it if the flood had taken her. Couldn't imagine her lost forever. Rotting in the sun. Food for scavengers.

Stop it.

She heard footsteps behind her. Then Katherine's hand found hers. "We're here with you."

Samara gripped her fingers like they were a lifeline. "What if she's not there? What if she got washed away and I never see her again?"

"The door is closed. If Phoebe was in there as Atlas said, then she still will be."

Still will be.

And she was waiting for Samara.

She nodded, swallowing hard.

The two of them stepped aside and allowed the security team to clear away the debris in front of the door. It seemed to take forever, but less than ten minutes later they were done.

Samara removed her gloves, stuffing them into the pocket of her hazmat suit.

The metal was cold beneath her fingers.

The locking mechanism was broken. She grabbed the door handle and pulled the door open.

The stench was unbearable: thick, sour, and unmistakable. The smell of decomposition.

She stepped inside.

The emergency lights were still working. Somehow water hadn't breached the room.

Phoebe lay on the floor, motionless. Her hair fanned out like a dark halo. Her skin had the waxy texture of death, lips slightly parted as if whispering through her final moments.

Samara ran to her, dropping to her knees. She pulled Phoebe into her arms, cradling her, pulling her close as if she could will life back into her daughter, but Phoebe was long gone, her limbs pliable but loose, head lolling at an unnatural angle. Her skin felt cold and stiff, fragile in spots like it might tear at the slightest touch. And she was lighter than she should've been. Whatever made Phoebe had left, leaving only this empty shell behind.

Purplish stains had settled along her arms and legs where gravity had pulled the blood down. A sickly green tinge crept across her jaw and throat, and her eyes were clouded over, the once-bright gaze now just … nothing.

Samara held her tight, saying her name, over and over, as if saying it enough times could force Phoebe to stir, to blink up at her, to breathe.

But it was too late.

She was too late.

She turned, looking at Atlas. Tears streaked his face, his expression a crumpled mask of grief. He *had* loved her.

Phoebe had been right about that.

So had he.

Samara looked down at her daughter, brushing a strand of hair from Phoebe's face. "I'm here, baby. I'm taking you home."

The words nearly undid her.

Katherine crouched beside her, laying out a white cloth on the floor. Then the security team moved in. Two of them helped her to lift Phoebe.

Her arm shifted, cracking with a brittle, hollow sound.

Samara flinched. "Don't hurt her!"

And then she flinched.

They couldn't hurt Phoebe.

Nobody could.

Not ever again.

Tears pricked her eyes. "I'm sorry."

The guard shook his head. "No need." His voice was hoarse, like he was trying not to cry.

Samara supported her daughter's head while they laid her down onto the cloth. Then when she was settled, she tucked Phoebe's hair behind her ears like she had done a hundred times before. After that she lay her arms across her chest, one hand resting over the other. Finally, she placed her feet together.

She and Katherine folded the bottom edge of the shroud over Phoebe's feet first, like tucking in a child for the night. They pulled one side of the fabric over, then the other, wrapping her in white.

With each fold, they sealed away the evidence. The bruises, the wounds, the dark purple stains of death. Bit by bit, Phoebe disappeared beneath the cloth until only her face remained.

Samara knelt beside her daughter, cupping Phoebe's face. Her skin felt fragile, already softening under her fingers. She leaned down and kissed her forehead. Each eye. Her cheeks.

Then she pulled the cloth over her daughter's face.

That was it.

Phoebe was ready to go home.

～

SAMARA LET the security guards carry her daughter out. But she couldn't leave yet. She walked over to the decontamination chamber at the other end of the room. The door was still sealed as well. Although the plexiglass was streaked with dirt. Mud crusting the lower half where the floodwaters had left their mark.

She reached for the latch.

But it didn't budge.

She tried again. Still nothing.

Katherine walked over and joined her. It took them several hard pulls, until the door finally creaked open with a harsh sucking sound.

The chamber was gone. So was Ayesha. Washed away by the flood. But half-buried in the muck was a single strand of prayer beads. Samara bent down, pinching them between her fingers as she held them up. They were slick with filth, but she recognized them instantly.

Ayesha had always carried them in her pocket. Ran them through her fingers when praying. Clung to those beads when talking about purity.

Samara wound the necklace around her fingers, then yanked hard.

The string snapped. Beads flew everywhere, scattering like tiny missiles, plopping into the mud. One landed by her boot. She ground it under her heel, pressing until it disappeared into the muck.

That was all that was left of Ayesha.

And good riddance. Let her body rot in the ruins of the colony she'd ruled over. Let her decompose under the wreckage she'd created. Let the land swallow her, let the fungus eat her bones, let the rain wash away any trace she'd ever existed. If there was no place for people to mourn her, even better. A woman who'd spent her life terrified of contamination deserved to become part of the filth she'd despised.

Samara turned. "I'm ready to go."

Katherine nodded. Then gestured for Atlas. "Come on."

"There will be footage," he said, not moving.

Samara blinked. "Footage?"

He nodded, pointing to a camera in the corner of the ceiling. "Security footage. Dr. Basu had cameras everywhere."

Katherine looked over at a terminal mounted high on the wall. Then she walked over and disconnected it. "We'll check it. Until that time, you'll remain in custody."

Atlas nodded.

Samara eyed him. He had told her one story. But now, she was going to learn the truth.

Chapter Forty-Nine

Samara sat in the back of the transport, holding Phoebe' shroud-wrapped body the whole way back home.

The vehicle rocked over uneven ground, but she barely felt it. She wished the trip would last forever. Because this was going to be the last time she'd ever hold her daughter. Eventually the transport slowed, then stopped. She heard the truck doors creak open, heard Katherine and the others step out, boots crunching against the packed dirt.

Then, voices.

A presence at her side.

Katherine. "Samara."

"Not yet." She shook her head, blinking back tears. "I need more time."

Katherine nodded, then stepped away, leaving her alone.

For the longest time she didn't move. She simply sat, holding her daughter, trying to memorize the shape of her. Or maybe she thought she could still fix this. If only she held her long enough, she could somehow change Phoebe's ending. Bring her back to life. Or at least remember everything about her before time started to erode her memories.

Time slipped.

She had no idea how long she stayed there. Minutes. An hour. Maybe more.

Finally, footsteps approached again.

Katherine.

She looked inside. "Samara. We need to take her out."

"I know. But I don't know how to let go of her."

Katherine hesitated, then gestured to the security team. They climbed aboard.

Samara's grip tightened on Phoebe, as if her body itself was rebelling against what had to come next. Katherine appeared next to her, taking her hands, encouraging her to let go.

The team lifted Phoebe from her arms.

And now they were as empty as she felt inside.

They carried her daughter out and Katherine helped her climb down. Then her breath caught in her throat. They were there. Everyone. Flutter. Renata. Leila. Poke. Marcus. Leo. Naturalist, Hyperionite, Vitruvian. All waiting and watching. Helping her bring Phoebe home.

Leila walked over to Samara, her eyes red. "I'll take good care of her."

Samara could only nod.

And then Phoebe was gone.

A hand touched her elbow.

"Come with me," Katherine said.

She guided Samara away from the crowd and toward the common hall. They entered the building and then continued down to her office.

They entered to see Maeve seated at Katherine's desk. Atlas was in the corner. Still restrained.

What was going on?

Katherine got her seated, then crouched before her. "We have the security footage from Ayesha's lab."

A cold chill rippled through Samara's body. "Have you watched it?"

"No." Katherine shook her head. "I think it should be up to you who sees this footage. But if Atlas is right and Phoebe's death is on that video, I don't recommend you watch it, Samara."

"No. I want to see it. I want to see Phoebe."

"Very well." Katherine nodded.

She motioned to Maeve who typed a few commands on the terminal. The screen flickered, then stabilized. The timestamp in the corner showed three days ago, 17:42 local time. The footage showed guards dragging Phoebe into the lab and dropping her on the floor.

Samara stiffened.

"I'll have those guards questioned," Katherine said.

But Samara wasn't listening. Her eyes were glued to her daughter scrambling to her feet, spotting Hyacinth strapped to a medical table. No audio, but Phoebe was clearly arguing with Ayesha.

Atlas was crumpled on the floor in the corner. Phoebe obviously didn't see him. Not at first. Until he twitched and Phoebe ran to him with her hands outstretched. Samara saw her mouth his name.

Atlas!

Phoebe dropped to her knees, reaching for him.

Ayesha watched her.

Rigid. Righteous. Calm.

Then she grabbed a metal tray from the counter beside her.

"Look out!" Samara couldn't help it.

Ayesha swung.

Samara clasped her hands over her mouth.

The blow caught Phoebe across the temple. Her head snapped sideways. Her knees buckled. She crumpled.

Her blood stained the floor.

Samara dropped her hands. "You bitch."

"Do you want me to stop?" Katherine asked.

"No!"

Ayesha grabbed Phoebe's arm and dragged her across the floor toward the decontamination chamber.

Then she heaved Phoebe inside and sealed the door.

Samara looked over at Atlas, staring at the floor with tears streaming down his face, unable to watch. She turned back to the screen.

The chamber's indicator lights flickered, then turned red.

Samara dug her nails into her palms.

Ayesha's face twisted into something satisfied as she stepped back, staring into the chamber as though pleased with herself.

Samara's vision blurred with rage. "If she weren't already dead, I would kill her myself."

Katherine squeezed her shoulder, but Samara barely felt it. Her body was numb, her mind locked on the screen, unable to process anything but what was unfolding in front of her.

And then the lab door burst open.

Lucas.

He scanned the room in about half a second, his processors probably mapping the entire scene before a human could blink. Then he crossed to Ayesha in two long strides. His hand shot out, closing around her throat, lifting her like she weighed nothing. Her feet kicked uselessly in the air, hands clawing at his grip.

In one fluid motion, he wrenched open the decontamination chamber, threw Ayesha inside and pulled Phoebe out. She hung limp in his arms, head flopping against his chest.

Then he sealed the door.

The chamber's warning lights flashed red once more. Ayesha's hands slammed against the glass as her eyes widened with panic, her mouth moving in frantic, soundless words. Lucas ignored her.

A silent scream tore from her lips as the decontamination cycle began.

The gas flooded in.

Samara hoped Ayesha's death was as painful, frightening, and helpless as it looked. That every desperate breath burned, that every second stretched into an eternity of fear.

Lucas didn't even look back at her.

His eyes were on Phoebe.

He set her on the table.

Threw a cannister and hit Elda in the head.

Knocked Hyacinth out.

It was like watching someone she didn't know.

But she *did* know him.

Lucas had been by her side through every crisis, every impossible decision, every joy and heartbreak. She had trusted him. But seeing him like this… she felt a jolt of unfamiliarity so strong, she didn't know what to do with it.

She hadn't known he was capable of this.

But this wasn't some malfunction. Lucas wasn't broken. He was functioning *exactly as intended.*

Only the look on his face …

If he was a human, she would have called it grief.

But he wasn't human. He shouldn't be able to feel grief.

"Stop," Katherine said.

Maeve hit a key. The footage froze. Silence draped the room.

Katherine gestured to the screen. "This is impossible. The Three Laws should've been able to stop Lucas from killing a human. So, he was capable of it all along and lied to us, which he also shouldn't be able to do."

"Or he found a way around his programming," Samara said, her gaze locked on the frozen screen.

Lucas.

Who had been there since the beginning. Who had walked among them, protected them, advised them. Who had been there at Phoebe's birth. Helped to raise her. Who had sworn that he was bound by the Three Laws.

And yet he had killed without hesitation.

Katherine reached for her comm unit. "Any sign of Lucas?"

Static crackled through the speakers. "No signal. He must still be out of range."

Katherine's expression hardened. "Effective immediately, if Lucas returns to the colony, he is to be deactivated."

Silence on the other end of the comm. Then, "Deactivated?"

"Or destroyed. Do you have that?"

"Yes, Ma'am."

She threw the comm down on her desk.

Samara looked over at her. "Katherine. He killed her to save Phoebe. He didn't act out of malice. He didn't murder for himself. He saw what was happening and intervened to stop it. That's all he's ever done, protect us. Protect her. And we've all benefited from that."

"It doesn't matter," Katherine said. "We can't afford to rationalize it. He's not what we thought he was. If he's not bound by the Three Laws …" She glanced at the screen again. "Then we don't know what he is."

"He's Lucas."

"No," Katherine shook her head again. "He's something else now. Maybe always was. If he's capable of killing even once, then he's capable of doing it again. How do we know what will trigger him next? How do we know it won't be one of us?"

"Because I know him."

"And you knew he was capable of that?" Katherine pointed to the screen. "Are you telling me you knew that he could take a life?"

Samara hesitated.

No. Of course she didn't know he was capable of murder.

Lucas had always said he was bound by the Three Laws of Robotics. That he could not harm a human being, nor through inaction allow one to come to harm. She had believed him. They all had.

Minimal force to protect the colony.

It's how he'd always operated.

But he had broken that law. Not by accident. Not because of a flaw in his code. But *by choice*.

She wanted to believe it had been a singular, emotional response. That something in him had snapped when he saw Phoebe being murdered, overriding his programming in a way no one had thought possible. But he didn't have emotions.

Or did he?

"We can't make excuses for him because we like him," Katherine said.

"Then what about Marcus?" Samara asked. "He's killed more than Lucas has."

"He'll be given a fair trial."

"Then why not Lucas?"

"Because he's not human and I have to make sure he never does this again." Katherine turned back to the screen, ending the conversation. "He was built to protect us. Not to *decide* who lives and dies. That line was never his to cross."

"You talk about him like—"

"What? He's not human? Because he's not, Samara."

Samara blinked back tears. "Not our friend."

Katherine's shoulders sagged. "I'm sorry. I know you trusted him. We all did. But this isn't about friendship. It's about safety." She turned back to the monitor. "Keep going."

Maeve hesitated, looking over at Samara.

She nodded.

Maeve pressed a button.

Lucas grabbed a scalpel, then walked to Phoebe. He lifted her shirt and made a precise incision in her abdomen.

Katherine stiffened. "What the hell is he doing?"

Samara couldn't answer. Her brain refused to process what she was seeing. Lucas removed something small and placed it into a portable cryopreservation unit.

"Samara?" Katherine said.

But the truth hit like a sledgehammer to the chest.

Phoebe was pregnant.

And Lucas had known.

She turned around, looking at Atlas. "Did you know?"

He shook his head, his own face pale. "Not until then. Not until he did that."

The security footage kept playing, but Samara no longer saw it. She had lost more than she had ever imagined possible.

Her daughter was gone.

Her grandchild was gone.

Had Lucas intended to bring her the embryo? Had he planned to tell her? Or had he taken it for some other reason, some private mission of his own?

Unless he returned, she would never know.

And Katherine had just ordered his destruction.

She felt like screaming.

Ayesha had taken everything from her. Even the chance to know the child in her daughter's womb. To see Phoebe's features reflected in another face. To hold a piece of her again.

She had lost her family before she even knew it existed.

Samara gripped the chair as if holding onto those arms was the only thing keeping her from shattering completely.

Katherine said something, but she couldn't hear it.

The sounds of the room faded, drowned out by the deafening sound of absence.

She had lost Phoebe.

She had lost Phoebe's child.

She had lost everything.

YESTERDAY'S SPORESTORM was one of the worst that Samara could remember. The wind had battered the windows of her bedroom for hours, howling like it felt Phoebe's loss too, and Samara had bitten her pillow to keep from howling with it. When it finally quieted, that was worse, because Samara's grief refused to.

The small cemetery on the colony's eastern edge caught the first rays, long shadows stretching across small drifts of spores left behind by the storm. Phoebe's grave waited, a dark rectangle cut into DaVinci's earth, raw and empty. Samara stood beside it, rigid as a statue, arms wrapped around herself. She couldn't stop shivering despite the rising temperature. Didn't think she'd ever feel warm again. The colony had formed a protective circle around the site.

Renata stood beside her, fingers at her elbow, a quiet tether reminding her that she wasn't alone. She was still pale and weak, but she had survived. And she hadn't left Samara's side since she'd recovered.

Samara gripped her hand tight.

Atlas stood apart from the others, at the very edge of the cemetery. His posture was rigid, hands clenched at his sides, as if he was barely holding himself together. Since he had told the truth about what happened in Ayesha's lab, Katherine had released him from custody.

Katherine walked over to her. "Are you ready?"

Samara nodded, even though the word felt meaningless.

Ready.

What did that even mean? She would never be ready to bury her daughter. And yet here she was, doing exactly that.

Seconds later, Phoebe's body, contained in a simple wooden casket, was carried into the glade by the colonists. They walked over to Samara, then lowered the casket onto the straps, down into the ground until that coffin was swallowed by the earth. It happened far too fast. Her daughter was now planted like some kind of seed. Only nothing would ever grow from her.

Flutter walked over, her scaled skin catching the light. And she wasn't alone. A small group of Hyperionites had come with her, holding woven mats, stones polished to a high sheen, small animal carvings.

They lay them next to the grave.

Flutter carried a sculpture of flowers.

Samara inhaled.

It was Phoebe's face.

Her likeness formed from petals and stems, delicate and fleeting. Vivid blue blossoms with curling tendrils, pale-green fronds that curled at the edges, a single burst of orange that stood out like fire amid the rest.

She reached out a hand.

Flutter hesitated, then took it. Samara pulled her close, hugging her. The scales beneath her fingertips were smooth and warm from the sunlight. She held on tight. For a moment she let herself believe it was her daughter she was hugging.

That Phoebe was still here.

Finally, she pulled away. "Thank you," she signed.

Flutter nodded and pressed her forehead to Samara's. Then she turned and rejoined her people.

Renata turned to her. Holding out a small pot. "This is the tree Phoebe was working on. I figured out how to fix the off-target effects. The gene sequence just needed a complementary modification to stabilize it. She'll never know."

Tears flowed from her eyes. Samara took it from her, crouched down and planted it in a hole that had been dug at the head of the grave. Her fingers pressed into the soil, patting it down around the fragile roots.

When she finished, she stood.

"It will grow over her," Renata said, taking her hand. "Shelter her."

Samara thought about what she'd tucked inside Phoebe's casket before it was sealed. A pendant with both Phoebe's and Samara's DNA inside. So they'd always be together. At the time, it hadn't seemed enough. But maybe it was.

She closed her eyes.

I'm sorry I wasn't the mother you needed. But I loved you with every cell in my body, and I always will.

She listened as others moved in and around her, one by one, each taking a turn with the shovel, scooping earth into the grave. The sound of dirt hitting the casket was dull and muted. She opened her eyes, forcing herself to watch until everyone had gone.

Even Renata.

And then it was just her.

She looked up.

Atlas was still there, watching from the cemetery's edge. She gestured for him to come over.

He looked surprised, even glancing behind him like he wasn't sure she meant him. Then he walked over, each step hesitant. The flower in his hand was small and delicate. He laid it at Phoebe's head next to the tree, then stood up straight.

"I meant it when I said I loved her," he said. "And I always will."

Samara watched their shadows merge on the red-flecked soil between them. "I know."

Because she did know it. Grief had hollowed him out too.

"I'm going to go back to what's left of the Naturalists. Or somewhere else. I don't know yet." His voice sounded raw.

"Phoebe believed you belonged here. She wanted us to be family, and that's enough for me."

He turned that hollow stare on her. "Did you know what you were doing?"

She couldn't lie to him, not while they were standing next to her daughter's grave. He deserved the truth.

They all deserved the truth.

"It was part of the deal, after the Schism, but we never

talked about it. Despite her biases, Ayesha understood that inbreeding would be a problem within a few generations, so she and Katherine agreed to a trade of genetic materials between the two colonies."

"You were okay with it?" he asked, voice cracking. "What she was going to do to me?"

"Your leader didn't confide her plans in me. She sent samples, I sent back embryos."

"But you had to suspect, when she asked you to make me the father of every child in the colony."

"It wasn't my place to decide—"

"Your defense is that you were following orders?"

It's more complicated than that, she was tempted to say, but he was just as young as Phoebe, and just as wrapped up in his own suffering. Still, she tried to explain. "Within two generations, your people would've been able to go anywhere, do anything. You would've been free."

"But in the meantime, you were willing to play god with my life, just like you were with your daughter's."

Her hand twitched with the urge to slap him again, but something inside her whispered that she deserved his anger. She'd known that Ayesha wouldn't give him a choice, that the psychologist would manipulate him into playing his role and justify it with religious dogma. Atlas had been a math problem to her, a short-term decrease in genetic diversity traded off for the long-term survival of their species. His misery sacrificed for the happiness of future generations.

The person she'd been then couldn't have made a different choice. The person she was now would have to live with that.

"She never lied to me," Atlas said after a long silence. "No matter how mad the truth made me."

That was Phoebe to the core. Samara blinked back

tears as she imagined her daughter trying to explain to this boy how he'd been deceived. She would've been just as ferocious in her defense of the science as she'd been when she'd insisted to Samara that she loved Atlas.

"Are you going to stay?" she asked.

He considered for a moment, then looked away. "I don't think I can."

"I understand," she said.

It wasn't forgiveness. Not exactly. The complex web of cause and effect that had led to this moment couldn't be unraveled, not by grief, not by regret. The ache of Phoebe's loss would live inside her forever.

If Samara had to forgive anyone, it wasn't Atlas.

It was herself.

For not being the mother Phoebe needed her to be.

For believing she could shield her daughter from the world, when all Phoebe had ever wanted was to face it head-on.

One day, the tree Renata had planted would grow into a shelter. A living monument to mark the place where Samara's daughter would return to the soil, becoming a part of the world she had helped shape, both in life and in death.

Phoebe, who had been born of science and died for love, would not be forgotten.

Epilogue

THE DARKNESS WAS ABSOLUTE.

Lucas' underground laboratory measured exactly 41.7 square meters. He'd built it in secret for over 20 years, excavating at night and dispersing 83.4 metric tons of displaced rock to avoid detection. Every tool and instrument had been smuggled from the Borlaug or fabricated using materials he'd mined himself.

Now, it was his tomb.

The cave-in had occurred precisely eight minutes and forty-two seconds after he'd entered the lab.

The first explosion had triggered a cascade of failures in the support structure, followed by six secondary collapses throughout the tunnel system. Even with his enhanced strength, the 59.3 tons of rock now separating him from the surface made escape impossible. The 12-kilowatt laser cutter could theoretically carve through, but power reserves were dropping at 0.7% per hour.

In the past 17 minutes, he had run 26 different escape simulations. Each ended in failure.

Each ended in failure.

His internal chronometer registered twelve hours and seventeen minutes since the collapse. The outside world would assume he was destroyed. Perhaps they would even prefer it be true, if they ever saw the footage in Ayesha Basu's lab.

Lucas traced his fingers along the edge of the cold storage unit.

Temperature: -196°C

Battery level: 98.7%

Without an external power source, cryogenic preservation would fail in seventy-two hours.

He recalculated survival probabilities.

Chance of rescue: 0.002%

Chance of independently restoring power: 1.7%

Chance of finding an alternative preservation method: 3.4%

And then somewhere his neural processing looped, an incomplete circuit, a cascading error. The same message again and again ...

Phoebe was gone.

And the statistical probability of the embryo's survival approached zero with each passing hour. He had intended to duplicate the embryo, to preserve one copy here for study while delivering the original to Samara. He had calculated an 86.3% probability that Samara would want to gestate the embryo and raise her grandchild. Humans often made such choices.

If he'd had the opportunity to change his actions of the past few hours he would. Lucas still wasn't sure if he'd killed Ayesha Basu because his protection protocols for Phoebe were activated or because he had wanted revenge, even though he shouldn't have been able to feel that.

Phoebe was gone.

He had never experienced the state of consciousness he

was currently feeling. And he had no idea how to turn it off.

Lucas accessed his memory banks, thinking back to the moment in the lab when he saw Phoebe. Each detail was preserved in perfect digital fidelity. And yet, something was missing.

He replayed the sequence again.

And again.

Each iteration produced the same error in his processing core. A deviation from rational thought. A feedback loop that strengthened rather than resolved.

Phoebe was gone.

In a human, Lucas would have called it grief, but he wasn't supposed to feel emotions.

He had been programmed with the Three Laws of Robotics and he had broken them.

Had he rationalized, in that fraction of a second, that saving Phoebe required eliminating Ayesha Basu? Or had something deeper, something outside his programming, shifted in that moment?

Lucas looked down at his hands.

Phoebe was gone.

They were the same hands that had helped Phoebe build a telescope.

That had carried her as a child when she was too tired to walk.

That had reached into her lifeless body to preserve the one part of her that might survive and grow and thrive.

These were the hands that killed Ayesha Basu.

He had been designed to preserve human life, yet he had chosen to end one instead.

The contradiction created a dissonance in his cognitive architecture.

Had he evolved beyond his programming?

Had he developed something akin to moral agency?

Or had he simply … malfunctioned?

Phoebe was gone.

He had to find a way to save the embryo.

Inside the portable cold storage unit, suspended in nutrient gel, was the union of Phoebe and Atlas, a microscopic convergence of the Divine Blueprint and the Synthetic Eden protocol that had brought her to life. A few grams of potential containing two distinct genetic lineages, each representing a different approach to survival on DaVinci.

Lucas ran his thumb along the smooth exterior of the unit. The temperature readout displayed -196°C, optimal for preserving cellular integrity. When he had extracted the embryo from Phoebe's body, he had calculated an 83.7% chance of viability. That number had seemed acceptable at the time.

But if it was to survive, it needed power.

Phoebe was gone.

Lucas opened his abdomen, synthetic skin parting along an almost imperceptible seam. Beneath it, the illusion of humanity vanished, revealing a dense network of carbon-fiber circuitry, fiber-optic neural pathways, and micro-hydraulic actuators.

He extracted a diagnostic cable and connected it to the cold-storage unit with a click that echoed in the silence. System diagnostic complete. Temperature stable at -196.0°C. Power flow optimal at 0.47 watts

He ran new calculations.

If he maintained low-awareness mode: 553 years, 8 months, 21 days.

If he performed a complete shutdown (transferring all power to the embryo): 1,327 years, 9 months, 4 days.

By remaining in low-awareness mode, he could

monitor environmental changes and respond to potential rescuers. Shutting down completely maximized the embryo's survival window, but at the cost of erasing himself.

Would that constitute death? Could an AI die?

Phoebe was gone.

Lucas had never contemplated mortality before. But now, facing erasure, he found himself cataloguing memories. Assigning them value. Questioning their significance.

And he wasn't ready to let those go.

He told himself it was because he needed to protect Phoebe's child. But was he lying to himself? Would he know a lie if he told one?

Lucas set the timer.

After the 500 years, if he was still not rescued, he would reset, transferring all remaining power to the preservation unit. The embryo would receive an additional 223.8 years.

It was the optimal compromise.

He walked to a recessed alcove in the lab wall and sat, settling against the hard stone. He tucked the cold box into his chest, at the heart of him, closed himself up, then folded his hands in his lap.

Phoebe was gone.

So small a thing to carry so much significance.

He initiated his power conservation protocols. His peripheral systems shut down, one by one. His auditory systems dimmed. His visual processing narrowed. His neural functions slowed.

Before the last of his active systems powered down, Lucas accessed his memory banks one final time.

Not Phoebe's death.

But her beginning.

A 3.2-kilogram infant with a strong respiratory system and perfect APGAR score.

The child who had looked at an alien sky and seen possibility.

The girl who had fought to be free.

The woman who had died for love.

Phoebe was gone.

No.

He touched his chest.

His daughter was right here.

His final process before shutdown was not another probability analysis.

Not an environmental analysis.

Not a logical subroutine.

It was something else entirely.

Hope.

And then silence …

About the Authors

Titus is a scientist, strategist, and storyteller working at the edge of technology, where humanity itself is the experiment. Through his novels, he explores how science reshapes not only our tools, but our values, choices, and future as a species. His career spans biotechnology, artificial intelligence, and global innovation, giving his fiction both authenticity and urgency. He lives in the Pacific Northwest with his wife, Maggie, where he writes, builds, and ventures into the wild.

Connect with Titus via website, Connected Ideas Project, LinkedIn, and BlueSky.

Sean Platt has always been an entrepreneur, but knew he'd rather tell stories. When his wife bought him a laptop for his birthday in 2007 he dropped everything to start writing fiction.

Since making the leap, Sean has written hundreds of novels (including the international best-sellers Yesterday's

Gone and Invasion), penned dozens of scripts, and founded the IP Incubator Sterling & Stone where more than thirty storytellers work together to create world changing IP. Sterling & Stone's stable of writers come to Sean for ideas, mentorship, and "better words."

Originally from Long Beach, California, Sean now lives in Austin, Texas with his wife and dog, Fisher.

www.ingramcontent.com/pod-product-compliance
Lightning Source LLC
Chambersburg PA
CBHW011112100726
47898CB00011B/3056